A
CONJUROR'S
JOURNEY

DAKOTA JANUCHOWSKI

Chapter One

I t started and ended with eyes. Glaring defiantly through the thick puffs of colored smoke, lurking over the long-awaited Coronation of Prince Daegon. High in the white towers, bronze bells rang out, their vibrations humming against the marble walls of Malachi. The sound drifted across Lake Kimset, disturbing the glass-still water. Daegon sat just outside the city, at the water's edge, brushing his boots through the stretching reeds. Ripples from jumping fish crashed onto the shore. He gripped the hilt of his sword, his knuckles turning white. Today, the crown would rest on his head.

Ten years of silence from the empty throne. Ten years since his father walked away and left him to rot. King Raynor had ventured off on some fishing trip on this very lake, always taking extravagant trips, removing himself from the duties of King. Of being his father. But he'd never returned, and the only remaining attachment to his father was Raynor's protector, Jordell, who'd washed up on the shores of Kimset three years ago. Daegon preferred that outcome. Jordell had always been there for him. He'd taught him the intricacies of politics, how to fight, and how to be a leader. Jordell was the father he never had. Or couldn't have.

This would be his last time at the lake before being crowned King. He wouldn't be able to sneak out from the Kingsguard anymore. He would often come to the spot when the pressures of the impending kingdom became too real. But now. Now there would be no more privacy, no more time to dwell on the isolation of his thoughts. Daegon sprang from the lush grass and swung his sword at a well-worn tree. The blade slashed into the trunk, becoming stuck. Daegon released the hilt and left the sword in the carved bark. He would be back.

The white stone wall, pristine and unblemished, separated his city from the forest. What would Raynor have thought of this day? Would he have been proud? Would he have encouraged him? Ignored him? Gone off on some other adventure, skirting the duties of both a King and a father? Daegon shook his head of the thought. This was an exciting day. Not a day for remorseful thoughts.

He took in Lake Kimset one last time as Prince of Malachi. The softness of the grass. The peaceful echoes of the rippling water. The succulent smell of honeysuckle. Daegon's nose tilted as a sharp scent cut through the sweet flowers. Sulfur and ash. Daegon frowned, tasting the grit on his tongue. Probably just part of the celebration. Fireworks blasted above the city, and packs of Conjurors created incredible displays of incendiary power in the city's streets. There usually wasn't a lasting smell, but there hadn't been a celebration in years. Maybe the Conjurors concocted some new elaborate spectacle.

He turned toward the city, meeting the glaring eye of Malachi head-on. The sigil of his city flew high, hovering over his people, obscured by billows of colorful smoke, promising protection wherever it looked. Daegon threw on his brown hood and blended in with the crowd flocking through the front gate. The royal florist decorated the ornate white marble gate with bouquets of fiery flowers. Because of the influx of people, guards patrolled the crowd more heavily, their bright armor guiding the citizens as they flooded into the city.

Daegon soaked in the happiness of his future constituents. Many weren't even from the city of Malachi. They bore the sun-weathered skin of hillside farmers, still shaded with their afternoon efforts. While he'd worked diligently at becoming the King his people deserved, he knew nothing of the efforts of those flocking to the city. He had never ventured much further than Lake Kimset. He'd never needed to, preferring instead to explore the vast passageways of Malachi's history. Daegon rested an arm on a shaded wall, watching the mass of people; all here to celebrate. To celebrate him.

Children ran through the legs of their adult counterparts, laughing as they threw small embers at one another. Conjuring was prevalent throughout Malachi. Many of its citizens were born with an innate ability to control the elements. While Daegon was one of the few without this ability, the internal presence of power pulled at his every movement. As Daegon continued through the street, incredible displays of color careened overhead. Crowds of people circled individuals performing tricks. An old man's fingers danced, tracing glowing blue sigils in the air. He tapped the cobblestones, and frost exploded outward. In a heartbeat, three hulking snowmen erupted from the ground, ice creaking as they formed. Children broke into the event, smashing through the snowmen. Daegon cracked a smile. The older man laughed and created additional ice treats, spritzed with their own personal snow flurries.

One child crashed into Daegon's leg, dropping his treat onto the ground. Daegon kneeled and picked the child up, dusting the city's scant grime from the treat. The young boy thanked him but grew wide-eyed at Daegon's appearance. Daegon smiled, shifted his hood to obscure his face further, and raised his finger to calmly shush the child. The boy returned a wide grin, nodded, and followed his friends down the street.

Daegon kept his head down and followed the winding streets, eventually funneling into the city center. A glowing white crystal towered over the crowd, providing shade from the sun's blistering rays. The crystal was the spiritual center of the town. No one knew how it came to be in the center, or why it existed, but its warmth radiated amongst all of Malachi's citizens. As he approached, a sweet melody hummed within his soul, and a quiet vibration rattled his teeth. He stepped into its shadow and the knot in his stomach loosened. It was hard to explain, but every Malachinian felt it. They were able to describe it despite their inability to identify why. Like the warmth from a fresh-cooked stew, or the view of a lover after returning from an adventure. Because of this omnipresence, all events began with a prayer of respect for the stone.

Behind the stone, five individuals dressed in dark scarlet cloaks sat in ornate chairs on the porch of Malachi Manor. The Cardinals. They rarely came to Malachi, but when they did, it was for some important event. Whether it was the *passing* of his father, or Founder's Day, the Cardinals were present, exerting their silent influence. Since Raynor's disappearance, they'd acted as Malachi's decision makers regarding its personal and political endeavors. But that ended today.

Daegon made his way through the crowd, avoiding the occasional cheering fist. Jesters and dancers performed on the front stage, twisting and throwing their bodies in intricate patterns. In front of the performers, white-clad swordsmen combed through the crowds. The midday sun crested above. He'd been out long enough. The Kingsguard were probably becoming worried. While he was yet to be crowned King, they were not obligated to watch over him. Despite his obvious royal ties to the Malachinian throne, this allowed him the ability to sneak away when life became too much, and besides, there hadn't been a King in so long, he wasn't sure if they could perform their job, anyway.

Daegon ducked into a closed alley and slipped through the hidden door that opened into the basement of Malachi Manor. He'd used the escape many times. Many of the guards didn't know about it and would often panic when they'd lost track of him. He closed the door behind him, and the roar of the crowd faded to a silent buzz in the background. As he tiptoed through the fallen boxes and crates, the older floor planks creaked, betraying his position.

"Where have you been?"

A familiar voice flowed into the dim basement. Daegon froze before dropping his heel, letting his boot thud against the floorboards. He said with a wry snicker, "I was just enjoying the celebration."

A large man with dark hair, clad in spectacular white armor, paced the basement. Geoffrey, the head of the Kingsguard. "We've been looking everywhere for you."

"Well, you're in a basement...You knew exactly where to find me..." Daegon's voice trailed off.

"Enough of your games, boy." Geoffrey's voice deepened as he grabbed Daegon by the shoulder and pulled him through the dark room. "You're about to be King. It's about time you acted like it."

Another set of footsteps clacked on the floor. An older man with gray, braided hair stepped forward and paused Geoffrey. "He's here now; that's all that matters."

Jordell. Thank the kingdom. While Geoffrey's dedication was admirable, Jordell had a levelheadedness that made sense more often than not. Made obvious by his rather mundane leather outfit for the Coronation. Daegon shrugged Geoffrey's hand from his shoulder and said to Jordell, "Can you believe everything out there?"

Jordell had been there for Daegon ever since washing up on the shores of Lake Kimset. He had been Raynor's closest friend and protector, but kept no memory of what happened. Jordell said, a particular vibration in his voice, "Yes, yes. And it's all for you." Jordell's gray beard cracked a smile as the old man opened his arms for a hug.

Daegon squeezed Jordell tightly, embracing the man who'd been there for him. Taught him everything there was to know about being a man, much less a King. Daegon's eyes glistened. "Thank you for everything."

Jordell released Daegon and put his hands on his shoulders. "You're going to make a fine King. I'm sure everyone's excited to have a Malachinian in charge once again."

He was right. The Cardinals had been in charge for the previous 10 years. While there were no outright revolts, there were internal groans when they would make decisions. Not that they were necessarily the wrong decisions, but just not the decisions

King Raynor would have made. Daegon shook his head at that thought and kicked a loose stone. *As if Raynor had ever made a decision that didn't involve a fishing rod or a cask of wine.*

Geoffrey groaned as the trumpets bellowed above, signaling the opening of the ceremony.

Before he could leave, Jordell grabbed Daegon. "Hold on, you have something on your face." He licked his thumb and wiped it across Daegon's cheek, smearing the trail of dirt from his face. Daegon pushed the hand away, but Jordell reached and shook his hair. "I'm proud of you."

Daegon opened his mouth, but Geoffrey grabbed his arm and hurried up the staircase into the main hall of Malachi Manor. The same seeing-eye crest of his people presided above their heads, watching the historic event. His head spun around the open room, darting through the paintings of the previous kings of Malachi. His father's painting hung to his right. His long jet-black hair and rune-covered sword pierced the foreground, stepping victoriously on a menacing fog. As he tracked his legacy, he wondered about his eventual place. Would he be beloved like his grandfather, King Gradius? His scant smile faded. *As long as he wasn't Raynor.*

Four guards immediately surrounded Daegon, all wearing matching white plate mail. It was time for them to begin their mission. It was time for him to become King. Geoffrey barked some commands, and the guards marched through the large doors leading to the porch. The light of the crystal blinded him, bathing him in the crowd's roaring applause. When his sight came back into focus, a sea of people cheered, casting conjurations through the air.

A smile appeared on his face. How could he not take pride in what was about to ensue? He had worked for this ever since his father had disappeared. Even though Jordell had taught him what it took to be King, like his father before him, that wasn't good enough. He had to be better. He would be better. Daegon waved at the crowd, evoking even larger applause.

And there it was again. That smell. It smelled hot. Like something was burning uncontrollably. The hair on Daegon's neck stood up. The crowd continued to cheer, oblivious to the hostile aroma, but the birds had stopped singing and the wind had died. He squinted as he scanned the crowd. It couldn't be a coincidence.

The trumpeting silenced, and the crowd followed suit as the Grand Cardinal took center stage. He wore similar red robes to the other Cardinals but also sported a distinct yellow sash around his neck. Whatever hierarchy the Cardinals maintained, Cardinal Sooman was at the top. "People of Malachi," he said, speaking as much with his hands as with his voice. "We are all gathered for this joyous crowning of Prince Daegon."

The crowd again erupted into cheers before Sooman waved his hand, creating a blanket of silence. Daegon looked out at the people, catching sight of many of the familiar faces that he'd met during his covert adventures into the city. Behind the mass of people, above the white stone buildings, an unusual purple and green smoke approached in the distance.

While the plume of smoke held his gaze, Sooman's voice droned on in a monotonous echo at the back of his mind. He snapped out of it quickly when Geoffrey nudged him in the back.

Sooman repeated, "If Prince Daegon would come to the front, we will now bestow upon him the crown of Malachi."

Daegon shook his head and stepped toward the Grand Cardinal. This was everything that he'd worked toward. His heart raced in his throat as the tapping of every step closer filled the silent courtyard.

Sooman took the ornate crown off the blue pillow and held it high above his head. "Kneel, Prince Daegon."

Daegon bent his head and knelt in front of Sooman. He was prepared to take the next steps as leader of his kingdom.

As they placed the crown on his head, the city shuddered. Crack! The ground splintered, surging through the mass of people. The crevice flowed up the nearby towers, sending stones crashing onto the streets below. That same purple and green cloud he'd seen earlier entered the courtyard, vining between the citizens and pulling them into the miasma. Shrill screams emanated from deep within the city, piercing the ceremony.

Chapter Two

Daegon fought for breath as the Kingsguard grabbed him from behind and pulled him into the keep. The purple smoke consumed his city. Stray tentacles struck out from the smog, reaching and pulling his people into the darkness. People scattered for safety, but wet gargles of slaughtered flesh quickly drowned out their screams.

The Kingsguard stepped in front with swords drawn and slammed the door shut. Geoffrey's chest heaved under his heavy armor. "What is going on?"

Cardinal Luminara trembled underneath her red cloak, her hands clutching at the sewn-in pockets. But Sooman? He stood like a statue, his face vacant, eyeing the smoke like an unexpected nuisance.

The female Cardinal stepped forward. "We have to get out of here now."

Cardinal Sooman interrupted her and waved her back to the others. "Pardon Cardinal Luminara. We are trained to always maintain a stoic position, even when facing death." His face darkened as he stared at the woman. "King Daegon, I believe your father created a passageway out of the city in the event of a potential siege?"

Jordell glared at the man before biting his lip and conceding the information. If there were an issue, there wasn't time to hash it out. The glass ceiling of the hall shattered, sprinkling shards of color across the ground. Jordell pushed through the Kingsguard. "Geoffrey, take the Cardinals to the catacombs and see if the escape still works." He reached for Daegon's shoulder. "Daegon and I are going to go to the tower and save what we can."

"We're what?" Daegon pushed the hand off, his voice frantic as the roaring cloud vibrated the keep. "Why can't we just go with them?"

Jordell unsheathed his sword and nodded to Geoffrey. "As the now King of Malachi, it's your duty to display strength and unity with your people."

Geoffrey returned the nod and ordered the Kingsguard to corral the Cardinals through a large wooden door behind the statue of Daegon's ancient ancestors. Before the Cardinals vanished, Cardinal Sooman turned to him. "We'll see you again, King Daegon." He bowed. "Keep the Memory."

Keep the Memory? Cardinal Sooman flashed a yellow grin as he turned away, but Daegon didn't have time to dwell on the interaction as Jordell rushed him down one of the keep's hallways. He ran past statues and ornate paintings depicting his family's history. The history of his people. Everything he'd learned, all of it becoming rubble as the mist ripped through the windows, spreading like a vine on the floor. Daegon covered his neck against the shattering glass as he sprinted up a staircase. His lungs burned. Every step was a battle against gravity. Through the arrow slits, flashes of purple light illuminated the dust, choking the air.

They'd finally reached the top, exiting onto one of the entry walls, Daegon's body fighting every step. He rested his hands on the stone railing, and his mouth dropped at the desolation. The mist had engulfed not just the courtyard, but crept up every building. The Grand Library folded in half, its white dome crumbling like dry bread. Twisting wood and shattering stone screamed at the forest, drowning Jordell's shouting. And there was that smell. It was always destruction. Always death.

The cloud was alive, swirling into areas of the city that still beat with some semblance of life. But it was hungry. And it couldn't be satisfied. Solid tendrils whipped out from the thick darkness, grabbing hold of buildings and collapsing them with ease. It was only a matter of time before the wall followed suit. On the ground just below, shadows of monsters scoured the streets, shredding what was left of *his* city. Daegon stepped back. "What is this?"

"It's called the *Scourge*." Jordell stepped closer. His voice was unnervingly calm amidst the chaos that surrounded them. He rested his hands on the edge of the wall. "I'll explain, but we have to go."

Everything was happening so fast. He had questions for Jordell, but now wasn't exactly the best time to have a chat. They had to escape. The two continued their sprint along the wall. Behind them, tremors and rubble filled the void. They heaved for breath; the smoke keeping pace and flowing under their feet. They had to hurry.

The wall shifted under the pressure of the swirling cloud, but they'd made it to the base of the tower. Pieces of the wall cracked and sloughed off into the darkness below. Jordell burst through the door. "We have to keep going!"

They scrambled up another staircase, bursting out at the top of the tower. *What now?* This *Scourge* was collapsing buildings, and Jordell had brought them to the tallest building in Malachi. Without an escape. Daegon gripped the window ledge until his fingernails cracked. Below, Malachi was gone. Swallowed by a sea of violet fog that burned through his city; even extending into the forest. The once incredulous screams became fewer, melting into the roar of the wind.

"What's the plan?" Daegon said. "You seem to know what this is." It came off ruder than he'd intended.

Jordell kicked a chest open. Without looking, he reached in and hurled a heavy object at Daegon's feet. Steel rang against the stone floor. The blue runes on the blade pulsed in the shadows. Jordell snickered. "You know how to use one of these, right?"

He's laughing? Now? What was he supposed to do? Fight the Smoke Monster? It was incinerating everything in its path. Before long, it would break through the door and come for them as well. If the building even held. Daegon grabbed the sword from the ground, his thumb tracing the familiar runes. "Jordell, what are we doing?"

"Now's the time, Daegon." Jordell closed his eyes, took a deep breath, and unsheathed his blade. "It's time to follow in your father's footsteps."

Daegon recoiled at the mere mention of his father. The smoke leaked under the door, tightening his throat. He opened his mouth to speak, but the door burst open, and the *Scourge* screamed into the room. The cloud surged forward and engulfed Jordell.

"No!" Daegon reached out, but the heat of the cloud repelled his hand.

He was all alone. Again. The smoke encircled him, cutting him off from his city. Daegon raised his sword, poised to strike. The roof split, exposing him to the churning sky. Around him, below him, the smoke suffocated all escape. The eye slowly formed above, and he knew. There was no escape. Daegon dropped the sword to the floor, preparing for the cloud to pounce. But the eye patiently stood above, promising a painful death. *Why had the creature not swallowed him yet?*

The cloud ripped open. A translucent maw. Falling rubble tore at Daegon's ears. The storm surged. This was it. This was how Daegon's reign would end. Before it even started. Daegon eyed the runes on the sword and grabbed for the hilt. One last time. Despite the futility, he would go down swinging. He wasn't his father. He wasn't a coward.

The creature opened its jaws, its black, beady eyes daring him to battle. It collapsed onto him. Daegon screamed and thrust his sword at the center of the mouth. Smoke flushed all around, burning not just his skin, but his thoughts. And the pain didn't cease, flooding into every crevice of his skull. The floor rushed to meet him, and the purple smoke filled his lungs, choking out the light.

Chapter Three

S teel rang against steel. Daegon lunged, aiming for the chest, but his blade was slapped aside, driven into the white marble tiles. Sweat beaded on his forehead, and he yelled out, thrusting the sword once again at his combatant. A parry jarred his arm all the way to the shoulder. His boots skidded on the smooth stone, and the world tilted. He hit the ground; the air leaving his lungs in a wheeze. He lay there panting, gasping for breath. Defeated.

"Better. But you're still fighting with anger, not eyes." The weathered voice of his opponent offered some solace to the blow to his young ego. Jordell sheathed his weapon, his chest barely heaving. "You strike before you see the opening. You need to see your enemy, anticipate their movements, and be ready to strike *only* when you know it's the right time."

"The right time, huh?" Daegon said, smirking. It was the same summary after every lesson. So far, his timing had never been right, and the older man anticipated Daegon's every move.

Still, he'd improved. And Jordell took notice. That made something inside him feel bigger, somehow. More capable.

Daegon pushed himself off the cold floor and walked to his mentor. "You're never going to let me win just one, are you, Jordell?"

Jordell rubbed his thick gray beard and gave him a wide grin. "Oh, why would I ever do that? What would that teach you?" He handed Daegon a leather flagon of water, and the two went to sit on the ledge of the central fountain.

As Daegon sat, resting his tired muscles, he grinned at the audience their battle had drawn. A dozen soldiers lined the walls to watch their simple sparring practice. To watch their future King. The entire kingdom would one day be his. He needed to be seen as a strong, competent leader.

He downed the last of the water, the coolness helping to lessen the heat of his exhaustion. With his energy restored, Daegon jumped from the ledge and grasped his sword, swinging it through the air.

Daegon's sword was a masterful work of metallurgy. Crafted with great care, it was slim, and the steel shone with the celestial warmth reflected from the city's central stone. Under Jordell's tutelage, his sword had become a part of him. Another appendage.

Still, he and his sword didn't have their timing right. Not yet. But they would. Jordell taught him the arts of combat and being a tactician. He also challenged him to improve each time they met so Daegon could better prepare for the machinations of being a ruler, despite his father, King Raynor, who had little good to say about his son and even less time for him.

The swoop and arc of the sword fell in elegant patterns. Daegon was light on his feet as he and his sword maneuvered across the tiled floor. He dipped the edge of the sword into the fountain, lightly spraying the water on his mentor.

"Watch it!" Jordell exclaimed, wiping the spray from his face. The older man beamed at his sword work.

A cold voice shot from the balcony, eroding Daegon's confidence. "Is that all?"

Daegon froze. That voice. It cut deeper than any sword.

"You'll never be good enough."

"Why can't you understand this?"

"When will you be the leader your city needs?"

Daegon shook his head of the persistent criticisms. Above, his father gripped the railing of a viewing balcony. Raynor wore a heavy, embroidered cloak, and his long, dark hair fell about his shoulders.

Raynor leaned over the balcony, lazily picking at a loose thread on his cloak. "You look like a child, dancing and playing with a stick." He shifted his ire to Jordell. "Is this what you teach him? Games and child's play?" Raynor turned back to Daegon. "Maybe a nursemaid would better suit your education."

Daegon hid the sting. He puffed his chest and looked up at the balcony, steadily holding the King's gaze. "If you think you can do better, come down here and face me."

As the words spilled out, Daegon squeezed his fists at his side. He'd played into his father's hands. He let anger and shame dare him into the challenge.

And in front of so many.

Raynor smirked, waiting for this exact moment. He dropped from the balcony, effortlessly landing on the cold white stone. He unclipped the golden eye-shaped brooch holding his cloak, allowing it to fall softly to the floor, and ran his hands through his hair.

Raynor drew his blade. The blue runes along the fuller pulsed, and with a hiss, the steel ignited. Flames licked up the length of the sword, distorting the air with controlled heat.

Jordell shook his head and sighed. "A bit dramatic, don't you think, sire?"

Raynor smiled and readied his weapon. Daegon broke from his daze and charged into battle, swinging his blade with the same vigor he used with Jordell. The flames spat from their swords, sparks flying when metal met metal. A gap opened in his father's guard. Daegon lunged. Raynor didn't even step back. He simply flicked his wrist, knocking Daegon's blade wide. The movement spun Daegon around, leaving his back exposed. The King used Daegon's own momentum to his advantage and threw him to the floor.

A boot slammed into his ribs. A distinct crack echoed, and Daegon collapsed, gasping as pain radiated through his chest. Blood pooled from his mouth, reaching into his nose. He lay on the stone floor. The victorious monarch towered over him, his black hair hanging like a planted flag.

There was a seriousness in the King's words, not just mocking. "You need to be faster."

Daegon raised his blade to continue the fight, but Raynor quickly slapped it to the ground. "You need to be stronger."

All of his training. It had been for naught. His fancy sword work. What good was it now? What did the soldiers think about their prince lying there, helpless?

Daegon gritted his teeth and pushed himself from the floor, swinging his sword and screaming with what little energy he had left. But it wasn't enough. Raynor simply caught the sword mid-swing with his blade. He closed his eyes, and in a flash, a sheath of fire engulfed Daegon's sword.

Daegon released the hilt as the heated metal singed his palm. He hit the cold floor again, unable to defend himself. Exhausted. Embarrassed.

Raynor stepped next to his son and dropped the sword. The flames withered, but Daegon didn't dare touch it. "You're going to be King one day. How can you hope to garner respect if you can't even defeat me?"

Daegon stared at the floor. Silence was his only shield. What could he say? Blood gushed from his mouth as Raynor walked away. There was no doubt about it. He was a failure in his father's eyes. Daegon beat his hands against the ground, and a tear rolled down his cheek. Jordell caught him by the shoulder and heaved him to his feet.

Daegon spat under his breath. "I hate him."

Jordell sighed. "He just wants you to be strong." He brushed the dust from Daegon's shoulders and wiped the blood from his lip.

Daegon used his sleeve to wipe the bloody sweat from his face, while his father faded back into the luxuries of the keep. "I'm going to be a better King than he ever dreamed of."

Jordell offered a hand. "Timing, lad. You let him dictate the rhythm. Next time, you set it."

Daegon winced and reached for his sword once again, readying it toward Jordell. "Again."

Chapter Four

Ice crystals crunched against his cheek. Daegon gasped, inhaling air so sharp that it felt like swallowing glass. He scrambled backward, his hands sinking into deep, wet powder. *Snow?* Daegon struggled to his knees and pushed aside the powdered mass. A thick cloud of fog circulated through the forest, but it wasn't the deadly violet that hunted him.

The stray singe of the *Scourge's* scent still lingered on his clothes, but the air was crisp and clean. Trees. Trees everywhere. Tall, thick evergreens with rust-colored bark. *A dream?*

He screamed into the abyss, "Hello!"

The frigid air returned the conversation, smacking his face with a sting. It was otherwise quiet. Disturbingly so. He muttered to himself, "What is going on?"

His hands brushed the cold blue steel of the sword Jordell threw him. He wasn't entirely alone. Stray memories of his father lifted from the raised runes; the remnants of heat from battle's past radiating from its core. Too bad the heat provided little comfort against the frigid winds and freezing temperatures that made it too cold to stay put. He wore attire for a Malachinian ceremony, which worsened matters. Ornate white robes and thin leather boots were all that separated him from the elements.

The ceremony.

He combed his fingers through his snow-dampened hair. *No crown.* He kicked through the snow, looking for the important piece of Malachinian history but found no trace of it. He searched the nearby trees, but violent shudders scolded him. He needed warmth. Warmth and shelter. He closed his eyes. The quiet comfort of his chambers called to him.

Daegon braced himself, set forth, and trudged through the snow without a particular direction in mind. At least the evergreens provided a reprieve from the blistering wind and a corridor for him to follow. But it was so dark. And everything blurred. There weren't any markers to suggest a particular point for him to get back to his crown. *That stupid crown.* Daegon shook his head at the thought and trekked forward.

He walked for what seemed like miles. The unrelenting wind peppered him with shards of passing ice. He had to hide. Had to escape and eventually found comfort within a copse of evergreens. The howling winds reached for him but relented at their failed attempts. Without shelter. Without warmth. It would soon return. He continued his trek, wading his way toward some unknown destination.

After some time, the sudden sound of flowing water reached his ears. Even if it wasn't life, the sense motivated him forward. A half-frozen stream of water peeked through the packed snow. Daegon kneeled and scooped the water into his mouth. The icy water instantly soothed the unmistakable taste of ash and death.

Yes, the water was a significant find, but his thin robes would eventually fail to the stalking cold. He looked around for anything he could use to create a shelter. Maybe even something to start a fire. The idea of warmth was a great motivator.

He pulled some branches from the trees and collected a small pile of twigs. When he'd gone on his father's hunting trips, he'd gleaned some knowledge about surviving in the forests. Unfortunately, he never quite figured out how to light a fire after he collected the twigs. That always eluded him. Another failure.

He sat at the edge of the stream, staring at his pyramid of twigs neatly stacked, ready to be engulfed by a flame he didn't have. He grabbed a pair of rocks and struck them against the sticks. A spark hissed into the wet pine needles and died instantly. He struck it again. And again. His hands shook so violently that the rocks slipped, disappearing into the snow. He stared at the useless pile of twigs, his throat tightening.

After a few more unsuccessful attempts at starting a fire, his meager pile of sticks tumbled from their neat stack into a messy pile of useless rubble.

Collapsing into rubble. Everything collapsing.

The tower. Jordell being consumed by the *Scourge*. It all hit him hard. Because of the blistering threat, Daegon hadn't even recalled those moments before he'd awoken here. Wherever *here* was.

Had Jordell died? Had everyone died?

As much as he wanted the answers, he didn't have time to dwell. The creeping cold and piercing winds converged on his position. Daegon looked about his surroundings and found another copse of trees with weeping branches. He stripped the branches from the trees and created a shelter with the sticky needles forming a barrier against the elements.

He used the treeline to help ease the biting wind, laying some of the stripped branches against the ground. They weren't soft, but at least they would keep the unrelenting cold away. The rest of the branches acted as a blanket, hoping to keep in the heat his body would produce. It wasn't much, but it would at least keep the stalking elements at bay. For now.

Daegon curled up in his cocoon of pine fronds and counted the unfamiliar sounds of the attacking winds. Now that he was out of the elements, at least slightly, his thoughts returned to those moments in the tower. Of Malachi crunching and collapsing, succumbing to the cloud. The squishing gurgle of his citizens played across the backs of his eyelids. All caused by the *Scourge.* And somehow, Jordell knew what it was.

What was it Jordell had said to him? "*Follow in his father's footsteps*". What did that mean? Had Jordell and the King seen the monster before? Did it kill his father?

Surely Jordell would have warned him if such an evil existed.

Daegon lay beneath the branches, pushing mounds of filtered snow into the crevices as the slithering cold laid siege to his shelter. After an hour, his fingers and toes grew stiff and numb. He needed to get up. He needed to move. But leaving what little warmth he'd established felt almost impossible. Only his full bladder gave him the final push to leave the bed of branches.

After relieving himself a little way from his bedding area and getting some of the feeling back in his extremities, Daegon scouted just a little more of the nearby area. It was still too dark to make out much of the landscape, and too cold to be away from his only source of warmth, but his mind needed something to occupy it, and maybe he could find some thicker fronds to add to his shelter.

He had only walked for five minutes when a plume of dark black smoke rose from the woods in the near distance. This smoke was different. Instead of the milky fog passively sifting between the trees, this one was created with intent. An innocent intent, like a cook's fire or a campfire.

An innocent intent. How strange my life has become.

The smoke wasn't too far away, and it offered some hope. "I guess any civilization is better than freezing to death," he whispered, readying himself for the short walk to what could be his salvation.

Daegon only had to walk a short distance to see the flickering flames. Like the rest of the area, the landscape here was much the same: bushes and conifers in small groupings sprouted from the frozen ground.

Daegon ducked behind a large fallen evergreen. The frozen remains blended perfectly with his Malachinian ceremonial robes, giving him adequate cover. He didn't want to surprise, or be surprised by, whoever created the fire. He hoped there'd be no trouble. There had been far too much trouble for his liking. He cautiously placed his hand on the hilt of his sword, his father's sword, and waited.

Two young men in amber-colored robes ran through the trees. Their panicked looks pushed Daegon deeper into his cover. The two bounced between the trees and screamed in terror, shooting balls of fire from their fingertips.

Conjurors! Did they escape Malachi as well? He couldn't help but hope he wasn't the only one.

Then, the trees shattered. A nightmare stepped into the clearing. Seven feet of black steel, clad in skeletal, encrusted armor, followed them through the frozen landscape. The two men stopped, standing their ground against the creature.

"Leave us alone!" One of the robed men yelled. He raised his sword and charged at the beast. The man's sword struck the creature squarely in the chest, but it did little damage. The beast shook off the hit and pulled its great sword from its back. It didn't hesitate, driving the weapon forward with terrifying speed. The blade punched through the robed man's chest like paper, lifting him off his feet.

Blood spewed from the man's mouth, and his body became limp. The creature waved its sword to the side, carelessly littering the snow. It realigned its direction toward the other robed man, who was frantically scanning the trees while trying to work some offensive conjuring.

He shakily spun his hands in the air, creating a ball of red and orange heat that was aimed at the creature. The blast landed a direct hit, spreading over the bony ridges of the black armor. He quickly conjured another blast, this time scorching not only the creature, but the surrounding trees and ground. A suffocating inferno engulfed the battlefield.

The robed man held the upper hand, but the flames engulfing the creature scattered into the trees. The beast stalked through the carnage, squeezing its palm shut, consuming the rest of the fire. The conjured flames dissipated, leaving the ground scorched but the creature, unfortunately, unharmed.

The robed man gasped and started shaking. He spun around to flee. Surely, he would try to escape from the creature. But the man held his ground. He defiantly faced the beast. Using his skills once more, he conjured two separate fireballs and screamed. The monster's eyes flared, reflecting the fire, and dashed through the blazes. The flames were mere nuisances.

Daegon's eyes widened at the creature's speed. It was unnatural, and before the man could create another volley of fire, the creature landed its sword through his shoulder blade, cleaving through his body and out through his hip. His body stood for a mere moment, eyes open in macabre wonder before falling to the snowy ground in two pieces, dyeing the stark white powder a scarlet red.

The monster placed a gauntleted hand over the corpse. A pulsing red light drifted upward, struggling like a trapped bird. Skeletal fingers reached around the orb, snatching it from the air and crushing it in its hand; the light extinguishing with a sickening pop.

Daegon crouched behind the downed tree, paralyzed. *What is that thing? Is it part of the Scourge?* The monster's helmet turned in Daegon's direction. *Could it see him? Or sense him?* He didn't want to sit there helplessly waiting to find out, and broke from his cover, sprinting into the forest.

The deep vibration of the creature's feet followed closely behind, pulsing just slower than the thudding of his own heart. He refused to suffer the same fate as those men. He had to escape. But the forest blurred in front of him. The same tall, thick trees provided the same cover as the previous ones in his path. There wasn't an easy way to evade or hide from the beast, and even if he could hide, it could probably just sense him anyway.

The snow and wind returned, accelerating into his face, blinding and disorienting him. A thick root broke the monotonous landscape and reached for his boot. He collapsed into the snow. Daegon reached for his blade and pulled it as he jumped to his feet. But it was already upon him. It lunged and swung its hulking sword. Daegon ducked under the blade and recoiled as their weapons met.

Move. Just keep moving. Daegon scrambled backward, his boots slipping on the ice, barely avoiding the backswing.

Daegon pushed the issue, swinging his sword. His attack was no different from the robed man's, bouncing off the creature's armor. He stamped out of the creature's counterattack, but his heel caught another root. Daegon flailed, crashing onto his back, the air exploding from his lungs. He looked up. The massive blade rose for the killing blow.

The blade plummeted, and Daegon squeezed his eyes shut. Boom.

Heat washed over his face. He opened his eyes. The monster staggered backward, its chest plate shattered and smoking.

Daegon scanned the tree line. *What happened? Who attacked the creature?*

A group of soldiers emerged from the trees and charged at the creature. They carried smaller swords and strange tubes that launched explosive rounds, mimicking the dead man's fireballs. And they were relentless, pelting the beast with the explosive rounds, preventing it from standing.

When they were close enough, they pounced on the creature, subduing it and slashing with their swords. Swords smoothly pierced between the creature's armor; into whatever lay underneath. It let out a ghastly howl, sending chills down Daegon's spine and splitting the quiet of the forest. Birds sputtered from the trees; watching animals shuffled away.

A violent black mist erupted from the creature's body. Daegon crept backward through the snow as it disintegrated. *Some type of conjuration?* His escape came to a halt when he hit the legs of a taller individual wearing a thick fur coat.

"Who are you?" The voice was sharp, commanding, but breathless from the fight. "Why are you out here?"

Daegon hesitated. He spun onto his hands and stared at the younger woman with dark hair standing over him. "My name is Daegon." He struggled to his feet before he continued. "From Malachi."

The woman cocked her head to the side and pulled her blade, placing it squarely on Daegon's chest. "Malachi, huh?" The question hung in the brisk air. "Malachi was destroyed one thousand years ago."

The forest swayed. Daegon grabbed a tree branch to keep from falling. "One thousand...?" The word tasted like ash. The snow, the forest, the strange soldiers. It all spun around him. He pressed the woman for more information. "What are you talking about? We were just attacked by...the *Scourge*...before ending up here in this forest...running from...what was that thing?" As he rambled, the dearth of his knowledge became clear.

"That Reaper did some damage, huh?" Her sword hovered over his chest as she carefully surveyed him. "We're in the Twinwood Forest, a long way away from Malachi." She sheathed her blade and waved over a member of her troop.

Her crew scoured through the dead men's belongings, covering the eyes and putting them to rest. He wasn't sure what to ask in the situation, so he said the only thing that came to his mind. "What is going on?"

"My name is Ellend, but my troop calls me El." One of her soldiers brought her a matching thick fur coat. "We're part of the Forlorn here in Shishbash."

Daegon took the coat and threw it over his shoulders, finally combatting the cold's relentless attempts to freeze his bones. It didn't matter that it was a little oversized; the cold nearly infiltrated his core. "Thank you."

She pulled the collar tighter on his fur coat. "From Malachi, huh? How about we get you back to our camp?"

Chapter Five

Heat. It wrapped around him like a heavy blanket. Daegon gasped, bolting upright. No snow. No biting wind. Just the snap of a fire and the smell of roasting meat. He'd been crowned King of Malachi just yesterday, and now he was lost. Abandoned in a frozen, unknown forest. The flickering flame of the fireplace jumped at him. He dug his nails into his legs, fighting the memory of the young man in the woods. That. Creature. *What did El call it? A Reaper?*

They'd brought him back to the Forlorn's camp and ushered him into one of the larger tents. The fireplace warmed the tent, finally dulling the chill that seeped into his bones. He sat on an enormous cot that took over half of the tent. It was stiff, but compared to the frozen roots of the forest, it was a throne. He dug his fingers into the furs—real heat.

The soft glow of the fire canvassed the tent's walls in orange. The faint aroma of hard work and campfire wafted from underneath. A glass of water and strange mashed food sat on a wooden crate placed next to the cot.

The tent flap swept open. El ducked inside, bringing a gust of cold air with her. She didn't smile; she studied him like a puzzle she couldn't quite solve. Gone was the fur coat. She now opted for a long gray tunic and a tight ponytail.

She grabbed a chair from the table next to the entryway, flipped it backward, and sat. "I hope the accommodations are to your liking." Her eyes flicked to the dirt floor.

The sarcasm was sharp enough to cut. Maybe he wasn't appreciative enough for the whole saving of his life thing. Or maybe she didn't believe his story about being from Malachi.

He took a drink of the water and pressed his hands on his knees before taking a breath. "The camp is amazing. Thank you...so much...for everything." He paused for a moment. "It's just been...a lot."

El contemplated him, still with a hint of mistrust. "Explain it to me," she asked, wiggling her hands in circles. "Everything. Like, how did you end up here in the forest?"

Daegon stared at the dirt floor of the tent, gathering his thoughts. "I was...it was my coronation." His hands shook. "The smoke. The purple sky. One minute I was in the keep, and the next..." He trailed off. "Is Malachi truly gone?"

El's expression remained motionless, even with the new information. "A King. Right. And I'm the Queen of the Ashes. You look good for a corpse, Your Highness. Most thousand-year-old men are a lot dustier."

He shook his head, squeezing his eyes shut, hoping to return to the white stone of his city. "I don't blame you. I don't know what's going on myself."

"And I don't recommend you go around telling people you're from Malachi. The place isn't exactly held in the highest regard anymore."

Another piece added to the puzzle of his confusion.

Daegon took a breath and scanned the tent. "So where am I?"

He didn't know what he'd been expecting. Something more than a frozen stare. She bit the inside of her lip before smacking the top of the chair in an enthusiastic motion. "That Reaper must have really done some damage!"

Daegon looked at her in confusion. "No, I'm fine. I know I'm in a tent. Just *where* this tent is what I'm asking."

She must have realized he was being serious as her tone shifted to be more comforting. "We're right outside the city of Shishbash. Sorry, we don't have a better fitting jacket. The Tundra festival caught us a little off guard."

Daegon reached over and ran his fingers through the hair of the fur coat he was wearing. It was coarse and exuded ample heat. He was finally warm for the first time since waking up in this cold, unfamiliar place. "What is the Tundra festival?"

El stood from the chair and walked over to the fireplace. "You hear those drums in the distance?" El pointed with her cup. "That's Tundra. Shishbash is throwing a celebration to send another poor kid to their death."

"Death?" Daegon asked.

"They call it a Journey. I call it murder. Those Conjurors never survive."

A Conjuror. Finally, something he could understand. At least a little. He closed his eyes; he knew how annoying he sounded asking all these questions. "What is the Conjuror's Journey?"

She shook her head. "You really have no idea..." She walked to a small cupboard that held a store of brown liquid and poured herself a glass. "Each major capital selects someone each year to begin their journey to gather a piece of every city's soul. They then combine the souls and use them to defeat the

Scourge...or delay it." She took a sip of the drink, wincing as it burned her throat.

"The *Scourge*!" Daegon yelled, jumping out of the bed. "That's what destroyed Malachi. That's what Jordell was talking about."

"Jordell?" El asked, pouring another glass of the liquid. She offered it to Daegon, who cautiously accepted it.

"My mentor. He was with me when the *Scourge* attacked." Daegon took a sip of the liquid, feeling the immediate, welcomed heat. Daegon's grip tightened on the cup until the wood creaked. Jordell. Dead. The thought hit him like a punch, hollowing out his stomach. "Everything...everything was gone."

El reached out her hand and patted Daegon on his shoulder. "I'm sorry about your friend."

Daegon nodded. "Thank you. But he was more than a friend. He was like my father." He hesitated and closed his eyes. "No, he was *much* more than a father. At least he was there for me."

El threw a bundle of clothes on the bed next to him, which brought him back to reality and his personal pity party. "I don't need to know about your family issues. When you're ready, get dressed. We have a mission that I'll need an extra body for." She forced back her drink and gave him a wry smile. "Considering we saved your life, I would think you owe us one...Your Highness."

Daegon reached for the clothes as El exited the tent. He still didn't know where or when he was exactly. He needed more information. Who were these people he was with? The Forlorn. They'd saved him from that creature, but who knows what kind of trouble he'd gotten himself into.

He could run. There was an opportunity. At the rear of the tent, a door invited him to sneak out. The commotion in the camp drifted toward the front and would probably hide his leaving. But where would he go? Into the forest? Back at war with the cold?

Daegon unrolled the bundle of clothing El had thrown at him. The faded brown wool clothes hid holes and pulled strings within their seams, but given the circumstances, they were sufficient and much warmer than Daegon's own. He hurriedly dressed and exited the front of the tent into the Forlorn's camp.

Upon stepping out, the wind returned its greeting, slapping him with a fresh reminder of its stalking presence. Ice pellets stung his face, forcing him to squint against the whiteout.

El called the event Tundra. Were they actually going out in this weather? Would they be able to see or navigate through the snow and wind? Would the horses even make it?

Lamps of burning oil provided a hum of orange light through the fog of the snowstorm. Despite the frigid conditions, the camp was a hive of activity. A woman with skin like polished obsidian sharpened a spear next to a pale giant who stood a head taller than any man Daegon had ever seen. He'd known Braccans, with their tan skin, carrying goods into his city, prepared to trade, but even these were different. He took a step back as a soldier with bright red skin threw a box to another soldier missing a left arm.

A powerful force pushed Daegon back from the doorway of his tent. A mountain of a man blocked his path. He had a mustache thick enough to nest a bird in. "Apologies," the giant squeaked. The voice was soft, lighter than a child's. The man reached down to help Daegon off the cold ground. "El requested I come grab you when you're out."

Daegon wiped the snow from his clothes and covered his face with the scarf El had given him. "Where are we going, exactly?"

Without answering, the large man put his hand on Daegon's back and ushered him across the camp. Daegon tried to pull away, but Krag's hand was a vise. The giant didn't even notice Daegon's struggle; he just kept walking, almost dragging Daegon along like an unruly child. Since the snow and wind made it too difficult to see anyway, Daegon decided he would just go with it. If El had sent the man to retrieve him, he was likely being taken to her, or at the least, to where he needed to go to assist in whatever she needed him to do.

"What's your name?" Daegon asked. Even though the wind was strong and the scarf muffled his voice, the man heard him. He at least wanted to know who was possibly kidnapping him if it came down to that.

The man released the pressure from Daegon's back, but the intention of continuing to move was present. "I'm Krag the Destroyer."

"The Destroyer?" Daegon questioned, with the slightest bit of laughter under his breath.

"That's right. I'm El's most powerful warrior." He pulled a large, chipped axe from his back and brandished it.

"Hey, I like a good nickname." Daegon rubbed the back of his neck. "Especially when it looks like you can back it up."

Krag huffed and motioned with his eyes for Daegon to continue. He didn't put his hands on Daegon, but he didn't need to. They soon came to the main section of the camp, where most of the Forlorn stayed.

The camp was lively and larger than he'd thought the Forlorn camp would look. Not that he had any reference, but a random ragtag band of soldiers exuded a certain idea. At least a hundred members all performed some duty for the betterment of the Forlorn.

The two stopped in front of a cart with six individuals sitting with cloaks covering their heads. Krag raised his hand, gesturing for Daegon to step up and into the cart.

Cloaks completely hid the snow-drenched soldiers. Hesitantly, Daegon climbed in and took a seat next to a small, covered individual. An unseen hand threw him a similar cloak and gestured for him to wear it. Daegon slipped it over his damp clothing.

A small voice peeped from the little person. "Can you fight?"

"Excuse me?" Daegon asked, unsure of what was happening.

"We're going to rescue one of our own. Can you fight?" The person repeated the question.

Daegon's hand went to his hip. Empty. His father's sword was gone. They must have taken it when they brought him into the camp. How was he going to fight? And most of all, what were they supposed to fight against?

A shock rippled through the cart. "Are we all ready to go?"

El tapped the cart two more times, and the entire crew returned the response in unison, "Aye!"

Krag sat down in the cart opposite Daegon, joining the mass of hidden bodies. The cart lurched. Wooden wheels groaned against the packed snow, vibrating through the floorboards and into his boots. Whips cracked through the air, picking up the pace; the cart's wheels straining under the load. He sat in the dark, surrounded by the heavy breathing of six strangers.

They had been moving for several minutes when a hiss stretched for his attention. He looked up from his cloak. Krag gestured down to the floor of the cart. A sword. Not his father's, but a rusty blade positioned right in front of Krag's foot. Daegon nodded, and Krag kicked the sword over to him. He reached down and held the hilt in his hand. It was salvaged and unkempt, lacking the balance he'd become accustomed to. Perhaps the spoils of a recent conquest?

Everyone's heads stayed down, staring at the squeaking planks layering the floor of the cart. He could try to escape right now. Eight on one. It was an option. Not a very good one, but maybe better than going off and fighting some unknown enemy. He'd seen animals that would send the cart careening through the woods. His father loved hunting parties, routinely rounding hundreds of Malachi's best soldiers, returning with few, but carrying the trophy heads of Ravabeasts and Marmoles. Both would present devastating opponents for this group of bandits.

The smaller person next to Daegon nudged him with his elbow, asking him the same question again. "You can fight, right?"

Why must he want to know so badly? Daegon leaned over and reassured him. "I can fight."

The smaller person deliberately rubbed his hands underneath the green tunic, excitedly chanting under his breath. Krag whispered to the person next to him, then directed his attention toward Daegon. "The Fluidguard captured one of our lieutenants, and we have to rescue her before they bring her into the city."

The little person interrupted, "It makes the rescue more difficult if they can make it into Shishbash."

Daegon kept up with the conversation, but he remained confused by all the details that they assumed he knew. "So, what do you want me to do?"

The smaller individual hissed back at Daegon. "We need you to fight. Create a diversion. Keep the Fluidguard occupied so that we can free Moan."

Krag said, "What Jovy is trying to say is that we need all the strength and manpower we can get in order to go up against the Fluidguard."

Daegon leaned back and thought about where he was, what he was doing, and how he got there. Between the clothes, the thick walls of the cart, and the cloak, at least he was warm. He didn't know about the Fluidguard, the Forlorn's mission, or his own expected role. For self-preservation, he would just continue following. At some point, an opportunity would come to escape, or maybe he would suddenly wake up.

Covered and inside the cart, the monotonous landscape dragged on. They were in the middle of nowhere, with only the moon cascading across the shimmering snow. It slipped through the crossed branches above, illuminating their path. Unfamiliar voices cut through the creaking cart. They were close.

It wasn't long before the cart came to a sudden halt. Shaking metal and the crunching of wheels echoed their movements.

Daegon and the others stayed quiet, unmoving in the cart, but still covered.

A man's voice ripped through the wind. "What is the meaning of this?"

El jumped from her horse, her feet landing softly in the snow. "I'm not sure. The old girl doesn't seem to want to move."

"You'll have to get that nag out of the way." He motioned to one of the other soldiers. "Perhaps one of my men can be of help."

The soldier wasn't satisfied. The distinct ring of steel shifted under their cloaks.

El said, "No, I don't think they'll be able to. She's a pretty stubborn gal."

The soldier quickened his voice. "Under the order of Shishbash, I'm going to order you to move."

El's feet crunched through the snow as she walked around the cart. "I'm afraid we're not going to do that."

The soldier pulled a large spear from his back. The soldiers guarding the prisoner's cart pulled their swords from their sheaths. The man in the front said, his voice firm, "I will not ask again."

El said, "You won't have to." She smacked the cart.

The Forlorn soldiers threw off their tunics and jumped out of the cart onto the snowy terrain. They drew their weapons and raced toward the prisoner's cart. The surprised soldiers hesitated for a moment before gathering their wits and putting up a small defense.

Daegon didn't think; he moved. Muscle memory from years of sparring with Jordell took over. He vaulted over the cart, the rusty sword heavy in hand. Two guards turned toward him, and he slid into a stance. Feet wide, blade high.

Metal swords clanged against one another. The Forlorn outnumbered the Shishbashi convoy two-to-one. Krag and his team overwhelmed the soldiers, knocking them to the ground and kicking their swords away. But there weren't any killing blows. Instead, they kept the soldiers pressed to the ground as Krag ripped the door off the prisoner transport.

The soldier fighting El yelled, "Don't let them escape!"

Jovy stayed at the prisoner cart, attaching some sort of contraption to the wheels while the rest of the team ran back to the Forlorn cart with Krag carrying a new person on his shoulder. Two additional men remained with their hands chained to the prisoner's cart. Daegon sprinted to the men and slashed at the metal shackles. He waved them away. Go. Somewhere. Anywhere.

"Let's go, new guy." Jovy's low, hissing voice yelled over the roaring wind. "You will not want to be here when these go off."

Daegon looked at the wheels where four boxes with lights flickered on and off. He wasn't sure what they were, but Jovy's wide eyes screamed danger. He needed to get away. Fast.

El continued her fight with the spearman. He was a much better fighter than the others. His sapphire armor glistened under the moonlight as he stabbed and spun effortlessly around. With their weapons locked, Daegon lowered his shoulder and drove into the spearman's midsection. The impact knocked the wind out of both, and they hit the snow hard, the soldier's spear flying from his grip. His helmet flew across the snow, and Daegon locked eyes with a blond-haired man who couldn't be much older than him.

The Forlorn fighters called from the cart, "We have Moan; it's time to go!"

Daegon sprang from the ground and hurried away. Expecting to be followed, he turned back. The man, lying in the snow, stared at Daegon, accepting a soldier's defeat. El jumped on the horse and whipped it to speed. The cart crunched as its wheels moved through the thick snow. The Forlorn soldiers high-fived and cheered when Daegon jumped into the moving cart. Moments later, Jovy pressed a button, detonating an explosion that rippled through the forest.

Boom.

The world turned white. A thunderclap slammed into Daegon's chest, rattling his teeth. The cart lurched sideways, lifting onto two wheels before slamming back down.

It went silent for several seconds, and Daegon shook his head at the unexpected pressure. But then, loud cheering and exuberance from the Forlorn members inside the cart broke through. They had completed their mission. Score one for the Forlorn.

Chapter Six

T he raucous cheers in the Forlorn camp were a twisted echo of his coronation. The Forlorn celebrated the return of Moan, their lead expert in planning. They were preparing for something. Something big, but Daegon had had no sleep since the *Scourge's* attack on Malachi and couldn't take part in any of the events. He spent the night and the entire day sleeping on his cot. A bed fit for a King. He scoffed. If only his court could see him now. Sleeping in a tent, smelling of wood-smoke and dried sweat. Though the scurry of the camp rattled outside the flap, he used it as white noise, falling deeper into a peaceful sleep.

Light flooded the tent. The dreaded bite of wind nipped at his feet. Daegon squinted at the silhouette standing in the entrance.

"Time to wake up. We have a mission." She yanked his covers to the ground and threw a sheathed sword onto the cot before leaving the tent.

Daegon gripped the hilt. The raised runes dug into his palm—a familiar, grounding pain. He looked up, but El had already left. She hadn't handed him a weapon. She'd handed him an invitation.

Daegon sat on his bed and closed his eyes. The outside noise had faded. Instead of the standard commotion of the day, the tent was filled with silence, replaced by the subtle clicking of packed bags and locked buckles. *Were they moving?* Daegon put on his warm clothes and lifted the flap. The camp was still a Forlorn camp, or how he supposed one should look. Only emptier. The boxes that littered the alleys were now packed away on carts, and the soldiers dispersed into the woods. While many of the tents remained, most people had already rolled theirs up and stored them for the trip.

Daegon stepped out, squinting against the glare of the snow. A few yards away, the team gathered around a large stump covered in a sprawling, charcoal-drawn map.

They didn't look up when he approached. They didn't need to. The air between them was already thick with the familiar tension of soldiers before a drop.

Krag was the first to break the silence. The giant polished the head of his axe with a rag that looked comically small in his massive hands. He nodded at Daegon, his voice a soft, high squeak that still seemed wrong coming from a chest that size. "Good to see you upright, little man," Krag said. "You took a hard hit when the explosion went off. Thought we'd have to carry you the rest of the way."

"I'm fine," Daegon lied, though his ribs still throbbed in time with his heartbeat. "Just a bruise."

"A bruise?" A sharp hiss cut through the air. Jovy sat cross-legged on the snow, his tail twitching as he packed black powder into a small clay pot. He didn't look up from his work. "You nearly missed your escape. If I hadn't waited to detonate, your 'bruise' would be scattered across three miles of tundra."

Daegon stiffened, remembering the chaotic scramble of the ambush. "I... I'll hurry next time."

"He'll learn, Jovy. Give the boy a breath."

The voice came from the shadows of the supply crates. Moan stepped into the light, favoring her left leg. Her armor remained scuffed from the Fluidguard restraints, and a fresh bandage wrapped tight around her forehead, but her eyes were sharp. She looked Daegon up and down, not with suspicion, but with a weary sort of respect.

Moan said, jerking her chin toward him. "If you hadn't helped, I'd still be in chains. Or dead." She offered a tired, grim nod. "You're one of us."

Daegon blinked, surprised by the acknowledgement. He managed a nod back. "Glad you made it out."

"See that you do," El said, cutting through the moment as she stepped into the circle. She dropped a heavy satchel onto the map, drawing everyone's eyes. There was no wasted time on pleasantries. "Since our royal guest is awake, Moan is mobile, and Jovy hasn't blown us up yet, we can actually begin. Eyes on the map."

She drew a knife and stabbed it into the circle marked near the center of the charcoal drawing. "Shishbash," she said. "We leave in an hour. We're the strike team for the mission."

Daegon said sheepishly, "Which is?"

Silence slammed into the group. Krag stopped sharpening his axe. El's eyes narrowed, sharp as daggers. Jovy's breathy voice said, "The Forlorn's mission is to protect the Conjurors and all of those they represent."

It seemed like a reasonable mission. *Why would there need to be an opposition? Who would oppose that?* Daegon nodded, which seemed like enough understanding as the team returned to El's drawings.

She continued with her plan. "We're going to sneak in through here." She pointed to a diagram depicting the sewers of a city. "Jovy, the tunnel will take us right to the keep. You're going to plant your explosives here." She finished pointing at the four corners of a large building.

"Explosives?" Daegon's eyebrows raised. "What are we blowing up?"

El balled her fists, remaining locked on her diagram. "I know you don't remember what the world is like, but the Congregation isn't good. You saw what happened to that young man in the woods. Slaughtered by the Reapers." El stabbed her stick into the snow, twisting it until the dirt showed through. "They send them like cattle to the slaughter. Another year, another kid thinking they can save the world. We're going to stop it." She took a seat on a log, wiping the snow from her brow. Her voice quieted. "It's like clockwork. The Congregation isn't righteous. Who sends its citizens on a perpetual death march and paints it as heroism?"

Daegon held El's gaze throughout the explanation, while the rest of the group nudged away from him and fidgeted in their seats.

"Any more questions?" El shot out.

Daegon shook his head. El returned to her planning. As he returned to the sanctity of his thoughts, her voice hummed against the quiet whistle of the wind. *What did he just get into?*

Daegon jumped at a coordinated clap. The briefing was over. Krag, Jovy, and Moan all dispersed throughout the camp, but El stayed sitting on the log, staring into the warmth of the fire.

Beyond the campfires, the forest was a wall of black pine. Above, the stars were impossibly bright; sharp points of light that Malachi's city glow had always drowned out. Maybe he could find the answers to what was going on in Shishbash? Or the Congregation? Whatever that was. Malachi was a trade partner with dozens of nations, but the cities discussed were strangers to him. There were Conjurors in Malachi. But people didn't revere them as individuals destined to save the world. They were far more common. Far more ordinary.

So many thoughts crowded his mind. While trying to make sense of everything, a random hand squeezed his shoulder. El approached with the bottle of brown liquid she'd been drinking earlier. Or something similar. The twinge of sour, bitter mash hung on her breath. She handed him the bottle. "Don't take the quiet personally. The team is on edge. We've been planning this mission since the snow started falling."

"Leading is difficult." Daegon took a glass from El's outstretched hand.

She took a swig and walked up beside him. "I just can't let anything affect the mission."

"No, it's okay. I get it. I'm just so confused, El." The wind died down, providing an uninterrupted view of the forest's sky. "I just don't know what's happening. I find myself in a world where I don't speak the same language. I don't know what a Reaper is. What Shishbash is. What a Conjuror does. What this Journey is. I'm just..."

"You're really just messed up...Your Highness." She flashed him a hidden smile. "I thought you were a spy," she said, taking a swig. "Convenient timing, showing up right before Moan got snatched." She took another drink of the liquid. "I believe you. You truly don't know what's happening."

Daegon shook his head, thinking of the potential compliment she'd just given him. "I don't." Daegon let the liquid enter his throat. The burning masked the frigid outdoors. "What we're doing is preventing Shishbash from creating a Conjuror?"

"Exactly!" El patted Daegon's shoulder. "We're saving the Conjuror's life. So many die to the Reapers when starting the Journey." She removed her hand and stared at the moon. "And that's before the end of their Journey, when the Grand Conjuror disappears altogether."

"Where do they go?" He followed her gaze up into the night sky.

"Nobody knows. The Congregation says that they're in a better place. Supposedly enjoying the spoils of their salvation."

Parades and applause splashed across his mind. From what he'd seen, defeating the *Scourge* was worthy of being called a hero. "You mentioned the Congregation earlier?"

"It's run by the Cardinals," she spat the words. "Five old fossils in red robes who think they own the world. They sit in their towers, preaching 'Keep the Memory' while the rest of us suffer."

Daegon's eyes snapped up at the mention of another familiar concept. The phrase ricocheted in his head like the collapsing stones of Malachi's keep. "Keep the Memory? A group of people called the Cardinals also led Malachi. Do you think they're the same ones?"

El finished the rest of her drink and chucked the bottle into the woods. "It's their phrase. Their greeting. Their goodbye. It's rather shadowy in meaning." She blew out a cloud of breath. "One thousand years? I assume it's a similar group. They've been around for as long as the *Scourge* has."

Daegon spun the glass in his hand; smudged fingerprints speckled the sides. "What are some of their teachings?"

"Their main teaching is to limit conjuring to only those approved to complete the Journey. Each city has a piece of power that grants the ability to manipulate the elements."

"Right, Malachi had Conjurors too."

"Ancient Malachi did. The city was destroyed because of its overreliance on conjuring. The conjuring of today is much more selective, and each city's guard controls for its unauthorized use." She crossed her arms. "Eventually, the Conjuror collects the power of each city, which allows them to defeat the *Scourge*." She tilted her head up at the moon. "Forever immortalized."

Daegon sighed, recalling the flurry of conjuring that illuminated his coronation. There was nothing controlled about it. One thousand years. The words bounced around in his head as he swallowed the last of the liquid. "Maybe I'll find answers in Shishbash."

El laughed. "We're not going on a vacation. It's an in and out mission." She put both her hands on his shoulders and patted them. "I'll tell you what, though. I can take you to our leader in Alexander. He might give you more answers than I can."

Daegon nodded. "That works. Thank you."

A voice yelled from inside the camp. "El!"

"Duty calls," she said. "We'll roll out soon. Be ready." El disappeared back into the storm.

Daegon stood alone at the edge of the light, staring into the frozen black of the trees. He wasn't a King here. He was just another soldier in a war he didn't understand.

Chapter Seven

T he small group of Forlorn soldiers gathered outside El's tent. They carried their weapons and Jovy's bag of explosives. Krag grabbed Daegon and threw him into position behind Moan. It wasn't a hard throw, but more of a "let me show you what to do" nudge.

El walked to the front of the group and barked orders. "Alright, men, it's about a three-hour march through the forest. With Shishbash as our target, we should return before sunup." El finished by raising her sword, using its point as a compass.

The group marched two-by-two through the moonlit forest. The snow had softened its persistent whipping to a light breeze; however, the damage had already been done to their walking path. Daegon's stride adjusted to the thick snow that flooded the forest floor. He marched next to Krag, who ignored the snow and trudged forward with effortless strides. Jovy, who walked next to Moan, complained about the stray giggles of the group as he was only a foot taller than the snow mounds.

"Are you excited for this, Jovy? We finally get to see how powerful your explosives really are?" Moan chuckled before finishing. "Let's hope they don't fail this time."

Daegon said, "This time?"

Moan brushed the hair from her eyes. "How ever do you think those Shishbashi soldiers captured me?"

Krag pulled the axe from his back and held it high above his head. "If they fail, I can destroy it."

Jovy looked like he was jumping from place to place in the snow. "Well, they worked pretty well to free you, didn't they?"

Moan put her hands through her dark brown hair. "For that, I am much obliged."

"Alright enough. We're all family here." El turned around to break up any squabble that might have developed, but she did it with a small smile peeking from the corner of her mouth.

Daegon cracked a smile, the tension in his shoulders loosening. Their bickering was better than the silence of the forest. The fresh snow stretched ahead, paving an endless road, and the constant buzzing of insects provided a backdrop for his wandering mind. El threw her balled fist in the air. Through the wintery haze, a large frozen gate loomed. Ornate blue ice dripped down the front like frozen tears. It wasn't just on the gate either. As he followed the outstretched walls of the gate, the beautiful blue hues of ice covered every surface. *Beautiful and practical.* The slippery ice was an ingenious defense, preventing intruders from scaling the walls.

Two fires burned discreetly, emitting their glow within the two adjacent towers. Daegon whispered, "So how are we going to break through that gate?"

El crouched and bunched the group together. "Were you not listening to the plan?" El patted Moan on the back. "Can you please show us the passageway you found into the city?"

Moan nodded and took charge at the front of the group. She led them to an area just beyond the city wall's sightlines. Any closer and they risked the guards spotting them. Moan pointed at the ground, and Krag sliced with his burly axe. It ripped through the thick snow until it clanged on a piece of metal. A hidden grate poked through.

"The best part about Tundra is that the cold should freeze over the sewers," Moan said, chuckling. "It should make for a smooth path into the city."

Krag ripped the grate from the ground and threw it aside. It landed quietly in the distance. If there weren't a layer of cushioning, the lug of a man might have given their position away.

El led the way into the hole. "Hey Jovy, let's hope we don't see any snow snakes."

Jovy shook his head back and forth. "Snow snakes. Why is she always trying to mess with me?"

The rest of the group slid into the sewers. By the time Daegon dropped in, El had lit a torch. Krag had to duck his head to walk, but the frozen river of water provided ample space. The wind from above no longer whipped them in the face, leaving them alone with their clouds of breath, their boots crunching along the frozen river. Shadows stretched long and thin against the curved walls, dancing with faint moonlight.

Moan, who knew the passageway from her review of the city's architecture, led the way. "It shouldn't be far now. It should take us right below the keep."

Jovy rubbed his little hands together. "Yes, yes. Then it goes kaboom." His excitement might have been enough to light the room without a torch.

Just ahead, a small glimmer of light crept through an opening in the ceiling, brimming with frozen drippings stretching for the floor. Krag jammed his axe at the ceiling, and pieces of ice collapsed. He looked at Daegon and Jovy. "I'll lift you two up through the hole."

Daegon said, "Me?"

El put her hand on the icy wall. "We still need you to prove yourself. You're obviously a capable fighter. I just need you to make sure Jovy is safe while he plants the explosives."

Daegon's head spun around. "What about Krag? Or you?"

El looked over her shoulder at Krag. "He's a little big to be sneaking about the city, don't you think?" She returned her gaze to Daegon, creeping ever closer. "I will man the tunnel to make sure it's safe for you to return."

Moan interrupted, "Sorry I can't be of more help. The keep is right above, and it's dark enough that you should be able to slide back in without being seen. It should be a quick job."

El's thumb raised at Moan. "See, should be a quick job."

Daegon rubbed the back of his head as he stepped toward Krag. "And if something goes wrong?"

El flipped her hands and let out a smile before thrusting a bag into his chest. "That's what Krag is for."

Daegon weighed the heavy bag in his hand. He was the expendable one. The distraction. If he got caught, the Forlorn lost a stranger. If Jovy got caught, they lost an expert. But did he have a choice? The grate ripped from the frozen ceiling, causing an echo to ripple through the tunnel.

El lovingly scoffed. "Could you be any louder, Krag?"

Krag's high voice chimed back. "Sorry." He gestured toward Jovy and Daegon. "Up you go."

Daegon entered Shishbash. The wall and gate were a prelude to the city's majesty. Brilliant dark evergreens lined the alleys, providing a green contrast to the decorative blue ice that crested each building. Snowflakes covered roofs, and intricate ice sculptures dotted every corner. Colorful streamers and wooden rattles sprinkled the stone buildings—flashbacks to his coronation.

Jovy bumped into him, interrupting his wonder. "Alright, remember the plan." Jovy pointed at the two large bags of rhythmically pulsing spheres. "You're going to go to the other side of the keep and plant them on the columns."

Daegon intended to disperse the bombs quickly. However, Jovy's size deceived the true load. The bag was heavier than it looked. The straps dug into his shoulder, and he had to hunch over to keep the spheres from clacking against his knees. How careful did he have to be for them not to blow up? Daegon didn't want to chance it, carefully throwing the bag over his shoulder and hoisting it to the backside of the keep. Thankfully, the snow was more managed in the city. The forest was a river of ice and frost that he had to wade through. But here? It was more of a dusting.

Prior to placing a bomb, Daegon's arms dropped to his side. High above the keep, a blue flag snapped in the wind. The Eye. His city's symbol, staring down at him in a foreign land. His stomach turned. He shook his head. He was in enemy territory. If anyone found him, he would have a hard time explaining anything, especially with a bag full of explosives.

He placed one sphere at the bottom of the column. The building's ice stretched across the surface and consumed it. Step one: complete. One last bomb and he would be out of here. Daegon hoisted the bag over his shoulder, this time slightly lighter, and walked to the last column.

A silent whimper trickled from the corner.

On the back of the building, a young woman with shiny black hair sat on the steps of the keep. Daegon crept closer, using the shadow of a frozen pillar to hide his approach. The bag of explosives bumped rhythmically against his hip, a heavy reminder of why he was here. But he couldn't take his eyes off the woman. She sat on the steps, looking out at the sleeping city. She wasn't wearing the mail of the Fluidguard or the rags of a commoner. She wore clean white wool that glowed in the moonlight. Her shoulders were shaking.

She was crying.

Daegon hesitated. The mission was clear. *Plant the charges. Get out.* But the sight of the Eye snapping above her, combined with her obvious grief, pulled at him. The scene was too familiar. It was the home he'd lost.

He stepped out of the shadows, his boots crunching softly on the frost.

"It's a chilly night for stargazing," Daegon said, keeping his voice low.

The woman spun around, her hand flying to her belt. She didn't reach for a dagger, but for a small pouch tied at her waist. Her eyes were red-rimmed, but the sadness in them instantly hardened into suspicion.

"The keep is restricted," she said, her voice tight. She scanned him, her gaze lingering on his strange clothes and the heavy bag at his side. "You aren't a guard."

Daegon froze. He forced his hands away from his sword, raising them slightly in surrender. He needed a lie, and he needed it fast.

"I'm a traveler," Daegon stammered. He gestured vaguely at the icy architecture around them. "I... I wanted to see the city before the crowds arrived for the festival. I didn't realize this area was forbidden."

"A traveler?" She didn't buy it. She took a step back, her fingers twitching over her pouch. "Nobody comes here just to look at ice."

"It's not just ice," Daegon said, the truth slipping out before he could stop it. He looked up at the frozen spires; the ghost of his own city reflected at him. "It reminds me of home."

The woman paused. The aggression in her stance softened, replaced by a flicker of curiosity. "Home?"

"Malachi," Daegon whispered.

The name hung in the cold air between them. Her hand dropped from her belt.

"Malachi?" she repeated, her voice softening. "The dead city?"

"Not dead," Daegon corrected, remembering El's revelations. The ache in his chest was sudden and sharp. "My father... he used to tell me stories about it. He said the walls shined like pearls when the sun hit them."

The woman looked at him, really looked at him, for the first time. The suspicion drained away, leaving only a shared, quiet loneliness. She turned back to the view, wrapping her arms around herself against the wind.

"My father told me stories, too," she whispered. "He said it was a place where hope was born. Before the *Scourge* took it all away."

"Your father was right." He wasn't lying anymore.

She wiped a tear from her cheek, replacing it with a practiced, porcelain smile. The kind of smile meant to hide things.

"It's rare to meet someone who knows about the old stories. Thank you."

Daegon nodded, the warmth in his chest fighting against the cold reality of the explosive bag at his hip. He lingered too long. Every second he stood there was a second closer to getting caught, or worse.

"I should go," he said, stepping back toward the shadows. "Before the guards realize I'm here."

He turned, the snow crunching under his boots.

"Wait," she called out.

He stopped, looking back over his shoulder.

"I'm Layla."

"Daegon." He held her gaze for a second longer, memorizing the face of the only friend he'd found in this frozen hell.

As he walked backward, memorizing her soft figure, she cleared her throat. "Keep the Memory."

"Oh. Yes. Keep. Keep the Memory." He hadn't gotten used to the phrase since the Cardinal mysteriously uttered it in Malachi.

As he turned the corner, he looked down at the pulsing bag at his hip. He closed his eyes and tucked the bag against the frozen pillar. Time to go. His job was done.

The front of the keep was as sleek as he'd left it. Jovy recently finished his job and slipped into the hole. Krag's arm leveraged the grate above the snow, leaving Daegon to snap his fingers about how smoothly the plan had gone.

The door of the keep slammed open.

"Stop!"

Daegon turned. Three men clad in blue scale armor raced out. Daegon instinctively put his hand on the hilt of his father's sword. *No.* His hand pulled off the sword, and his feet churned toward the opening in the ground. Something caught his foot, sending him sprawling. His foot was now encased in ice. He smacked the foot against the cobblestone, shattering the cage and freeing his toes. He sprang to his feet and limped to the hole.

Another ball of ice smashed his arm, and the cold crept through his wrist and shoulder. Daegon tried to shake it free, but the weight of the ice shifted his center of gravity. Another piece of ice hit him on his good leg. He was mere feet away from escape, but he couldn't move. Another ball smacked him in the back, taking his breath away and dropping him to the ground. With his remaining arm, he pulled himself closer to the sewers, but the ice glazed his eyes.

"Sorry, Daegon." Krag's voice echoed.

They had to be close. The sound of the grate scraped against the stone. They were going to leave him.

Another voice sounded in the darkness. El. "We'll come back for you, but if not, thank you for your sacrifice." The grate slammed onto the hole, and Daegon was back to being alone.

The ice encircled him, restricting his movement and breathing. With a groan, he turned onto his back and looked up at the snow flurries. Out of the corner of his eye, Layla stood, her mouth agape. The ice surged over his face, pressing against his lungs. Cold and suffocating. The crunch of boots on snow filled his ears before the world went white. Then black.

Chapter Eight

Daegon inhaled. The frigid air shredded his throat. He was alive. He opened his eyes. White mist filled the air before him. Breath. He wiggled his fingers, no longer encased in ice. That might've been preferable. His shoulders shivered at a stray breeze that slid across the nape of his neck. At least he was still wearing his Forlorn cloak. As his vision focused, bars came into view, blocking the lone exit. A cell? Daegon stood from the bench and walked to the metal bars, his warm hands sizzling on the cold steel. "Hello!"

There was no one else. Only him and the faint flicker of a stray torch lighting the hallway out of the dungeon. Daegon shook the bars, rattling ice onto the unkempt floor, exposing the smooth metal underneath. There was no point. He turned back toward the bench and sat. A narrow window provided natural light into the cell. While it was too small to slip through, he stood on the bench and peered out of the slit. Footsteps clacked in rhythmic cadence, marching across the icy cobblestone. He closed his eyes and leaned his head against the window. Drums thundered against the stone walls, shaking the dust from the ceiling. Outside, Shishbash was screaming in celebration; inside, the silence was deafening.

The bombs must not have gone off as planned. Or they hadn't gone off yet? The parade of people continued for what seemed like hours, and what he thought were bombs rippling through the city turned out to be fireworks of what he assumed was the Conjuror's celebration. An explosion of color painted the inside of his cell.

The hallway across from the bars rumbled, and Daegon sprang from the bench, thankful that he hadn't frozen to it. A voice questioned him from the darkness. "Ah, you're up."

Daegon said, "Who's there?"

A taller man stepped forward, grabbing the torch from the wall. The blonde-haired soldier from the ambush stepped into the dungeon.

"I am Sir Gallant. And you are the filth who tried to blow up my city." The man gradually stepped to the edge of the bars, brandishing the flame in Daegon's face. "It's not every day that we catch a member of the Forlorn alive."

Daegon stepped forward, meeting Gallant's approach. "I'm not part of the Forlorn. They found me in the forest. They saved me from a Reaper."

Gallant spat at the excuse. "You expect me to believe that? You're being charged with attempting to murder the Conjuror, and now you're no longer with the Forlorn?"

Daegon scanned the empty cells and frozen moss that reached for the ceiling. He had no leverage. El told him not to bring up Malachi, but what if that had been a lie? It was worth a shot. "It's true. I was being crowned King of Malachi when the *Scourge* destroyed my city. I woke up alone, for dead, in the forest outside of a Forlorn camp. They brought me in, and I followed along." Daegon's voice petered out, matching the cadence of the whooshing flame. "I don't know what's going on."

Gallant narrowed his eyes. "Malachi, huh? You're a little far from those ruins, aren't you?" Gallant slammed the torch against the bars. Sparks showered the floor. "Where is Alexander? Tell me where the rats hide, and I might let you keep your tongue."

"Alexander?"

"Enough with the games!" The soldier's voice bounced around the empty cell.

"Like I said. I don't know what's going on. I wasn't part of the Forlorn." Daegon fell back onto the bed.

Gallant's eyes again narrowed, and he violently spun, sticking the torch back in its holder, and retreated out of the room.

The door slammed, leaving Daegon to once again sit idly with his thoughts. The celebration outside his chamber rattled the room, and shards of icicles periodically fell from the ceiling, providing some much-needed excitement to his captivity. What were the Forlorn doing? Given how little they knew Daegon, he wasn't surprised that they'd abandoned him. Leave the loose ends to fix themselves.

He waited in the cell for hours. Eventually, the sound of the celebration died, and the footsteps outside the window walked in the opposite direction. During his time alone, he'd created an amusing game. Watching his breath slowly freeze before it reached the ceiling. It wasn't much, but it kept his thoughts from suffering the same fate. One nearly reached when the same door slammed open at the end of the hall. *Not him again.* Daegon stood from his bench, prepared for whatever punishment the soldier could threaten.

Gallant slammed the torch into the bracket on the wall. The flame sputtered, casting deformed shadows across the cell. "I don't have time for games," Gallant growled. He pulled a dagger from his belt. It wasn't a weapon of war, but a thin, cruel blade meant for skinning. "You are with the Forlorn. You planted the explosives. Tell me where Alexander is, or you won't have fingers left to point with."

Daegon pressed his back against the cold stone wall. "I told you. I don't know who Alexander is. I don't know where I am."

"Lies." Gallant stepped forward, the blade gleaming orange in the firelight. "You'll talk. They always talk."

"Stop."

The voice was soft, but it hit the room like a hammer. Gallant froze.

Layla stood in the doorway. She wasn't wearing the soft wool from the night before. Instead, ceremonial white furs draped her slender figure. A crown of woven frost adorned her dark hair. Regal. Powerful.

"My Lady," Gallant said, sheathing the knife and bowing his head. "You shouldn't be down here. This prisoner is dangerous."

"He wasn't dangerous last night," Layla said, stepping past the soldier. She stopped at the bars, her blue eyes drilling into Daegon. "He was lost."

Daegon straightened, meeting her gaze. "I told you the truth, Layla. I am Daegon of Malachi."

Gallant scoffed. "He is a lunatic, my Lady. A heretic claiming to be a dead King from a dead city. Let me finish him."

"No," Layla said.

"My Lady?" Gallant's jaw tightened.

"Open the cell," she commanded.

"With all due respect, I cannot..."

"I am the Conjuror!" Her voice rose, cracking with a sudden, sharp authority that silenced the dungeon. "The Stone awaits me. The people await me. And I want him there."

"You say you're a King?" She looked back at Daegon. "You say you know Ancient Malachi? Then come witness the ceremony. If you are a liar, the Stone will reveal it. And if you try to run..." She glanced at Gallant. "Then Sir Gallant can have his fun."

Gallant stared at her for a long moment, his face flushing red. Finally, he spat on the floor and jammed a key into the lock.

Click. The door swung open.

"One wrong move," Gallant whispered to Daegon, his hand hovering over his sword, "and you die before you hit the ground."

Daegon stepped out of the cell, the chill of the dungeon replaced by the icy tension between his captors.

"Lead the way," Daegon said. He shrugged his shoulders and stepped past Gallant, who was fuming at the decision. The groaning continued until they approached a door outlined in light.

Layla opened the door into the city of Shishbash. The bright, reflective shimmer of the city blinded Daegon. *He couldn't have been in the cell that long.* His body cracked with every step, as if thawing from the dungeon's frozen clutches. He stood at the entrance and admired the sleek design of the city, glistening in the sun sliding off the icy glaze.

Gallant nudged him from behind. "Let's go, Your Majesty. The Conjuror has to complete the ceremony." The words practically pained him to speak.

The crowd from earlier swarmed the keep. Where he'd met Layla. Where he'd planted the explosives. A giant, pulsing blue stone, which they'd wheeled out of the building, was planted at the center of the crowd. The stone hummed the melody of his childhood. A subtle vibration that started in his teeth and rattled down to his boots. It called to him. Wanted him. This was what El was talking about. What gave the Conjuror's power. *Could it have done the same to Malachi?*

They shuffled their way to the front of the crowd. He was glad that the crowd didn't know who he was or what he did, as they probably wouldn't take kindly to someone trying to destroy all that they had been celebrating. Daegon's eyes widened as an older man dressed in a dark red cloak made his way to the center stage.

"Presenting Cardinal Bilari," a voice resonated over the crowd.

Cardinal Bilari was one of the five Cardinals presiding over Malachi. While impossible, it was clearly him. Was he over one thousand years old as well? Daegon stepped onto the snowdrift platform, biting his lips. None of this made any sense.

Cardinal Bilari was frail, but his contrasting deep voice easily stretched over the crowd. "Today begins a magical journey. Our dearest Layla has taken the reins, following her father, prepared to harness the power of Shishbash to vanquish the *Scourge*."

The crowd roared with applause. Bilari continued with his speech, but Daegon had a difficult time understanding any of it. Or hearing any of it. Everything became a blur as he thought about all the times the Cardinals were present in Malachi. There was an answer to where he was and why he was there. And the answer had something to do with them. He was sure of it.

Bilari requested Layla forward, but her mind must've wandered during the speech. She stood, eyes wide and unmoving. Eventually, Gallant nudged her, and she cautiously treaded to the front. Layla stepped toward the pulsing stone and offered her hands. The stone lit with a vibrant blue as her hands trembled. Her back arched, and blue light flooded her veins. She gasped, straining to keep her feet.

After a minute of holding the pose, Layla's hands erupted in white light, and she dropped to the ground. Her billowy white cloak swallowed her figure. She looked up from her knees and forced that porcelain smile she had shown him on the steps. She braced to her feet, held up her hands, and a snowy flurry shot from her palms. The crowd responded with raucous applause.

Cardinal Bilari returned to address the crowd. "Congratulations, Layla." He flourished his hands, enabling the crowd to increase their volume. "Your Journey begins now, but it is not without danger. May you and your protectors complete the quest and vanquish the *Scourge* for good. Keep the Memory."

Cardinal Bilari shook Gallant's hand and froze when he made eye contact with Daegon. The two held an uncomfortable gaze before Cardinal Bilari turned away, retreating into the Shishbashi keep. Fireworks thundered overhead, contributing flashing colors to the mystical frozen landscape. Daegon stared at the painted sky. If the Forlorn's bombs had worked, this would all be ash. A roaring crowd flooded through the frozen streets, partaking in the festivities that only made him miss home. *Why would they want to stop this?*

Daegon leaned into Gallant. "I know Cardinal Bilari. He's from Malachi too."

Gallant shook his head. "Impossible. Cardinal Bilari has been the protector of our Stone for decades. If he were moonlighting as an ancient Malachinian, I think it would be blatantly obvious." Gallant shook off Daegon and walked to Layla, helping her to maintain her balance.

But Daegon knew Cardinal Bilari from his childhood. He was kind and taught the wonders of conjuring to the children of Malachi. He had a fondness for showing off snowmen during the winter or for creating whirlpools in the fountains. It made sense that he was associated with Shishbash.

Daegon ran to Layla, but Gallant's hand swiftly reached for his spear. Daegon took a step back and raised his empty hands. "Woah! I'm not your enemy."

Gallant huffed, sliding his hand from the spear.

Daegon lowered his hands, refusing to give Gallant any opportunity to strike him down. "Is there any way we could have a meeting with Cardinal Bilari?"

Layla's eyes narrowed, and Gallant translated, "He thinks that Cardinal Bilari is from Malachi, like him."

Layla bit the inside of her lip and provided a sheepish smile. "Of course."

Gallant rolled his eyes, but she waved her hands, and a series of guards escorted them into the keep. With how long he had been in the dungeons, they glared at him, but Gallant raised his hands. "Calm, we would like an audience with Cardinal Bilari."

The guards stepped out of the way, and the door swung open. A guard led them into the central chamber. Instead of the frozen architecture of the city, the inside was warm, complete with flowing streams and waterfalls decorating the chiseled walls. A booming voice chimed in from the opposite side of the chamber. Daegon looked around. Cardinal Bilari leaned against a second-story rail, staring at them.

"Welcome Layla. I did not expect to see you so soon." He walked down the staircase adjoining the platform. "Congratulations on attaining the power of liquid from the stone."

Layla's cheeks rose as she thanked him. Gallant and Daegon stepped up beside her.

Cardinal Bilari continued. "Sir Gallant, it's always nice to see you." His voice slowed inquisitively as he stared at Daegon. "And who might you be?"

Layla interrupted the conversation before Daegon could speak. "This is King Daegon of Malachi."

The older man rubbed his chin. "King Daegon...of Malachi?" The man paused, thinking over the information. "Malachi has been destroyed for all but one thousand years, has it not?"

Daegon finally had the chance to talk. "So everyone says. Have you ever been?"

The old man shifted his stance. "To Malachi? Of course. Many of the Congregation travel to Malachi. A monument to the consequences of irresponsible conjuration." He pointed his hand at the water, its form shifting under his power. "Take only as much as we need, right, Sir Gallant?"

Gallant nodded, but Daegon pressed with his questions. "There was a Cardinal Bilari in Malachi. He was there on the day the *Scourge* destroyed the city. Was that not you?"

Bilari pulled at his robes, their scarlet features contrasting with the cool tones of the room. "The *Scourge,* you say? If you survived an encounter with that monster, I'm not surprised you're more than just a little confused about your reality." Bilari turned away from the group. "I truly am sorry that I am not the Cardinal of your memories."

Daegon stepped forward ready to ask more questions, but Gallant's hand slammed into his chest, pushing him backwards. Gallant intervened. "Thank you for your time, sir. Our friend here has been...confused as of late. We're sorry if we impeded."

Cardinal Bilari said, "No impediment, Sir Gallant. Take care of Layla and bring peace to our land. Keep the Memory."

Gallant offered a hand signal to the Cardinal and repeated the phrase before pulling Daegon by the shoulder. Layla stepped back, watching the Cardinal gently ascend the staircase. They exited the Shishbashi keep and returned to the snowy stage, where the crowd remained. Fervent cheers erupted from the crowd as Layla returned into view.

Gallant chuckled. "We forgot the most important part of the ritual."

Layla smiled and stared at her hands before flinging them into the air. Crack. A surge of blue energy erupted from the sky. The snowflakes falling from the clouds shone a brilliant blue. The sky parted, and the ground melted as if the grass and stone were drinking the snow. Trees stretched toward the warming sun, shaking off their frost, and the statues that adorned every building released a refreshing, misty spray that sprinkled the skin. The Festival of Tundra had ended. The Conjuror's Journey had just begun.

Chapter Nine

A misty glow bounced between the dew-soaked buildings. Now that the frozen layer had eroded from the structures, Shishbash was more ordinary than thought. Rows of thatched houses intermixed with decorated brick houses, their fireplaces chugging suffocating black plumes of smoke. The melting ice exposed the rustic, choppy cobblestones beneath. Recently thawed fountains peppered the surroundings with fresh water, and the remnants of ice sculptures that adorned every building pooled on the pathway. Water danced through the streets, twisting into impossible spirals before splashing into the gutters. The city was weeping its decorations away.

"Do you mind helping, Your Highness?" Daegon jumped, nearly dropping the crate. He hadn't heard Gallant approach.

Gallant grabbed multiple crates of supplies, loading them into the carriage to prepare for their journey to Terratoria. Gallant's tunic was already stained dark down the back. He wiped his brow, leaving a streak of grime. "This heat is unnatural," he grunted.

Daegon grabbed one crate and heaved it into the carriage. He was about to grab another when Layla approached. She wore much lighter, traditional Conjuror robes and carried multiple bags of supplies. She tied her dark hair in a ponytail and wore a crest bearing the unknown symbols on the flag above: a fish with a snowflake.

Gallant groaned at the sight of the bags. "You know we're making a Journey, not going on a vacation?"

Despite the protests, Layla threw the bags into the cart and gave Gallant a hug. Daegon leaned on the cart, his foot propped up on the final crate. He couldn't help but notice the many eyes that stared at him through the crowd. Did they know what he had done? He was an outsider here, after all, and Daegon had no idea where he was or what he was doing. He'd already been a part of the Forlorn and their stupid plan. Now he was joining their direct enemy? If enemy was the right word. Daegon shrugged off the glares and strapped the supplies into the cart. They were ready to go.

Daegon found Gallant at the front, standing with his arms crossed, eyes fixed on a group of children taking part in a combat lesson. Their swings and movements were familiar. When he was young, Jordell taught him similarly. Blade high. Blade low. Step into the enemy. Parry. Down. And what meshed it all together? Timing. Jordell always talked about timing. The old man used to say, "You don't have to be the best dancer; you just have to know the rhythm."

Daegon said, "Do you know any of them?"

Gallant scoffed. "They're orphans. Taken in by Shishbash hoping to become Fluidguard of the Congregation."

"So, you trained them?" Daegon filled the space next to Gallant.

Gallant stared past him, his knuckles white as he gripped his own biceps. He looked like a statue. Cold, hard, and unmoving. "You wouldn't understand."

"What does that mean?"

"You say you're a King. Of Malachi." A grim laugh rumbled from his tight jaw. "If true, you woke up every day pampered, without even a shred of worry that you'd live to see the night."

"You act as if I were—"

"Regardless of how you were. We, Shishbashi, have to fight for our safety. Every day we risk the wrathful eyes of the *Scourge*, its Reapers, or some monster in the forest." Gallant's gaze finally dropped to Daegon. "The very hands that risk their lives trained our children. To be the best."

Daegon opened his mouth, but Gallant brushed past him, crashing into his shoulder and continuing to the cart. Daegon looked back at the kids dancing to the beat of their blades. Their every step was perfectly coordinated, and their shrunken plates of armor jingled as they moved. Combat was reserved for the royalty of Malachi. It was their duty to protect those who couldn't protect themselves. He reached into his waistband, fingers tracing the ridges of his father's hilt.

As he walked back to the cart, a colossal statue stood high above the center of town, its arms crossed with a hood draping its familiar face. The carved robes were reminiscent of Layla's current attire, and the base of the statue rippled with water that reached into the city. Layla already sat in the cart, staring up at the statue and moving her hands in some prayer formation.

He tapped the cart, surprising her. "Someone you know?"

She said, "Something like that."

She was about to continue, but Gallant jumped on the cart and readied the horses. "It's time!"

Crowds lined the streets to say their goodbyes. Streams of water sprayed over their carriage, replacing the snow flurries and mounds of ice. The splashes cooled their sun-kissed skin. Daegon remembered the crowd at his albeit short-lived ceremony, but the number of people to cheer on Layla's journey was unquestionably more. *Could Layla mean this much to these people?* He caught Cardinal Bilari's eye, who stood on the porch of the keep, staring at them with his hands behind his back. The door to the city slammed shut, no longer encased by the brilliant patterns of ice, but now flowing with pristine waterfalls.

"No turning back now," Gallant exclaimed before snapping the reins of the horse to speed deeper into the forest.

***

The hooves of the horses dug deep into the ground. Gallant pulled back on the reins. "We're making camp here for the night."

They had been traveling for most of the day. The sun peeked behind the trees, casting a red glow through the forest. They had stopped in a small clearing with pieces of stone jutting from the ground. It was almost too perfect of a clearing. Daegon stretched and jumped from the cart. The ground wasn't just dirt; it felt unnaturally solid. He rubbed his boot through the surface. Hard stone lay beneath the spongy grass, hiding forgotten rubble. "Where are we?"

Gallant tied the horse to an outcropped piece of stone. "This is Whisperwind. Right on the border between Terratoria and Shishbash."

Daegon reached for the shapes. Faded words fought back against his touch. They weren't random rocks, but collapsed structures that time had forgotten. "We're safe here?"

Gallant kicked a piece of blackened stone. "You see this rubble? This used to be a town. They relied on Conjuring too much. Now? It's a graveyard."

Layla joined. "All Conjurors pass through when they begin their Journey. It grounds us in the reality of what we're about to undertake."

Daegon paused and ran his fingers through his hair. "What are those rules?"

Gallant ambled up to him. "Only as much magic as you need. Too much is a burden on life as we know it. Hundreds of years ago, the town of Whisperwind found that out the hard way." He shook his head and reached out his hand. A sharp knife dropped into Daegon's outstretched palm. "I'm going to find some firewood. Can you please find us something to eat?"

"Something to eat? Like what?"

"Rabbit, fish, snake, I don't know, and I don't care," Gallant retorted, turning back toward the tree line. "You know how to hunt, don't you, Your Highness?"

That remark stung. Of course, he knew how to hunt. The number of times his father had taken him hunting. It was his father's favorite thing to do; the only memory that didn't make him hate the missing King.

Daegon stepped across the crumbled walls of the town and into the forest. With his father's sword firmly at his side, he sifted through the foliage, searching for any signs of wildlife. Scratch marks on the trees, trampled patches in the grass. *This is just like one of the royal hunting parties.* A trickle of running water turned him toward a stream. *There had to be an animal around here somewhere.* Daegon grunted and walked further into the woods.

"Why is this so hard?" he asked himself.

Birds scattered from the trees as he disturbed the bushes and stepped on branches. While green and red berries were plentiful, Gallant had surely packed fruit. They needed protein. Something to be at the core of a meal. Something fresh. A twig snapped. The sound cracked through the silence like a whip. Daegon froze, his hand hovering over his hilt. Gallant and Layla's conversation had become a distant whisper.

He crouched and stalked his way toward the noise, shaded by the unique shapes of the canopies above. Daegon unsheathed his blade, prepared to capture whatever lay behind. The rustling betrayed something large. With his free hand, he moved the curtain of green to the side. Metal shrieked against metal. A gauntlet of black steel and bone punched through the foliage. A massive sword followed, cleaving a sapling in half as it swung for Daegon's head.

He moved out of the way, deflecting the sword into the ground. Daegon screamed for Gallant. For Layla. For anybody. After the attack, the Reaper stood there, silent. Daegon scrambled backward, his boots catching on roots. He raised his sword, but his hands were shaking. His heartbeat pulsed through the back of his head, and his breathing steadily raged out of his mouth.

The Reaper's monstrous arms moved once again, mechanically shifting under the armor. The creature lifted its foot in Daegon's direction. He stepped back, but his foot snagged on forest overgrowth, and he collapsed into a thick bush.

A voice rang through the trees. "Daegon, where are you?"

It was Layla. *What was she doing without Gallant?* He scrambled up, leaves sticking to his sweat-drenched face. "No, Layla! Run!"

Layla appeared between two trees, following the stream of water to his location. Daegon reached for his sword and spun around, ready to die. But the blade hit only air. The forest was empty. No heavy breathing. No crunching footsteps. Just the wind mocking him with a low whistle. He spun in circles, hands gripping his scalp. Something that big doesn't just disappear. His voice shook. "There was a Reaper right there." He pointed at the undisturbed pile of leaves.

Footsteps rustled behind them, cracking branches as they approached. Daegon didn't think. He lunged for Layla, shoving her behind him. He raised his sword, putting his body between her and the noise.

Gallant broke through a thick wall of bush. "Is everything okay?" He breathed heavily, surveying the scene before lowering his guard. The woods were empty. "Have you never been in the woods before, Your Excellency?"

Daegon lifted his shoulders and directed Gallant to the Reaper. "There was a Reaper. Right there."

Gallant snickered. "If there were a Reaper, we'd all be dead."

Daegon released Layla's hand, and she followed Gallant back toward the camp. Gallant must've been successful with the fire as a plume of smoke rose through the forest. He took a breath. The cold steel of the Reaper's blade still hung in his mind. He winced; the phantom sound of metal cleaving wood still rang in his ears. He sheathed his sword, but refused to release the hilt.

Chapter Ten

T he roaring fire blazed at the campsite. Dusk stretched shadows across the ancient town's crumbled architecture. Daegon sat on a stone slab as Gallant pulled fish from a roasting spit and passed them around. "We're about a day's walk, now, from Terratoria." He used his teeth to rip off a piece of stubborn twine. "Once there, Layla, you'll complete the ritual and we'll restock on supplies. Should be quick."

Daegon took a bite out of the roasted fish. The savory crunch of the skin was a relief after the last few days. The fire popped, sending sparks into the night air. For the first time since the tower fell, Daegon's shoulders dropped. No running. No fighting. Just the heat of the coals and the smell of roasting meat. Layla hadn't touched her food. She just stared at her fish, pinching at the crisped skin from the once colorful body. He'd seen Conjurors before. He'd become so accustomed to them he rarely glanced at them anymore. But in Malachi, there weren't any stones that people harnessed their power from. They were just born with it.

"There will be a Reaper...eventually," Layla whispered, staring up from the coals. "They're drawn to the power of the stones, like the *Scourge*."

Gallant covered his mouth, hiding his food. "Don't worry, Layla, I will be there to protect you."

Layla caught herself and forced a smile. "Of course, I know."

Gallant lifted himself from the ground and tended to the crates, strapping down their extra supplies for the journey tomorrow. Layla put down her skewer. "So, you really don't know about the *Scourge*?"

Daegon shook his head. "All I know is that the *Scourge* destroyed Malachi." He placed his skewer on the rock surrounding the fire. "And I ended up here."

"The power of the stones draws the *Scourge*. If there's too much conjuring being used in any one place, it comes and cleanses the land."

Daegon rolled the skewer across the rocks. "Is that so?"

"That's what the Congregation preaches. That's why the stones are so far apart, leaving each of the individual nations with its own." She hovered her hand over her cup, attempting to pull an uncertain stream to her fingers. "Shishbash maintains the power of water. Terratoria. They control earth."

Daegon rubbed his thumb against his palm, trying to make sense of the rules of the world. "In Malachi, we kind of just had conjuring. We used it freely. It didn't require any sort of stone or ritual."

Layla said, "Maybe that's why the *Scourge* destroyed Malachi? To cleanse it of an overreliance on conjuring?"

Daegon sighed, the glow from the fire brightening as the sun descended behind the trees. "Then why did I survive?" He shook his head and asked. "Cardinal Bilari mentioned your father was a Conjuror too?"

The radiance of the fire contrasted with her blue eyes as her eyebrows dropped. "He was Shishbash's last Conjuror," she whispered. "He'd completed the stones and was about to destroy the *Scourge*. Then a Reaper found him. It didn't just kill him, Daegon. It erased him."

The crackle of the fire faded. "I'm..." His words failed him.

Layla shook her head, a tear falling from her eye. She forced a smile, masking the sadness. "No, it's okay. It made me realize how important a Conjuror is to people. No matter how dangerous the Journey is, people can't live in eternal fear."

Daegon bit the inside of his lip and watched her feet ruffle in the dirt. "Layla, it's okay to be afraid."

Her smile shook from side to side. "It's good to give people hope. Even when it's hard. Even if we die trying. To know that someone is working to end the suffering, it's worth it." She wiped both her eyes and took a breath. "I'm living up to my father's memory."

Daegon hesitantly reached for his fish. "I wish I could say the same."

Layla seized the chance to change the subject. "Is your father here too?"

Daegon scoffed. "No. I don't know. He disappeared 10 years ago." He took a bite out of his fish and sarcastically said, "King Raynor of Malachi."

Layla perked up at the name. "Raynor!"

Daegon raised his eyebrows. "You know him?"

A voice chimed in from the darkness, and Gallant reappeared. "Grand Conjuror Raynor was the previous Conjuror to defeat the *Scourge* and bring the Peace."

"What?" The heat of the fire rushed across Daegon's face. "My father? A savior? That's impossible. The man couldn't be bothered to raise a child, let alone save the world. And besides, he lived what? 1000 years ago?"

Layla tilted her head and said, "You're here, are you not?"

Gallant sighed, taking a seat beside Layla. He lowered his voice. "About 10 years ago, Grand Conjuror Raynor completed the Conjuror's Journey and destroyed the *Scourge*."

Daegon looked from Gallant to Layla. "Destroyed the *Scourge*?"

Gallant rubbed his hands down his face and sighed. "I forgot you truly don't know what's going on. The *Scourge* never truly dies. We get a reprieve from its destruction, but it regenerates with time."

Daegon said, "If it returns, why do it at all?"

Layla said, "We call it The Peace. Even if it's not permanent, the time when you don't have to worry about surviving is precious."

Gallant stood from the fire once again. "And as for your father, if it is your father, Grand Conjuror Raynor. The Congregation says that they've entered the holiest of places. No one's sure where that is, but our teachings say that defeating the *Scourge* gives you eternal salvation."

Layla looked down at her feet, which had created a divot in the ground. "If you really are Grand Conjuror Raynor's son, maybe fate brought you to us? Maybe we can destroy the *Scourge* once and for all?"

Fate. A cruel coincidence in the form of the *Scourge's* defiant grin. It had to be something. Daegon forced a smile. "It's worth a shot!" Renewed vigor filled his voice. "Let's get the stones, find my father, and destroy the *Scourge*!"

Layla held out her hand, palm open to the fire. "To the end?"

Daegon looked at her unblemished palm, then at his own father's sword leaning against the log. He placed his hand on hers. "To the end."

Gallant didn't join. He just nodded, his eyes reflecting the flames. "I'll keep watch."

Chapter Eleven

A light dew spritzed the rubble in Whisperwind. Daegon stretched from his makeshift bed. Gallant had already loaded the cart. The sun gleamed through the trees, carrying with it the subtle sounds of tweeting birds. He walked to the fire, where two crimson fish roasted. Layla raised her hands, practicing her newfound powers in a pot of water. So focused, she missed his approach. The water shook, but shifted under her control, raising and lowering, and twisting into spirals.

Daegon said, "That's pretty impressive. What's it been? Two days?"

The water splashed into the pot. Her cheeks blushed red as they peeked around the edges. "It's not something that comes naturally."

Daegon sat beside her. "In Malachi, the Conjurors would do all sorts of tricks with water. They would create snowmen, rainbows, anything to create a bit of laughter."

She manipulated her fingers before emptying the pot of water and chuckled. "It sounds wonderful."

Gallant's footsteps were heavy. He wore his traditional Shishbashi armor, decorated in ornate blue metal, gleaming under the blistering sun. "We should get to Terratoria by midday."

Layla nodded and stared at the collapsed camp. "I've never been outside of Shishbash." Her words were barely audible against the soft breeze.

Daegon stood and touched her shoulder. "If it means anything, I've never been to any of these places."

Her arm covered her mouth, hiding the laughter. She reached and touched his hand; the warmth rippled through Daegon, causing him to pull back. Layla ignored the recoil and said to Gallant, "I didn't know you were such a chef."

The knight plopped down next to them and pulled a perfectly crisp fish off a skewer. He pointed it at Layla and said with raised eyebrows, "You know, I've learned a thing or two about survival in these woods."

Daegon took a bite of the fish, savoring the flaky flesh melting in his mouth. "She's right, Gallant. It's not half bad."

"That's Sir Gallant to you." He spat a piece of the charred fish onto the ground. Gallant's smile didn't reach his eyes. He spun the spear in his hand, the heavy wood whistling through the air. "You were pretty scared back there when you thought you'd seen a Reaper."

Daegon frowned. "From what I'd seen back in the Twinwood Forest, they don't exactly seem the friendliest." He was about to take another bite when something heavy smacked him in the chest. His sword.

"You talk a big game, King. Let's see if you can actually hold a blade." Gallant rose from the campsite and walked to the center of Whisperwind. He pulled his spear from his back and pointed it at Daegon. "Shall we?"

Layla raised her hands and attempted to keep Daegon seated. "Now? I don't think we need to do this right now, do we?"

Daegon shrugged and pulled his sword from the scabbard. "It's okay. I get it. He doesn't trust me." He readied himself with the stance Jordell had taught him all those years ago. Foot back. Weight balanced. Sword raised. "I don't blame him."

Layla sat back at the campsite, front and center for their duel. Gallant thrust his spear at Daegon's midsection, which Daegon successfully parried away. The dance had begun. Daegon raised his sword and slashed at Gallant's plate mail, trying to avoid swinging for any of his vulnerable areas. *It was just for fun, after all.* Gallant locked his sword with the base of his spear and crushed his shoulder into Daegon's face. Iron stung the inside of his mouth. He expected the metallic taste of Gallant's armor, but blood dribbled down his cheek. *Or so he thought it was for fun.*

Daegon balanced himself and waited for an opportunity. It was always about the timing. Gallant whipped his spear around once again and stabbed at Daegon's midsection, but he sliced at the spear, bouncing it away and kicking Gallant in the stomach. Gallant clutched his stomach, gasping for air.

From the campfire, Layla pleaded, "Can we be finished now?"

"No!" Gallant jumped at Daegon with his spear angled above his head.

Daegon didn't think; he pivoted, letting the spear tip graze his ribs. He snapped his sword up, stopping the cold steel an inch from Gallant's throat. Gallant stepped back and sliced his spear at Daegon. The blunt side of the weapon bounced against Daegon's back, knocking him to his knees. Gallant readied his spear and went in for another stab, but Daegon rolled to safety, allowing the point to plant into the dirt.

Layla screamed from her seat. "Stop!"

Daegon and Gallant's eyes locked, sweat beading down their foreheads. They were breathing in heavy unison. *It was supposed to be for fun.* Gallant nodded, to which Daegon mirrored. Gallant wiped his brow. "So you can fight."

Daegon made his way to his feet. "Did you think I was lying?"

"One can never be too careful. Especially in protecting our Conjuror." He pointed his gaze toward Layla. "I think you're in good..."

An arrow whizzed out of the forest and landed in the bark of a tree surrounding the campsite. The morning sun created a layer of red glare along the tree line that made it difficult to discern any attackers. Another arrow blew past Daegon's head, causing him to run and tackle Layla to the ground.

"Get down!" Daegon yelled.

Gallant readied his spear, covered his head with his protected arm, and hurried toward the arrow's origin. "Bandits!"

A war cry flooded the field. Figures burst from the tree line. Small, fast, and ragged. They moved like a pack of starving wolves and wore pieces of tattered clothing, complete with matching masks all bearing the symbol of an eye with a scratch through the center. *Forlorn? No, they wouldn't be this bold. Would they?*

Daegon pushed Layla close to the log and covered her with a nearby blanket. "Stay down. Gallant and I will handle this."

Their duel had been a warmup for the proper event. Daegon readied his sword and approached the attackers, using Whisperwind's raised ruins to navigate the rain of arrows. Two bandits jumped into the clearing and raised their weapons, prepared to strike, but they were unlike any weapons he'd seen in his days of combat. Instead of swords, spears, or mauls, these weapons were chipped stone, curved at the handle, and just sharp enough to pierce flesh. He doubted they would do anything to Gallant's Fluidguard armor.

Another arrow blew out of the tree and bounced off Gallant's plate armor. Even the arrows couldn't hurt them. Daegon and Gallant both ran at the intruders, immediately causing them to retreat into the forest cover. *What were they doing?* Three attackers dropped from the trees above. *Surrounded.* Their weapons were of the same variety, and their armor had a similar disordered mix of patterns, still bearing the scratched eye.

Daegon and Gallant prepared their weapons when the ground exploded. A jagged wall of rock erupted from the earth, slamming into the bandits with the force of a battering ram. Daegon turned his blade toward the wave of stone where a man with long dark hair wore a purple set of Conjuror's robes. He waved his hands, tracing a pattern he'd envisioned in his mind, and stomped his feet, causing spikes to spear the edge of the forest.

The enemy attackers initially stepped on the spikes before retreating deeper. The clamor of battle died as quickly as it started, replaced with the serene mumble of insects moving about. Gallant and Daegon leveled their weapons at the man stepping into Whisperwind.

"Relax," he said. "I am not your enemy." The man lowered his hands, his chest heaving. Dust fell from his purple robes. "You're lucky I was passing through."

Gallant stepped forward with his spear aimed at the man. "You're lucky we don't take care of you right now. Who are you?"

"A Conjuror. My name is Fabian." He flourished his hands and bowed, his black hair staying tightly kept behind his ears.

Layla peeked above the log, and Gallant gestured for her to stay down. He said, "Where is your protector, Conjuror?"

Fabian hesitantly stepped closer. "His name was Reyxor. Sadly, he passed away protecting me from a Reaper." Gallant refrained from attacking, allowing Fabian to step closer. "For the last week, it's been me, just trying to make my way to Shishbash to gain the power of yet another stone."

Gallant huffed but ultimately lowered his spear, prompting Daegon to follow his lead. Layla made her way up from the log and said, "I'm sorry to hear that. Do you need anything?"

Fabian smiled at her. "I could smell your cooking from a mile away. I bet it's some delicious fish."

Gallant sheathed his spear on his back and ushered Fabian to the campsite. *We're just going to trust him? Like that?* Fabian sauntered to the log and took a seat, resting his forearms on his knees. Gallant dropped to his knees and tended to the fire, stoking the fire to cook the remainder of the fish. Layla offered a cup of water to the Conjuror.

Daegon cautiously returned to the campsite and stood behind Fabian. Dirt and dried sweat matted the Conjuror's dark hair. Based on his ability to manipulate earth, he must've come from Terratoria—their next destination. His protector had succumbed to a Reaper, wincing at the steel arms and skeletal designs that refused to vacate his mind. The isolated journey of the man reaffirmed Daegon of the dangers that loomed ahead.

After consuming some fish, Layla asked, "You were on your way to Shishbash?"

Fabian wiped his chin. "We were. However, we were ambushed just outside of Terratoria." He looked down at his feet. "We'd only attuned to two stones. I didn't think we'd be in that kind of danger so quickly."

"But you survived," Gallant interrupted. "We can help you find another Protector. You can even join us as we travel to Terratoria. Continue the Journey. Keep the Memory."

"Keep the Memory." Fabian chuckled under his breath. "I don't know if that's the right decision."

Daegon said, "What do you mean?"

Fabian looked back at Daegon and said, "I'm not sure if I want to continue. If it's even worth it."

Gallant stood from the log and yelled, "You would brand yourself a Loneseeker? That's sacrilege!"

Fabian pushed himself from the campsite and brushed his robe with his hands. "I can tell that's not something you agree with."

Gallant stepped toward the Conjuror. "As the head of the Shishbashi Fluidguard, I would have no option but to arrest you."

Fabian bit his lip and stepped back. "So says the Congregation. Their Journey killed Reyxor..."

Gallant interrupted, "You understood the risk. The Conjuror's Journey isn't about any individual person. It's about bringing the Peace. No matter the cost."

Fabian turned around and looked at the trees. The morning sun had peaked over the canopies, and a wave of birds fluttered above. "I'm not so sure anymore." The fading embers prompted him to stand. "I feel like I might have overstayed my welcome." He took a step toward the forest.

"Where do you think you're going?" Gallant pulled his spear from his back and pointed it at the Conjuror. "If we let you go, we endanger everyone you come in contact with."

"What are you going to do? Kill me?" Fabian shook his head and continued to walk toward the trees. "I'm not coming with you."

"If I must." Gallant lunged at the Conjuror, but tripped onto the ground. His feet had frosted over with a layer of ice that held him steady.

"Let him go," Layla whispered.

"We can't! It's not allowed."

"I said, let him go." Layla stood from the campsite and moved to block Gallant's path. "As my Protector, you must do as I say."

Gallant's knuckles turned white on the spear shaft. The veins in his neck bulged. For a terrifying second, Daegon thought he would strike Layla to get to the deserter. Gritting his teeth, he said, "As you wish."

Fabian wiped the sweat from his brow and waved off the group, disappearing into the forest. Daegon walked up beside Gallant and put his hand on his shoulder. Gallant shrugged off the hand and lumbered to the cart, returning to pack for the trip.

Daegon said, "Is he going to be okay?"

Layla crossed her arms. "Gallant is the most devout member of the Shishbashi Fluidguard and has been there for me since my father passed away. He's the best of all of us. He will be fine."

Chapter Twelve

After the bandit attack, breakfast went down faster than usual. Gallant heaved the rest of their supplies onto the cart. They would be at Terratoria soon. Maybe he could meet with the Cardinal? They might have more information about where he was and how he got here. Or maybe they knew about his father. The idea of his father being this grand savior didn't mesh with his memories.

Daegon rubbed his hands over the faded etchings of a Whisperwind ruin, trying to discern the history of the architecture. The faint images of conjured water lapped against the stone, but time had erased the remaining carvings—another worn-down victim of the *Scourge*.

With the fire crackling in the background, Gallant cracked his whip, causing the horses to drag the creaking cart along the faint trail. After a few hours, the ground shifted. Shishbash was natural, complete with tall conifers and thick, emerald blades of grass. The dense rows of trees filled the forest with walls of nature.

Now, the trees grew fragile and dingy. Between the large swaths of dirt, the grass turned brown, patchy, and starved for water. Before their eyes, and without so much as a tell, the lush forest had morphed into a barren desert.

The air swelled with copper and dry earth. Daegon wiped sweat from his brow. The cool breeze of Shishbash was a distant memory, replaced by a suffocating heat that radiated from the cracked ground. "So, does Terratoria celebrate an incoming Conjuror with a desert ceremony?" A tinge of sarcasm brandished the question, but he never knew what could or couldn't happen in this world.

Gallant actually chuckled. "No, no, this is just how Terratoria looks." The group scanned the endless beige void. "They're one of the center nations, meaning Conjurors come to their cities more often. More conjuring, more possibilities for the *Scourge*. They're never really given the opportunity to rebuild."

Daegon winced at the image of the *Scourge,* its toothy maw collapsing down on him. Teleporting him into this future world. He leaned onto the cart's edge, gripping the edge as the memory clenched its teeth onto his mind. In the distance, a dust cloud kicked up, and the faint shadows of fighting peaked through. Metal shrieked against metal, and a plume of fire erupted from the dust, orange and angry against the beige horizon.

"Fire?" Daegon whispered. "Is that a Conjuror?"

Daegon pointed, but the knight had already seen the battlefield. He jerked the cart in the direction and snapped the reins. Gallant pulled the spear from his back. "Ready to fight, Your Highness?"

Was it a point of endearment or resentment at this point? Did he seem like someone who wasn't able to use a sword? He pulled his father's blade from the sheath and held it above the ledge. "I'm ready."

They circled the fighting cloud. Within, a family in a carriage staved off attackers, their horse slain in the sand. The short offenders sported matching makeshift weapons and tattered clothes. Their matching sigils—a scratched eye—marked them as the same crew from Whisperwind. Except this time, instead of a few hidden bandits, dozens of attackers overwhelmed the family. But the father held them back, throwing balls of fire into the group. A Conjuror.

Daegon and Gallant jumped from the cart and raced toward the battle, his father's blade reflecting the unobstructed sun's rays onto the dusty ground. They deflected a hail of stones and rusted scrap metal into the shifting sands. Like the group at Whisperwind, the attackers' armor wasn't professional. More raggedy and thrown together, with an intent to confuse rather than protect. Gallant pushed in front of the family, avoiding the man's flames, daring them to strike. Multiple swords darted at him, their weapons swinging wildly. Gallant parried the attacks, his spear spinning rapidly. Daegon watched, mesmerized, until a stray blade nearly took his foot.

The enemy changed its target, screamed, and lunged at Daegon. The cloud of dust kicked up from the fighting made it difficult to follow the moving figures, but he fell back on the swordplay he'd learned from Jordell. Step, step, parry. Step, step, swing. Timing. The beautiful song that carried the beat of each strike. Through his timing, he tamed their blows, deflecting their haphazard weapons into the sand.

Before long, the attackers retreated. Gallant twirled his spear and walked toward them. The tornado of sand barreled in their direction. They screamed some obscenities, but the noise lay mute against the attacking sands. More dust shot up from their escape, allowing them to disappear behind one of the sandy hills. Daegon wouldn't let them escape. He sprinted after, but they'd vanished. At the top of the hill, a small opening in the sand succumbed to the stray grains. Gallant put his hand on Daegon's shoulder and pulled him back toward the family.

"Thank you!" The man crashed to his knees in front of his broken-down carriage. His family hid inside, clearly unsure about who they were. "Thank you for saving us from those savages."

Gallant didn't say a word. He simply stared at the man. Surveyed the family. His chin indicated the direction of his gaze.

Daegon stepped in front. "Who were they?"

The man picked himself up and wiped the sand from the front of his green tunic. "Those were the orphans. They're a group of bandits around here. Thugs."

Daegon sheathed his sword. His father had helped him out enough today. "I saw you using fire. Are you a Conjuror too?"

The man's face grew worried. He stuttered, "Oh, no, not at all." The man looked at Gallant and his glistening blue armor, unaffected by the dusty air. "Please, I was just protecting my family."

Gallant whipped his spear at the man's throat, stopping just short of puncturing the windpipe. "You're a Loneseeker." His voice grew deep with a scratchy roar. Even when he was transporting Moan, Daegon hadn't heard Gallant speak like that. Such ferocity.

"I didn't ask for it!" The man fell to his knees, clutching his wife's cloak. "It just happens when I'm scared! Please, sir, we were just trying to get to the city!"

There were so many unwritten rules to the land. Or maybe everyone knew them, and Daegon simply didn't. What was a Loneseeker? And more so, why was it a crime to be one? Daegon reached to lower Gallant's spear. "How about we just talk this out?"

Gallant whipped Daegon's hand off the spear. "You realize his presence endangers everyone here. That there's two Conjurors could very well send the *Scourge* our way."

Tears welled in the man's eyes. "Please, sir, I'm begging you. I was just trying to protect my family."

Gallant glared at the man's wife and child. They hid behind a crate, tucked into the cart. He closed his eyes and grunted. "I have to take you to Terratoria. They'll decide what to do with you there."

At the news, the family yelled out in pain. Gallant walked up to the kneeling man and placed a pair of locks around his wrists. "Please, sir, we were just escaping Terratoria. It's becoming worse by the day."

Gallant directed the man to stand and oriented him toward their cart. As he did, hooves clattered in the background. Gallant released him and reached for his spear. Daegon unsheathed his father's sword once again. A troop of horses raced toward them. *Could this be the orphans? Returning with backup?* Gallant directed Layla to lie down in the cart.

The thundering hooves circled, and Gallant spun around, locking eyes with the leader as they closed in. They wore unique clay masks and worn-out green armor, not too dissimilar to Gallant's regal garb. Daegon and Layla threw their hands in the air. They were outnumbered.

The leader pulled his horse into the air. It whinnied and slammed its hooves to the ground. Dust kicked at their cart, and the masked man slid down from the saddle. A muffled voice spoke behind the ornate mask. "You're a long way from Shishbash, soldier." The man approached with his hand firmly planted on the hilt of his sword while the rest of the horsemen sat idly watching their leader.

Gallant adjusted his posture and shot a comforting glance toward Daegon. "Peace. We're the Conjuror's party from Shishbash." Gallant brandished his bare hands. "This lady right here is Layla, our Conjuror. And that is Daegon. We're her Protectors."

The masked figure stared. Daegon wasn't sure exactly what he was staring at as the clay façade betrayed no emotion. His horse scratched the ground and snorted; the silence was almost as intimidating as the throng of soldiers bearing down on them.

The man sheathed his weapon. "We've been expecting you. Cardinal Mesa received word from Cardinal Bilari that you would be coming through."

Daegon and Layla lowered their arms. They were friendly. Or so it seemed. Layla shouted from the cart, "And who may we be talking to?"

The man grabbed the underside of his oversized mask and revealed a weathered gray-haired and bearded swordsman with a scar traced across his face. Daegon froze. His breath hitched in his throat. The gray beard. The scar across the cheek. The steel-gray eyes. He looked so much like Jordell. But the warmth was missing, replaced with the cold competence of a career soldier.

"My name is Sir Maybin. Head of the Terratorian Shield-guard. Cardinal Mesa has instructed us to bring you safely to Terratoria."

Gallant took a deep breath, almost expecting a brawl to take place. He reached out for an embrace with his arm. "Keep the Memory. I am Sir Gallant, head of the Shishbashi Fluidguard." With a deep laugh, Gallant said, "This place has seen better days?"

Maybin looked around at the barren landscape. "Yes, Keep the Memory. The *Scourge* has actually spared us these last couple of months. There's been fewer and fewer Conjuror's even attempting the Journey anymore."

Daegon caught the clay eyes of the surrounding soldiers. "Why's that?"

Maybin shrugged his shoulders. "I'm not sure. Perhaps that's a question for your Conjuror." He looked past Daegon and stared at the man Gallant had captured. "And who is that?"

Gallant walked over to the cuffed man and lifted him off the ground. "This is a Loneseeker."

The prisoner screamed, "I'm not a Loneseeker!"

Maybin eyed him before letting out some clicks with his mouth. Two horsemen closed in and grabbed the prisoner, throwing him onto the horse's back. "Unauthorized conjuration is a crime against the Congregation." He lowered his head and closed his eyes at the revelation.

The man continued to protest, but Gallant nodded in agreement. Were they really going to imprison a man simply for protecting his family? Daegon's hand drifted to the hilt of his sword as the additional soldiers scooped up the man's family and carried them back to the city. Gallant glared, warning him against a fight he didn't understand. Maybin clicked his teeth again, and two soldiers lined up next to their cart.

"Follow closely. Despite the appearance of nothing, there's a lot of danger in these lands." Maybin climbed back onto his horse and kicked off into the wasteland.

The group returned to the cart and followed. The encircled party of horses fell in line both in front and to their side. Layla sat straight, observing the mass of horses click their way through the dusty sand. Muted trees and stray bushes provided guidelines along the barely visible path. Gray birds perched on the dilapidated branches, their heads rotating as the wheels passed.

Daegon sat next to Layla, looking over the edge, the wheels of the cart digging into the sand. "Other than the *Scourge*, what else is out there?"

Pulling at the reins and centering the carriage, Gallant said, "You only really see the *Scourge* if the Reapers fail."

Daegon nodded. "Right, and their job is to stop the Conjuror's from defeating the *Scourge*?"

Layla said, "Nobody really knows what the Reapers are and why they are associated with the *Scourge*. Like the *Scourge*, the more stones you've visited, the more they're drawn to you."

Gallant interrupted. "I've just assumed they were the *Scourge's* minions, protecting their master."

Daegon closed his eyes. "I saw one. When the Forlorn saved me. It had just killed a Conjuror and his protector. It sucked the essence out of his body and crushed it."

Gallant kept his eyes on the path. "You're lucky to be alive then. One-on-one, those things aren't exactly forgiving. There's few who've fought them and even fewer who've lived to talk about it."

Layla touched Daegon's leg from across the cart, her sheepish smile warm against his mind. "There seems to be a lot of luck with you, Your Highness."

Your Highness? Gallant was rubbing off on her. She turned back toward the front of the carriage. Daegon followed, squeezing the edge of the cart as an imposing shape stretched across the horizon. Before long, the great gate of Terratoria came into full view. The stone structure spanned hundreds of feet high. Dozens of soldiers manned the guard towers that peppered the wall, stretching endlessly in both directions. It wasn't just built; it was woven. Massive stone fingers interlocked hundreds of feet in the air, holding the desert at bay.

Gallant took his hands off the reins and leaned back. "I've never been this close to the wall before." He rotated his head from side to side. "They say every new ruler adds to the wall, creating the incredible layers."

The lower layers were older, more weathered and muted, but as Daegon's eyes drifted up, he was greeted with an abundance of unique colors and patterns.

Layla leaned over the edge of the cart and whispered, "It's beautiful."

Daegon's head burned with the hidden eyes of a nearby observer. He broke from the wall's intense trance and scanned the environment. Five tiny figures stood atop a dune, silhouettes against the dying sun. They didn't wave back. They just watched, their eyes white marbles in soot-stained faces. Vultures waiting for a carcass.

"Who are they?" Daegon questioned aloud.

"Scavengers." A voice appeared alongside the cart. Maybin had been listening and enjoying the group's immense wonder.

"The city has fallen on hard times. More and more people are begging for food or leaving altogether."

Layla interrupted Maybin. "You said the *Scourge* hasn't attacked for a long time?" She turned to the children. "Why have so many fallen on hard times?"

Maybin looked toward the wall, taking his time to respond. "It's the fear of the *Scourge*." The Territorian rider continued alongside the carriage, waving his hand toward the gate operator. "We haven't been getting Conjurors, traders, visitors, anything." He closed his eyes. "The city has grown stagnant, and our citizens are suffering."

Layla turned back toward the soldier. "I see. Cardinal Mesa hasn't been able to fix things?"

"Cardinal Mesa is a good leader. She tries, but the Congregation sees Terratoria as a pit of despair. Where they stick the vagrants and apostates. Why have a wall if you're not going to use it?"

Layla offered a smile. "Maybe we can bring the city back to its original greatness."

Maybin loosened like everyone when Layla smiled at them. He nodded and struck a smile himself, before kicking at the horse and speeding to the front of their cart. The large gate swung open, scraping across the sandy floor. The city's streets erupted into view.

Maybin said, "Welcome to Terratoria."

Chapter Thirteen

The grandiose view of the wall faded into a sprawling city. Alleyways stretched like veins, and storefronts dotted every corner. Emptiness filled the crevices. What should've been a busy marketplace now resembled a trickling stream that had recently dried up. There were no vendors, no urchins trying to rob them, and a layer of untouched dust glazed every structure. As they made their way through the city, citizens poked their heads from the windows of the coated structures and stared at the cart with open mouths. The Conjuror. The hope.

Maybin directed them to one of the more cared-for towers. The building hadn't endured the torture that most of the city's buildings had suffered—structural cracks and open holes. A smaller archway echoed the city, shielding the guests from the desperate eyes of the starving populace. As they entered the courtyard, two guards greeted them, wearing the traditional green armor of the Terratorian Shieldguard.

Maybin took Layla's hand and assisted her out of the cart. Daegon and Gallant followed closely behind as the guards led them up a spiral staircase. Someone had clearly maintained this building. Or at least cleaned prior to their arriving. Maybin unlocked the door to their room. "Welcome to Territoria." He ushered Daegon and Gallant into the room. "Obviously, we've seen better days, but with you, Layla, we may one day return to our great heights."

Layla smiled. "I hope to see that."

Gallant scanned the area, picking up items, moving shelves, and looking under surfaces. "All clear."

Maybin frowned. "You don't think we'd try to hurt you?"

Gallant chuckled and patted Maybin on the shoulder. "To be honest, I don't trust many people. And you can never be too clear with the Forlorn. They'd already tried to stop us back in Shishbash."

"They did?" Maybin's eyebrows raised.

"Yeah. They planted bombs around our stone's keep to kill Layla." Gallant's eyes flicked to Daegon.

Layla interrupted, "But I'm safe now." Her optimism was always enough to calm a room. "Thank you, Maybin, for directing us here."

Maybin nodded and stepped out. "Of course, ma'am. Cardinal Mesa will let us know the next steps, but please enjoy the city if possible. Our citizens would love to see a Conjuror. They need some hope."

The door slammed, and Daegon looked out of the window. On the ground, within the courtyard, away from the guards' view, those children from beyond the gate stared at them. More than a few piled out of a manhole not far away. "For such a giant wall, security doesn't seem too tight around here." Daegon broke eye contact with the children and turned toward Gallant and Layla. "It looks like it's pretty easy to break in." He returned his gaze toward the children, but they'd disappeared. Back into the sewers.

His gaze ventured toward the cityscape. It really was expansive. They were but a small pinhole in the sea of buildings. Their tower, being one of the higher buildings, allowed him a sweeping view of the entire city. Despite the decay, shards of beauty peeked through the cracked roofs and collapsed statues. He saw the purpose. The promise. The pristine curves and lines, now eroded by time.

Gallant gathered a satchel and sheathed his spear to his armor. "Daegon, can you protect Layla and go into town for supplies?"

Layla said, "Where are you going?"

"I'm going to the prison. That Loneseeker wasn't alone. I need to know if there are more of them in the city before I feel comfortable continuing."

Daegon stepped away from the window and placed his sword on the table. "Um, sure. I think we'll be fine. Right, Layla?"

She looked at him and smiled. "Of course."

Gallant's feet plodded across the wood floor as he exited down the spiral staircase.

Daegon paced the room for a moment before turning toward Layla. "So, let's say we check out the market?"

Layla nodded, gathered their belongings, and headed into the dusty city. The streets were wide, peppered with what used to be market stands. A few remained open, mostly old men peddling food. Small crowds of green-cloaked civilians sifted their way through the market. Daegon approached one vendor stationed under an awning with what looked to be fresh produce. The vegetables were vibrant green, only slightly frosted from the prevailing dust. Daegon smiled at the vendor and asked, "So what would you recommend?"

The old man's wrinkled cheeks pulled back. "These sand peppers are always a favorite." He reached into the pile of produce and held up a gnarled, yellow fruit covered in thick spines. "Or sun-pears," the old man rasped. "Tough skin, but sweet inside. Only thing that grows in this dust."

Layla covered her mouth, hiding her laughter at the man's eagerness. She nudged Daegon's side, evoking a response. "Perfect. We'll take some of those. And whatever else you think is delicious."

The vendor packed up a large canvas bag and threw it across the table toward Daegon. Layla placed a small bag of coins on the table and nodded in his direction. The old man flipped the money between his fingers, feeling the grooves of the golden images: a fish with a snowflake. Coins from the treasury in Shishbash, given to Conjurors to fund their journey. The coin dropped from the old man's fingers.

He stared at the snowflake sigil, then up at Layla, his eyes widening. "Shishbash," he whispered, dropping to his knees. "You...you are the Conjuror?"

Layla provided her characteristic smile, causing the old man to yell in excitement. A swarm of people descended on their position. Daegon stepped toward her, his hand on the hilt of his sword, but she put her hand on his forearm. The warm, soft grasp called for him to fade away.

He obliged and took a step back as people surrounded her, bowing at her feet. A young woman asked, "Did someone send you to save us?"

A group of small children brought her flowers. Was this the hope Layla was talking about? The mere presence of a Conjuror created so much excitement. As she interacted with the people, warmth spread through the masses. Being around Layla, Daegon felt it too. Like the great stone of Malachi. The sorrowful faces of the citizens morphed into a rosy hue. Layla spun around, simply touching as many people's hands as she could. Daegon stood on the outskirts of the sudden shift, his shoulder pressed against a sandstone pillar, grinning as the marketplace transformed.

After Layla had met every individual, she jumped through the group to Daegon. Random flowers and tokens decorated her attire. He could do nothing but admire her. "You're incredible."

The red on her cheeks broke through as she coyly covered her face. "Thank you for being there."

Daegon chuckled. "I thought I was going to have to fend off all of those people!" The statement evoked a new type of smile from Layla. One that showed all her teeth. A genuine smile. He threw the heavy bag of food over his shoulder and turned back toward the tower. "We should probably get this back to Gallant. I wonder what food he's going to whip us up tonight."

Layla grabbed Daegon's arm, sparking a sudden jolt through his chest. His shoulders faded, and he looked down at her dark hair before heading back toward the tower. The weight of the supplies slowed him, and it didn't help that the sand from the seldom-walked street had built up like the snow on his trek to Shishbash. Despite that, the hairs on his neck perked with the pressure of a million individual eyes beaming at them. Daegon froze in the middle of the street.

Layla looked up at him. "Is everything okay?"

A blur of motion slammed into Daegon's back. He stumbled, grit tearing into his palms as he hit the ground. The canvas bag was ripped from his grip before he could draw a breath. He stood and pulled his sword, only to catch the boots of a lanky boy in tattered clothes sprinting away.

Daegon checked to make sure Layla was okay. "Stop!" He took her hand and chased the child.

The child curved through the streets. He slid through slight openings and weaved through sudden statues. But Daegon and Layla stayed in pursuit. There were only so many more places to go without alerting the guards. The child paused at the end of the street, his head scanning the wall, tauntingly spinning as they approached. He smiled and sprinted down a side street where an avalanche of barrels fell from the top of the buildings. Daegon pushed Layla against the side of the building to avoid being crushed by the obstacles. When there were no more barrels, Daegon resumed the chase but quickly came to another dead end.

Daegon spun in a circle, his chest heaving. The alley was empty. Just three stone walls and a pile of refuse. "He didn't just fly away," Daegon snapped, kicking a crate.

Daegon scanned the walls and the rooftop, but there was no way the child could have climbed out. Layla walked to the end of the alleyway and found a grate hidden in the sand. The same type of grate the children were escaping into at their tower. Daegon squinted, bent down, and outlined the rusty edges. They were rubbed raw. He pulled his hand to his eyes; the rust flaking between his fingers. Daegon lifted the grate from the ground and reached for Layla's hand. "Do you trust me?"

Layla looked at the dark hole, then back at the empty alley. She took a breath, steeling herself. "I'm following you." She gripped his hand.

Together, they stepped off the ledge and vanished into the city's underbelly.

Chapter Fourteen

S and drifted through the windows of the Territorian prison. Shieldguard soldiers, their emerald armor glazed in the gritty mist, stood ready at the front gate. Builders constructed the prison cells into the side of a mountain adjacent to the city. Gallant rushed to Maybin, who transported the prisoner they'd picked up on their way into the city. The shackled man bled from his nose and slumped in Maybin's grasp, his swollen, half-open eye tracking his eventual imprisonment. Remnants of a feeble escape attempt. He'd stopped fighting at this point.

Gallant said, "Has there been an increase in these unauthorized Conjurors?"

Maybin waved his hand, passing the guards into a deeper chamber of the prison. "Sometimes, I wish. That would explain the *Scourge's* random attacks on us."

The mountain sucked the light from the prison. An eerie dripping mixed with the echoing click of the lock sealing behind them. Two guards followed close, wielding torches to cut through the darkness. Their voices trailed off the etched walls. Unwashed bodies and stale ammonia permeated the air. Gallant wrinkled his nose; it smelled like a stable that hadn't been mucked in weeks.

"What do you mean?" Gallant asked.

Maybin opened a chamber at the far end of the hallway and pushed the man onto the dusty ground. The shackles released as he entered the cell, and he sprawled onto the sandy floor. The cells were rather empty, with their own distinct flair. Not unlike Shishbash, which prided itself on its frozen conditions, these cells suffocated and squeezed the life out of their inhabitants. They used the weight of the mountain as a punishment itself.

Maybin locked the door and sighed. "The *Scourge* used to be more...predictable." He paused over the exact wording. "When we had too many Conjurors passing through, we anticipated an attack. Expected it. Could preemptively move people to safety."

They walked toward a back room, the cracks of the door lit by the faint glow of a freshly lit fire. Gallant cocked his head. "Now?"

Maybin stood at the door, his hand pressed into the wood, his eyes tracing the misshapen patterns carved into the floor. "Now it's become random. As if the monster's throwing a die every morning, deciding if it wants to attack us." He pushed the door open, revealing a small stone room hidden from the dust. It was dark, the only light coming from the fire, but also unusually comfortable. Two wooden chairs sat in front of the fire, and an assortment of colorful liquors lined the back wall. A room meant to combat the constant reminder of destruction that flocked outside of the cave. "Our people can't handle the random attacks."

Maybin waved the accompanying guards away and gestured Gallant toward a wooden chair. Gallant sat stiffly, his armor clinking against the wood. "And you don't think that these Loneseekers have something to do with it?"

Maybin huffed a dry chuckle and poured some of the brown liquid into a recently washed glass. "Loneseekers? No. No, they're simply men who were born with an innate ability to conjure." He poured a second glass. "There have always been those who've been able to bend the elements."

"They break the Congregation's teachings." Gallant remembered the lessons of his childhood that taught salvation would come from reducing reliance on conjuring. How their overreliance brought an end to great kingdoms. Like Malachi. Gallant's grip tightened on his knees. Ten years ago, he would have struck a man for saying that. Today, he just basked in the roasting coals.

Gallant stared deep into the fire when Maybin shook a glass of liquor in front of his face. "You really think that kid you're traveling with is from Malachi?"

Gallant took the glass and rested it on the arm of the chair. He leaned back and took a breath. "Malachi? How did you hear that?"

"Cardinal Mesa. The Cardinals all talk to one another. We were told to be on high alert for your Conjuror party and, in particular, that boy from Malachi."

"I don't know. Layla sure seems to believe he was." Gallant took a sip of the liquid, wincing as it burned his throat. "He also claims to be Grand Conjuror Raynor's kid."

Maybin's eyebrows raised. "Was Raynor from Malachi as well?"

Gallant raised his glass in a covert toast. "Apparently?"

Maybin groaned as he removed his armor. His gray hair flaked with specks of sand, and his undershirt dripped sweat onto the floor. He rubbed his hand along the divot in his face. "You know, the older I get, the more I question why."

Gallant took another sip of his drink, the sting fading. "What do you mean?"

"Why are we alive? Spared by the *Scourge*? Why can't we conjure? Terratoria used to be a beautiful sanctuary for trade and travel." He closed his eyes and placed his hands on the table. "It wasn't that long ago."

Gallant eyed Maybin's assertions and grimaced. "I remember traveling through here when I was a kid. I remember being mesmerized by the wall."

Maybin dropped his armor on the ground and fell into his chair. His knees creaked, matching the chair's wooden legs. "Now we're just a bastion of despair. If the Congregation's teachings truly worked, why? Why aren't we spared?" The question was rhetorical, if not sacrilegious, but Maybin ignored the shifting glances and sipped his drink. "I feel like a cog in a greater game."

Gallant sat straighter. "You know, even speaking like that can be considered an act of heresy?"

Maybin still eyed the fire and chuckled darkly. "I'm just an old cynic, Gallant. I just want to one day rest easy without the morning sun beaming a warning of death."

A rattling cage inside the prison shook Gallant out of his chair. He stared at the door, waiting for a prisoner to come barging through, but after seconds had passed, nothing.

Maybin continued his ramblings. "We're instructed to clean up the city. Remove the remains of the perished. The orphans. The lepers. It never feels right."

Gallant placed his glass on the mantel of the fireplace. "You're following Cardinal Mesa's orders. Following the Congregation's orders."

Maybin chuckled, swished his glass, and stared at the bubbles rising to the top. "And I proudly do it. Without question. But I can still feel at odds." He threw the drink down his throat and closed his eyes, taking a deep breath. "We're not even fighting an enemy anymore." Maybin stared at his drink, the condensation dripping onto his scarred hand.

A sense of malaise and exhaustion blanketed the minds of even the most devout. Even Gallant's blue armor had dinged from the Territorian dust. "What do you mean?"

Maybin leaned back in the chair. "There used to be a huge Forlorn contingent opposing us here. Blocking every opportunity at welcoming Conjurors. But even they seem to have left. Moved away to more relevant cities."

Gallant remembered the bombs surrounding Cardinal Bilari's keep. "Like Shishbash."

"Eh, wherever they go." Maybin shrugged his shoulders. "All I know is that we've lost the message. It's become a war of our own. Until the day when the *Scourge* finally finishes the job. And now Cardinal Mesa has begun sending our own away to the other cities."

"To other cities?"

Maybin scratched the dust on his scalp. "It started yesterday. Many of our best scholars and most influential tradespeople received orders to go to Embre. To Corporeal."

Gallant placed his drink on the arm of his chair. "Without reason?"

Maybin's nose huffed in bemusement. "None given. I doubt the people giving orders even know."

Gallant looked at his calloused hands and grabbed his necklace. There couldn't be any truth in Maybin's words. It had to be the cynical words of a soldier past his prime. Certainly, Cardinal Mesa and the Congregation had some plan for Terratoria? Some reason for all the movement. One that didn't involve sitting idly on their hands while a once-great city delved deeper into bleakness.

Gallant stood, his hand remaining on the sigil on his chest, the metal pulling him back to his vow. "Keep the Memory," he whispered, though for the first time, the words rang hollow.

Maybin shook his head and laughed. "Keep the Memory."

Chapter Fifteen

Dripping water echoed off the walls of the dark chamber. Layla held Daegon's arm as they stepped through the tunnel. They were back in the sewers, but this one was unlike the previous one. Instead of a frozen, open tunnel, the dried-up center stream of water provided a divot for them to follow. Poorly replaced manhole covers filtered shafts of dusty light throughout the shadows. The kids weren't just hiding; they were moving.

Multiple paths branched, creating a maze without a map. They tiptoed through the darkness, traversing so as not to alert the enemy to their position. The walls displayed paintings and etched designs. Without a light, it was difficult to determine their content, but the familiar eye of Malachi periodically stared back at him, complete with a scratch through the center. Daegon furrowed his brow at the eye. It was his father's sigil. The symbol of his home, now twisted into a mark of rebellion. His stomach turned.

They followed the path with the most carvings until the tunnel came alive. Footsteps danced in the distance. He held onto the wall and crouched, using the cold surface as a guide through the maze. A proud voice arose from the dark. "Foreigners are too easy to steal from."

Laughter vibrated the chamber. It wasn't just a single assailant. Daegon peered around the corner of the tunnel into the main chamber of the sewer system. A large central light revealed a group of children rummaging through the stolen supplies. There had to be ten to fifteen children all gathered around, dressed in tattered rags, wearing headbands ripped from their clothing. Cloth hung from the walls, pinned at the corners with hammered weapons, filled with dingy blankets and pillows. Poorly carved cutlery sat atop a pair of weathered crates. They lived here.

Daegon stepped into the light, his hand resting on his pommel—a warning, not a threat. "That's enough."

The children scrambled into the shadows; ten pairs of wide, terrified eyes locked onto him. A scant echo of dripping water replaced their conversations. The lanky child, who ran off with Daegon's bag of supplies, stepped forward from the group. "How did you find us?" he demanded, stepping into the light. He held a rusted dagger like he knew how to use it.

"You aren't exactly quiet," Daegon said, keeping his hands visible. "And you left a trail."

The boy sneered. "This food feeds us for a week. You want it back? You'll have to kill us."

"I don't want to kill children," Daegon said softly.

"We aren't children," the boy snapped. "We are the Forgotten."

"Forgotten?" Layla asked, stepping out from behind Daegon.

"Failed apprentices," the boy said, his voice cracking with anger. "We trained to be Shieldguards. We bled for the Congregation. But we weren't strong enough, or fast enough, or obedient enough. So they threw us away."

"They...threw you away?" Layla whispered.

"Cast out," the boy corrected. "Cardinal Mesa didn't want failures walking her streets. Bad for morale. So she sent us down here to rot." He pointed his knife at Layla. "And now you bring a Conjuror here? To give us more false hope? The *Scourge* will eat you just like it ate the last one."

Layla stepped forward, her smile beaming with the same hope she'd displayed in the marketplace, but the boy spat at her feet, waving his blade between the two.

Daegon closed the gap between them and the boy. "Layla will complete the Conjuror's Journey and save everyone."

The boy thrust his blade back at Daegon. "You don't understand!" He looked back at his group before returning his gaze. "The Conjuror doesn't survive. They never survive. It's always just false hope peddled by Cardinal Mesa."

Daegon didn't move at the threat of the blade. "This one's different. I promise." His face remained stoic in the presence of the point.

The boy sighed and dropped the blade. "It's never different. We've met Conjurors before who've said that. Everyone abandons us." A tear cut through the dirt on his cheek.

"I think..." Daegon reached for the boy, but he stepped back.

"You would think that ripping us from our families was enough. And we were told it was the noble thing to do. We didn't question it. Relished in it. Made to believe that we'd develop new bonds. We embraced the Congregation as our family, and they cast us aside. Like trash."

Daegon reached over and grabbed the boy's bony shoulder. "Layla's different."

The shoulder slouched under the weight of Daegon's hand. "This city used to be beautiful. There used to be dozens, hundreds of Conjurors attempting to defeat the *Scourge*. But, according to Cardinal Mesa, the constant presence of conjuring made us a target for both the Reapers and the *Scourge* itself. I remember as a kid when it ravaged us." The boy wiped the tears from his face and tilted his head at Daegon. "That was the day my life ended. And this one began." He looked back at the group of children. "Our life."

"So, you really are outcasts." Daegon softened his voice.

The boy pushed Daegon's hand off his shoulder. "Forgotten! Scattered to the wayside. Better dead than alive." His voice bounced off the walls of the chamber. "Forced to scavenge and survive, but also hunted by the Shieldguard because of our concerns. They call us the Orphans, but we call ourselves the Forgotten Ones."

Daegon sighed and nodded. "I know what it's like to be alone. I'm trying to return to my people too." Daegon kneeled to be more in line with the rest of the group. "Layla is the best way of returning to my city. To my people. She's going to do the same for you." As he finished, he flashed a warm smile toward Layla.

The boy mockingly chided Daegon. "Like I said, everyone says their Journey is different."

"I know." Daegon closed his eyes and waved his hand at the boy. "Keep the supplies. Your group needs it more than ours." There wasn't a point in arguing any further. The gnawed apple in a younger girl's hand browned with age. He looked at the boy's shaking arm, trying to hold the heavy knife steady. They weren't enemies. They were starving.

"You won't fight us for your food?" The boy sounded disappointed at the lack of aggression. "You're not going to turn us over to the guards?"

"We're on the same side. Defeat the *Scourge* and bring the Peace?" Everyone was on the same side. The Forlorn. The Congregation. These children. So why were they fighting?

Daegon turned away, and the kid yelled through the chamber. "The name is Kazi."

They returned the greeting, and Daegon took Layla's hand, escaping the darkness. Terratoria was rotting from the inside out. If the Congregation treated their own children like this, what were they planning for Layla?

Chapter Sixteen

Gallant didn't laugh. He slammed his fist onto the table, rattling the cups. "You let them take her into the sewers? Are you insane?"

"They were children," Daegon shouted. "They had nothing. It wasn't their fault."

The steam faded. "Yes, Maybin mentioned them. They're a danger to the Conjuror. Apparently, many of them have defected to the Forlorn."

Daegon remembered El. And Krag. And Jovy. "The Forlorn only cares about saving the Conjurors."

Gallant again slammed the table with his fist. "The Forlorn blow up buildings, Daegon. They don't care who is inside, as long as the message gets out." He sat in a chair. "Are we going to join them? Save them?"

Daegon refused to turn from Gallant. How didn't he understand? They were all on the same side. Was he so brainwashed by the Congregation not to see that everyone wanted the same thing? "I just feel like our purposes align. There has to be a common ground, right?"

Gallant chuckled. "I'm sure there is. Let me grab the Shield-guard. I'm sure they'd love to talk to them."

Layla grew tired of their arguing and inserted herself into the conversation. "I'm sure they mean us no harm."

Gallant sighed and shook his head. "Maybe. But we're much too busy right now to do anything about them."

The tension in the room was thick like syrup, only disturbed when multiple loud knocks shook the door and a guard shouted through the thick wood. "Letter from Cardinal Mesa for Conjuror Layla."

Gallant sprang toward the door and snatched the letter. His eyes lifted from the writing. "It appears Cardinal Mesa would like to have a meeting alone with Daegon. Tonight."

"A meeting with me?" There had to be a link between the Cardinals he knew and the Cardinals that he was meeting. "It can't be a coincidence, right?"

Gallant read the letter again and bit his lip. "I stopped questioning or trying to figure out your past shortly after we met." He put the letter on the table and dusted his blue armor. "All that matters is that Layla believes you."

She smiled and placed her hand on his shoulder. "You're related to something in this world. Maybe Cardinal Mesa can help you realize what that is?"

Daegon nodded and strapped his father's sword to his belt. Maybe the Cardinal would recognize something from it. Raynor was one for extravagance and could've etched the unique characters on the blade into a new sword. He took the letter and pushed through the wooden door leading out of the tower.

***

The cathedral spanned the center of the city, constructed of the same durable and ornate sandstone that housed them. Cardinal Mesa ensured that her quarters were immaculate. Serpentine statues stretched across the top of the keep, their beady eyes following him along the path. Two guards with strange clay masks allowed Daegon into the courtyard, tusks jutting from their domed mouths. *Were they used to disguise their faces or shield their eyes from the splattering dust?* His stomach churned at their vacant stares.

A hulking wooden door creaked open into a hall with lush foliage. Green orbs radiated a subtle glow, and large olive leaves reached across the path. Daegon swept his arm through the maze of green, clearing a path to the faint noises behind. They were cool to the touch. Wet. Freshly watered? He took in the sweet smell that wafted past his nostrils and followed the mural of a night sky stretching across the seemingly endless ceiling. *Was this what Terratoria was?*

A scolding, deep voice cut through the bushes. Daegon couldn't make out the words, but a competing soft voice begged. Pleaded. *For what?* He tried to focus on the tearful words, but all he could make out was the desperate peaks of an attempt to placate the man. Daegon hesitated, eventually crouching behind a broad fern leaf to better hear the conversation. A tall, slender man without hair and a long gray beard wedged the door open. Through the crack, Cardinal Mesa slumped into a chair, resting her head in her hands. He recognized the old man stepping toward him. Another vestige of Malachi. Grand Cardinal Sooman.

Two Shieldguard soldiers escorted Sooman, with his crimson robes and yellow sash. Their armor matched the leafy foliage of the room, and their faces were just as obscured as the soldiers manning the front. They came right at him. Daegon searched, but there was nowhere to hide. *Why did he have to hide?* Daegon stood from his crouch and caught the vacant eyes of the guards, who gave a firm nod.

Cardinal Sooman held his hand out and slowed them. "Ah, and who do we have here?" His smile stretched wide, revealing his cork-colored teeth. "Yes, you're that boy King that I keep hearing about?"

"It's Daegon." He managed only his name before Sooman's deep voice continued.

"Yes, I've heard a lot about you." Sooman rubbed the frail gray of his beard and smiled, stretching the skin on his face too tight. "The Congregation has taken a great interest in your backstory."

"Me? Why?"

Cardinal Sooman rubbed his index finger across his greasy thumb. His words came out with a gravel that threatened the nearby shrubbery. "Your Malachinian life."

"So, you know? Or believe me?" Daegon questioned.

"We know how important it is to believe in the impossibilities of life. I've requested a formal meeting with your team when you arrive at Corporeal." The Grand Cardinal swept his hands, and the two guards guided him out of the building.

Corporeal. Again, another city that he hadn't heard of, but he was sure Gallant, with all his infinite wisdom about the Congregation, would know. He hadn't noticed the sticky air coating his skin. It wasn't hot, but the spray from the nearby stream peppered the leaves with a fine mist of refreshing moisture. His brow dripped into his vision.

A voice once again called to him. This time softer; more pleasant, but still just as demanding. "Hello Daegon, King of Malachi."

Daegon reoriented himself in the chamber. Cardinal Mesa stood outside the small room where Cardinal Sooman exited. Tears had ruined the intricate design on her face, and she wore a tight but opulent green dress.

Daegon said, "You requested my presence?"

She dipped her toes into the stream winding through the room. The surface reflected the luminous green from the floating orbs. "Does this city remind you of Malachi?"

Daegon pictured the decaying buildings. The empty market. The dust that caked every surface. "It's not exactly a spitting image." *What was she getting at?* "What's going on, Cardinal Mesa? Why are we here?"

Her face paint cracked as she measured her words. "We? I don't know what you're talking about." Mesa walked into the stream, the water lapping over her bare feet. She didn't seem to care that it ruined the hem of her expensive gown. "Grand Conjuror Raynor used to talk about Malachi. The alabaster walls and gardens. So full of life. Oh, how beautiful it must've been. Do you not think that it's a coincidence that the son of the last Grand Conjuror joined us as well?"

Daegon's heart raced. "So, you knew him? Where is he!"

Mesa squinted her eyes. "He completed the Conjuror's Journey. Destined for a life of eternal salvation."

That didn't answer his question. "What do you want? Why do you want to meet me?"

"Cardinal Bilari let us know another King of Malachi was present in Shishbash." Cardinal Mesa crept closer. Slowly, but with a curious intent. "Raynor is a hero to everyone in this city. I wanted to extend a thank you for continuing in your father's footsteps."

Daegon's stomach dropped. There was that line Jordell had uttered before the *Scourge* consumed him. She knew something. *Why couldn't they just come out and say it? Why did everything have to be a riddle or a denial?* "Enough games. Tell me what happened. To Malachi!"

Mesa was feet from him. "Malachi was destroyed a thousand years ago. A city of bliss, without want or starvation." She paused. "A city too reliant on conjuring to exist." She reached her hand into the air, and specks of dirt coalesced into her palm, forming a ball of earth. "If the city of Malachi couldn't wield the power, why should any other nation take on that burden?"

Daegon looked down at the cobblestones. "The *Scourge*."

"The *Scourge* righted the balance and offered an example to those who couldn't withdraw completely from their desire to be governed by conjuring."

"But how am I here? Why is it that I remember everything so vividly? Why do I know that King Raynor is my father?" Daegon returned his gaze to Mesa, their eyes locked on one another.

"Once we got word of a Malachinian, I read through the archive and couldn't find anything about a King Daegon. You offered that your last memory of Malachi was being consumed by the *Scourge*?"

Daegon nodded slowly, shifting the piercing eyes of the *Scourge* from his memory.

She placed her hand on his shoulder. "Perhaps in surviving the *Scourge,* the trauma has caused you to take the memories of those around you? Perhaps the Cardinals you remember aren't us, but false memories? Maybe you're not the King of Malachi? Maybe, just maybe, you're more damaged by the *Scourge* than you thought."

Daegon opened his mouth to argue, but the words died. Could she be right? The headaches...the gaps in his memory...was he just a madman echoing a dead King? Everything felt so real. He winced at the memory taking hold; the pain and stench of the swirling cloud as it consumed everything he loved.

Cardinal Mesa broke from their face-off and twirled back toward her chamber. "Regardless of what I think, Grand Cardinal Sooman would like a meeting in the capital city of Corporeal.

"About what?"

Cardinal Mesa flicked her fingers, and two guards stepped through the indoor forest. "We don't question the authority of the Congregation."

The guards grasped Daegon's shoulders. Firmly, but without hostility. Before they pulled him from the room, Daegon said, "I can't wait."

Mesa laughed to herself. "Keep the Memory, young King. Keep the Memory."

***

Daegon cracked the door to the tower, bracing himself for Gallant's inevitable questions about the meeting. Instead, silence greeted him. The moon cast highlights across the room, illuminating the dust dancing in the stillness. Gallant lay sprawled on the bed, still in his full armor, legs crossed in a surprisingly relaxed pose. Trying to be quiet, Daegon tiptoed through the room, his boots barely whispering against the stone floor. Sound asleep. He scanned the rest of the room, but Layla was nowhere to be found.

A single torch burned on the balcony, its flickering light casting long shadows. Layla leaned against the railing, gazing out at the sprawling city below. Daegon pushed aside the thin, woven cloth separating the room from the Territorian dust and approached. She wore white robes with a vibrant green sash wrapped around her waist, a token of their time here in Terratoria. She gasped at his sudden presence but quickly offered her usual hypnotic smile that drew him deeper into her gaze.

"It's a beautiful night," she murmured, her voice a soft whisper against the city's distant hum.

Daegon rested his hands on the dust-covered rail. He had become all too familiar with the gritty texture that covered everything. The suffocating night revealed the city's supposed beauty. By day, the carnage of the *Scourge's* constant attacks were stark and undeniable, visible in the scars of fractured buildings and scattered streets. But at night, the flaws remained hidden, and the vast expanse sparkled with individual blips of golden light, each a tiny testament to life amidst the ruins.

The wall, so impressively imposing by day, truly came alive at night. A persistent flame pulsed atop, creating a protective layer of fire that circled the entire city with a vibrant, unwavering shield against the shadows.

"It is," he agreed, his voice a low rumble.

"Did you find what you were looking for? About your father?" Her question cut through the quiet.

Daegon shook his head, the unproductive conversation still fresh in his mind. Cardinal Mesa seemed more interested in merely verifying his existence than genuinely assisting him in his search. "Just more dead ends," he sighed, the words tasting like ash.

"I'm sorry," Layla said. "Maybe Embre will have more answers?"

Daegon cut her off. "Cardinal Sooman was there. He wants to meet at Corporeal."

"The Grand Cardinal is here?" Her mouth dropped in surprise, and her hands tightened on the rail. "He rarely leaves Corporeal. I wonder what brought him here." A flicker of concern crossed her face.

Daegon could only think of one thing: him. He wished he'd listened more closely to Cardinal Mesa protesting in her room. "I'm not sure, but it's the only direction I have right now."

She scooted closer to him along the railing, their arms brushing lightly. "We'll find your father and find out how you came to be here," she promised, her voice laced with genuine hope.

The tension drained from his shoulders like water, and a tinge of heat flushed across his cheeks. How was she able to do that? "You're incredible, Layla. What you did in the market today. The hope you gave those people."

Her face flushed a delicate rosy hue, and she looked away. A bashful expression on her face flashed before fading to that small, fake smile he'd constantly seen during their adventure.

Daegon leaned on the railing with his elbows, turning to face her more fully. "Your hands are shaking," he said softly.

Layla looked down, clenching her fist. "They stopped shaking hours ago."

"No," Daegon said. "They didn't."

That statement took Layla aback. Her forehead furrowed in a thoughtful frown, and she bit her lip. A silent question pulsed from her eyes, caged by her perceived duty.

Then Daegon leaned over the railing and screamed into the city. Layla took a step back as his voice echoed across the rooftops. "Sometimes you just have to let it out! You can't be perfect for everybody all the time!" She froze at his sudden outburst. "Go ahead and try!"

She shook her head; a slight tremor ran through her, and she stepped back from the railing, but he reached for her hand. Her skin was cold from the desert night, but her palm was damp. She didn't pull away. She leaned in, the distance between them shrinking until he could feel the ghost of her breath on his cheek. "Try it. I promise," he encouraged, his voice softer now.

She took a deep, shuddering breath, then yelled into the midnight city. Her voice, at first tentative, then growing stronger, careened off the tiny buildings and disappeared into the vast expanse. She stood there for a moment, listening to the echoes, before yelling again, a little louder this time. After two more powerful yells, Daegon caught her as she stumbled back from the wall, a wave of exhaustion washing over her. The two of them laughed. It was an honest, unrestrained sound that finally revealed Layla's genuine smile, the one he had seen so few times.

"Don't you feel better?" Daegon said, his words punctuated by their shared laughter.

Their eyes locked, and there was a moment of suspended time. Daegon felt their shared breaths battling for rhythm. Her blue eyes contrasted brilliantly against the darkness of the night, shining with a newfound freedom, sucking him closer. Daegon reached for her hand. He expected her to recoil, but she instead lifted her fingers into his palm.

"What is with all the yelling?" Gallant appeared from behind the curtain, his hair disheveled, a look of sleepy confusion written across his face.

Layla pulled from Daegon's grasp, returning a deep breath that had eluded her in their shared moment. Daegon turned to Gallant and laughed. "You don't want to join us?"

Layla joined Daegon in the laughter, to which Gallant shook his head and returned to his sleep. Alone again, with the echoes of their shared amusement bouncing between the vacant buildings.

Chapter Seventeen

A sharp and insistent light pierced Daegon's eyes, and he groaned, rolling over onto the hard ground. A jolt of disorientation hit him at the conspicuous absence of both Gallant and Layla. A guard dressed in green-hued mail that shimmered faintly in the light slammed open the door. Daegon managed a weak smile and sank onto the bed, holding up a hand to signal that he was alright.

The guard's posture relaxed. "Good morning," he said, his voice a low rumble. "Conjuror Layla wanted me to let you know they were going into the city for the ceremony. For you to catch up when you awoke."

What time was it? Daegon peered out the window. Instead of morning fog, the sun was high and bright. Midday. He should've jumped up to race toward the market, but he sat there, a soft smile playing on his lips, the memories of the previous night warm in his mind. He waved a dismissive hand at the guard. "Thank you."

Daegon walked to the window, the faint warmth of the sun grazing his face. A crowd of green-cloaked citizens already gathered around the center keep, the very place where he had his strange meeting with Cardinal Mesa. During their trek into the city yesterday, the market was empty. *Where did these people come from?* Daegon rubbed a hand over his face, shaking off the lingering sleepiness, and hurried down.

Horns blared through the streets, their deep, resonant calls echoing off the buildings. Yesterday, the streets were a graveyard. Today, they were a sea of green. But it didn't look like a celebration; it looked like a summons. The lack of exuberance pushed Daegon to tiptoe through the crowd. Their gaunt faces vacantly faced the keep, silent and waiting.

Daegon wandered among the surging mob, still in awe of their sheer numbers. On top of the building to his right, Kazi and a small group of children sat, their gazes fixed on the central platform. They shared a silent nod as Daegon remembered the promise he'd made in the sewers. Sir Maybin stood on guard, leading a group of clay-masked soldiers guarding the stage, their tusks decorated with bouquets of flora.

As he drew closer to the front of the swelling crowd, a booming voice reverberated through the street. "Today we celebrate another opportunity for peace." The clamor around Daegon hushed, and the thousands of whispers fell silent almost instantaneously. "Conjuror Layla is completing the second stone of her Journey to defeat the *Scourge*."

The crowd erupted into practiced applause as Layla stepped onto the stage. She was now dressed in a Terratorian green gown, the rich fabric flowing gracefully as she moved. Gallant followed closely behind, his Shishbashi blue armor a striking contrast to her attire. Layla smiled and waved at the crowd. Her cheeks were flushed, but when her eyes scanned the crowd, they stopped on Daegon. A small, secret smile touched her lips. Not the performative smile she gave the crowd, but the real one she'd found on the balcony. The man who had introduced her ushered her to the front and, with a sweeping gesture, once again beckoned for silence from the audience.

She spoke, her voice clear and carrying across the plaza. "Thank you. There's nothing I want more than to bring safety and joy to Terratoria. To know that when you rest your head at night, you'll wake in the morning. To return to the thriving markets that once connected our nations, and the bustling streets that spurred your growth." She finished, providing that familiar smile she'd been so meticulously trained to give.

The crowd erupted in a thunderous wave of applause as Layla gracefully retreated from the platform. Daegon wove through the crowd and caught Gallant's eye, who gestured to join him on the stage. As he entered, two Terratorian guards crossed their swords and blocked his path.

Daegon pointed past their dusty armor. "I'm with…"

The guards pushed with their swords, but paused when Gallant rolled his head and swept his arms, inviting Daegon onto the stage.

Daegon crept up beside Gallant, his voice low. "You could have woken me up."

Gallant chuckled. "Don't throw me in the brig, Your Highness."

Daegon rolled his eyes. "I think something's wrong." Gallant's eyes, usually so open, narrowed slightly at the corner. "The meeting with Cardinal Mesa was strange. Cardinal Sooman was there, and they were fighting."

Gallant's expression hardened, and he whispered back, his voice barely audible above the lingering murmur of the crowd, "Cardinal Sooman?"

There wasn't much time to take in the information. Cardinal Mesa, dressed in an ostentatiously green dress, indiscreetly hidden under her traditional scarlet Cardinal robes, walked across the platform and waved, drawing all eyes to her.

"I'm pleased to present Conjuror Layla with a piece of Terratorian history," she announced, her voice resonating with seriousness. She held out her hand, and in her palm rested a glowing green stone, pulsating with an inner light. "Through all the destruction, may it offer a glimmer of hope that one day the *Scourge* will be eradicated."

She unfurled her hand and beckoned toward Layla, who stepped forward and reached for the stone. As her fingers brushed the surface, she choked. A rush of energy radiated through her body. A flutter started in her stomach, but this time, it traveled upwards, through her chest, and into her mouth. She gasped a soft, breathless sound.

"Thank you, Cardinal Mesa," she managed, her voice filled with awe. "I won't let you down."

"Oh, I don't think you will." Cardinal Mesa's voice cut through Layla's vow. Her sharp gaze lifted from Layla, finding Daegon in the background. A crooked sneer spread across her face, her brow furrowed in recognition.

Daegon froze, unable to break eye contact with the Cardinal until Layla, oblivious to the silent exchange, approached them, eager to display her newfound power. The ethereal green crystal, which had pulsed with light moments prior, slowly faded in her hands. But the now dim stone still exerted influence. It pulled at the iron in his blood. Daegon tried to resist, but the familiar hum started in his fingertips, vibrating up his arm, demanding to be touched.

Gallant grabbed Daegon's wrist, his grip bruising. "Daegon! Your hand!" His eyes grew wide, reflecting the stone through Daegon's translucent flesh.

Daegon waved his hand. "Layla? What's happening?"

"I'm not sure," she replied hesitantly.

Daegon yanked his hand away from the stone and tucked his arm into his cloak. The three exchanged quick, panicked glances. He pulled his arm out, and to his immense relief, his skin returned its rosy hue. His heart hammered against his ribs.

Before he could utter a word, a deafening crack rippled overhead, followed by a series of brilliant flares, lighting the already bright midday sky with a burst of vibrant colors. Fireworks, loud and celebratory, were unleashed to commemorate the continuation of the Conjuror's Journey. Daegon stared intently at his hand for another moment before looking up at the interested eyes of Cardinal Mesa. She didn't look at the fireworks, but instead tracked his form, as if there were a ghost in the crowd. She squinted her eyes, maintaining that look of intrigue, before turning toward the podium, her flowing dress rippling in the wind, and declared, "Let's celebrate this joyous occasion!"

Chapter Eighteen

T he red setting sun dusted Territoria. Though the celebration had been going on for hours, the tower provided a peace absent in the Congregation's subtle glares. Besides, celebrating had never been Daegon's favorite activity. He much preferred to keep to the side, letting the exuberance of the crowd pull a smile across his face. But it was all for Layla.

He sat on the bed and rubbed his wrist. The skin had returned to its normal color—tan, solid, scarred. But the phantom cold still clung to his bones. He flexed his fingers, half-expecting them to vanish again.

Layla sat beside him and asked, "Maybe you're a Conjuror too? Like your dad?"

Like his dad. The sentence he never wanted uttered by anyone, much less Layla. He cut his gaze to her hands. "Where's the stone?"

Layla dug through her pocket and pulled out the dull rock, no longer exuding its green glow. He reached for it, expecting his arm to once again fade away. But nothing happened.

Gallant gruffly said, "Layla's absorbed the power by now."

So why didn't Layla make him disappear? Daegon nodded in agreement, and Gallant cleaned the layer of dust from their supplies. A thin layer of grit coated their armor, weapons, and food. "So with the extra stone, we're more likely to encounter the *Scourge?*"

Gallant refused to look up from wiping the supplies. He exhaled. "The *Scourge*, or his Reapers, yes. This is where our job really begins. Remember. The mission at all times is to protect Layla."

Layla leaned back, closing her eyes. "Two stones down," she whispered. "It almost feels...manageable. Like we might actually do this."

It really hadn't been hard. They'd already visited two of the cities, and the next one wasn't too far away. Gallant called it Embre. A name Layla had mentioned on the balcony. Apparently, the home of the Conjuror who succumbed to the Reaper when he'd first arrived. The screams still pierced his thoughts; the image of the giant blade ripping through the red cloth wouldn't leave him.

Shadows stretched across the room, providing some much-needed shade from the sun. He sank onto the bed, relief washing through his legs as he finally put his feet up. As Daegon lay on the bed and closed his eyes, a scream emanated from deep within the city. A twinge of fire seared his nostrils. He knew that scent.

Gallant sprinted to the window, his body shaking. "The *Scourge.*"

A roar ripped through the city, and the screams intensified. The *Scourge? Now?* Daegon frantically swiped through supplies and grabbed his sword. A nightmare reborn. "We have to get out of here."

Gallant took a breath and nodded, throwing his spear onto his back and surveying the area. They needed a plan. They needed one fast. The purple and green cloud descended on the city, slowly snuffing out the bright lights of its people.

Daegon raised his hand. "The tunnels the children used to move through the city!"

They didn't have time to argue about the merits of the plan. Before Gallant could even complete the sentence, Daegon had already busted through the door to the tower. The steps shook as the monster drifted closer. The city had endured attacks from the *Scourge* before, but not without countless loss of life and destruction. Malachi's walls rumbled through his mind, swallowed by the same sinister vines now reaching for Terratoria. He shook his head of the thoughts. There had to be a plan for Terratoria. They'd survived before.

As they entered the courtyard, the *Scourge's* green and purple mist reached into their minds. Daegon shook it off as it fluttered aimlessly. Outside the gates, multiple soldiers clad in green armor ran with their swords drawn. To their death. For their city.

The swirling sandstorm that pestered the city shifted the ground, covering the manhole where the children had escaped. Their vacant stares burned into his mind, pinpointing their location to right...there. He kicked the sand away, revealing the escape. They had nothing but the weapons on their backs. But survival was of the most importance. He lifted the cover and ushered them into the hole before following behind, enclosing them in the darkness of yet another sewer.

The *Scourge* unleashed a roar, and the cave shook with the fragile cracks of a collapsing building. Screams leaving lifeless bodies played like an endless song. The ceiling was the only thing that separated them from the monster. Daegon and Gallant surrounded Layla as they walked along the narrow chamber. Red light filtered in from small holes, but even they exuded a fine purple mist. Layla reached out and created a ball of bright white ice that illuminated the chamber, giving them direction. They were in the tunnels earlier, but the familiar curved paths all looked similar. Ahead, the tunnels split, leaving Daegon to randomly select the direction leading toward their escape.

Where the tunnels escaped to, it was unclear, but the children had sprung up all throughout the city. He first saw them on the outside of the wall, probably curious about their entry. Then they were at the entrance to their courtyard. They had to lead out, eventually. To somewhere. They continued following the stretching tunnels until they emptied into a large cylindrical room with a glowing-red skylight above. It branched into five separate tunnel systems. Five choices, and every one led into a different dark. Remnants of purple mist lingered in the room, bringing with it the charred remains of burned flesh.

Gallant lowered his spear and walked to the front of the group, stepping over the crumbled wreckage of the worn passageway. Burrowed divots where water used to flow allowed them to walk unabated down the passageway. Despite being empty, the faraway dripping graced their ears. Gallant grunted, "You've been in enough sewers. Which way do you think is out?"

The subtle reminders of the destruction above remained. The eye of Malachi, along with the slash protesting its duty, tagged multiple passages. Other than the occasional Orphan carving, the tunnels were indistinguishable. Just endless cylinders of darkness. He walked up beside Gallant and rubbed his chin, looking for any discernible tell.

Gallant shrugged his shoulders. "What does your royal instinct say?"

Daegon couldn't help but crack a smile at the comment. He shook his head and pivoted to Layla. "What do you think?"

Layla rubbed her hands across her waist and pointed toward the chamber on the far right. It didn't look any different from the others, but maybe there was a Conjuror intuition. Gallant clapped his hands; a smattering of dust shot into the air. "Then it's decided."

Daegon smirked and walked to the front of the chamber. He pressed his palm against the smooth, burrowed walls, straining to hear anything over his own pulse. Only a cold, heavy silence greeted him.

Gallant's voice ripped through the room. "It's found us!"

A thick plume of smoke billowed out of the skylight in the center, replacing the red highlights of the sunset with the dark hues of despair and pain.

Gallant ran to the front and pulled his spear, pushing Layla to hide within the tunnel. "As a King, what exactly have you fought before?"

Daegon's heart raced, and he pulled his blue sword, running to join Gallant. "Tell me what we're fighting, and I can give you a better idea."

The purple smoke congealed and developed a shape. What was originally a lifeless wisp of smog sprouted spiny legs, a long, slender tail, and two sharp claws. Sharp teeth sprouted from the mist, screaming in their direction. Gallant patted Daegon on the shoulder. "That. That is what we must defend Layla from."

The creature roared as its teeth sliced in their direction. They rolled out of the way in separate directions, avoiding the razors.

Daegon shakily raised his sword at the monster as it rushed him, and his ribs cracked as he was thrown to the side of the chamber. He'd never felt strength like that before. It wasn't an animal. The monster rebounded for the killing blow when a spear pierced its side. It reared in pain. The screams ripped through the enclosed space, ricocheting off the walls.

Gallant panted. "Get up! There's not a way to fight this right now."

Daegon bounced to his feet, wincing as a sharp heat bloomed in his side, and squared himself toward the creature. Gallant pulled his spear and readied himself. A gurgling rattle echoed through the chamber, and the beast rushed them again. Daegon raised his blade as the beast speared its razor-sharp talon at his chest, but he parried the arm out of the way. A second arm swung for a counterattack. Gallant deflected the shot at the cost of his spear, which splintered onto the stone floor. The creature's teeth shifted in the mouth, and it plunged at them once again. Relentless.

Daegon closed his eyes and imagined his death. Quick. Painless. But not with this creature. It would probably take its time, ripping and devouring his flesh. *Why hadn't it happened yet?* He opened his eyes. The monster's mouth bit into an enormous wall of earth. Daegon spun. Layla stretched her arms at them, wielding the ground as a shield.

She yelled from inside the tunnel. "I can seal it!"

Without a second thought, Daegon and Gallant sprinted to Layla. The creature pulled its mouth from the block of earth and screamed, digging its talons into the ground and sprinting after them. They made it into the tunnel when Layla raised her arms and swung them powerfully into the ground. The ceiling collapsed, crushing the monster under the weight. Its screams died out as the stream of rubble continued to flow, locking them into their chosen path.

Layla collapsed onto her knees and heaved a breath. Daegon rolled over from their landing, unable to see through the darkness, whipping his hand through the cloud of dust. He laid his head back on the stone ground and laughed. Gallant, too, laughed.

Layla pushed herself from the ground, holding another block of that prismatic ice. Through the grainy passage, she too smiled through the fatigue. They'd survived their first encounter with the *Scourge*, and they'd done it together. Gallant nudged Daegon's chest, prompting them to spring to their feet.

The group hugged, and Daegon, through strained words, said, "I can't believe you did that. That was amazing."

She took a small step back, allowing the ice to fill the tunnel. "We have each other's backs. Whatever happens, we'll find a way."

Their eyes locked, and the two traded smiles. Gallant turned toward the collapsed rubble and kicked a dislodged stone across the passage. "Perhaps we should get going before the *Scourge* realizes we're still alive."

There was only one way out. Daegon said, "I guess we go straight?" Gallant shot him a narrow gaze, laced with a wry smile.

While the trio's footsteps provided a quiet ambience for their escape, the vibration of the fallen city followed their slow descent into the passageway.

Chapter Nineteen

The carnage. The destruction. The death. All reminiscent of his last moments in Malachi. The screams of pure terror rang through Daegon's mind. He clamped his eyes shut, pushed forward, and continued through the tunnel. A glowing shard of ice illuminated the dark from the palm of Layla's hand. They hadn't encountered any more instances of the *Scourge*. There weren't any monsters or Reapers. No more acrid air burning their nostrils. Just darkness. With the rumbling vibration of a city being decimated. As Daegon walked along the tunnel, the ground softened, turning from stone to a damp, sucking puddle that smacked at his boots. Stagnant water and rot choked the air.

Gallant, who was leading the pack, raised his hand and said, "I see an exit."

In the distance, the faintest crack of light pierced the blanket of black. The smooth walls of the tunnel converged, but instead of an exit, the tunnel ended without a way to escape. Layla touched the sides of the tunnel and pushed. A glowing layer of ice grew from her hand toward the flicker of light.

Crushed stone filled the path, blocking their only way forward. Foliage and moss swallowed the collapsed stones—proof that someone had sealed off this passage ages ago. Gallant threw his shoulder against the boulder, grunting with effort. Veins bulged in his neck, but the rock didn't budge. He kicked it, cursing his own weakness.

Layla stepped forward, latched onto the debris, and let out a deep breath. The stones shifted, turning outward, and pushed into an opening. Light flooded the darkness as Layla stepped back, her hands shaking. Daegon caught her from behind, ensuring she didn't fall. Her body was weak in his arms.

She pressed against the wall, wiping a line of blood from her nose. "Just not used to the power of the Earth Stone."

Daegon squeezed tighter and guided her out of the tunnel. The trio exited onto the dusty Terratorian landscape. But this time, it was even more desolate. Even more barren. More depressing. The stars were gone. In their place, a bruise of purple smoke stretched across the horizon, choking the moonlight. Terratoria wasn't just burning. It was being erased. The pungent smell of fire and flesh festered in the air. Daegon sat in the sand, his hands resting on his knees. "So, do you think the *Scourge* knows we escaped?"

Gallant found a nice, thick tuft of sand and sat. "I don't know." His voice was hesitant as he stared at the smoke pluming in the distance. "We should probably keep moving though. Make sure we're as far away from Terratoria as possible and build a shelter for the rest of the night."

Daegon helped Layla onto the ground. Her positivity continued to shine through even in the darkest moments. The pain was physical, yes, but the emotional toll hollowed her expression. She held her hand over her heart. "We can't let Terratoria's destruction be for nothing. They trusted me with their future."

Daegon forced a smile to compete with Layla's and wrapped his arm around her. "Then we have a plan for the night."

After another hour of walking in the direction opposite of Terratoria, they settled next to a stream to make camp. The terrain shifted as they approached Embren territory. Dusty outcroppings grew sparse; replaced with patches of green foliage. On the horizon, massive tree trunks with humongous leaves hung from thick branches. The ground below them sprouted thick blades of grass. Territoria was eroding.

The smoke from their campfire contributed to the canvas of destruction that persisted above. Daegon pulled a log and took a seat. Gazing into the blue of the toasting fire, Daegon turned to Layla. "Now that you've faced the *Scourge*. Do you think it's all still worth it?" Layla cocked her head and sat down beside him. The warmth of the fire was a gentle reminder of their first meeting. He continued, "Why are you doing this? I understand the Conjuror's Journey, but why you specifically?"

"I remember the day he left," Layla whispered, staring into the flames. "The city threw a parade. Flowers, drums, cheering. Everyone was so...so happy."

She picked up a twig and snapped it.

"They cheered when he left, and then they cheered when the news came that he was dead. They thought that he'd saved them. Sacrificed himself to defeat the *Scourge*. They didn't mourn the man; they worshipped the act."

Daegon studied her, the firelight casting deep shadows across her twisting face.

"So that's why?" Daegon asked. "To be a sacrifice?"

"No," Layla said, her voice hardening. She threw the broken twig into the fire. "I'm doing this so no other daughter has to watch a parade and wonder if her father is coming home."

Daegon leaned in and put his hand on her. "I'm sorry..."

She waved him off. "That feeling of being so close to saving everyone, only to have it replaced with hopelessness. It spread throughout Shishbash. It consumed me." She closed her eyes, and a tear formed at the corner. "People need a reason to believe there's a future. That the darkness is temporary. That my father didn't fail."

The wind blew through the trees and caused the fire to twirl. The cool breeze welcomely contrasted with their previous days in the cloudless Terratoria. Daegon watched the fire spark and flicker. "That's why it had to be you."

Layla, with tears streaming down her face, shakily said, "It always had to be me. To instill that faith in my city. If I wasn't backing down to the *Scourge*. To the Reapers that slaughtered my father, then my people could sleep at night knowing that one day their pain would end. Life is finite. But through me, my father's Journey would be complete."

Daegon sat up and brushed the tears from Layla's eyes. So much pain behind that constant smile. She carried the burden of an entire city on her shoulders and did it without the faintest hint of agony. He wanted to hold her. Wanted to let her scream into the smoke-drenched sky. But coming from someone who'd lost his own father, he knew nothing would replace the feeling. He looked her directly in the eyes and said the only thing on his mind. The only thing he could say that would make sense at that moment. "Thank you."

The crackling fire played background to their somber conversation. She sniffled her nose, wiped her face, and said, "I met him, you know?"

Daegon sat straight. "What?"

"Your father. When he first came to Shishbash."

Daegon pushed at the lump developing in his throat, but words struggled to develop. Layla reached for his hand. "He was kind. He'd heard about my father and pulled me aside."

"What did he say?"

"He told me about Malachi. It's sprawling beauty." She gazed into the fire. "I thought it was just stories, created to make a sad girl smile. But then you showed up."

Daegon rubbed his chin, remembering their conversation behind the Shishbashi Keep. Her immediate intrigue with Malachi plastered across his memories. It wasn't just blind intrigue that fueled her desire to trust a stranger. There was a history. A shared history.

Layla sat straight and wiped her eyes as Gallant returned from his short fishing trip. She greeted him with a smile, and he threw four large fish on the stones in front of the fire. Gallant's eyes dropped to the tears on her cheeks, and he reached for a piece of his cracked spear. "Is everything okay here?" His voice adjusted in pitch.

Layla nodded and continued with a grin before beginning to laugh. "You aren't seriously thinking about taking out the great King of Malachi, are you?" She nudged Daegon with her fist before jumping from the log and grabbing one of the fish.

Gallant angled his chin. "You know, if he hurts you, it would be simple work."

Daegon raised his hand in protest. "I think we proved at Whisperwind who would win that fight."

Gallant brushed off the comment, causing Daegon to laugh as he tended the fire. Layla's fire-lit cheeks peeked through the bouncing flames. Daegon rested his chin between his fingers, staring into the fire, anticipating the heat of their adventure. Tomorrow, they would make their way to Embre, the city of flames.

Chapter Twenty

Daegon dug his face into the pit of his elbow, smearing the settled ash across his dry eyes. The smoke from the previous day's destruction had dissipated, returning the skies to their deep blue. All that remained of the destruction of Terratoria were the memories the three carried with them. Hopefully, someone survived. What had happened to Cardinal Mesa? To the children in the sewers? The *Scourge* follows the stones. That was the prevailing thought. Now that the group had multiple of them, would the *Scourge* home in on them with more regularity?

The three walked through the now lush jungle, cutting away obstacles and wading through the thick web of uncut grass. Daegon kind of missed the barren desert of Terratoria. At least there he wouldn't have to worry about stepping on, or in, something that might kill him. Or at least that was what Gallant had warned him about. Unseen creatures climbed through the canopies above. The dusty ground had vanished; now slightly damp as the thickness of the grass choked the warmth of the sun from evaporating its moisture.

Gallant, at the front of the group, shouted, "We shouldn't be far now." He pointed off into the distance. "The volcano at the center of Embre creates soil ripe for all this jungle to grow. The larger everything gets, the closer we are."

He wasn't kidding about the magnificence of his surroundings. Everything was large. The trees. The flowers. The blades of grass. He didn't want to see the animal Gallant had warned him about. If it could be described as an animal.

Layla was at the center of the trio, focusing her attention on the denseness of their surroundings. Daegon cautiously stepped through the thick grass as the gusting wind slammed into the dark bark of the trees above. The sun was scorching. When it could peek through the thick brush above, it warmed his skin. But the humidity quickly cooled him as they continued to trudge deeper. Daegon stared at the rich patterns above, mouth agape at the incredible scale of the forest, only to be halted by Gallant's blue armor.

Gallant abruptly stopped and clenched his fist in the air. Hesitation grabbed his voice. "This grass has already been cut." He reached out to feel the significantly shorter blades of grass, outlining a path for them to follow.

Multiple sections split in opposite directions. As if a giant scythe wildly traversed the wall of grass. Searching. Layla stepped next to Gallant and kneeled. "What could do this?"

Gallant put his hand on the hilt of his shattered spear, shorter, but now properly pointed after a night of sharpening. "I'm not sure, but it's best we keep moving. I don't want to find out."

Daegon too readied his father's sword, coiled like a spring, prepared to combat whatever enemy positioned itself in their future. Between the heavy cover and constant clamor above, they were vulnerable. Out in the open. Unable to properly detect the location of their enemy. But the path outlined for them pointed toward Embre. The blazing plume of volcanic ash peaked in the distance.

They crouched and followed the curved path toward the city. Whatever had sliced through the grass was large. Large and apparently unsure of what exactly it was looking for. Gallant paused at the intersecting paths, poking his head to ensure they were safe. Was this the animal Gallant had been concerned about? Sweat beaded on the back of his neck, and his assortment of inappropriate quips remained silent. Which, based on his typically stoic demeanor, made Daegon quiver.

Daegon said, "I think we need to get off the path. Whatever it is, it's looking for something."

Gallant and Layla both turned around before emitting an audible gasp in his direction. Daegon shuddered at their faces. Their fear. He turned around to see what he'd been dreading the entire Journey. Memories echoed from Shishbash, where the hideous creature ripped apart the young Embren Conjuror. He closed his eyes and reached for his sword. The mechanical crunch proved that this wasn't the phantom that attacked him at Whisperwind. No. The stones had lured it to them. A Reaper.

The creature, with its bony face, leaped at Daegon, hefting its oversized sword with ease. Daegon successfully unsheathed his sword and met the Reaper's blade just in time.

Clang!

Metal clanged in the successful defense. The Reaper's red eyes bloomed, and it swung its arm at Daegon's already weak chest. The arm collided with a pop, sweeping Daegon into the grassy walls before returning its sights to Layla.

It ignored Daegon's attempts to move and advanced with a terrifying singular purpose. Its eyes locked on Layla as if drawn by a magnet. Gallant stepped in front, his shattered spear looking pathetic against the Reaper's massive blade. They wouldn't be defeated this way. He roared as the creature's gigantic blade swung down on him, but he safely guided it to the grassy floor and attempted a counterattack. His spear squeaked off the armor, leaving Gallant defenseless. Its metal-clad arm met Gallant's chest and pushed him away. Air escaped his lungs as he gasped. He lay on the ground as the Reaper lumbered toward Layla. He cried out, but his words were hollow.

The Reaper stepped forward, now within mere feet of Layla. She staggered backwards and put her hands up to prepare for the creature's incoming blow. It hefted its sword into the air and swung it at the Conjuror. But the ground shuddered under Layla's feet as she called on the power of the stones. The earth groaned. A pillar of stone shot up, intercepting the blade with a deafening crack. The emotionless creature staggered as she pushed her hands at the grounded sword, encasing it within a tomb of earth.

The Reaper pulled at the unbudging sword, and Daegon reappeared from the forest. A flash of gray appeared just beneath the monster's arm. He didn't hesitate. He lunged, driving his blade into the gap in the armor. The monster's arm severed from its body. Shuddering, it tried to retreat, but Layla pressed on, coating its feet in an earthen shell. It collapsed onto its back and shook the battlefield. Gallant sprang from the ground into the air and drove what was left of his spear between its eyes.

The beast shook violently. Daegon stepped in front of Layla, blade drawn, ready for whatever came next. Gallant held the spear squarely in the creature's skull, driving it deeper as it screeched. Grinding metal emanated from the convulsing beast. Its hands shook, and the Reaper disappeared. The now-hollow armor collapsed inward. The creature didn't rot; it evaporated, melting into a foul-smelling black steam that hissed as it touched the grass. Gallant stepped back and watched the creature, hands grasping his spear, until it faded away.

Layla's feet had buried into the ground. "Is...it...gone?"

Gallant lowered his weapon. "I believe so." His voice continued to tremble until his breath eventually cracked, releasing a noticeable sigh.

The Reaper's body left a black, matted stain where it had lain. A yellow glimmer winked from the matted grass. He carefully walked through the would-be remains and picked up a piece of what looked to be jewelry: a golden necklace with a circular insignia comprising an eye. Daegon held it in his hands and stared. It seemed...familiar. Like everything in this land, there were hints of his life before. Malachi, the Orphans, and the cities all bore a similar crest.

Gallant broke him from his trance. "Hey! What did you find?" Daegon held up the golden eye, and Gallant went pale. He reached for his neck, pulling out his own chain. The golden eye in his hand matched the one from the Reaper. "Corporeal," he whispered. "This...this is a soldier's medallion."

Layla approached Daegon. "What's a Reaper doing with that sigil?"

Daegon ran his hand through his dark hair. "I'm not sure." He paused before looking up at Layla. "Maybe the Reaper stole it from a soldier?"

Gallant said, "When we get to Embre, we can meet with the Cardinal about what we found."

Daegon interrupted, "I don't know if that's the right decision." He closed his eyes as the wind swirled in the trees above. "Something's not right about the Cardinals, Gallant. Are you sure we can trust them?"

Gallant's eyes grew hard, and his voice became hoarse. He clenched his fist around the necklace. "Stop," he said, his voice shaking. "Don't say it. Reapers kill soldiers. They steal trophies. That is all this is."

Layla held up her hands and attempted to quell any dissension. "Maybe Daegon's right?" She pointed at Daegon. "Didn't you say that Cardinal Mesa was terrified of Cardinal Sooman prior to your meeting?"

Daegon nodded, but Gallant said, "What does that have to do with anything?"

Layla kept her hands raised. "Maybe Cardinal Sooman warned Cardinal Mesa about the *Scourge*."

"Warned her? As if he's able to control that...that thing." Gallant was practically spitting.

Layla lowered her hands. "I don't know. I just think we need to be careful. Can we at least do that?"

Gallant's voice tapered off. "I've been with Cardinal Bilari for years. He practically raised me."

Daegon and Gallant's eyes were unbreakable. Daegon said, "What about Cardinal Sooman? Do you trust him?"

Gallant squeezed his fists and looked at Layla. "Let's just get to Embre. We can figure everything out once we're in the safety of a city. Do you understand?"

Their gaze broke, and Gallant flicked his cloak in their direction. Daegon pressed further, "Gallant."

He looked back at Daegon, and for the first time, fear darkened Gallant's eyes.

"If you're right," Gallant whispered, "then we're already dead."

Daegon hesitated before pocketing the Corporeal sigil and returning a somber nod. In the distance, a volcanic eruption radiated from the mountain at the center of Embre, beckoning them closer.

Chapter
Twenty-One

Daegon and Gallant crawled across the damp ground and peered from the top of a nearby hill. Embre was now within reach, its volcano spewing a black cloud that shaded the city from the scorching rays. The humidity that pestered them in the forest dampened their armor, creating an environment that was initially pleasant, but slowly grew more oppressive. Daegon wiped the sweat from his eyes and squinted at the commotion occupying the front gate. Hundreds of people swarmed, all dressed in various shades of green, pushing against the guards attempting to quell the dissent. Citizens of Terratoria. Survivors of the *Scourge*.

The front gate poked into the crowd, comprising multiple towers topped with the jagged features of the Embre Sigil: a serpent with ruby eyes. Thin plumes of lava flooded over sections of the wall, filling a surrounding moat that prevented intruders from getting too close. While the area near the city was lush, the strips of land closest to the wall were barren. A consistent clatter of noise emanated from the people. Rowdy, indiscernible commands were barked from the wall and from within the crowd. Daegon searched the origin, but it didn't sound human. Just faint syllables playing alongside a mechanical scratch.

He scanned the mass for Cardinal Mesa, Kazi, or Sir Maybin, but the uniformity of the sea of green made it difficult to discern features. An unseen weight pulled at him. He searched the unruly mass below, certain someone was tracking their movement. Then, a break in the shifting sea of green revealed him. A figure in a dark blue cloak stood frozen, hood angled directly toward the hill. Daegon blinked away the stinging salt in his eyes, but the spot was empty. The figure had vanished into the rot. *Who was that? Or what was that?*

Gallant gestured for Daegon and Layla to follow, and he slid down the hillside, meeting the outskirts of the refugees. Decay wafted from the crowd. Combined with the burning smell of the *Scourge*, Daegon did everything he could not to throw up. And yet, they pushed through, holding arms so as not to get lost.

Once inside, dust flogged his eyes, and the injured limbs and scarred bodies were a map of the destruction he left behind in both Malachi and Terratoria. While initially a static, chaotic mass, the wave of people began to shift, skirting the moat of lava that surrounded the volcanic city. Stray limbs bumped and pushed them away from one another, eventually succumbing to the flow of the group. Daegon spun out and reached for Gallant or Layla, but the gritty hands sucked him in. Eyes. There was that singular figure. Even though their face was covered by their hood, their gaze was distinctively fixed on him. A gray beard peeked from under the hood when a refugee smacked Daegon in the face, dragging him along with the wave.

Embren guards corralled the refugees. Their stone-colored armor, pocketed with glowing red cracks, provided a stark contrast to the sea of green. They wore machines on their mouths that attached to the backs of their helmets, and their voices bellowed with a metallic rasp. The guards pushed the people along, aggressively guiding the crowd away from the front gate. Their mechanically amplified voices fueled the chaos that plagued the refugees.

Gallant erupted from the crowd and grabbed Daegon's arm. "Stay together!"

Thankfully, Layla had been with Gallant the whole time, and the three were now locked in arms, pushing toward the outside of the group. Someone ushered them into what looked like a courtyard, but it too swelled with the stench of evacuees. The crimson-scarred guards watched idly on the walls above, directing the crowd with their barbed whips.

They continued pushing until they sprang from the pile. Daegon collapsed onto the dusty floor and his chin met a glowing red boot. He looked up as a blade sang through the air, stopping inches from his throat.

Gallant lunged forward, hands out. "We're from Shishbash. This is Lady Layla, a Conjuror on her Journey to defeat the *Scourge*." His voice was too loud, too forceful. The tone of a man trying desperately to prove he belonged. If he wanted to belong.

The Embren guard shrugged off Gallant's arm and sneered. "Yeah, and I'm the Grand Conjuror from Embre." The guard raised the hilt of his sword and swung it down on Daegon, but a wall of earth erupted, clamping the steel in a stone vise.

"I am the Conjuror from Shishbash," Layla said affirmatively. Her eyes pierced the man's armor.

The guard bit his lip and glanced at his guardsmen. They exchanged passive nods. The guard ripped his sword from the stone and sheathed his weapon. *Everything was suddenly okay?* His voice, while still gruff and angry, became less abrasive. Less hostile. "Welcome to Embre, Lady Layla, Keep the Memory. Cardinal Drone has been expecting you. We're sorry for the disturbance." He reached for Daegon, and hoisted him to his feet. "We have received more refugees since Terratoria was destroyed."

Layla lowered her stance and walked in the guard's direction as he beckoned them out of the mass. As they followed the guards into the narrow alley within the wall, an additional guard watched every few feet, eyeing them through the tubing on their machines. The defense was incredible, if not unnecessary. All were ready, prepared to strike or defend at a moment's notice.

Daegon turned back one last time. A back gate in the city swallowed the refugees, but in the middle of the mass, a hooded figure stood unmoving, staring coldly at him. Darkness continued to shroud him, but this time a familiar glint bit through the shadows—a bearded gray chin and a deep scar carved into his jaw.

Could it be?

A hand grabbed Daegon by the shoulder, spinning him away before the memory could take root.

They were led through an inner path in the wall, containing an elevated platform that rose high above the flowing river of magma. Daegon peered over the edge as flames ripped through the carefully dug canals. The heat radiated from the crevices, slowly searing his skin. "Was this city built over a volcano?" The question escaped his lips before he could stop it.

Gallant bit his lip, and sweat beaded heavily on his brow. "It sure looks like it." He wiped his brow and said, "One heck of a defense system."

They followed along a narrow passage until a bridge appeared, leading to a dark wooden door carved into the side of the mountain. Daegon blinked. The searing heat vanished, replaced by the unexpected scent of rain and blooming jasmine. Massive cooling vents pumped mist into the street, feeding the lush vertical gardens that lined the rustic stone walls. Along the paths and between the buildings, the city planted the same leaves that shrouded them in the forest. After a few steps, Daegon stopped to admire the mountain nestled at the heart of the city. Streams of molten lava flowed down the mountainside, creating slim cracks of fire that stretched alongside the buildings.

The main street raced up the volcano, culminating in what was presumably Cardinal Drone's chamber, ornate and ostentatiously perched from an outcropping. Embre was not like Terratoria. There were no cracks. No debris or dilapidated buildings. Properly spaced thatched houses mixed with regal meeting places, and its red-cloaked citizens roamed the streets. Every citizen maintained a machine wrapped around their necks, as if prepared for noxious gas to come pouring down on them. Daegon scratched his throat to clear away any potential toxins.

Layla's mouth was agape. She'd never left Shishbash, and after escaping Terratoria, this was the first functioning city she'd seen. Her eyes followed the fresh plume of smoke from the tip of the volcano into the sky. The group had moved, but her feet were locked in place, the juxtaposition of the city steeling her breath. It wasn't until Daegon grabbed her hand that she started to walk.

She said, "How can so much life exist next to the potential for so much destruction?"

Chapter Twenty-Two

T he guards came to an abrupt halt at the entrance of an enormous gate flowing with red magma skirting the sides. While the lava spewed into a river dividing the building from the city, a singular pathway stretched to the gate, fully wreathed in fire. The guard leading them approached and said, "Cardinal Drone is inside. He requested an immediate audience."

Gallant narrowed his eyes, assessing the guards, before giving a sharp nod. "Lead the way." He peered at Daegon and Layla before beckoning them forward and through the fiery path.

The gate creaked open, narrowing to a single-file entry through the door. They quickly entered, and the gate behind them crashed, sealing them within.

Gallant whispered, "Why would Cardinal Drone demand an audience with us when he didn't even know we were here, or alive?"

Daegon squeezed the Corporeal crest picked up from their battle with the Reaper. "I'm not sure...should we be worried?"

Gallant unclipped his spear and slowed his pace in the narrow hallway. "Just stay on alert."

The heat struck them like a hammer. Curving stone walls bled warmth, and the air carried the sharp sting of sulfur and ash. Sweat vanished from Daegon's skin the moment it formed, leaving behind a dry, itchy salt. Twin canals of flowing magma churned on either side, their orange light pulsing against the ceiling. The narrow walkway widened, but only slightly, now allowing two people to walk simultaneously. Thick green bushes clung to the walls and rocks that jutted from the magma canals, a defiant splash of life against the sweltering cave. Three guards stood at the end of their path, shrouding a throne, steam piping from their breathing devices. Their armor was brighter and more ornate, and they readied their hands on their sword hilts.

A brown-haired man dressed in fire-red robes and a long, pointed beard made his way to the center. "Hello, Lady Layla and her...protectors. Welcome to the city of Embre."

Layla rested her hand on Gallant's shoulder, interrupting him before he could respond. "Cardinal Drone, why does it feel like we're not exactly welcome guests?"

Cardinal Drone looked at his guards, their hands still prepared to strike. "It seems you've become quite the lightning rod for the *Scourge*...for the...Reapers, haven't you?"

Gallant interrupted, his voice on the defensive. "How did you know Reapers attacked us?"

Drone's hand brushed through his brown hair before whipping into the air. "It was only an assumption. What...with the three of you being the reason for the absolute destruction of Terratoria?"

Layla motioned for Gallant to back down. "Yes, we were attacked, but we defeated the Reaper. We defeated one of the *Scourge's* monsters too."

Drone laughed and put his arms in the air in celebration. *Was he mocking them?* "Yes, yes. Of course you did. Because you three are different. You will bring an end to the *Scourge*...once and for all."

Layla's hardening confidence faded at the presence of Cardinal Drone's taunts. His voice was calm, collected, and calculated. As if every word were prepared beforehand. Scripted with meticulous forethought. Layla narrowed her eyes. "What did you want to meet with us about?"

Drone stepped closer, his fiery robes swishing against the stone. He opened his arms. "It's nothing personal. I wasn't even certain you were alive. I instructed my guards to bring you to me immediately if you were spotted." He reached for Layla's shoulder, but she brushed it off. Drone's tongue flicked across his lips. "I can only allow you a short stay. I cannot allow Embre to suffer the same fate as Terratoria. I trust you understand."

Layla stared into his crimson eyes. "But what of the stone ceremony?"

"Yes. I was told to make sure that happened. It will be short and discreet." Cardinal Drone shot back his answer before turning his gaze toward Daegon. "And you...have you determined how you arrived from Malachi?"

The pointedness of the question. *Was it all real?* Daegon stepped next to Layla, fully occupying the width of the narrow path. "I haven't figured that out yet, but I'm sure it has something to do with the stones. Everyone could conjure in Malachi."

Drone's eyes narrowed. "The stones?" The Cardinals truly didn't know how he'd arrived there either. In every encounter, they'd probed him for information. A test to be solved. As if he had done something that broke some unwritten rule. Drone continued, interrupting Daegon's realization. "Why is it that the *Scourge* saved its greatest nemesis's son?"

Daegon looked at the now outstretched hand and thought of his father, King Raynor. He was promised eternal glory after defeating the *Scourge*. But where was he? Where were all the Conjurors who'd completed their Journey? "So, you believe me?"

Cardinal Drone dropped his arm and turned back toward his throne. "The Cardinals were there...were they not?"

A small chuckle stemmed from the bearded man, goading Daegon to take a step forward, his hand drifting to his hilt. "What do you know?"

The three guards intervened, stepping in front of Cardinal Drone, blades hissing from their scabbards. Gallant reached for his spear to prepare for an attack, but Drone continued his subtle laugh. "Peace, young King...I can promise you that I do not know how you returned from Malachi. The rest, though...will be explained...in due time. Keep the Memory."

What was he doing reaching for his sword at that moment? He was outnumbered, essentially sentencing Gallant and Layla to death had he attacked. Drone knew more than he was saying, even if the other Cardinals remained oblivious. What was the dark secret the Congregation was hiding, and what was his place in it?

They would have time to dwell on those thoughts. Cardinal Drone waved his hands, and the guards directed them out of the chamber.

Layla stepped forward and questioned, "How do I get the Embre Stone?"

Cardinal Drone dropped onto his throne and slumped his shoulders. "Yes...we've established a temporary living space for you on the far side of the city. Our priest will be there shortly to perform the ceremony and grant you its power."

Cardinal Drone flicked his hand, and the guards rushed to their sides to usher them out. Daegon dug his heels into the ground, a futile attempt to squeeze the questions from Drone, but Gallant grabbed his arm and whispered in his ear, "Now is not the time for answers. We'll regroup and figure this out once we're safe."

A sudden heat squeezed Daegon's hand, draining the mounting anger from his chest. He flinched, half-expecting a stray splash of magma to have found him, attempting to suck him under. But as he recoiled, his eyes met Layla's. The touch was subtle, but the silence was a promise. They would find the truth. Together.

Chapter Twenty-Three

Specks of fire flickered throughout the city. Daegon peered out of his tall window, counting the torches that lined the streets, flickering against the canals of piping magma flowing freely through carefully carved paths. Thick green foliage filled in the gaps between the buildings, creating a sense of jungle. As if the city were attempting to hide amongst the landscape. An impossible task. The volcano in the center spewed its dark smoke, mixing with the twilight sky. Daegon took a breath, closed his eyes, and replayed the green and purple smoke surrounding him, sucking him into this world. The *Scourge's* razor teeth and piercing black eyes stared back at him. Its visage burned into the back of his skull. *Why didn't it just kill him?*

Two enormous thuds shook their door, and Gallant jumped from his chair, his hand grasping for his spear. After the hostilities displayed by Cardinal Drone and his guards, the furniture was a little less inviting. The Embren guards from earlier returned, now carrying their own sets of spears, wearing their customary glowing red armor. The lead guard stepped forward and said, "We're here to deliver the city's power to Lady Layla."

Layla stood from the floor in front of the fireplace and walked to meet him. She outstretched her arm, meeting the wrinkly hand of an old cloaked figure. He wore ceremonial red robes, complete with a tall, gilded headdress. Through his grizzled beard, he blew into their clasped hands, causing their embrace to emit a vibrant red glow. Layla closed her eyes, felt the heat of the moment, and absorbed the power. She gasped and jerked her hand back, revealing nothing but ground-up ash sifting to the floor. She stared at her hand, clasped her fingers, and nodded.

The old man retreated behind the guards and said with a dry, creaking voice, "If there's anything else you need, knock. One of our guards will be sure to take care of you. Keep the Memory."

The guards slammed the door, the iron locking mechanism clicking with finality. Footsteps descended the staircase until they were alone.

Daegon turned from the window and sank into a chair at the heavy dining table. "Why does it feel like we're in prison?"

Gallant offered a dry, abrupt laugh. "Considering you're the only one here who's been in a real cell, I'll take your word for it."

"Hey, hey, hey. That's not fair," Daegon shot back, but a grin broke through. Comfort settled between them, fragile but real, as Layla fluttered her fingers. She snapped, and a patch of the rug erupted in flames, causing her to cry out in panic.

Gallant lunged, smothering the fire before it could cause any actual damage. "Your new power, I assume?"

Layla nodded and laughed. "I guess I need to practice this one. The last two stones weren't as dangerous."

Daegon crushed his hands on the table. "We still need to figure out what our plan is for tomorrow. Obviously, we're not welcome here." He felt the Corporeal crest in his cloak pocket. "Cardinal Drone was strange, wasn't he? He knows something about the *Scourge* or my father."

Gallant nodded and took a seat at the table. "Yes, let's figure it out." He closed his eyes, detesting the fact that he'd agreed. "Something is strange in this city. As the leader of the Fluidguard, we're trained by the Congregation to accept the reality that bringing in a Conjuror has the inherent risk of an attack by the *Scourge*. Being a Cardinal, he knows that. Preaches that. It makes little sense why we're being shunned." He folded his hands and placed them on the table, obviously uncomfortable with the fact that he questioned the very religion where he'd been raised.

Daegon slammed coins on the table, outlining the layout of the cities. "Well, how about this? We are here," he said, sliding a coin toward the edge. "And Sooman is here."

Gallant pressed his thumbs to his temples. "Corporeal? You still want to go to Corporeal?"

"We need answers," Daegon said. "And the only person who has them is Sooman."

"That medallion came from the capital. If we go there, we could be handing ourselves over to the enemy."

"We're already in their hands," Daegon countered, gesturing to the locked door and the guards outside. "Drone knows who I am. Sooman knows. If they wanted us dead, we'd be dead. They want something."

"And you intend to give it to them?"

"I intend to find out what it is," Daegon said. "Grand Cardinal Sooman is the head of the Congregation. If there is chaos in the order, it starts with him. We go to Corporeal. We get the Corporeal Stone. And we confront him."

Gallant looked at Layla, who was practicing with a small flame in her palm. The fire danced across her knuckles. "It's a trap," Gallant whispered.

"I know," Daegon said. "That's why we're going to spring it."

"Fine," Gallant sighed, moved his hands to some papers, and scribbled a map of the area. "Right, well, here's how we get to Corporeal."

The two worked out their next movements while Layla practiced her newfound magic in front of the fireplace, the embers dancing across her knuckles. Metal clanked and echoed from the door as the guards below them moved about. Outside, the mountain's thick smoke pulsed with a chugging smog, echoing the *Scourge's* deadly cloud.

After they completed the plan, Daegon stood from the table and stretched his arms. "Regardless of what we do, we'll be ready for anything. We'll find a way."

Gallant nodded and placed his spear on the bench in front of the fire. Layla had recently fallen asleep to the melodic crackles. Stoking the flames for one final consistent blaze, Gallant said, "I can take the first shift tonight, if you want to get some rest."

Daegon scoffed. "Taking shifts? You really must not trust this place."

Gallant peered down at Layla and shifted a stray blanket onto her shoulders. "I think it's best if we stay prepared. For anything."

Daegon collapsed into the chair. "*If* I can get some rest." He held onto the first word a little longer than normal, realizing that sleeping in enemy territory wasn't exactly easy.

He placed his scabbard next to the dining room table, still ready to go at a moment's notice, slouched into the chair, and closed his eyes. The consistent creaking of shifting metal played just underneath, lulling him further asleep.

Chapter
Twenty-Four

Daegon peered around the corner, down the hallway leading to his father's quarters. The King's quarters. The room he would eventually occupy. However, with his father's disappearance, the room had remained vacant, continually patrolled by two Kingsguard. Their blank armor shimmered in the light that leaked through the windows. Six candles burned brightly, lining both sides of the hall that ended in wooden doors. Ever since King Raynor's disappearance, the room had remained off limits to everyone, including himself. It was the King's private quarters, but shielded from his own son? A stoic smile slipped through the shadows. Today would be the day when he would finally figure out what was behind the doors.

He turned from the occupied hallway and followed the art-filled corridor of Malachi's keep. Images of his father decorated the walls, detailing incredible feats of conjuring ability. The signature flaming blade his father carried appeared in every piece, specifically showing the many adventures he'd undertaken to create a better Malachi. *It had to have been a lie*. Daegon knew Raynor. And he'd never known him to be much of a savior. Never known him to be much of anything to strive toward. But these heroics occurred prior to the death of his mother. Daegon had never known his mother, who'd died in childbirth, leaving the King to raise him on his own. Whispers from within the kingdom implied his father had changed after his mother's death. While running a kingdom and raising a child without aid was difficult, the lack of his father's praise caused Daegon to turn toward others for guidance. Mostly Jordell. But he too disappeared. With his father. The irony.

Daegon opened the door onto the streets of Malachi, bustling with the midday assortment of traders and citizens engaged in the transfer of goods. Malachi had everything anyone could ever want, clear by the heavenly smell of freshly baked bread loaves mixed with the spicy sparks of carved steel. Daegon took a second to admire the work of his city, or what would eventually be his city, and parsed through some of the produce brought in by the outsiders.

True Malachinians matched the pale hue of their armor. Of the white bricks that built up every wall. Outsiders were noticeably different. The men peddling goods in this area of the city were tan and maintained heads full of hair, dusted with the spoils of their morning hunt. But they were good at their job and maintained crowds of people rummaging through their supplies, throwing gold coins into their collection baskets. He'd always known them as Braccan. Some took offense at the phrase, but Daegon had been taught the etymology to mean outsider.

Daegon waded through the crowd, his hood covering his obvious appearance outside of the keep's walls. One of the Braccan traders attempted to stack a crate onto the carriage when it tipped. The man was unaware of the collapsing box, but Daegon jumped to his aid and prevented the box from crashing into him. Daegon couldn't save everything, allowing a few of the red fruits to fall to the ground. The man winced and ducked, but quickly turned to Daegon after the immediate danger had passed.

"Tha...thank...thank you, sir," the older, tan-skinned gentleman said. He wore a brown cap that extended over his ears and a matching tunic that distinguished him as someone who'd been a trader for longer than Daegon had been alive.

Daegon pushed the box onto the carriage, turned toward the man, and tipped his hood.

The man's mouth opened wide. "You're the King!"

Daegon pressed a finger to his lips and quieted him so as not to cause the crowd to collapse on them. "Not the King yet." He put his hand on the older man's shoulder and offered a smile. "I just do my best to help." He pulled out a couple of coins from his pocket and slid them into the man's hands before nodding and being on his way.

The quiet rumble of noise faded from Daegon's thoughts as he made his way down an alleyway and to the base of Malachi Keep. He'd always been able to sneak in and out of the city using the crevices in the stone architecture. But he'd never attempted to climb the Keep itself. He'd never had a reason to. Based on the structure, it couldn't be too difficult. The general idea was the same, and the original architects of Malachi had too much hubris to think that anyone could scale them. With how beautiful the city looked from the top of the Keep, who could blame them? Malachi was a bastion of peace, and for as long as he could remember or read, it had never engaged in conflict with any of the neighboring territories.

The entrance to his father's room quietly loomed six stories above. Daegon pressed his foot into a divot and began the ascent to the top. The white stones jutting from the wall offered secure footing, and he navigated the maze of footholds with ease. Halfway up, the heavy stomp of armored boots vibrated the stone. He pressed himself flat, using his white cloak to blend seamlessly with the marble. It'd worked sneaking into the city when he needed time away, and it worked again now.

Daegon reached for the window and pulled himself through before cushioning his fall onto his father's wooden floor, revealing a large circular room with all the amenities common to most Malachinian citizens. A long-curved dresser stretched from the door, ending in an ornate bed crafted with the eye of Malachi burned into the headboard. Always on watch. A wooden chair was pulled from the desk next to the window where he'd arrived. Undisturbed. A relic of the day his father had disappeared. The shiny down blanket still lay disheveled on his bed, and his drawers still bore his open cloaks. With the candles cold and unlit, only the window aided Daegon's search. From behind the door, the soldiers' shifting armor scraped, like a branch too close to a building, alerting him to maintain his stealth. He left a disturbed layer of dust as he searched through the forbidden room.

Daegon approached the desk and found an open book covered in a gritty layer of dust. The pages crinkled as he touched them, but he brushed the filth from the leather cover. The book hummed under his touch, a vibration that rattled his very bones. A pull that he'd felt so many times. The shining stone, peeking outside the window, pricked at his neck.

He opened it. There were no words—only images that swirled like smoke trapped in paper.

On one page, a city of white marble stood tall. Malachi. On the opposite page, a city of black stone mirrored it, dark and jagged. Corporeal.

Between them hovered a stone, surrounded by images of the various elements: fire, water, earth, light, and shadow. Coalescing in a chaotic, blinding vortex.

The Aether Stone.

The name whispered in his mind, not read but felt. The source of all conjuring. *Not innate.*

In the book, armies clashed beneath the contrasting stone. Soldiers in white slaughtered soldiers in black. Then, the stone began to crack, and a shadow leaked from the fracture. Formless. Hungry. *The Scourge.* It stretched from the page into the room, slowly consuming the shadows that played against the chamber's walls.

"Complete my Journey." A quiet echo traced the back of his mind.

He dropped the book as the moving ink bled from the page and stained his fingers.

A gravelly voice jerked his gaze toward the front door. "The boy. Where is he?" The soldiers shifted under the weight of their plate.

When he returned to the book, absent pages greeted him, silently hiding their story. Daegon put the book down and shuffled to the door, putting his ear against the wood to amplify the noise behind. He recognized the voice. Geoffrey. The head of the Kingsguard. *Why would he need him all of a sudden?*

After the guards let out confused grunts, Geoffrey said, "We need to find him now. It's regarding his father. Somebody just washed up on the shores of Lake Kimset." He disbanded the troop to search the halls, leaving the front door unattended.

If there were ever a time to sneak into his father's chambers, now would be it. Scaling the wall wasn't even necessary. His ears, though, perked up at the mention of someone washing up on the shores of Lake Kimset. Could it have been his father? Maybe his body, decomposed after all these years, nibbled on by the Longo Eels in the dark depths. He waited for the guards to clear the hall, and creaked the door open, sliding out into the candle-filled hallway. He carefully closed the door behind and made his way to Geoffrey.

But when he turned the corner, two guards greeted him, their helms opened to their faces. "Daegon! What are you doing down — never mind? Geoffrey is looking for you. Come with us." They reached for his arm.

Daegon pulled away. "What's it about?"

"You have someone requesting you. Just washed up on the shores of Lake Kimset." They grabbed Daegon once again, but he rebuffed their attempts.

"I'm no longer a child. I don't need to be escorted anymore. I can follow along."

The soldiers nodded and walked him to the food hall on the second floor of the Malachi Keep. The glaring eye of Malachi, etched into the entryway, watched as two additional soldiers now guarded the room. *Who could it have been that there needs to be security?* The soldiers nodded to one another and opened the door. Geoffrey's back prevented Daegon from immediately seeing the individual. Geoffrey turned toward Daegon and shook his head in disbelief. *Was it his father?* Geoffrey moved to the side, revealing a gray-haired man with tattered robes dripping onto the pale floor. A scratch ripped under his eye as he looked up.

"Hello kid."

Daegon froze at the entry. Along the walk, he'd thought of all the things that he would say if it were his father. His mind rotated between disdain and surprising excitement but didn't account for the man sitting before him. It wasn't the King. It was the man who had raised him.

Jordell.

Chapter Twenty-Five

I n between the quiet billows of smoke, a canvas of stars peppered the brilliant night sky. Crackling torches sprayed outside, and the low rumble of the mountain vibrated the room. Daegon was only half-asleep. How could he be anything but? Even in his dreams, he was still conscious of the outside world, ready to react at any hostile thud or crack. He couldn't allow his mind to fully rest. There were too many pieces that didn't fit. The Cardinals didn't just know something. They knew everything. About his father, about the stones, about the *Scourge*. The thoughts rattled in his mind like ice in a cup.

Gallant sat in front of the roasting fire, repairing his spear, mumbling a hymn under his breath. The sting of his metal spear pierced the room as a whetstone slid across the point.

Layla woke up on the floor and scooted toward Gallant. "Is everything okay?"

Gallant paused in grinding his spear and gave a comfortable grin. His brow had lines from furrowing. "I'm just ready to leave this place and get back on our way."

Layla nodded and crossed her legs. She gestured toward Daegon, barely visible at the edge of the firelight. "I'm glad he's getting some sleep."

Gallant glanced over his shoulder at Daegon, whose mouth was wide open, drooling from the corner. "I don't think it's as comfortable as he wants it to be."

Layla's cheeks peaked. "Still, we all deserve a break. Even you, Gallant." She blocked him from cleaning his spear and gestured for him to lie on the cot.

He shrugged her off and continued sliding the piece of stone over his weapon. "I'll be fine. I promise."

Gallant wiped his forehead of the sweat that had suddenly beaded on his brow. The fireplace maintained its gentle roar, but the room had warmed at an unnatural speed. Gallant's ears perked as the crackling torches outside swelled, sounding less like streetlamps and more like a bonfire. He shot to his feet and threw a pillow at Daegon.

Daegon shuddered awake, instinctively grabbing his sword. "What's the danger?" he shouted incoherently.

Gallant's head spun around the room, trying to find the origin of the heat. Of the crackling. "I'm not sure." He gripped his spear, walked to the window, and stared at the expanse of the city. Everything seemed normal. Or normal enough for less than the day that they'd been there. The volcano sustained its quickened billow, and the torches lining the streets continued to flicker. As he made his way around the city, searching for the noise, he stepped back as his eyes caught the base of the tower. "We have to go. The tower is on fire!"

Daegon sprang from his chair and ran to the door. He pulled the handle, but it refused to budge. The locking mechanism clicked in his mind. He cursed under his breath and scanned for something to rip the door from its hinges. The heat had radiated into the room, and small puffs of smoke slipped through the cracks in the wooden floor. "What are our options here, Gallant?"

Gallant, in his blue armor, stood pensively in the center of the room, weighing their options. "Layla, do you think you could freeze the hinges? We might be able to shatter them?"

Layla nodded, closed her eyes, and thrust out her arms. A pale blue frost shot from her fingertips, coating the iron hinges in ice. The metal groaned. Layla shuddered as her arms fell from the task, breathing heavily but affirmatively.

Gallant patted Layla on the shoulder and offered a smile. "That'll do." He hefted his newly sharpened spear and stabbed at the hinges, shattering them into shards. "Alright, Daegon, pull the door down. Layla, stay close. We don't know what we're up against here."

Daegon ripped the door from the frame and stepped into the dimly lit stairwell. His breath exploded out of him, and he crashed into the wall as one of the crimson-clad guards tackled him. His back cracked, and blood spewed into his hand as the glow of more red climbed the staircase. *No time to think about the reinforcements.* Daegon couldn't reach his sword. The guard reared back for an additional attack, but Gallant sprinted out of the room and kicked the guard down the overheated staircase. Two additional guards stopped his fall. The guards, wearing their brass respirators, drew their blades and sped up the staircase.

Steel clashed in the hallway as Gallant stepped forward onto the staircase to meet the attacks with ease. Gallant chided Daegon, still dazed from the guard's attack. "If you want to get up and help, that'd be great."

Daegon jumped from the ground and pulled his blade, joining the fight in the narrow corridor. Every swing of their sword was about gaining one additional step out of the burning building, making it to safety, and escaping this hostile city. The stairwell had become blisteringly hot, and Daegon sweated through his cloak, his sword slipping with every swing. The heat from the fire bled through their boots, quickening their steps. Daegon parried a swing from a guard, locked blades, and sliced through their glowing armor. They fell backwards and slumped onto the blazing stone. An opportunity for Daegon and Gallant to push.

The remaining two guards retreated down the staircase, their glowing armor lighting a path for them to follow. "It's time to go now!" Gallant shouted, swinging his arms and ushering them down the staircase.

Flames had engulfed the entire first floor of the building, clogging the stairwell entry, slowly climbing like vines toward them. Daegon stared into the blaze, shaking his head at the heat before diverting his gaze to Layla. "Anything you can do about the fire?"

Layla squeezed her hand and focused intently on the rising flames. Like the fireplace, just bigger. Whether it was because of the escape or the exhaustion from using her abilities, she shook ever so slightly. Regardless, she closed her eyes and reached into the chaos. The flames flickered away, clearing along the steps, and creating a tunnel of fire for them to enter.

Layla fell to one knee, her breath becoming labored. Daegon attempted to help, but she brushed him away. As she stood, she said, "That should be enough."

The three darted through the opening. As they completed their descent through the staircase, Daegon shouted ahead at Gallant, "What's the plan once we make it out? They're obviously waiting for us."

Gallant didn't respond. He just continued through the ashen furniture of the first floor, to the entrance of the building, prepared for whatever would meet them on the other side. Gallant quickened his pace and rammed his shoulder through the door, but it disintegrated on impact. He collapsed onto the Embren cobblestone, coughing and gasping for breath. Daegon and Layla followed shortly behind, not realizing how little they could breathe until they were out of the building. Now in the burning building's shadow, Daegon looked up from his crouched position to face at least fifteen guards, all dressed in their red, pitted armor, pointing swords in their direction.

One guard stepped forward, his dark hair curled under the illuminated helmet, his machine attached to his mouth. His voice distorted as he said, "There's nowhere for you to run. Surrender."

Gallant stabbed his spear into the ground and used it as a crutch to stand from the cobblestone. Exhausted, his voice struggled to find the breath the fire had sucked away. "We're trying to stop the *Scourge*, protect Embre and the Congregation. Why are you trying to kill us?"

The guard leered at him, his fingers flickering a command in their direction. "You were responsible for the murder of thousands in the city of Terratoria. We have our orders."

The words struck Gallant harder than any blade. He froze, his spear dipping an inch. "What? That's a lie!"

He raised his spear toward the circling guards. This was how he would fall. Following the teachings of the Congregation. The guards lunged toward Gallant, but a jagged slab of cobblestone erupted from the ground and cut them off. Layla held her arms above her head and yelled at them, "We have to run!"

Gallant regained his footing and retreated to Daegon and Layla, and they sprinted down the main street of Embre. Torches lit their path, crackling with a more controlled ember than the one currently engulfing their quarters. Daegon glanced behind. Dozens of guards spilled onto the street. "We will not escape the city at this point. There must be a different way."

Gallant, keeping pace, nodded his head in agreement. They turned a corner, out of sight of the intruding guards, allowing Daegon the ability to scan the area. Boxes, buildings, lava plumes. All would either lead to their quick death or eventual capture. He kept searching before finding the deep green foliage that stretched around every building. The same thick green leaves and undergrowth that concealed the Reaper outside of the city. It was their only option at this point. Daegon pulled them into the brush and shrouded themselves in the foliage.

The three crouched deep in the brush and watched as guards scampered down the street. The guards frantically conversed, and Daegon wiped the sweat from his brow at the knowledge that they had escaped. At least temporarily. He put his hand on Layla's back and waited for the group to pass. The guards yelled louder in confusion before spreading through the side streets and alleyways.

Gallant pointed toward the wall. "That street over there...it leads to the door where we came in."

Daegon nodded in agreement. His hand continued resting on Layla's back, providing veiled assurance that they would make it. When enough of the guards had scattered, the three hugged the green edges of the canopies and sprinted across the street. Daegon paused in the middle, admiring the now erupting volcano, angrily watching over their escape. Layla brought him back to reality by pulling him into the leaves near the doorway.

Still crouched, they successfully made it to the entrance in the wall. The heat from the inside radiated through the wood. The narrow walkway and flowing rivers of magma would meet them inside.

Gallant reached for the handle, making sure that it was safe to grab, and twisted. "If I remember correctly, it should just be right on the other side of this room."

The door opened, and the trio slipped into the chamber, gently closing the door behind. Half expecting to be caught the second they slipped through the door, they instead met the thundering sounds of the erupting volcano, which called on the flows of lava to reach onto the paths. The waves of fire spilled onto the walkway, leaving scorch marks and soot in their wake. The heat in the room was visible, pushing against them as the magma whipped. But there weren't any guards. What few they could see quickly exited through the surrounding doors.

Gallant took the first steps through the treacherous chamber and pointed at the door on the far side. Their way out. The ground crunched under their feet as they trepidatiously walked around the flowing canals of magma. Sulfur pungently burned Daegon's nostrils, prompting his hand to the hilt of his blade. *Now would be the time for one of those machines the soldiers were wearing.*

As they approached the exit, Gallant laughed. "I guess the guards were too busy looking for us in town."

Daegon wiped the sweat from the nape of his neck. "I mean, the lava in this place doesn't exactly feel safe."

As Gallant turned the handle, the door violently swung open, and a portly man in glowing red armor burst through. The guard pushed Gallant into the grainy ground.

The Embren guard bellowed a devilish chuckle. "And what do we have here? Where do you think you all were going?" Two more Embren soldiers followed the guard, laughing and joining the lead as they cleanly drew their swords. "Cardinal Drone is going to make me captain once I bring you three in."

Gallant and Daegon drew their weapons, and Layla braced herself in the burned sand, hands raised, prepared to defend. The large guard swung his blade at the downed Gallant, but he parried the weapon with his spear. The clanging metal acted as an alarm for whoever else to know their location. Daegon jumped in and met the additional guards in combat.

Layla pushed out with her hands, still weary from her conjuring earlier. The guard battling Daegon fell to the ground, his feet encased in a tomb of earth. Daegon reversed his sword and butted him in the back of the head, knocking him out. He rushed to Layla's side as she collapsed to her knees. She was weak, sweating, and her voice wavered. The small guard laughed as he slid the sharp of his blade through his hand, strolling toward them. Daegon stepped in front and dug his feet into the ground, surveying the situation.

Gallant held his ground against the leader, but they would soon be out of time. More of Drone's guards would be descending on them any second. They had to think of a plan to escape the heated tomb.

The guard's laugh morphed into a wet gurgle. He buckled, eyes bulging as a long, silver blade erupted from his chest. Panic surged through Daegon, and he stepped in front of Layla. Standing over the corpse was the hooded man. The mask shrouded his features, but the gray, scarred chin was unmistakable. *It couldn't be.* He yanked the steel free, and before the second guard even knew what happened, the stranger dashed forward.

A blade flashed, and the burly man screamed as his arm hit the pavement, severed at the elbow. Gallant didn't hesitate. While the guard was distracted by the loss of his arm, he drove his spear through his throat. He withdrew the point and aimed it at the masked figure.

Through the tattered clothes, he pushed the spear away and gestured with his arm for the group to follow. Daegon and Gallant exchanged a wary glance, then shrugged. *It was die here or potentially die outside.* The heat from the chamber pricked at the back of their necks as they made their escape.

Chapter Twenty-Six

The hardy moon flecked their path as their masked savior led them through the dense green foliage, up what seemed to be a never-ending hill. A blaze of fire backlit their escape, presumably from their quarters in Embre. Ash and fire painted their palette as they finally caught their breath from the carnage. Or so they thought. Who was the person who'd saved them? Daegon caught the muted eyes of the masked individual for a split second, bringing up memories of old Malachi. As he watched the tattered rags guide them through the jungle, the person's bounce, or limp, to their gait felt familiar. Daegon's mind raced with the events of the previous hour, half-expecting the man to be an assassin hired to clean up the job. But Gallant and he had sheathed their weapons, fully resigned to the possibility of a sneak attack.

Tiny insects searching for flesh smacked Daegon's face, testing his constitution, but when he turned to account for the group, Layla's bright smile greeted him, shining through the darkness. She had regained some of the strength she'd lost, tightly squeezing his hand as they moved through the thick leaves. The uncut vegetation felt like razor blades, sawing against his already taut flesh.

A hand shot into the air, and the stranger stopped in a partially covered clearing. Humongous leaves still surrounded them, hiding them from the looming volcano, but the moon's gaze slipped through the canopy's cracks onto a smooth space of land. The man said with a familiar, raspy voice, "We're far enough away now; we should be safe."

Daegon scanned the campsite. Charred logs were stacked against the nearby trees, and divots marked the earth. *The man had used this area before.* "Why did you save us?" Daegon said, still holding Layla's hand. "Who are you?"

The man turned, pulling back the hood to reveal a face etched with the lines of a thousand years.

"Hello, kid."

Daegon gasped and released Layla's hand. He stepped forward and froze. Everything spun. His head. His legs. His entire body convulsed, locking him within the memories of a fallen idol. "Jordell?"

Gallant and Layla both choked at the man's name. Gallant raised his voice above the quiet chirping of the surrounding insects. "The great Jordell? One of Raynor's protectors?"

Jordell chuckled, refusing to break eye contact with Daegon. "The one and only."

Daegon stared. *He was supposed to be dead.* Everything about Malachi had been a dream. A convincing one at that, but still just a dream. There were pieces of Malachi that cleanly fit into this world, but nobody had knowledge of his city, or belief in him. Now Jordell? Daegon clenched his fists at his side, gritting his teeth, the pain straining out. "What happened, Jordell? To Malachi? To everything?"

Jordell stepped forward and wrapped his arms around Daegon. That embrace Daegon had been missing. Yearning for. "I promise I'll explain everything I know. Let's set up shelter, and we can talk?"

Jordell was real. His squeeze was tangible proof that what he remembered existed. It validated that his life had happened. A tear welled in his eye as he stood there, accepting the embrace. He took in a large gulp of air and closed his eyes, remembering their last encounter. The green and purple smoke sucked Jordell away before collapsing and consuming him. *How could either of them have survived?* And then, the thought of Jordell knowing about the *Scourge* flickered through his mind. Everyone else in Malachi was so oblivious. So unprepared. In any other time, Daegon would have fought for the truth. But now, the dissonant information didn't matter. Daegon lifted his arms and squeezed back. The world made at least a little more sense.

***

Embers wafted from the crackling fire, contrasting with the array of twinkling lights filling the night sky. They were alone in the forest, joined by the persistent white noise of chirping in the canopies above. Gallant returned from the treeline with chunks of wood and threw them onto the burn pile. Setting up camp had become a routine behavior, but losing their supplies made things more difficult, though Layla's newfound ability to create fire sped up establishing an effective base camp. While she was still learning and mastering her craft, Daegon caught her practicing in her free time. With the press of her hands, she could move mounds of earth to create a platform for a bed, extract the water from the flora, and now start a fire at the snap of her fingertips. While she hadn't mastered the art, her power was growing, and with it, the target she was becoming for the *Scourge.*

Daegon stared blankly into the fire opposite Layla. Scorch marks tattooed their skin, and dark soot stained their clothes. They were exhausted, but her smile cracked through his stoic face as he caught the blue swirls of her eyes. She always knew how to make everyone around her feel comfortable. At ease. She was in deep conversation with Jordell, expressively moving her hands and explaining their last few weeks. Daegon wanted to listen. He just couldn't. The sound of the crackling fire drowned out his already encumbered thoughts. Thoughts of Malachi. The last words Jordell had said to him. "Now's the time to follow in your father's footsteps." He looked up at the old man, who was grinning and rubbing his beard. *What did he know? Is this even the same Jordell?*

He returned his gaze to the burning wood. The fire leaped from timber to timber, consuming the wood with a hunger that mirrored the *Scourge* swallowing Malachi. Daegon closed his eyes, returning to the tower where this life began. His fingers grazed the handle of his father's sword. Jordell had no fear in his eyes. Being in that building was almost intentional. He shuddered at the razor teeth ripping through the stone bricks. A piece of damp wood popped, jarring him from his trancelike state. Jordell and Layla turned in his direction.

Layla, with her ever-present smile, asked, "Are you okay?"

But Daegon maintained his frozen posture. The mere sight of Jordell rendered him unable to speak. And even if he wanted to, what would he say? What could he ask that would make the last few weeks make sense?

Jordell put his hands on his knees and pushed himself up. His body clicked with experience. "I think he and I need to have a little talk. It's been a pleasure to meet you, Lady Layla." He reached down and kissed her hand before crossing the fire and pulling Daegon from his seat.

Daegon, both numb and despondent, eventually complied, walking to the edge of the forest just outside their campsite. Shadows wound through the woods from the glow of the campfire. Once the two were out of sight, Daegon woke from his trancelike state. The pain of loneliness surged through his bones. He understood so little about this world, and yet he had survived. Thanks to this man. Who'd...left him. His hands crashed into Jordell's chest. "Where were you!"

Jordell stumbled backward, catching his breath. "I understand. I deserved that."

Daegon pressed Jordell once again, unrelenting in his assault. "I said where were you!"

Jordell once again stumbled backwards, this time bracing his feet and centering himself, prepared for another attack. "Look, kid, I know you're confused right now..."

Daegon jumped at him once again, his voice straining. "I said where..."

Jordell grabbed Daegon's arms and locked him in a tight squeeze. He was trapped. Most would have squirmed and fought to escape. But not at this moment. The vice grip brought a much-needed reprieve from the pain of being alone. His life wasn't a lie. Jordell's voice rasped, "I can explain. If you let me."

Daegon relented, and Jordell released. But instead of slumping to the dirt, he spun around and embraced the old man. Tears bounced from his cheek and drenched his cloak. "You weren't there, Jordell."

Jordell took a breath and hugged the young King back. He hadn't seen Daegon since the *Scourge* either. "I know, kid. But I'm here now."

Daegon pulled back and walked to a fallen trunk to catch his shaky legs. So many questions. *Where to begin?* "What happened in Malachi?"

Jordell hadn't moved. He just stood in the forest watching Daegon. Calibrating the events until that point. He eventually exhaled and closed his eyes, replaying the scene in vivid memory. "The *Scourge* took your father and me on the day we disappeared."

Daegon's eyes rose at the revelation. "You said that you were lost at sea?"

"We were. Taken and marooned outside of Shishbash. Your father, with his ability to manipulate fire, was accepted as the next Conjuror...with me naturally being his protector."

"When you returned...why didn't you say that? Why did you keep this a secret?"

Jordell chuckled and took a seat next to Daegon. The distant roasting fire burned brighter, illuminating their faces. "Would you have believed me? That we teamed up in a distant land to destroy a smoke monster and saved the world?"

"Saved the world...where's my father?" Daegon looked down at his sword, remembering his father lighting it ablaze as they fought in the Malachi courtyard.

Jordell closed his eyes and leaned back on the log. He stroked his beard, matted from his days in the woods. "The *Scourge* killed him. It ultimately wins. Always."

Daegon's throat closed, unable to create a coherent question. All this time. He'd thought King Raynor had died on one of his stupid hunting trips. But he died saving the world. A hero. "But...he defeated it...it was gone for a decade...?"

"It was. But the *Scourge* always comes back. It was inevitable. And we knew it." He placed his hand on Daegon's back, and he shuddered at the touch. It was real. "We didn't want to believe it, especially Raynor, but we knew what would ultimately happen. Upon that realization, I found a way back to you and fulfilled Raynor's wishes. Watching over you as you became the King of our city."

Daegon couldn't imagine Layla succumbing to the same fate. A brief reprieve, only to be forgotten in the annals of time. His father. Layla. Was it worth it? "Layla's different, Jordell. We're going to find a way to defeat the *Scourge*...once and for all."

Jordell's hand squeezed tightly around his shoulder, and he looked back into the campfire, where Layla and Gallant laughed. "Raynor had the same enthusiasm."

"She is!" Daegon wasn't sure why that assertion came out so aggressively. Daegon bucked his hand off and embraced the sound of Layla's laughter. So much levity after what had just happened. They'd just survived an attack, and now the Congregation was hunting them, but she could make everything that much better. "How did you even find us?"

Jordell's chuckle grew more audible. "It's easy to find you three. Everyone's talking about the next protectors of the realm.

The boy from Malachi really gave you away. And after the destruction of Territoria, the next, most logical place would be Embre."

Daegon looked over his shoulder, back at Jordell, and remembered their fencing practice. Timing. Jordell had a knack for it, being sure to find them right before succumbing to the Embren guards. "Are you going to help us beat it?"

Jordell returned his gaze and nodded. "If you'll have me. Are you going to let me continue your father's wishes?"

Daegon's voice couldn't rise through his throat, catching halfway up and preventing him from providing Jordell with the affirmation. This forced him simply to nod.

"Then let's finish the Journey. Once and for all."

Their shadows stretched tall as they approached from the dark forest. Daegon did all he could to wipe away his bloodshot eyes, but Layla's inquisitive gaze meant he had failed. She offered a scant smile, which he reciprocated, but everything felt heavy. Heavy enough to question why they were even continuing forward. He knew the reason, and unlike his father, they wouldn't fail.

Jordell broke the heavy silence and pointed at Gallant's creation in the camp's corner. "You call that a bed?"

Gallant peered at his sticks and blankets, strewn together from the surrounding trees. "If you want to try your hand at something better, be my guest."

Jordell sat next to the knight, chuckled and smacked his back. "Oh no, I rarely sleep. I'd just assumed it would be a little more complete, what with how long you all have been on the road."

Gallant squinted his eyes. "I'm sorry, we weren't exactly able to get supplies from the burning building back in Embre." He spat out as Jordell smacked his back once again.

Jordell provided a raspy chuckle. "I'm just messing with you, Sir Knight. Daegon's father and I set up camps far more uncomfortable than this monstrosity."

Gallant shook his head at the assertion but ultimately conceded a friendly smirk. Gallant and Layla had been roasting freshly harvested meat. While Gallant may have been a poor bedmaker, his ability to track down food in an instant was exceptional.

Gallant grinned, offered Daegon a skewer of crisped meat, and with a full mouth said, "We need to figure out our next step. Drone probably knows that we've escaped at this point. Should we assume that if one Cardinal were against us, all of them are?"

Was Gallant really saying that? Besmirching the Congregation that he served.

Layla said, "We only need two more stones. One from Luminary, and one from Corporeal."

Gallant nodded and put his soot-covered hand to his chin. "If we head to Corporeal, maybe we can get an audience with Grand Cardinal Sooman? Maybe we can explain everything and get some help?"

Daegon jumped at the assertion. "Didn't you just say that they were all out to get us?"

Gallant shook his head at the thought. "Grand Cardinal Sooman is the wisest of the group. I'm sure there was some misunderstanding that he could correct."

Daegon remembered Cardinal Mesa in her chambers. Crying. Protesting. Only to be greeted by Sooman. Then the

Scourge struck. Everything seemed too coincidental, and yet everyone just passed it off as a plausible occurrence. Daegon fell back onto the log with his hands folded in his lap. "I...don't...know." *What would his father do?*

Jordell kicked his boots into the fire, crossing his legs as he leaned back, obviously comfortable. "I've been staying in a local village. If you want to create a plan there, the local innkeeper is a longtime friend who's helped me more than I can say."

Gallant finished chewing his thick piece of meat. "Could this *friend* help us gain the Luminary Stone? Because I don't know how else they're going to help us."

Jordell chided back, "Perhaps we should take a step back. Why are the Cardinals trying to kill you? If we could answer that, it might allow us to proceed quicker."

Daegon noticed the word *us* when he spoke. It felt good to be back together. "And they could answer that?"

Jordell waved his hands in uncertainty, creating amusing shadow puppets on the trees behind them. "With his help, I think that we'd be able to talk it through a little clearer."

Gallant moved his head through the group, catching everyone's trust in the plan. "Let's just hope it gets us on the right path."

Jordell clapped his hands, the sound echoing through the canopy. "Then it's settled. Sleep while you can, even on these monstrosities Gallant calls beds." A sly grin tugged at his beard, prompting a muffled laugh from Layla. "And in the morning, we'll head to Talman."

Chapter Twenty-Seven

W ater rushed over Daegon's face. Gallant's laughter greeted him as he sat up from the makeshift bed. Through the morning sun, they had already packed their campsite. Not that they had much stuff anymore. A conjured stone pot of liquid bubbled above the smoldering campfire, its puffs of smoke staining his cloak.

Gallant offered a warm, "Good morning, your highness."

Jordell chimed in, chuckling as he spoke, "Yes. Good morning, Your Highness."

Daegon shook his head, still rattled from the fog. After weeks of Layla rebuking his pokes at Daegon, Gallant had finally recruited another. Daegon pressed his hands into his eyes. "Not you too."

Jordell and Gallant laughed in unison, which Daegon ignored. He stumbled over to Layla and nudged her awake. She too awoke with a start. With what had happened the previous week, who could blame her? Layla's warm smile quickly returned as she focused on him with a gaze that meant "good morning."

It was almost time to move on to the next city. *What did Jordell call it? Talman?* Their Journey moved at a breakneck pace. This campsite, simple as they'd constructed it, allowed them time to consider their options. Catch up on what had been. Take in the scenery. But outside of the strict outlined path of the Conjuror's Journey, he wasn't even sure what they were walking into. He'd traveled through thick snow, across barren deserts, and now they were surrounded by the large, sticky leaves of the jungle. He should've appreciated the previous cities more.

Jordell poured the bubbling liquid into stone cups and handed them to Daegon and Layla. "A little warmth to start your day, will you?"

Daegon stared at the piping hot drink. Small leaves floated in the milky concoction. *Some sort of tea?* "You don't happen to have any food, do you?"

"My masterpiece isn't good enough for you?" He crossed his arms, huffing at the comment. "We can eat in Talman; it's only a few hours walk from here. And the food will be better than anything we can catch?"

Daegon stretched his fingers through his dark hair. "Shame. I was getting used to Gallant's forest delicacies."

Gallant shook his head and winced at the bitter taste of the drink. "Do you think they will have anything stronger than whatever this is?" He shook the now-empty glass above his head.

Sweat already dripped from their unkempt hair as they finished packing up the rest of the camp. Dousing the flames of the fire introduced black smoke into the sky, mixing with the lingering smoke from the nearby volcano. *How had the Embren soldiers not found them yet? It was better to be lucky in this instance.* Assuming that they would eventually meet a whole troop of the Embren military, his eyes glazed over the scant weapons they carried, knowing that they wouldn't be able to fight back. But Jordell seemed confident he could escort them to safety.

At least there was an upside to losing their supplies. Without the unnecessary weight, Daegon's legs were livelier as he moved through the forest, quickly avoiding sharp rocks and jutting tree roots. Jordell carved his way through the forest, leading the way and cutting through hanging tree limbs. The volcano's plume of smoke cast intermittent shadows through the forest canopy, and the oversized trees and leaves continued to obscure their vision. Combined with the sticky humidity, the lurking sun created a rather oppressive trip.

While the previous forest felt well-traveled, this one was unforgiving. They blazed their own trail, following the sun and the occasional wet finger pressed against the sparse wind. The cautious pit in Daegon's stomach mixed with the fear of the hidden eyes lurking passively in the shadows. Gallant had repeatedly warned about the dangers of the woods, and yet, they had thus far been spared from its deadly grasp.

But this time was different. This forest was different. Broken sticks and indented segments of soil vined around them. It wasn't as large as the Reaper's haphazard path from earlier, but it still meant that they weren't alone. Creaking limbs above lifted Daegon's hairs, and every sudden step caused him to reach for his sword. His father's sword. The hero's sword.

Suddenly, Layla's scream filled the silence of the forest, careening off the scattered trees. If there were anyone looking for them, they could surely pinpoint them now. Gallant and Daegon pulled their weapons and stepped in front of Layla, who was backpedaling from a mass of twigs and leaves. The scream had frozen Layla's mouth open, and her normally warm face grew pale. Daegon scanned the woods, looking for the attacker, before eventually stumbling on the cause. The mass of sticks hid the decaying remains of several skulls. The skin pulled tight over the bones, cured like leather by the sun. Empty sockets stared up at the canopy.

Jordell jumped back to help defeat the unknown foe but sheathed his longsword at the sight of the dead men. He kneeled, examining a broken rib. "Blunt force. Not a Reaper. Not a bandit." He looked at the trees, sliding his tongue over his lips. "Something worse."

Daegon's heart clicked at the skeletons. Deep holes burrowed into the yellow bones; some monstrosity had stabbed and brutalized them. He slowly sheathed his weapon and stepped with Gallant, escorting Layla back in line with Jordell. Whatever it was, it wasn't safe to stick around and find out.

The midday sun acted as a compass, directing them to the edge of the forest and exiting into an open field. At the center of the field, a small wooden wall, tall enough that Daegon and Gallant could probably work together to shimmy over, attempted to protect a small town. Multiple thatched houses with their own personalized smokestacks spewed soot from their chimneys. There weren't more than twenty. Daegon exhaled heavily at the knowledge that their travels were almost over. That they were so close to safety.

Jordell pressed into the open field with his hands raised above his head, waving at the guards sitting at the front gate. Daegon, Layla, and Gallant followed closely, stepping over the various spikes and arrows that littered the field. Sharpened sticks jutted from the ground, acting as what appeared to be defensive traps. With how easily they could maneuver around them, it couldn't be for people. Daegon peered behind at the forest, the taut skin of the skulls stretching across his mind.

The guards wore beige cloaks, not unlike Jordell's currently tattered and soot-stained outfit. Their matching brown hats tipped at Jordell. They looked more like farmers than soldiers. "We weren't sure if you were ever coming back this time."

"I always come back." Jordell laughed. "You know that. And this time, with friends." He swept his arms toward the group.

The guards motioned them forward, through the maze of traps, and cranked a shaft. Mechanical gears groaned through the field, and the gate exposed a dirt street. Daegon had only seen Shishbash, Terratoria, and Embre. Talman was grittier, more resembling the various camps they'd constructed than the clean sprawling cityscapes that'd housed them on their Journey. Every thatched building was visible from the entrance, huddling together against the forest's edge like a herd of frightened animals.

"I must check on somebody." Jordell took a deep breath, taking in the musty smell of the city before pointing to a building in the distance. It was one of the largest thatched buildings in the space, complete with a thick cloud of dark smoke billowing from its chimney. "Let's meet at the Crossed Swords Tavern in an hour."

Daegon nodded as Jordell left down an alley. There weren't many places for someone to disappear. Daegon spun back at Gallant and Layla, shrugging his shoulders. "I guess we're on our own."

Gallant shrugged his shoulders and motioned past Daegon. "Crossed Swords Tavern, I guess. I could go for that drink. Still have the taste of whatever he made in my mouth."

Layla stepped with Gallant and jerked Daegon's hand to follow along. While full of buildings, the town was devoid of specialty shops. Being a city on the edge of a capital, it was usually an exporter of trade rather than a marketplace all its own. The blacksmith and grocery, clearly marked with matching sigils, contained lines of civilians conversing and showing off their goods. A dusty building with a porch that had collapsed on one side slowed him. Stacks of books cluttered the front, and the faint shadow of someone sweeping moved against the drawn curtains. Daegon's eyes narrowed at the building; a weathered eye slashed across the center, carved into the lintel. He scanned the rest of the building for another touchstone, but Layla pulled him through the town.

The exterior of the tavern was noisy. Despite the midday sun beaming overhead, the patrons inside were bustling. A large iron door separated the inside from the dusty Talman streets. Two slightly rusted crossed swords were emblazoned above the door. A board stabbed with various papers stood next to the door. Bounties. Every letter detailed a different shade of nightmare. Some called it a demon. A monster. But they all mentioned similar details: "Sharp teeth." "Capable of killing 1000 men." "Transform into the forest itself."

Daegon pulled the handle of the door. It was much heavier than expected. As it creaked, the bottom scraped across the dirt-covered ground. They filed in, their feet tapping across the wooden planks that lined the open room. Evenly spaced tables blanketed the floor, and a long bar stretched across the back wall. The noise outside the tavern was deceiving, as there were only a few patrons being served. However, combined with their raucous cheering and the background piano, the tavern swelled with excitement.

The three awkwardly stood at the front before a loud voice yelled for them, "Welcome to the Crossed Swords Tavern. Have a seat where you can."

It didn't take long for them to find a table. They had their pick of the room but chose one far enough from the piano so that they could maintain a conversation. Within seconds of sitting, a larger man with long, braided red hair and a full mustache approached. "You three aren't from here, are you?"

Gallant provided a conversational smirk. "We're actually traveling from Shishbash."

The man glared at the group before softening his expression. "I haven't been there in a long time." He touched his chin, his eyes sweeping across them. "But everyone's welcome here at the Crossed Swords Tavern. The name is Aramide, and I own this establishment."

Layla's smile relaxed the innkeeper's shoulders as she spoke, introducing both Gallant and Daegon.

"Since you're from Shishbash, I have an incredible wine from the region if you want to try it? Ever heard of Icerni?"

Gallant perked up and gestured with his finger. "I, for one, would love some Icerni."

Daegon shook his head and waved Aramide off. The way Gallant reacted to the Icerni wine, one would have thought that it was some nectar sent from the gods. Aramide left to grab the booze, leaving Gallant gesturing with his head toward two men sitting a couple of tables down. The dimly lit room cascaded shadows across their faces, masking their intent. Friendly or foe?

Daegon, realizing he had been staring at them for maybe a second too long, found himself locked eyes with the larger one. The man's eyes were razors. An unnatural red hue glared back from the shadows of his hood. He wiped the blade of his abnormally curved knife between his fingers, the steel hissing against his calloused skin.

Gallant sprang from his chair and slammed his hands on the table, the wood groaning under the impact. Layla and Daegon jumped in their seats. Daegon peered at the ceiling and rolled his eyes. *Why couldn't they just have a second where they weren't fighting somebody? Something.*

Gallant yelled, "Can we help you with something, gentlemen?"

The two men slunk out of their chairs and plodded over to their table. The stench from their unwashed trench coats flowed with them. Through them. The larger man growled, "You aren't here for our bounty, are you?"

Gallant looked at Daegon, his eyebrows raised, before returning his attention toward the men. "I can honestly say that I have no idea what you're talking about."

The man slammed the knife into the table, its blade sticking firmly into the wood. "There's a demon in these woods. Able to take down one hundred men with a snap of their fingers." The man rubbed his arm across his nose and slammed a crumpled piece of paper onto the table. The crude image depicted a cloaked figure absent of discernible features. "Talman has promised 5000 gold pieces to the hunter who can rid the woods of the demon."

Daegon stared at the obviously human figure and remembered the bodies just outside the city. The desiccated and mangled remains of their skulls and limbs. What kind of person would do that? If the image was any sign, it placated the fear of the worst: Reapers. But now there was a separate fear.

Gallant pushed the paper back in the man's direction. "I believe the paper says one thousand men, not one hundred."

The larger man pulled his knife and lifted it at Gallant, who put his hand on the hilt of his spear. "You think you're smart, do you?"

The tavern quieted, and all eyes shifted to the standoff. Gallant sighed, took his hand off his spear, and raised his hand in surrender. "I don't believe we're interested in hunting your demon...but let us know of your success."

The gruff man huffed, pulled his knife from the wood, and spun back toward their table. He grabbed his partner by the shoulder and shoved him into a seat. Their persistent bickering mixed with the piano returning to fill the room. Daegon's heart had almost returned to a normal cadence when it rebounded from the thudding of large glasses smacking the table.

"You know, it's rare I get visitors from Shishbash. Or really anywhere anymore." Aramide pulled up a chair, his aroma concerningly pleasant for a barkeeper, and made himself part of the group. "The last visitor I had..."

As he was finishing his sentence, Jordell approached from behind and patted the innkeeper on his shoulder. Aramide twisted, jerked Jordell by the arm, and pulled a knife out from his belt. So fast. But Jordell laughed. Daegon didn't even realize that his hand was on his hilt before Aramide returned laughter. Jordell gestured for the group to relax. "You haven't slowed with age, have you, my friend?"

Aramide lowered his knife back into his pocket. "Jordell!" The two embraced in a deep hug. "We haven't seen you in weeks. Thought you'd left...again."

Jordell pulled a chair to the now-crowded table. "I see you've met my friends. This is Sir Gallant of Shishbash, Lady Layla, our Conjuror from Shishbash, and this one...." He paused. "This one is Conjuror Raynor's son, Daegon."

Aramide's jaw fell at the revelation, and his leg crossed in thought. "Is...it...really?"

The way he studied Daegon made the hair on his neck stand up. "Is that a bad thing?" Daegon asked, his hand drifting toward his sword.

"No...no." Aramide swept his hands through the air as if brushing away a ghost. "You see, Jordell and I were his protectors when he defeated the *Scourge*."

Daegon shot up from his chair, catching himself on the table. "You knew my father, too?"

"I did. Jordell, does he know about..."

Jordell interrupted Aramide, "...that the *Scourge* killed his father? I already told him about that."

The two old men shared a stark glance. Aramide's green eyes shrank. Daegon sat back in the chair before continuing. "Jordell, did you find who you were looking for? Is it going to get us the next stone?"

Gallant chuckled, "You know, I doubt getting the Luminary Stone is going to let us just walk right into Corporeal."

Jordell took a sip of Gallant's wine. "We don't even know why they were trying to kill you. Perhaps if we do some research, we'll get a better understanding of what we're working with?"

Jordell twitched in his chair. Daegon had known him long enough to know all his tells. All the faint lines and movements that gave away an uncomfortable knowledge. As if he had some story he couldn't say. Didn't want to say?

Jordell said, "Callah is a local historian and a bookkeeper. She owns a shop down the street. If there's anyone who's going to give us any sort of advice on what all is happening, it's her."

Gallant rubbed his chin but ultimately agreed with the plan.

Layla, who had patiently listened throughout the meeting, said, "I don't think it requires all of us to go. Daegon and I can do it?"

The corners of Daegon's cheeks raised at the suggestion. Daegon and Layla were on an adventure, no matter how big, once again.

Chapter Twenty-Eight

Dust wrapped its gritty fingers across every surface. Daegon and Layla meandered through the street, passing smiling citizens wearing dirt-scratched clothes performing their mundane jobs. An armorer hammered away at a green-hued piece of metal, and a butcher sliced a strung-up, skinned rat. Or at least, it looked like a rat. It was the size of a large hog. For the first time since the Journey began, Daegon truly felt safe. Buildings were sparse, connected by horse-beaten paths that branched through the thatched walls.

After just a few minutes of walking, they made it to the far side. The faded porch beckoned closer; its windows stacked with columns of haphazard books. A layer of age hid the carved eye above the door, but it still glared, watching their every step. A scratch through its center—the Forgotten Ones. Daegon and Layla exchanged silent nods and approached.

The gray porch wood squeaked as they stepped up to the door. The books in the front were more for show, damaged by periodic rainfall, and faded from the midday sun. Layla ran her fingers across their blurred covers. "I've never heard of some of these."

Daegon picked up and put down two books, their pages stiff from disuse. "I don't think you've read every book there is."

"No, but the Congregation makes it a point to have aspiring Conjurors read as much as possible." She pushed off the book and walked toward the door.

As they pushed the door, it creaked, and a bell rang, alerting anyone to their presence. Dust-coated books lined the inside door of the shop. Daegon picked up the first book he could see and smeared the caked-on layer of dust from the cover. *A History of Corporeal.*

A dry, shriveled voice stretched from the abyss of books. "Who's there?"

Daegon wrapped his arm around Layla and pushed deeper into the towers of books. "We're just some visitors looking for information. We were told you may be able to help us."

The tall stacks of books obscured the light in the room. The bookkeeper seemed to be aware of this issue and sprinkled candles at points that provided just enough light to navigate the entries. Every step caused dust to fly into the air, coating the back of Daegon's thoughts.

"Information, you say?" A head popped out from a stack of books. "My name's Callah, the head bookkeeper in this town. What kind of information were you looking for?"

Daegon squinted. Wrinkles crested over every inch of her face, and her spindly gray hair stretched in all directions. Her voice scratched through the air but reverberated with a twinge of excitement at the opportunity to spread her knowledge.

"My name is Daegon, and this is Layla. She's a Conjuror, and we're trying to find any way possible to gain the power of a stone without traveling to a city."

"Ah." Callah glided past her mountain of books. "And why can't you travel to the city?"

"It's..." Daegon began but was quickly interrupted.

"It's complicated right now," Layla stepped in front of Daegon. "But Jordell said you'd be able to help us out?"

"Jordell, you say?" Callah turned her eyes squarely on Daegon. "And you must be that boy he told me about. You're like him? From Malachi?"

"I am." Daegon's heart raced at the mention of his history, and his eyes narrowed on the woman. Unlike almost everyone who knew his secret, she didn't appear to be in disbelief. Instead, she leaned forward and examined him as if he were an experiment. "If you know Jordell, would you know how we're here? Everyone keeps telling me that Malachi was destroyed. If that were the case, how are we a thing?"

"That," she paused, "I cannot help you with." At that assertion, she rummaged through one shelf in the rear of the store. "However, I can tell you it is possible to retrieve a stone without actually traveling to a city."

Layla's mouth opened, and she darted toward the old lady. "How?" Her question seemed to fall out of her mouth.

Callah flipped through the pages, and her long, bony fingers settled on a dusty picture. "You simply have to seize the stone from a Conjuror who's already in possession of the one you seek."

Daegon softly questioned, "You mean kill?" His mind flashed to the Reaper snapping its hand shut around the glowing orb outside of Shishbash.

Callah's sharp eyes rose from the book before she slapped it shut with both hands, coughing at the cloud of dust that erupted from the ancient pages. "I mean seize. However, you're able to rip the power away from the Conjuror."

Layla's open mouth slammed shut, now replaced with a shroud of dread at the thought of destroying someone who had dedicated their life to saving the world. She rotated her gaze between the two before responding. "How would we find someone who'd abandon their quest? Their life?"

Daegon put his hand on her shoulder. "Maybe we can find someone who's given up in the middle of their journey?"

Layla fixated on the various rows of dust-layered books. "No, that wouldn't be right. The stone's power constantly draws the Reapers. If you were to stop, they'd soon come for you. Right?"

"So, you've been told, yes." Callah folded a page in a book and threw it to Daegon. "But you'd be surprised at the number of lies we're told every day."

Daegon acted quickly and caught it, opening to the pre-folded page. Callah gave him an expectant look. *The Aether Stone.* Quickly scanning the words, he said, "What...is this?"

Callah plopped onto a stack of books, smacking at the dust that had been kicked into the air. "You said you wanted a why. Well, to understand the stones, you have to know their history. Take that and see if you can learn something."

An image of a giant stone filled the center of the page. It seemed...familiar. He'd seen it before. In the center of Malachi. Yet another thing from this world that existed in his history.

Layla broke the stilted silence. "There's not another way to gain the power of a stone?"

Callah leaned back, using the books as a large chair. She took her time to answer, more interested in watching Daegon flip through the pages of the book, but eventually glanced at her and said, "Sadly, there is not. But there is a rumor of a Loneseeker living in the woods that may be of...help."

Daegon peered up from his book. He'd heard those words before. Gallant used it with Fabian and the man outside of Terratoria. "A Loneseeker?"

Layla touched his arm and provided an answer to yet another mystery word. "A Conjuror who's abandoned their Journey."

Callah nodded, sitting up from her stack of books before darting toward another bookshelf. She flipped books behind her and moved with a haste that threatened the integrity of the thin pages. Layla stepped closer, both admiring and surprised at the sprawled mess developing in front of them. "How could a Loneseeker evade the Reapers? Evade the *Scourge*?"

"Like I said earlier. You'd be surprised at the number of lies we're told every day." Callah jumped in excitement and scurried to Daegon with the newfound book. "King Raynor exists in the annals of history."

Daegon traced the worn leather of the history book. *The Reign of Raynor, King of Malachi, 12th Age.* "What...is...this?"

Callah's finger shot into the air. "This is probably why people believed your father was crazy when he showed up in Shishbash all those years ago." Callah rested her arm on Daegon's shoulder and peered into his eyes. "Your father was an incredibly gifted Conjuror, Daegon. Probably stemming from his Malachinian bloodlines."

Gifted Conjuror. His father used fire to quell his enemies and impress his people. He wasn't this savior everyone made him out to be. His signature war cry featured an ignited blade spinning through the air. He'd thought nothing of it simply because of Malachi. Almost everyone could conjure, and his father, no matter what image he put forward, was no different.

Almost as if Callah were reading his mind, she approached. "Your people were the keepers of the *Aether Stone*." As she offered that morsel of information, her bony finger hooked toward the drawing of the central gem.

Daegon's heart hammered against his ribs. He recognized the gem. It sat in the heart of Malachi, a pulsing anchor of light he had walked past a thousand times. Daegon puffed and ran his fingers through his hair, now crunchy from the settling dust. "I...I still don't understand. Do...I exist?"

Callah perked up at that assertion. "All valid questions. All questions Raynor had as well when he stopped in this town with sweet Jordell and our Aramide. I'm sorry to say that I cannot answer what you are; however, I can tell you that all Raynor's memories can be validated in that book, showing that he did," she cleared her throat, "you do exist."

Layla reached for Daegon's arm, both frozen and shaking at the revelations. "Did he travel through time to be here?"

Callah spoke quicker, and her voice squeaked. "I don't know how your young prince came to be, only that his history actually happened. Take that for what it is. Read through your history, and maybe you'll find something that I couldn't understand."

Daegon peeked from the depths of the book and nodded at Callah. "Thank you for pointing us in some direction." Even if it wasn't the right direction, it was still a direction. Finding Jordell validated his existence. That he wasn't living some dream. Interacting with Callah validated that their shared past had happened. He somehow fit in the puzzle of this world; he just had to figure out how.

Daegon and Layla retreated from the bookstore, every step lifting more motes of dust into the air. As they opened the door, Callah's voice bellowed from the depths of the store, "The six stones have incredible power, Layla. May you be the one to bring us everlasting peace. Keep the Memory."

Was it dread? Was it a promise? The hair on Daegon's neck bristled at the statement. They barely acknowledged her, closing the door and entering the streets of Talman. Manure and roughed up dirt replaced the musty, damp smell of the bookstore. *Six Stones?* There were only five cities that possessed a stone. Five cities that comprised the Journey. Where were they going to find the sixth stone? The *Aether Stone*? And what was its purpose?

The setting sun brought the sound of boarding windows clicking through the streets. The village had prepared its end-of-day meal, clear in the savory waves of roasted meat and vegetables. Daegon held his hand under his chin, knowing it was too late to act. "So, we need to find the Loneseeker in the woods, right?"

Layla's lips squished in thought. "There must be a way to take the power without killing them. But yes, finding them would be the first step."

Daegon flashed a smile. "Agreed. I'm going back to the tavern to read. Something about the *Aether Stone* just seems...off?"

Layla glanced around before stepping in and embracing him. Her arms wrapped around his back, and she burrowed her face into his chest. As long as she was around, how could he feel alone? She whispered into his ear, "Everything is going to make sense. Remember that. Keep the Memory."

Daegon squeezed and took in the intoxicating breath of her hair, still as sweet as the day he'd met her on those cold steps of the Shishbashi Keep. After savoring the moment, he stepped away and returned to the Crossed Swords Tavern, fresh on the hunt for the meaning of the pulsating stone at the center of his city. *The Aether Stone.*

Chapter Twenty-Nine

The Aether Stone. What was it? Daegon recognized it, sure, but he knew it as the center of Malachi, not some celestial stone with unlimited power. Why would there be a Journey to harness the power of the five individual stones, instead of just searching it out?

Daegon sat in the middle of the Crossed Swords Tavern, armed with the stack of books Callah had given him. The piano player from earlier had left, leaving him alone in the quiet room. With how difficult it was to navigate the items on the table, it was understandable why the town packed up and ceased activities at night. Daegon squinted over the pages, guided only by the scant candlelight framed in the windows. Periodically, glasses pinged at the counter as Aramide performed his nightly rituals.

A large glass of cream-colored liquid dropped onto his table, and Aramide sat with his apron draped across his shoulder. "How's it going there, son of Raynor? It's late, so I brought you something to loosen the mind."

Daegon declined, continuing to flip through the pages. The dust from the books stained Aramide's freshly cleaned table. Where was he going to even start? What was he looking for?

Aramide flipped a seat and sat with his arms hanging off the back. His clothing had stains, and his auburn hair was slicked back. "Anything I can help you with? If you can point me in a direction, I might know something. You know, Jordell and I completed the Journey you three are on."

How true that was. Daegon perked up. "Callah said there were six stones of power. Have you ever heard of the *Aether Stone?*"

Aramide's mouth widened, and a half-smile crested from the side. "She's misreading her history if she thinks there's six stones."

Daegon squinted his eyes even tighter to pierce the mystery. "What do you mean?"

Aramide scooted his chair closer and flipped through the section detailing the *Aether Stone.* "If you're thinking about the *Aether Stone* as a separate stone, you're wrong. The *Aether Stone* is all the stones."

Daegon had already skimmed the section Aramide had flipped to. There was no mention of the *Aether Stone* being a progenitor stone. Instead, it was a map of all the territories, corresponding to the stone each possessed. Aramide's deep voice began a story. "You will not find it by reading the books. You must've had a history with the stones; completed the Journey to defeat the *Scourge.* To truly understand the power of each, and to truly know what the *Aether Stone* is, you have to travel to Malachi."

The words stung in his mind. "You've been to Malachi? My Malachi?"

"Has Jordell really not told you anything about our Journey?"

Daegon shook his head and stared at his book, sighing at the onset of confusion that had been so prevalent since landing in the Shishbashi woods. "Everything about this place is so familiar and foreign."

"Malachi was originally a melting pot of conjuring ability," Aramide said as he remained on the page with all the territories. However, he now drew a new shape on the map. "The *Scourge* one day appeared and ravaged anything that conjured." He scratched out the territories one by one. "What you're familiar with is the *Aether Stone*. The center of Malachi and the reason there were so many Conjurors in your city."

Daegon sat back in his seat, deciphering the deluge of information. "If each city controls an element of nature, what does the *Aether Stone* control?"

Aramide once again drew lines from the surrounding cities to Malachi. "Memory. The *Aether Stone* didn't just control the elements; it remembered them. It held the blueprint of the world. Every tree. Every city. Every person. Some say it could even restore what was lost."

Daegon remembered massive paintings of war and conquest on the walls of the Malachi keep. Despite Malachi being in what seemed a perpetual peace, his father used to regale him with stories of their ancestors standing up against their enemies—a city mirrored in black. He tried to remember exactly what'd happened, but he was too young to truly grasp the magnitude of why their history was so important. "What happened to Malachi?"

Aramide's drawings morphed into swords and arrows. "A war broke out between the cities for the power of the *Aether Stone*. Too much power is terrifying for people who have too little. But the war soon ended when the *Scourge* arrived. A penance for the war over the ability to conjure, drawn to the power of conjuring itself."

"What happened to the stone?"

"To ensure that each of the nations survived." Aramide split the drawing of the *Aether Stone* into five sections. "The *Scourge* hungered for the power of the *Aether Stone,* eliminating all who worshipped it and fed off it. To survive, they separated the Stone's power into the five elements of the five cities we know today."

"And what of Malachi?"

Aramide scribbled Malachi from the page, relegating the ancient city to the silence of the inn. "Without the *Aether Stone* to protect it, darkness didn't just destroy the city; it erased it. Every brick. Every bone. Suffocated by the oppressive cloud of the *Scourge.* Never to exist again...That is until your father appeared all those years ago."

Daegon remembered the day his father disappeared. The day he was abandoned. What was supposed to be a simple naval hunt turned into a city without its leader, under the stewardship of the Cardinals, until the day he would one day take the crown. He remembered his shock when Geoffrey told him the news. The immediate pain quickly numbed as the days passed. He was no longer shackled by the scathing demands of his father. Free to explore, learn, and grow as the leader he always wanted Raynor to be.

Aramide interrupted Daegon's thought by passing him another glass of opaque liquid. "Is everything okay?" The older man genuinely seemed to care, contrary to most he had met in this world, who more so wanted to prod him for information about his mysterious past. In fact, between Callah and Aramide, Daegon hadn't felt this understood since before the *Scourge*.

Daegon snapped back into the present. "What was he like?"

Aramide snorted behind his thick red mustache. "Who? Conjuror Raynor?"

Daegon acknowledged.

"He was rough. Always running headfirst into every situation, leaving Jordell and myself to always bail him out." That sounded like his dad. A know-it-all who could take on any challenge regardless of the inherent risk. "But he talked about you constantly. How incredible a fighter you were. How incredible a politician you would become. He said you could talk your way out of any situation, absent in using your sword."

That didn't sound like his old man at all. He questioned Aramide about the authenticity of his statement, but his darkened tone caused Aramide to raise his eyebrows. Perhaps they weren't talking about the same person.

"Yes." Aramide's voice was more encouraged than doubtful. "All he did along the Journey was talk about how you'd be able to make peace with the fiery Embrens or make trade with the isolated Luminarians. How you would be twice the King he ever was."

The words clashed with every memory of his childhood. Really, his entire life. His father never expressed even a fraction of the admiration, the love, Aramide was spewing. Raynor was more likely to find a flaw in his fencing practice than to praise his ability to compete against his Kingsguard. "It..it couldn't be the same..."

Aramide's chair screeched across the wooden floor. "The one and only King Raynor of Malachi. I heard it over and over again. He couldn't wait to show you the world one day. A world absent in the *Scourge*." Aramide sensed the dissonance in the young King and pushed the untouched drink closer. "Have a sip on the house, would you? It's rare that I have royalty in here."

Daegon's stoic façade broke into a mild chuckle, and he finally relented to the foaming liquid. The cool bubbles popped against his lips. "Jordell came back to Malachi? How was that? If you three were so close, why didn't I ever meet you?"

Aramide followed with a sip of his own before closing his eyes. "That...my boy...is not my story to tell."

Daegon breathed out, exasperated at yet another dead end. Another roadblock to exploring his past. His future. He slammed his hands on the table, shaking the drinks. "Then whose story is it? I have a right to know what's happening in my life."

Aramide lifted the drink and nestled it into the palm of his hand. "Ask Jordell for the truth. If you push him, he'll explain everything." He exhaled, "It's what caused him and me to drift apart, and I think he'd give you a much less jaded version of the story."

Daegon rubbed his chin, frustrated by yet another failed opportunity at discovering the mystery of his life. The Cardinals had some knowledge of him, or of Malachi. Aramide apparently knew something important. And now Jordell wasn't telling him the whole truth. The sting of that revelation hurt more than any sword. Daegon chugged the rest of his drink, scooped up the books. "Thank you for the drink. And for the history of Malachi. I suppose our next step is to hunt down a Loneseeker? Will you be joining us?"

Aramide sank into his chair and cocked his head, still twiddling with the rim of the drink. "A Loneseeker now?" Aramide's brow arched once again before shaking his head and letting out a subtle laugh. "I assume to gain that Luminary stone."

Daegon stood from the table. "So it is true? It can be done?"

Sipping his drink, Aramide stared aimlessly at the wood grain of the table, their shadows flickering in the surrounding candlelight. "You know, Jordell and I protected your father from the very thing you're planning on doing. If it truly is a Loneseeker, don't take them too lightly. They can survive quite a long time on their own."

Daegon nodded, and images of others hunting Layla flashed across the backs of his eyelids. "I'll see you tomorrow then."

Aramide raised his glass and smiled, allowing Daegon to quietly exit the tavern as he pondered his father's adventures. His father really defeated the *Scourge* and brought temporary peace to this destroyed world. And he did it for whom? Himself? He kept asking if Aramide had even known the true Raynor, but did he even understand him? He walked the silent streets of Talman. The moon hung heavy and bright, watching him like an eye. He scratched his boots against the soil, needing the sound. Needing to know that at least the ground beneath his feet was real.

Chapter Thirty

A sharp clatter jolted Daegon awake. The thumping hooves of a snorting creature plodded through the Talman streets. The rhythmic beat suggested a friendly beast. He spun out of bed and darted to the window; the earthy aroma filled his lungs. Wagons with abnormally full wheels, pulled by furry, muscle-rich animals, spanned the streets, indenting the soft ground as they marched. The soft bustle of footsteps and tapping dishware drifted up through the floorboards. Daegon closed his eyes and soaked in the stillness. He wasn't being rushed. Nobody was trying to kill him. Everything was just...calm. Serene. He threw his cloak on, grabbed his scabbard, and headed downstairs, catching the wafting scent of freshly cooked bread.

"Good morning!" The innkeeper shouted as he creaked down the wooden staircase. She was a portly woman with long, curly hair. "Can I interest you in some warm tea to start the morning? Just got a new shipment of spicy tea from outside Embre."

Daegon smiled and took the tea, the warmth of the ornate glass seeping into his palm. The scent entered his nose before even receiving the glass. It wasn't pungent, but pleasant, and spiky, crimson berries floated on the surface. He thanked her for the beverage and surveyed the homey lobby of the inn. "Have you seen any of my friends this morning?"

The woman brought her hand to her chin and flicked her wrist. "The young lady and two men? The young blonde one incredibly handsome? They came down about an hour ago. Not too many places for people to go here in this town, so I bet you'd find them at Aramide's tavern."

Daegon thanked the woman, finished the drink, and headed toward the Crossed Swords Tavern. The streets remained unexciting. Like Daegon, the town was just now waking up. As the morning sun greeted the roofs, steam rose from the dew-dampened thatch. A bead of sweat dripped into his eyes. In the distance, the cold Embren volcano bloomed with a billow of smog; still on the prowl for the deserters.

He passed Callah's bookstore, recalling the revelations Layla and he had learned the night before. Jordell's secret. As he opened the heavy door of the tavern, Layla, Gallant, and Jordell sat around a large wooden table, talking and laughing. A freshly opened oven wafted through the air, mixing with the stale beer that lingered from the night before, and the piano player had returned, gently beginning the day with a morning melody.

Jordell gestured Daegon toward the table with a hearty wave. "I wasn't sure if you were ever going to wake up this morning."

"Yeah, well, I had a late night." Daegon approached the table, yawned and rubbed his hair as he sat down. "Learned about the *Aether Stone* and the entire history of what happened to Malachi. Aramide also told me some stories of your adventures with my father."

"Did he now?" Jordell looked up at Aramide, who was behind the long bar polishing glasses. "Well, did you learn anything of value?"

Daegon nodded, reaching for one of the steaming glasses in the center of the table. "Aramide essentially confirmed that defeating a Loneseeker will give Layla the Luminary Stone."

Jordell opened his hands in a joyous fashion. His bellowing voice boomed with relief at the onset of a new quest. "Then that is the mission of the day!"

Daegon locked eyes with Jordell, knowing full well he already knew about the Loneseeker. Jordell's tongue shifted behind his cheek, and his foot tapped a nervous rhythm under the table.

Gallant interrupted their stare-down. "So how are we going to find this Loneseeker? And how has he avoided the Reaper's grasp for so long? The Congregation says that both the *Scourge* and the Reapers are forever drawn to those harnessing the stone's powers."

Layla spoke up, leaning on the table. "Callah implied that the monster on the outskirts of town was a Loneseeker."

Gallant's face contorted at the possibility. Based on everything he knew, Daegon had the same initial reaction. An unbelievable beast had to have mangled the bodies outside of town. Not a human with the power to conjure. By the very nature of the job, those undertaking the Conjuror's Journey were ultimately good-natured. It made little sense for them to cause that much unnecessary carnage. That much pain.

Aramide sauntered over and smashed a piece of paper onto the table. It was the bounty report the hunters had been holding the previous day. "You don't think an animal is causing this much damage, do you?" Aramide's freshly trimmed mustache shook under the motion of his mouth.

Gallant glanced at the sketch, a smudge of charcoal that looked more like a shadow than a beast. "This monster? Killing dozens of people. You think it's a Loneseeker?"

Aramide chuckled. "Now, I never said that. But I know the hundreds of creatures in these woods. Sure, I could think of a few that could do this once or twice to a couple of amateur hunters, but I don't believe there's one that has the capability of consistently avoiding capture."

Layla interrupted once again. "It's our best lead. I say we look into it."

Gallant's gaze shifted from Aramide. "I can think of quite a few dangerous things that could kill us in these woods. One of them is a Reaper, which I assume is out there, hunting us."

"Hunting *me*," she quickly interjected.

Jordell shot across the table, diffusing the situation from the sudden flames. "Of course. And we're not going to let anything happen to you. You have three of the very best."

Layla's demeanor had blossomed since their escape from Embre. Her stare had hardened, and her voice had become more pointed. When their eyes locked, a smile pricked from her cheeks, and that signature optimism radiated from deep, warming him like the morning berry tea.

He shifted to Jordell, who was chuckling with Gallant. His old mentor was hiding something. About his father? About Malachi? He wanted to throw the tea off the table and yell, but his restraint was for the better. Instead, he kept it buried, letting it simmer, waiting for the moment to boil over.

Gallant chugged the rest of his drink, his armor clanking as he stood up from the table. He might as well have been ready to leave. His shimmering blue armor contrasted with the rather muted and earthy insides of the tavern. "So that settles it then? Let's go find this Loneseeker. Meet at the front gate in one hour."

Jordell raised his steaming drink above his head. "Sounds like a plan. Make sure your weapons are sharp. Layla, make sure your mind is right." He finished the rest of his drink and pushed it to the center.

Gallant and Jordell both exited the tavern, leaving him alone with Layla. He jumped when something soft smacked his head. The culprit: a crumbled piece of bread. Layla covered a sly smirk. "Is everything okay? You're not usually this down."

Daegon put both of his elbows on the table and massaged his eyes. "I'm not sure. I hope so." Another piece of bread crashed into his head, causing a smile to pierce his lips. "You really need to knock that off."

Layla crossed her arms, sinking back into her chair. "Or what, Your Highness?"

She always knew how to get through to him. Daegon rose from the table and pressed his palms into the wood. "Just you wait...we have an entire day of traveling and I'm going to get bored at some point."

Layla's cheeks blushed, and she covered her mouth at the playful threat. "I'm so scared."

Daegon tried to speak when another piece of warm bread hit him. They both burst into laughter. He wished the entire Journey would end there. At that moment. Nothing else but them. *Was it really necessary? Necessary to continue?* Realizing that he was still in his robes, Daegon walked to the entrance, but as he passed her, she grabbed his arm, slowly following it to his hand. They locked eyes, and she whispered, "Whatever it is, know that I'm here for you."

The words fluttered around his head, and the corners of his cheeks raised as he pulled away from her grasp. He exited the tavern onto the now busy streets of Talman.

***

It didn't take long for him to grab his sword and wear his chain armor. When he arrived at the gate, Gallant was already there, whittling a piece of wood into an unfamiliar shape. His traditional Shishbashi armor, tinted blue with icy patterns, sparkled after a fresh wash. Jordell approached wearing similar chain-mail to Daegon, shrouded by a new Talman green cloak. Layla followed Jordell and wore tighter robes than usual, colored with a unique purple hue. Jordell and Gallant both bore packs, stuffed with supplies for the unknown trek into the wilderness.

The gate wrenched open, revealing the familiar forest that had led them here. The trees hugged one another, creating a perfect circle around the town. They contained a monster. Daegon studied Layla. The potential for destruction loomed behind her eyes. *Impossible.* A stiff wind seeped from the darkness and cooled his thoughts. Whether it was real was irrelevant; Daegon's skin prickled at its presence nonetheless.

Gallant was the first to take a step forward, leaving the safety of the Talman walls. "We've already been through these woods once and lived. What's another trip?" He grinned as he stepped through the uneven terrain, avoiding the traps and spikes prevalent on the ground.

Layla followed Gallant closely, while Daegon walked beside Jordell in the rear. Daegon kept pace with Jordell and said, "Aramide told me you're not telling me everything about Malachi. That there's a secret you're keeping."

Jordell continued forward, his head fixed on the forest in front of them. Muscles in his jaw flexed. It was like he was trying to speak. Wanting to speak, but something was holding him back.

"Whatever it is, I can handle it. I deserve to know."

Eventually relenting, Jordell said, "Now's not the time."

So, there was something. Daegon squeezed his fist at the confirmation and grabbed his arm. "You are going to tell me what you know about Malachi. About my father."

Jordell sighed at the sudden hostility from Daegon. "I swear, when we get back to the Crossed Swords, I will tell you everything." He raised his hands, offering surrender. "Aramide is as much a part of that story, and it's probably best told with us both there. Is that okay?"

It wasn't okay. "I'm just tired of being in the dark. I want to know where I am, why I'm here, and what happened to Malachi."

Jordell lent Daegon an outstretched arm. An olive branch. "I promise when we return, you'll know everything. I know it may not be what you want to hear, but the middle of this mission is not the best time to hear it."

Daegon caught something he'd never seen before. Scars carved into Jordell's skin, detailing a story of pain and anguish.

He'd always been there for him. And he was there for his father. He'd never kept anything from him before. Maybe it was right to give him the benefit of the doubt. Daegon bit his lip and grabbed the arm, squeezing it under the lock of a promise.

A voice called from the tree line, shaking them from their confrontation. Layla and Gallant waited, beckoning them with enthusiastic motions. Daegon and Jordell quickly regained their composure and hastened their pace to catch up, leaving their squabbles trapped in the open field. They had a Loneseeker to hunt.

Chapter Thirty-One

The edge of the forest spoke with the sound of a new world. Something Daegon had become accustomed to. Desolate rows of trees carved the forest, but persistent cracking branches and whistling wind filled the silence with an air of dread. As they stood at the edge of the endless rows of trees, a cold breeze stretched its fingers around them, drawing them closer. Gallant's hand remained on the hilt of his spear, prepared to combat the creeping chill. Their shadows followed closer than usual, appearing when the canopy parted for the mid-morning sun.

They had walked for most of the morning when Gallant punched his spear into a nearby tree. The point dug deep, and he turned toward the group. "We've been walking for hours. When do you say we head back?"

Jordell expressed amusement at the knight's statement. "What. You've grown tired already?"

Gallant slumped to the ground and rested his back against a rotund tree. His blue armor shimmered under the peeking light as he muttered, "It feels like we're hunting a ghost. No clues, no tracks. Just wandering aimlessly through the woods."

Jordell walked to the nearest tree and rested his palm against its trunk. Layla looked around at the group, noted their sudden exhaustion, and collapsed onto a log. "I think it's okay if we take a break?"

The rest of the group nodded in agreement, gratefully groaning at finally being able to sit. The sun and humidity were difficult during the night and within the town's walls. But in the forests, hiking without a clear aim, the elements were oppressive. Daegon pulled his sword from its sheath and pushed a little deeper into the forest, still within view of the group. He scratched the ground with the point of his blade, inspecting every lip, crevice, and hole. There had to be a clue pointing them in some direction. Any direction. Remnants of his father's hunting excursions peppered the landscape. Every ridge and carefully tread blade of grass led them closer to their bounty.

As he rounded a hulking tree, he recoiled, his sword slicing at the unknown enemy. Hanging like grotesque ornaments, the tree bore the mangled bodies of the two men from the tavern flailing against the stalking wind.. *The bounty hunters*. The Loneseeker had carved them, stripping away the human traits that made them so loud and arrogant only a day prior. Daegon clamped down on his rising stomach and yelled for the group.

Jordell and Gallant flanked Layla as they bounded forward, their hands clutching the hilts of their weapons. Layla screamed at the sight of the withered bodies. It was how the bounty had described: a monster in the woods, slaughtering the villagers. Her eyes failed to leave the disfigured arms of the once-talkative body. "Is this really the work of a Loneseeker?" The thought alone caused her to look at her hands.

Jordell shook his head. "Whatever it is, we'll protect you." His hand squeezed the hilt of his sword. Daegon had always remembered Jordell being calm under pressure. It was that calmness that allowed him to tackle so many challenging obstacles without the fear of failure. Even when the *Scourge* was destroying Malachi, the old man skirted bewilderment. As if he'd met the monster before. Knew every move that it would attempt.

Jordell swung his blade at the rope that strung the two men up, and they collapsed to the leafy floor. Gallant kneeled in front of the men and ran his hands over their wounds. The injuries crushed, slashed, and even burned parts of their bodies. He whispered, "Could a Conjuror cause this damage?" He squished a piece of the ashen skin between his fingers, allowing it to disintegrate into the wind. After examining the bodies, he lifted the men's cloaks over their faces. "The monster can't be far off. The body's still warm. Stay on your guard."

The bitter wind returned and brushed past Daegon's ears. Despite the sudden flooding of his senses, the emptiness of the forest beckoned him. That same emptiness that had stalked them from Talman. The green leaves in the canopies waved as the wind quietly whistled between his outstretched fingers. Daegon walked toward the cooling breeze. Each step caused the leaves below to crack under his weight. He put his hand on one of the towering trunks and pressed into the bark, allowing it to scratch into his fingertips. A flicker of movement shifted in the distance, quietly lurking behind a tree. He squinted his eyes, unsure at first. Then it appeared. A man dressed in a familiar green cloak watched them.

Without thinking, Daegon lunged forward. "Hey! Who are you?"

The man bolted from his spot, cascading deeper into the woods. Gallant and Jordell readied their weapons, but Daegon was already out of sight. Needing to decide on a plan, Gallant hastily yelled for Jordell to stay. He sliced through the forest after Daegon. Jordell ushered Layla against a tree, surveyed the area, and dug his feet into the leaves below.

The trees provided a never-ending maze for Gallant to navigate, only made more difficult by the blur of brown and green undertones merging as he raced faster. The noise of the canopies above suddenly sucked out of the air, and he found Daegon at the edge of a small clearing. In the center of the clearing stood a black-haired man wearing a green cloak, coated in muck and branches.

Daegon didn't acknowledge Gallant's approach. He just stood there silently, staring at the man, his sword ready at his side. Gallant approached. "Daegon, is everything okay? Who is that?"

A deep, booming voice radiated from the slender, cloaked man. "Are you here to hunt me?" The voice pierced their thoughts, amplified and dissonant from the body that produced it.

Daegon said, "You're the Loneseeker?"

The man spun his cloak around, revealing a youthful face—a pointed chin and shaggy black curls. Dark circles pulled under his eyes, and a dense story of holes and forest debris covered his cloak. His voice shook Daegon, booming one more time, filling the noiseless space. "I'll ask again. Are you here to hunt me?"

Gallant stepped beside Daegon and said, "We are in need of the Luminary Stone in order to progress our Conjuror's Journey."

The man creaked a wry smile and narrowed his eyes. "Then you come with the same purpose." He suddenly vanished into nothing.

Daegon and Gallant looked at each other with wide eyes before something swept Daegon off his feet and threw him into the tree line. Gallant swung his spear, stabbing at the empty air. The earth shifted under Gallant's feet, pulled out from under him, and thrust him onto his back. Daegon bounded back into the battle as the man returned to the middle of the clearing. His eyes vacantly stared at them, still absent a weapon.

Daegon charged and thrust his blade, but a wall of earth quickly deflected it. The man pushed into the tomb of earth and sent it crashing against him. Daegon pushed against the collapsing earth, but eventually succumbed to the forest floor.

Gallant steadied to his feet and reached for his spear, but grabbed air. It had vanished. There wasn't time to search for his weapon, and he ran at the Loneseeker, attempting to tackle him. But before he could reach him, Gallant's vision became black, and he crashed to the ground, absent from his attacker.

Gallant yelled out, alone in a world of darkness. Ostracized from those he cared about. From his family. The Congregation. They were no match for a Conjuror, nonetheless a Loneseeker. The raw power. The speed. The sheer will to live. All without the Congregation's rules holding it together. The ultimate killing machine. Why was he even in charge of protecting Layla? If this was what was possible, what chance did he stand? Was it she who was protecting him? Grief and fear clawed at his mind as he braced for the end. His end. The grinding sound of metal pinged through his ears. This was it.

Daegon blocked Gallant's spear from ending the knight with a well-placed parry, causing the metal to ping within feet of his face. Daegon, through panted breath, yelled, "We don't want to kill you, but we need the stone." He pushed against the spear and separated the two weapons.

The man stood idle, now wielding not only the power of a Loneseeker, but the sharpened spear of a Shishbashi warrior. He snapped his fingers, and Gallant gasped loudly. The Loneseeker's voice had morphed into something more characteristic of his soft features. A proper accent befitting his looks. "Where is this Conjuror of yours?"

Daegon splayed the fingers on his left hand and lowered his sword. "She's here with us. We're all on the same side. We were told that to take the stone from a Conjuror, we have to kill you. Is that true?"

The man threw the spear at Gallant's feet. "Once a Conjuror attunes with a piece of the *Aether Stone*, that piece becomes a part of them. It's impossible for the Conjuror to give it up willingly."

Gallant picked up his spear as if he were picking up a fragile twig. "I don't take it you're wanting to give up that stone?"

The man's voice hissed. "And why would I?" He disappeared once again and reappeared behind the knight. "I've survived this long."

Gallant stabbed out, catching his breath. "You abandoned your quest! Abandoned the Congregation!" The man dodged the attacks and vanished.

A laugh echoed through the trees, and the hissing voice continued, "The Congregation? You believe they care for their precious Conjurors? Why do you think I ran?"

Gallant stood tall, certain of his morals. "Because you fear the *Scourge*."

The man's ever-present laugh sounded again, and he appeared between Daegon and Gallant. "The Congregation wishes only to continue the cycle of destruction in perpetuity. What do you even think happens to the Conjurors who defeat the *Scourge*? Do you even have the slightest idea?"

Gallant scanned the area, suddenly second-guessing his next attack. Nobody knew what happened to the Conjurors who defeated the *Scourge*. The Congregation's teachings claimed they ascended to heavenly status, resigning themselves to a life of extravagance and splendor. His voice wavered at the sudden questioning. "They become forever enshrined by the Congregation."

"When a Conjuror defeats the *Scourge*, their body, their soul, combined with the five pieces of the *Aether Stone*, are then used as the vessel for a reincarnated *Scourge*." The Loneseeker appeared closer to Gallant, his laugh echoing off the trunks. "When a Conjuror finishes their quest, they're rewarded with becoming the very thing they set out to destroy. How does that sound as a trophy? Forever enshrined by the Congregation." He spat on the ground. "In darkness, performing the bidding of your pathetic Congregation."

Daegon and Gallant both shouted in unison, "You lie!"

The Loneseeker narrowed his eyes. "Why else would I abandon eternal glory? Why else would I resign myself to this life, constantly unsure if there will be a tomorrow? Your Congregation lies to you, and I'm sure on some level, your Conjuror knows this too."

Daegon thought of his father and all the times he'd wished he'd never existed. What did that mean? He was never sure. But he would never wish for someone to become the *Scourge*. His mind flitted to Layla. Could she really become *that?* "My father is High Conjuror Raynor. If what you say is true, then you're saying he's the *Scourge?*"

The man cocked his head to the side. "High Conjuror Raynor's soul is being used as the vessel for the *Scourge*. I am not sure how much of him is left." A crumble of remorse chewed at the edge of his revelation.

Daegon lowered his head, feeling the weight of his eyes heaving against the front of his skull. Why should he be upset? His father was never there. Never. Not when he mastered the art of sword fighting. Not when he successfully hunted his first Elderdeer. Not when he became King of Malachi. His father wasn't there because he had sacrificed himself for the good of this world? Even that was pointless. The *Scourge* would always come back. Daegon's voice shook. "How do we stop it?"

Gallant trembled. His entire world was crumbling with every passing sentence. In a measure of passion, he pulled his spear and directed it at the Loneseeker. "The Congregation has protected us from the *Scourge*, not wielded it!" He ran at the man and plunged the tip of his spear into his chest.

But the Loneseeker deftly moved to the side and pulled the earth from beneath Gallant's feet. Gallant collapsed onto the dirt floor and lay there, shaking. There was no counterattack. No spiteful retort. Instead, the man's voice grew quiet. "I went through the same emotions. Imagine being the most important piece of your religion. Promised eternal gratitude, only to discover that you were lied to. Walking yourself into your own slaughter."

Gallant rolled onto his back and cast aside his spear. A sign of surrender.

Daegon fell to his knees, his tears staining the ground below. "There must be a way to stop it. Stop the cycle. We can't let it happen again."

The man walked to Daegon and pulled his shoulder. "My name is Vrest. Grab your Conjuror. I can take you to my shelter. If, after everything I say, you still want the Luminary stone, then I will let you take it."

Daegon agreed and approached Gallant, hoisting him from his sudden stupor. He refused to respond to Daegon's attempts at conversation, shaking in the confines of his thoughts. Daegon threw him over his shoulder and followed Vrest through the maze of trees, burdened with more truth than he could carry.

Chapter Thirty-Two

The familiar sound of a crackling fire bounced off the makeshift thatch house constructed from leaves, twigs, and logs sourced from the forest. Jordell and Layla sat around a fire talking to Vrest, painted by the red hue of the setting sun. Blue fireflies had made their way out of the forest, offering a friendly glint of color to the dour conversations. Gallant lay inside the house, still despondent following the revelations from their battle with the Loneseeker. Daegon ambled to the fire and joined.

Vrest's voice had returned to a normal tone as he asked, "Are you okay?" They were supposed to be hunting a monster in the woods. That question alone contradicted the carnage he'd seen.

Daegon rubbed his arm, fingers tracing the raw edge of a new scar. "Nothing but a few scratches. How were you able to teleport back there?"

Vrest hovered his hand over the fire, causing the flames to contort before ultimately disappearing. "I started in the capital, Corporeal. They have the power of influence. To alter and shape the realities we perceive." Vrest removed his hand, and the fire reappeared.

Layla said, "We started in Shishbash and also have the power of Terratoria and Embre."

Vrest shifted a log in the fire, splattering sparks into the soon-to-be night sky. "Do the stones even matter? After everything I've told you, you still want to complete the journey?"

Layla clasped her hands together. "I...don't...know."

Jordell interrupted Layla. "We just need enough power to find another way. There's got to be another way."

Daegon kicked a piece of flaming wood, causing it to hiss in protest. "You knew, didn't you?"

Jordell met Daegon's gaze. "Excuse me?"

Daegon, now with a rasp in his voice, said, "You were my father's protector. You and Aramide knew exactly what happened to him."

Jordell's eyes shifted to the flames as he said, "I was there when King Raynor defeated the *Scourge*. Combined with his innate conjuring ability, it was a rather easy victory. We had won. The world was at Peace. Or so we thought. Soon after the victory, Raynor became weak. His eyes, always full of adventure, became black. Cold. He was no longer himself." Jordell closed his eyes. "His body faded away, and a void grew. That void, I learned, would become the *Scourge*. Reincarnated."

Daegon shot from the log. "And you couldn't tell me!"

Jordell leaned his head into his palms. "I'm sorry. I wasn't sure how to tell you, especially with your life in Malachi. Everything was perfect for you. I was scared. But I *was* going to tell you."

Jordell emphasized that last sentence, but it didn't matter. Daegon had already learned everything from Vrest. Jordell had every opportunity to tell him about his father, and he missed every one of them. Daegon bolted from the fire and sprinted into the trees, disappearing among the blue fireflies. Jordell sighed and angled his eyes at Layla, who quickly stood from the fire and followed.

"Wait!" Jordell called out. Layla turned back to Jordell while continuing to backpedal. "Just in case."

Jordell picked up Daegon's sword, admired the familiar runes, and threw it toward Layla. With a huff of breath, she disappeared into the firefly-lit forest.

Vrest leaned back on his log, staying out of the fight. "It's not easy when your entire world becomes a lie. I can tell you that."

***

Daegon shot through the forest, the fireflies painting a frantic trail as he dodged hanging limbs. Tears obscured the forest, forcing him to a halt. To his right, a luminescent stream glowed a consistent blue, drawing him closer. Daegon stepped into the stream. The crisp water bit at his skin, refreshing but unable to wash away the anguish. He replayed the scene of the *Scourge* consuming him, dragging him into this world. *Why?*

Daegon sat in the stream, ankle deep when he heard a crackling from behind. He reached for his sword. His father's sword—no, the *Scourge's* sword—but realized in his quick escape, he'd forgotten it at the camp. Unable to protect himself, he closed his eyes at Layla's comforting smile.

"I'm sorry if I startled you. I wanted to make sure that you were okay." She reached out with his sword.

Daegon pulled it from her and turned back to the flowing water. The soft current provided an ambient undertone to the creaking forest. "There has to be a way to end the cycle." He bit his inner lip at the thought of Layla succumbing to the void. "Did you know?"

"I knew I was on a Journey that I wouldn't return from, yes. But I didn't know that the Conjuror became the *Scourge*."

Daegon stepped deeper into the cool water, the refreshing blue current lapping over his knees. He dipped his hand into the water and watched the stream flow between his fingers. "Why?"

Layla's ears perked and her head cocked at the question. "What do you mean?"

"Just why? Why take the Journey? It's always going to come back?"

She waded into the water after him. "In Terratoria, when we were in the market. The joy on those people's faces when they saw me. That measure of peace, regardless of how long. Is that respite from destruction not worth my life?"

Daegon continued to the middle of the water, the glowing light illuminating his face. The fireflies from the trees followed along, providing an uninterrupted view of Layla. "But you'll just return as the *Scourge*." He wiped the tears welling inside. "I can't let that happen."

Her heart kept up with the pace of her chase. "There's not another option."

His eyes grew heavy, and he slipped under the cool surface. The muffled sounds of the flowing stream drowned out the chaos. He sprang from the depths, water cascading from his hair. "I'm going to find one. We're going to save the world. We'll end it for good." He dipped his chin, breaking the surface once more. "I won't let what happened to my father happen to you."

Layla offered one of her signature smiles, though it frayed at the edges. "Because you've always found a way?"

She lunged forward, wrapping her arms around him, her tears searing into his chest. Daegon pulled her back, locking onto her matching blue eyes. The moon hung above them, mirroring its lustrous presence in the stream. "I told you," Daegon said, "I'm not going to let anything happen to you."

Daegon's heart was telling him a million things, all in contrast. But he just did it. Their lips parted. The feeling he'd buried since Shishbash rushed to the surface, undeniable and overwhelming. He'd expected her to push away, but she locked her arms behind his back. Her fingers laced through his hair, drawing him deeper.

In that moment, it was just them. From the beginning of the Journey, sitting behind the Shishbashi temple, seeing her black hair flow over her shy shoulders, to now, alone in the forest, hunted by the remnants of his father. The fireflies sparkled and fluttered around them in rhythmic motion. The kiss lasted for what seemed like minutes, but all that mattered was Layla. Life had stopped. Just as he had wanted all along.

Chapter Thirty-Three

Vrest and Jordell sat around the now-roaring fire, soaking in the warmth of the blaze. Jordell's head remained in his hand as he gazed into the fiery abyss. A cup of steaming moss tea stung the underside of his nose, causing him to jump back.

Vrest snickered. "It's safe, I promise." He gestured toward the thatched house where Gallant was resting, still despondent on the bed. "I take it your friend in there was pretty attached to the Congregation?"

Jordell put his finger into the cool cup. The liquid bubbled, eventually releasing steam into the air. "I'm not sure. Of the three, the only one that I truly know is Daegon."

Vrest almost dropped his cup as he jumped back on his log. "A Loneseeker too, then?"

Jordell offered a low, weary chuckle. "Oh, this. No. Where I'm from, almost everyone has some form of conjuring ability. It's innate."

Vrest's eyes narrowed. "And where exactly are you from?"

Jordell sipped some of the liquid, pausing before he answered. Answering with the truth was never the easy option, but Jordell, over the past few days, saw the ramifications of avoiding it altogether. "Malachi. Or the ghost of it."

Vrest set his drink down, folded his hands, and leaned into Jordell. "The *Scourge* destroyed Malachi. Hundreds of years ago."

"Over a thousand years ago, actually," Jordell interrupted.

"Okay, over one thousand years ago. The point is. I've seen it. The ruins. How could you be from there?"

"Yes, yes." Jordell had answered the question multiple times over the years and was well-versed in the direction the conversation typically traveled. "When Raynor and I appeared here, we were told the same thing. And at first, I believed them. Had my entire life been a lie? But after he succumbed to the effects of the *Scourge*, things failed to make sense. I started searching."

The insects filled any void that Jordell allowed to develop within his story. Vrest leaned so close that he nearly fell in the fire. "And what did you find?"

Jordell looked at the night sky and the swath of stars that gazed down on them. "You see, Shishbash chose Raynor as their Conjuror after he displayed exceptional ability to manipulate fire with no attunement with a stone."

Vrest leaned forward, looking into the fire. "But how can that be? That ability was lost with the destruction of Malachi, wasn't it?"

Jordell finished the drink and gently placed the cup in front of the flames. "There's always been individuals with innate ability, but they're quickly taken away by the Congregation."

Vrest looked to the shadows. "Of course. Can't have their order mucked up."

Jordell's voice softened. "Yes. We were told that they were abominations. Branded as Loneseekers. Separate from the teachings of the Congregation. A blight on the world. A target of the *Scourge*. But the Malachi I know, Raynor knew…Daegon knows…it's like the one you describe. I should've seen the cracks when they so willingly allowed Raynor to become the Conjuror."

"You couldn't have known."

Jordell huffed into the steaming liquid. "Following Raynor's transformation, I confronted the Cardinals."

"I'm sure that was productive." A sense of sarcasm dripped from Vrest's voice.

"In a way, yes. They listened but ultimately wouldn't give me any advice…or direction." Jordell closed his eyes. "But soon after, they hunted me. Reapers attacked. I had hidden my ability to conjure, and yet they still followed, pushing me into the shadows."

"You were asking too many questions. Breaking their hold on the world."

Jordell sighed and beckoned for another cup of the liquid, to which Vrest quickly obliged. "My partner Aramide and I set out to unravel the secrets of the Congregation from that point on. We followed Raynor's…I mean the *Scourge's* movements, hoping that there would be some semblance of his consciousness left… And we were right. It led us right to it. Malachi." His voice trailed off, becoming a whisper, "Daegon."

Green liquid dripped from the sides of Vrest's open mouth. "The city still exists?"

"It exists. And its surrounding forests are guarded. Protected. By Reapers and the…*Scourge* itself. They act as a barrier, shielding the city from the outside world."

Vrest handed a freshly refilled glass of the liquid to Jordell. "And it's just protecting the city? Why Malachi?"

"That's what I thought too, but it wasn't the city itself. It's what the city held. The source of every Conjuror's innate ability."

"The *Aether Stone*," Vrest whispered.

"I believe so."

Amid Jordell's story, the fire smoldered, but he hovered his hand over the dying flame and pushed a spark into the center, reigniting its vibrant blaze. Once again, the flickering sparks caught Vrest in their magic. "And you think the *Scourge* protects the *Aether Stone* from those that get too close?"

"Or too powerful," Jordell finished. "It's why Aramide and I believe the *Scourge* takes the soul of the Conjuror who defeats it. A perpetual cycle of augmenting its strength."

"That explains the Journey." Vrest spat into the dirt. "We're continuing this cycle of destruction, unknowingly allowing the *Scourge* to exist. To prosper."

"That would explain why you've survived for so long without even a modicum of aggression from the Reapers."

"Because they didn't know I was here." Vrest stood from his log and gazed into the trees now ablaze with blue fireflies.

"That's essentially what we learned. The Congregation and its Cardinals control everything."

"But...why? It can't just be to hoard the power of the *Aether Stone*?"

Jordell shook his head. "I could never figure that out. It could be that simple."

"That explains so much." A voice reverberated from Vrest's shelter.

Jordell and Vrest both turned their heads toward the thatched building. Gallant stepped from the shadows, looking at the fire as if it were the only clean thing left in the world. "We saw the crest on the Reaper outside of Embre," Gallant said, his voice hollow. "And Cardinal Drone...he knew. He was protecting the secret."

He ripped the chain from his neck. The golden eye of the Congregation stared at him, glinting in the firelight. A symbol of the lie he'd worn against his heart for a decade.

He didn't just drop it. He cast it into the white coals, watching the metal blacken and warp. "I wasn't protecting the world," Gallant whispered. "I was just guarding their secrets."

Vrest rubbed his chin, surprised by a sudden laugh. "I wasn't so crazy after all."

Chapter
Thirty-Four

Layla sat with Daegon on the bank of the water, her head resting on his shoulder. She wished for the Journey to pause. What better time for everything to stop than now? In the middle of a moonlit forest, shrouded in fluttering blue fireflies, surrounded by the subtle roar of the flowing river. She squeezed his hand and pressed her hair deeper into his arm. "Should I just abandon everything? Become a Loneseeker?"

Daegon rubbed his chin against her hair and nestled his lips into her scalp. "I don't know what to do just yet. But we have time to figure it out. No one has to die."

Dying wasn't what Layla was worried about. Not anymore. She closed her eyes and allowed herself to be held. She felt safe. With him, she didn't have to maintain the walls that shielded her, instead allowing her emotions to flow freely. She could go back to Shishbash. Life was so much easier before she'd become a Conjuror. She understood things would be different after taking her father's mantle, but if the ending truly was futile, what was the purpose? Especially when the end becomes the beginning of another's Journey. When starting the quest, the answer was so much clearer. Now, being with Daegon, her Journey was split between two futures that couldn't coexist.

A flock of birds darted from the canopies above, and a cacophony of cracking branches collapsed into the stream. They'd been away from camp long enough. Perhaps Jordell and Gallant were coming to find them? The cracking grew louder, morphing into inhuman snaps and crunches. Layla's stomach coiled as the ripples in the water mirrored the dense vibrations of the coming stomps.

Daegon pulled her into a thick bush and poked his head out to glimpse the creatures. Multiple monsters wearing skull-encrusted armor crashed through the trees, armed with hulking blades strapped to their backs. Reapers. There were so many of them. They'd killed one, but there had to be at least ten searching for them. Hunting them. "Stay down."

With every passing step, their blades ripped into the earth, dividing the forest floor and sending creatures scattering. The fireflies swarmed, imparting a lustrous blue shine to their otherwise jagged, obsidian armor. They headed directly for Vrest's shelter. From here, it couldn't have been more than a ten-minute walk. Daegon scratched the back of his neck, now covered in goosebumps, and nodded to himself. He slid from the bush. Layla touched his back and reached for his arm, but it was too late. Without a second thought, Daegon jumped into the stream, splashed, and yelled for the monsters. He sprinted into the woods, opposite Layla and the shelter.

***

Jordell snapped his fingers, and a small fire twinkled from the tips.

Vrest cleaned the green soup that had stained the rocks surrounding the fire. "Can you feel the heat?"

Jordell shook his head and extinguished the flame. Gallant joined them now, sipping from Jordell's used cup, covered in one of Vrest's disheveled cloaks. He didn't acknowledge Jordell's power, simply brushing it aside, and stared into the depths of the steaming soup. The pot of liquid rippled, causing Jordell to grab the hilt of his blade.

Gallant's eyes drifted up. "Is everything okay?"

Birds escaped into the sky, bringing the dense canopies alive. The fireflies dispersed, fading the ethereal blue from the campsite. Jordell stood and huffed, glaring into the darkness. "Gallant, ready your spear. Vrest, be ready. We have company."

They nodded to one another and separated into the trees. The crackling branches erupted into fallen trunks crumbling onto the smoldering fire. Five Reapers flooded their campsite. They swung their massive blades through the flickering flames, shredding the thatched walls of Vrest's shelter. Jordell had hunted Elderdeer many times with Raynor, but these dwarfed even those. Their persistent grunting echoed through the empty forest, scattering what animals remained. Jordell counted five. Even in all his travels with Aramide and Raynor, no more than two had ever appeared at once. But with their escape from Embre, the Cardinals must ensure that they finish the job.

Jordell whistled from behind a tree, and the Reapers ceased their rummaging almost simultaneously. They turned toward the root of the sound, but Vrest, who was on the opposite side, shot a bright light from his hand, bringing the campsite out of the darkness. Two of the Reapers flipped their gaze from Jordell's direction and moved toward the light.

As they approached the edge of the camp, Vrest jumped from the trees, pirouetting over the hulking monsters and slashing their legs with his rapier. His sword clanged against their metal armor, vibrating in his hand. The Reaper lifted its sword and crashed it into the ground next to Vrest. Jordell appeared from behind his tree and created a wall of fire separating the Reapers, but they pressed through, their encrusted skulls absorbing the heat and glowing red.

Gallant jumped from the bushes and stabbed the nearest Reaper with his spear. Its point initially bounced against the solid metal armor before slipping into a crevice. The creature recoiled at the attack and swung its sword in retaliation. Gallant was ready this time. He ducked out of the way and stabbed through the creature's arm, sloughing it off. The monster's sword collapsed to the ground, and Gallant darted back into the bushes. It roared and thrashed about with its remaining arm.

Two other Reapers wantonly swung their swords, blinded by both Vrest's rays of light and Jordell's wall of fire. Jordell raised his arm and pushed out, blasting the Reapers with a wave of flames, causing them to stagger before attempting a counterattack. Jordell ducked out of the way and stabbed the Reaper's chest piece, piercing through the shiny metal. He attempted to retreat with his weapon, but the monster's chest swallowed the blade. He jumped back and heaved a fireball at its skull-like helmet, penetrating the creature's armor and leaving behind a crater of glowing red metal. Jordell wiped the sweat from his face and cracked a smile.

Four to go.

Vrest raised his hand, snuffing the light out of the Reaper's immediate surroundings. The creature spun, its sword lashing at the empty air. Vrest yanked at the ground, shaping a piece of earth into a floating step, and bounded onto the creature's head. The Reaper swung its sword upward, but Vrest vanished. The massive blade crashed into its own skull, crumpling the beast to the dirt.

Three to go.

In all the chaos, another Reaper charged Vrest. Thinking quickly, he held up both hands, calling on the ground to freeze the creature's feet in place. It worked. Initially stuck, it ripped through the inconvenient obstacle and deftly swung its blade onto Vrest, slicing him in half. Blood, or what looked like blood, splattered across the campsite.

"No!" Gallant yelled from the bushes.

The Reaper withdrew its blade from Vrest's lifeless body, but it moved even more stiffly than normal. It dropped its sword and convulsed before eventually crumbling to the ground. Vrest appeared underneath the beast's neck and thrust his sword squarely through its chin. He cheekily waved at Gallant as the beast slumped to the floor. "Corporeal's stone lets me control perception, remember."

Two to go.

The two remaining Reapers stood back-to-back, lashing out with their swords. Jordell shot another wave of fire at the pair while Vrest pulled them into the ground. They glowed with a crimson heat, reminiscent of the Cardinal's red robes, their bodies buried up to their waist. Vrest fixed his ray of light on the two, who were now blindly slashing at the air. Gallant stepped closer to the beasts and maintained his spear on the creature with one arm. How could something be so feared, and yet so vulnerable? Gallant launched his spear between its eyes. Direct hit. The spear pierced through the monster's skull, ripping through the back side.

One to go.

Vrest vaulted onto the remaining creature and lifted a stone from the ground. He slammed it into the Reaper's face, and it recoiled with a fearsome roar. Another stone shot from his hand at the monster. And another. Vrest refused to relent, continuously slamming stone after stone at the now crushed head, until it eventually slumped, its lifeless torso leaning to the cold forest floor.

All the Reapers. Defeated.

Chapter Thirty-Five

Just keep running. Daegon sprinted through the dense woods, hurdling tree roots and downed logs. He swung his blade through the hanging vines and followed the luminescent glow of the sapphire fireflies that carved a path. He wasn't far ahead of the Reapers. Their thumping vibrations warned that they were plodding ever closer, matching his every move. *He just had to keep them away from Layla.*

Daegon wished he could've gone farther, but he had to halt at the edge of another body of water. The reflection of the moon above glistened on the mirror-like surface, not unlike the river he shared with Layla. If it weren't life or death, he could've stayed here, enjoyed the view. Instead, he peered over his shoulder at the familiar sound of snapping trunks and branches. Two Reapers appeared, heaving their monstrous swords over their shoulders. Daegon stared into the abyss of the helm where eyes should be. Glowing red orbs tracked his movements. He contemplated his options. There weren't many. And there wasn't time to improvise. They steadily walked closer, pulling their swords to the front.

Daegon readied his sword and monitored their slow steps. They were coordinating their attack, flanking him from the sides. It didn't help that he couldn't retreat. His back foot slipped into the lake behind. This was it. This was his time to fight. All the sparring with Jordell and Gallant came to fruition in this moment. Daegon dug his feet into the ground and bent his knees. The Reapers sprang. Daegon raised his blade, parrying the heavy swing into the dirt before pivoting aside to return the slash. *It's all about the timing.*

***

Layla remained hidden for what seemed like hours. Only minutes had passed, though the rumbling in her bones stretched the waiting. She parted the thick bushes. Every sign of danger had vanished. Nothing remained but the rushing water of the nearby river and the penetrating silence of the now-absent canopies above. She pushed through the bush, crouching along the riverbank. *Daegon ran off into the forest, opposite Jordell and Gallant. She had to warn them.* She jolted up and started toward Vrest's camp, but collapsed to the ground. A tear traced the curve of her cheek, melting into the dew on the grass below. What was a peaceful moment had morphed into a memory she'd pain to forget. *How did they know they were here? Why were there so many?*

Layla pushed through the fear and crept closer to the shelter. She'd never needed to be stealthy, but it came naturally. Without thought, she jumped from tree to tree, peering around every corner to avoid any hidden enemies or surprises. Just ahead, above the branches, plumes of dark smoke billowed from the shelter's fire. The black whiffs stretched above, but dissipated without a plan. She followed the deep indentations in the earth carved by the Reaper's sharp swords until she arrived at the camp. Five motionless Reapers littered the camp, but there were no signs of Jordell, Gallant, or Vrest.

Layla ran her foot across the sooty scorch marks that blazed through the camp. The shelter's walls had caved in, and slash marks scored nearly every surface. The oversized weapons of the defeated Reapers were embedded in the dirt. She approached the two Reapers buried halfway in the earth and reached for their armor; a shudder rippled through her. *They can't hurt you now.* The skeletal designs etched into their armor gracefully wound throughout their plate, as if planned with meticulous forethought. She ran her fingers through the breastplate and around the shoulders; the armor trembled and collapsed upon itself. Like the Reaper outside of Embre, the beast hissed and faded into a noxious mist. She stepped back. It was empty. Within seconds, the remaining beasts followed suit, crumbling into ash and drifting along the quiet wind.

The fireflies surrounding her followed suit, disappearing into the trees and leaving her in a veil of darkness. Thankfully, the bright moon illuminated the campsite. Gallant's blue armor lay buried under the tattered thatch of Vrest's destroyed shelter.

A nearby puddle of water rippled, and a pit returned to her stomach. Initially, the thudding felt like her heart, still coming off the high of escaping those dreaded beasts, but as the vibrations grew louder, it was worse. She scurried around the campsite before diving into the destroyed shelter, wrapping herself in a bundle of ripped thatch. The camouflage was better suited for hiding in a grassy outcropping than inside a shelter, but this wasn't the time for being picky. A roar ricocheted through the camp and sent a shiver down her spine. Through the slivers in the shattered walls, multiple Reapers approached the camp.

She lay in the thatch. Motionless. Breathless. The warmth of Daegon's embrace from earlier that night felt like a lifetime ago. *Was that the last time she'd see him?* The thundering footsteps of the Reapers grew louder until they were all she heard. And then. Silence. Quiet. The walls of the shelter ripped from around her, and she was face to face with the scarlet hollows of the creature, its cumbersome sword sheathed on its back.

It reached for her, but she shot a blaze of fire and rolled out of the thatched bedding, making her way to the center of the camp. The rumbling grew louder. Suffocating. Encompassing her completely. She waved her hands, and pieces of stone shot at anything that flashed in her vision. Waves of skeletal metallic hands reached for her. One landed and squeezed her wrist, but she instinctively stomped her foot into the ground, sprouting a wall of sharp stone that severed the appendage. She stepped back, screaming in exhaustion, and conjured a fireball.

They kept coming. For every one she slowed, another quickly took its place, stalking closer. Air rushed from her lungs as she backed into a wall of solid steel. She whipped around, fire erupting from her fingertips, but it was too late. The fire had weakened to embers, and her vision darkened. The monster's booming footsteps reduced the world to a low rumble. She was alone, aware of her life through the slow, ragged rhythm of her breath. The cold steel of the monster's armor squeezed against her body. She tried to push away, but her limbs no longer functioned. Captured. Alone. Numb.

***

Daegon swung his father's sword at the creatures, meeting their heavy strikes blow for blow. For their intimidating size, he kept up with their strength, shrugging off the advances and ducking under their lumbering swings. They were ankle-deep in the lake, the water splashing with every blow. Every step was a slog, but the disadvantaged landscape worked both ways.

He rolled out of the way, gliding through the water, continuously avoiding their relentless onslaught. He spun out of his roll and met the creature's heave with his own. The creature wrenched the sword from Daegon's grip, sending it splashing into the moonlit water. *If only defeating his father were so easy.* Suddenly, he was weaponless. Face to face with two hulking monsters. The creature returned to its attack, and Daegon danced out of the way, combating the clinging mud that sucked at his feet.

Splash!

Daegon collapsed into the water and choked as the cool wave flooded into his hacking lungs. This was it. In the surface's reflection, the Reaper raised its blade for the killing blow. Now swordless and stuck, Daegon closed his eyes for the impending slash. Its flooded armor creaked as it hefted its sword above its head and brought it down on the young King.

But the pain of the strike never came. Instead, heat scorched his face. A roar of flame tore past him, striking the beast. Jordell sprinted from the tree line, hands ablaze. He unleashed another fireball, striking them off balance into the muck. Daegon's jaw opened, but words failed to develop. Jordell had never conjured anything before, much less a flurry of deadly fireballs. Roaring fire replaced his thundering heartbeat. He dug his hands into the water and found his blue blade. *Let's finish this.*

Gallant followed behind Jordell and aimed his trademark spear at the beasts. He deftly flipped his hips as he neared the edge of the lake and heaved it at the remaining Reaper. The spear slid through the creature's skull, sending a wrenching scream through the forest. Gallant splashed into the water and pulled his spear from the beast. "You can't have all the fun, can you?"

Daegon hardly recognized him, no longer enshrouded by the shackles of his Shishbashi armor. "I tired them out for you guys."

Gallant brandished a smile to which Daegon imitated. They couldn't have come at a better time.

Vrest appeared in the water and scanned the battlefield. "That should be all of them. They came for us too."

Daegon slogged to the shore and crumpled to the mud. His breathing slowed, but his armor felt twice as heavy as it had that morning. Jordell approached and placed his hand on Daegon's back. The last person Daegon wanted to see, and yet, the subtle embrace was everything.

"Are you okay, kid?" Charring blackened Jordell's gloves and stretched through to his sleeves.

Daegon said, "Since when have you been able to shoot fireballs?"

Jordell stared at his own palms, a faint smile touching his lips. "I guess there's quite a bit I haven't told you." He laughed, his touch becoming more of a pat. "Where's Layla?"

At that thought, Daegon jolted to his feet. "Layla!" His heart rate spiked. "You didn't see her when you came this way?"

Gallant shook his head. "She was coming to see you."

Daegon squeezed his head. His voice was quick. "She *was* with me. But then there were so many Reapers. I tried to lure them away."

Vrest walked onto the shore. His voice was calm and certain. "I'm sure she's fine. Let's retrace our steps and see if we can find her."

Easy for him to say. Vrest had survived as a Loneseeker for years by avoiding Reapers. But Layla? Alone against a flood of them? No Conjuror could survive that single-handedly.

The sapphire fireflies returned to the trees, re-illuminating the dark corridor of the forest. The path back to her. Daegon didn't wait for the others. He took a deep breath and sprinted.

Chapter Thirty-Six

Daegon ripped through the forest, guided by the neon blue light of the flocking fireflies and the grumble of the upcoming river. It couldn't have been much further. And yet, every step was met with the increased ferocity of his beating heart. He had to find her. She had to be safe.

Finally, he'd made it. His boots squished as he approached the gentle flow of the passing river, where Layla and he had shared their moment of peace. *That moment.* The memory vanished as quickly as it had surfaced, and he jolted to the bushes. His hands tore through the jagged leaves until the truth stopped him cold. She wasn't there. A small sliver of purple fabric clung to the sharp sticks. Daegon bit the inside of his lip and sprang to his feet. "Layla!"

"Shhhhhh." Vrest kicked through the water. "We were just swarmed by Reapers. Perhaps we should quiet down. Just a bit."

Daegon frantically spun and dug in the nearby bushes. "She's not here. What if they have her?"

Gallant approached and searched for clues to her whereabouts. It was his duty to protect her as well. "Maybe she made her way back to camp? If she saw you running in one direction, maybe she thought the shelter was safe?"

The camp? Why would she even risk that? Without another thought, Daegon took off into the woods. Vrest raised his eyes at Gallant and shrugged his shoulders before following behind.

Daegon broke into the camp and reeled from the carnage of the earlier battle. The blood drained from his head; the trees blurring and doubling. He pulled his sword from the hilt and kicked over whatever boxes remained. *She has to be here.* He pulled the cloth scattered along the ground and smashed through the countless layers of collapsed tree limbs. "Layla! Are you here?"

Gallant and Vrest approached, stepping forward to help. But the camp wasn't as they'd left it. Sure, the camp had seen better days when they darted into the woods after Daegon and Layla. But now? Now there were battle scars they didn't cause. Footprints, large and small, trampled the dirt. The shelter, while it had been destroyed before, was ripped from its foundation and hurled dozens of yards away, and its once sturdy frame was mangled and twisted around a tree. Scorch marks covered every surface, and conjured stone stabbed from the ground.

Jordell finally caught up and stood at shoulders with the others. He steadied his breath and allowed Daegon to dig. And flip. And search. But he knew. "Daegon."

Daegon kicked the ground and continued his frenetic search through the thatch of the shelter. *She has to be here.* He flipped a table without legs and lifted the torn remains of the shelter's blankets. He scoured the camp again.

Jordell's voice rose, ricocheting across the moonlit campsite, "Daegon!"

She's not here. Daegon fell to his knees, and tears cascaded to the forest floor. His back heaved in desperation. "They have her, don't they?"

Gallant expanded his search and stepped into the deep footprints left by the Reapers. Through the chaos, an uneasy discovery of order pointed north. A row of at least a dozen separate Reapers indented the earth, all walking in unison. It had to be something. "This direction. Where does it take you?"

Vrest looked at the moon and walked to a tree. He rubbed his hand on the green, sticky moss, the cool midnight air biting his skin. He took a breath, the words scraping his throat, "That's North. That would take you to Corporeal."

Daegon sprang from the tear-soaked ground and darted down the path. He stopped at the absence of additional footsteps. Unable to hold back the tears, he waved his arms toward them. "What are we waiting for? Let's go save her!"

The three didn't budge. They stood motionless as Daegon writhed in urgency. Jordell shook his head. "It's not that simple. There could be more."

Daegon rushed back to the three, begging them to follow. "We just defeated how many Reapers? We could easily take them? We have to try!" Daegon turned back and ran toward the path.

Jordell reached out and snagged his cloak, ripping him back toward the group.

"Let go of me!"

"Daegon! There could be more than just Reapers. If the Congregation is controlling *everything*, what stops them from simply unleashing the *Scourge* at us?"

Daegon's shoulders shuddered at the thought of the *Scourge* surrounding them with its suffocating mist. Suffocating her. Tears streamed down his cheeks, and his knees gave out from carrying his trembling weight. "So, what do we do? Do we just let them take her? Kill her?"

Jordell sighed. "We just have to think of a plan. I told you I would tell you everything when we got back to town." Daegon's eyes veered up at him. "There's a group there that could help us save Layla."

In Talman? Who? How? Daegon rubbed his eyes with his forearm and steadied his way to his feet. "Aramide?"

Jordell smirked. "You didn't think he would go from Protector to the High Conjuror to a simple tavern owner in a throwaway town, did you?"

Daegon's eyebrows contorted in opposite directions. "What do you mean?"

Jordell gestured for the group to follow. "Come with me back to town. Let me introduce you to the leader of the Forlorn."

***

Aramide wiped the inside of a half-empty glass of beer when the door to his tavern slammed open. He took a breath and gently set the glass onto the freshly polished table, leaned onto his counter, and peered intently as the group flooded into the Crossed Swords Tavern. This time, a new adventurer joined them. Matted black hair. Tattered green cloak tinged with dirt. A man of the forest. Aramide lifted off the counter and met them in the center of the room. "I take it you found the Lone-seeker."

Jordell led the group into the space. "We did. This is Vrest. I believe the source of Talman's monster rumors." Jordell directed his attention toward the young man, who playfully bowed. "Aramide, we need your help. Corporeal captured Layla."

Aramide closed his eyes and snickered, finding the nearest chair. "I don't know what all I can do, Jordell. Do you want me to liquor you up and help you all forget your troubles?"

Jordell held his gaze on Aramide for an uncomfortably long time. The room grew silent, the flickering of the candles casting an eerie glow across the group. The roof creaked from the outdoor wind, prompting Jordell to slump into a chair next to the tavern keeper. "Aramide, we need your help."

Aramide looked through Jordell to the three who stood as hopeful as Jordell sounded. "I take it he knows everything?"

Jordell looked back at Daegon and nodded. "Everything."

It was Aramide's turn to create the deafening silence. He sat in his chair, studying Daegon. His mouth, while closed, contorted through his cheeks, but ultimately culminated in a thick sigh. "Because you're Raynor's kid." He stood up from the chair and walked back to his bar. "I have to reach out to some people, but let's make a plan to meet here in the morning."

Jordell let out a sharp breath and stood from his chair. "Thank you, Aramide!" He patted Daegon on the shoulder. "We will probably travel soon. Let's make sure that we're ready to go when we do."

Daegon followed Jordell with his eyes as he left the tavern. Was that it? Just...wait? They would regroup and prepare while the Congregation did what to Layla? The stillness in the tavern made him want to scream.

Gallant sensed Daegon's discomfort and approached. "A well-thought plan is better than rushing in and getting us all killed."

Daegon knew that was true. But he just couldn't ease the image of Layla sitting in the bushes. He'd left her. The mere thought stung with the pain of abandonment. A feeling he'd known all too well. Was there something else he could've done? Daegon squeezed his fists at the pain and gritted his teeth. "Vrest, my room is down the road. Let's get you cleaned up."

Chapter
Thirty-Seven

The morning sun crested over the tree line. It should've been another peaceful morning in Talman, complete with the characteristic smell of fresh dirt and the sounds of a soon-to-be bustling town. Should have been peaceful. Would have been peaceful. Daegon sat on a bench and stared out at the billowing plumes of smoke persistently poking over the horizon. A subtle trickle of shade offered a reprieve from the humid heat. He couldn't sleep. He'd already gotten ready and, instead of resting, sat idly, sharpening his father's blue blade. The mirror finish reflected the glow of the sun into the dimly lit room.

Vrest shook his hair dry, now wearing thick leather armor that held a familiar green hue. His black hair was slicked back, and his skin rinsed of the grime that once tattooed his body. He walked to the couch in the center of the room and kicked his feet onto the table. "Who do you guys think that Aramide guy was reaching out to?"

"Whoever it is, it must be important." Gallant shrugged his shoulders. He wasn't sure of anything nowadays. Gray leather bracers stretched from his armor to his shoulder. He'd left his glistening Shishbashi armor back at Vrest's shelter. It represented the lie he'd been living his entire life. He reached for his chest to squeeze his necklace, but his fingers grasped only empty air. He let his hand fall, the phantom weight of the golden sigil still heavy on his neck. He willingly perpetuated the oppression of the Congregation, and enforced their self-serving rules, converting his people to their teachings. He did so without a second thought, and his compliance earned him the Fluidguard's captainship. His eyes closed, and he tightened the leather cords of his breastplate. It was lighter than his Shishbashi chain-mail, wrapping around his body, and allowed him to glide as he flourished his newly sharpened spear.

After everyone cleaned up and readied their weapons, Daegon stood and pressed for the door. They'd already waited too long. There was too much that could've happened in the hours they'd delayed. Aramide said meet in the morning. It was morning. It was time.

Rows of torches lined the dew-covered streets of Talman. The few people who dotted the town stretched and yawned, preparing for another honest day of work. Hammering anvils and bubbling pots of stew steadied their march. Everything came alive. Everything was open. Except one building. Aramide had flipped the sign of the Crossed Swords Tavern to *Closed*.

Daegon pushed the door open. The tables and orderly seating had vanished. The tavern had transformed into a war room. A singular, excessively large round table replaced the battered bar tables, and thick brown chairs encircled the edge. The windows, normally filtering stray streams of light, were covered with a cloth that encapsulated darkness. In the dense candlelight, Aramide sat back, facing away from the table with his arms crossed, hunched over a tattered map pinned to a board. He murmured to a familiar woman with dark brown hair.

Daegon shouted from the door, "El?"

The woman broke from Aramide's conversation and gave him a familiar sly grin. He hadn't seen her since she'd found him freezing, alone on the outskirts of Shishbash. She'd helped him survive his encounter with the Reaper. And even then, she and her crew left him for dead, to be slaughtered by Gallant and his Fluidguard in the frozen Shishbashi dungeons. She looked different now, though. Most notably, she'd shed her thick winter jacket. The humid heat of Embre contrasted with the frozen forests of Shishbash during the Tundra ceremony. She now wore a tight black coat with a thin sword strapped to her waist.

She leaned over the map, her shoulder brushing Aramide's as she traced a line with a gloved finger. "I didn't know this was the kid you were talking about." She followed the outline of the table to Daegon. "We thought you'd sacrificed yourself for the good of the Forlorn."

Daegon raised his hand. "To be fair. You left me for dead."

El waved her hand dismissively. "Semantics. You're alive, aren't you?" She smashed her hand onto the table and more squarely faced her body toward Daegon. "You're a survivor!"

The words hissed through Daegon's ears. Survivor. He remembered his first encounter with that Reaper. The fear and shock as it tore the Conjuror apart. His frozen boots, both figuratively and literally, were unable to move as it tramped toward him. He was alive because of her. Daegon stepped back from the table, a lump swelling in his throat that required considerable effort to clear. "Yes...well...where's everyone else?"

Aramide put his arm between the two to prevent the growing hostility. "You two know each other?"

El shot Aramide a smile and pressed his hand. "Oh, Aramide." Her voice always had a tinge of condescension. "Daegon here helped us save Moan from the Shishbashi Fluidguard and helped disrupt the Tundra ceremony."

Gallant said, "You!" The two caught eyes. The electricity between them caused Daegon and Jordell to step back.

El pushed from the table, stalking toward the blonde-haired man with a predator's grace. "Ah. This must be the fallen Shishbashi warrior. You've finally come around to the atrocities of your beloved Congregation, huh?" She was a foot away from him when she finished. "At this point, you can probably see that we were on the right side of history."

"You tried to kill innocent people…"

She broke his sentence, her voice filling the space. "We tried to prevent you from sacrificing an innocent woman to the Congregation." She took a deep breath, and the corners of her cheeks slowly lifted, returning to a warm gaze. "And you see where it eventually led. Now we have to save that very person from what?"

Gallant remained speechless. He glared at her until Jordell broke up their squabble. He, too, had cleaned up and freshened his armor, replacing it with shiny chain mail.

Vrest said, "Are you all that is coming? It's going to take a lot more than that to break into Corporeal."

El's footsteps creaked across the wooden planks as she walked back to Aramide. "The entire Forlorn has been called to help. Being the leader of the Shishbashi Forlorn, I answered the call on behalf of my people." She picked up a glass of beer from the counter. "Imagine my surprise to see you." Her eyes narrowed on Daegon.

Jordell interjected. "It's all to help Layla."

El shot back. "Yes, the Conjuror." A laugh fluttered behind the fizzing bubbles. "Had you listened to the Forlorn in the first place, we'd never have been in this predicament." Her eyes slid from Daegon to Gallant. She lived to antagonize.

Gallant shook his head. His mission was always to protect Layla. At all costs. Even if the Congregation had morphed into some evil monstrosity, his duty remained the same. "My name is Sir Gallant. Head of the Shishbashi Fluidguard. I beg you to assist us in saving Layla."

El's laugh crashed into his plea. "You know the world is ending when a Fluidguard grows a conscience," she smirked, "and realizes his holy Congregation is a lie." El's head cocked to the side. "Wait...I know you. From our ambush?"

Gallant scoffed, but Aramide interrupted their back-and-forth banter by throwing a map into the center of the table. The piece of parchment had to have been hundreds of years old. The stained creases in the paper created inky grid lines for Aramide to follow and establish a battle plan. "This is a map of Corporeal and the surrounding territory."

Vrest snickered and said, "Are you sure it's even up to date?"

Aramide's eyes shot the Loneseeker a glare before they returned to the page without retorting. "I've reached out to all Forlorn pacts for assistance. At the moment, El is the only one who's answered the call." Aramide rubbed his forearm across the paper, flattening it out. "But I feel like a small group should be able to take advantage of Corporeal's many passageways, slip in, grab Layla, and make our way out."

El pushed the corner of the paper and added, "Like the Loneseeker said, we're going to need more help. The second they even sniff us, we'll be swarmed with Corporeal soldiers."

Daegon added, "or worse."

Vrest doubled down. "Reapers and the *Scourge* are also in play as combatants."

Aramide had obviously informed El of the updated information regarding the enemies, as her surprise was nowhere near where it needed to be. He rubbed the braided red knots at the edge of his mustache. "So what are our options then?"

El touched a spot on the map, central to their location in relation to Corporeal. "There's a group not too far out of the way I helped establish a little while ago. They're small, but they could definitely help."

Daegon slammed his hand on the table. "No more detours!"

El bit her lip. "Look kid. I get you have feelings for this girl, but we all need to come back alive."

Aramide said, "Agreed. I think the passages are our best option for getting into the city, but we need to distract whatever enemies lie beyond the wall."

"And that's where my group comes in. They can cause some ruckus outside and keep them occupied."

It wasn't the answer Daegon wanted, but he knew it was a solid plan. There was only a finite amount of time before something happened to her. He winced at the images of Layla becoming the *Scourge*.

Jordell and Gallant closed in on the map and traced the many underground passages that led directly into the center of Corporeal's outer keep. Gallant had studied the battle between Corporeal and Malachi when he was a young Congregational student. He leaned across the table and traced his hand along a particular tunnel starting under the surrounding lake. "The passages are ancient and were used both to allow citizens to escape and to ferry in supplies during the war with Malachi."

Everything always came back to Malachi. Daegon stepped up to the center of the table. "So that's the plan then? The passageways?"

Aramide sat back in his chair, grabbed his beer and propped his feet onto the table. "Unless somebody has a better one?"

"You don't think the Congregation has those things monitored?" Vrest's voice drifted from the back wall

"Oh. I expect them to be. But we have a Loneseeker." Aramide gestured his glass toward Vrest. "We also have High Conjuror Raynor's personal protectors, to go along with his son." He took a long swig of his beer before slamming it onto the table. "I'll take my chances with this crew every day. Plus, we'll have more Forlorn helping on the outside."

Jordell nodded. "I've heard of worse plans."

Vrest chuckled. It was quiet at first but bubbled into a contagious cadence of laughter. Jordell followed, then Aramide. Before long, the rest of the group joined in. Aramide pushed Daegon a beer. He initially rejected the drink, but after an affirmative nod from Jordell, eventually conceded to having a sip. They all raised their drinks into the air.

"For Layla!"

Chapter Thirty-Eight

The jungle was a wall of noise—insects, wind, shifting leaves—but the group moved in silence. Aramide, Jordell, and El took the lead, leaving Daegon to trail with Vrest and a sullen Gallant. While the terrain maintained a sea of deep green foliage and oversized trunks, the rows of untouched trees stretched their branches into the path, slowing their travel. The remnants of a once-traveled path wound ahead, slipping through the forest.

Daegon rubbed the back of his head; the sweat from a half-day's walk soaked his scalp. "Strange seeing El again, isn't it? After everything in Shishbash?"

Gallant turned his nose at the comment. "Whatever we need to do to get Layla back."

El's neck wrenched back, cracking a smile. She peeled away from Aramide and Jordell. Gallant scoffed at her presence, quickened his pace, and ran ahead with Vrest. El shook her head as they crossed.

Her thumbs pointed at Gallant. "Is he always that grumpy?"

Daegon let himself chuckle. "Since the day I met him."

"You know...we weren't leaving you for dead back in Shishbash."

Daegon looked down at the tall grass attempting to snag his feet. "It sure felt like it."

"Oh, I bet it did. But it was all for the good of the Forlorn. Can you imagine what would've happened if they'd caught all of us?" She put her hand on his shoulder, ducking under a low-hanging branch. "At least now you see why we must continue."

Understand? That was an understatement. Since the Reapers took Layla, he, like the rest of the group, had truly seen just how much the Congregation had seeded their dastardly fingers into the misgivings of the world. They controlled fear and death itself, with the help of his father. But why? Why would the Congregation want the *Scourge* to destroy? And not just destroy, but erase? Was it control? In some sick way, were they protecting something? Keep the Memory—the constant phrase that sprinkled against the Journey. What memory? He shook his head. There was no excuse for what he'd seen in Terratoria. In Malachi.

His attention fixated back to El. "Where's the rest of the group? Krag, Jovy, and Moan?"

Just the mention of them brought a smile to El's face. "We'll see them soon enough. They were pretty shaken up when you left. Created some wild plans to break you free."

Daegon laughed. "They sure had a way of showing their affection. I didn't exactly feel the warmth in your camp."

El's face went deadpan. "It was Shishbash's Tundra festival...everything was frozen."

"No...I mean like I didn't feel..."

She smacked his back. "Relax, I'm just messing with you. They have their way of showing that they care. You jumped in and helped us without a second thought. You bested your knight-friend up there when we needed it most. It was always appreciated."

They weren't family. But they were the first ones to take him in when he'd ended up here. Alone. Scared. They were the Forlorn. The word had been a pull of emotions and confusion since he'd arrived. At first, they were some righteous group, rising against an oppressive offender. Then, they were terrorists attempting to stop Conjurors from saving the world. Turns out his first impression was correct. And he was glad. They seemed so...so normal.

Daegon relented with a nod, and she walked back ahead to the front with Aramide and Jordell, leaving Daegon alone to take in his surroundings. He closed his eyes and allowed the persistent chirping to fill him. He imagined Layla holding him. Their first kiss. It wouldn't be their last. It couldn't be their last.

El yelled ahead, stopped, and held her hand up. The group scanned the branches, but the trees followed the same pattern. Except for the sound. The unrelenting bugs had stopped. The silence stretched between them, causing their feet to brace into the ground. Their hands reached for the hilts of their weapons. And then, the noise returned. A ripping whistle filled the space. Another whistle shot from the far side of the forest. If they hadn't prepared for a sneak attack, it would have sounded like an echo. But it was instead another assailant. A familiar orb of bright light shot out from the forest. Luminary's power.

The light extended, casting a canvas of blinding white across the group. They covered their eyes to avoid the pain, and a hand remained firmly on their weapons. A multitude of branches snapped, and Daegon looked up from under his sleeve. Dozens of attackers pushed toward them. The light faded, allowing them to drift their gaze to the enemy; their swords remained sheathed.

Was this the Forlorn cell? The brightness forced their forms into shadows dotting the edge of the tree line. But they were outnumbered, and one of the assailants was a Conjuror. Or what he learned, a Loneseeker. Like Vrest. As the light faded, chain mail and pointed arrows threatened them. The man in the middle held up his hand, tracing patterns in the air. He wore purple robes and tied his shaggy hair into a ponytail.

"Fabian!" Gallant yelled.

The younger man with long dark hair and excessively large robes glared back at the group before lowering his hand. "Gallant? Daegon?"

Daegon's face stretched into a smile when the rest of the figures came into view. A hulking man held an oversized axe, and a small mouselike human sheathed their even smaller sword. Daegon yelled out, "Krag! Jovy!"

While everyone obviously knew each other, drawn weapons prevented Daegon from simply running and meeting the two for a long-time hug. But at the cordial greetings, they naturally lowered. They dropped them even faster when Aramide laughed and commanded them to sheathe their weapons. "I guess we found our Forlorn!"

Fabian walked ahead with Gallant discussing who-knows-what. *It had to have been about the Congregation.* Their last interaction ended without a friendly resolution. But the now-full party made it difficult to hear anything. Krag, who always had a difficult time understanding how big he truly was, gave him a hard squeeze from the side.

Jovy, with his scratchy voice, hissed, "Krag, you're going to hurt him."

"We just missed you, Daegon. We're sorry we left you in that Shishbashi dungeon. Moan and I devised a plan with explosives to break you free."

Jovy rolled his eyes. "That was the extent of the plan. Shock and awe. Get in without a way of getting out. It seems to me the kid is doing just fine."

Daegon laughed, remembering Jovy's harshness. "It's good to see you too, Jovy."

The camp they arrived at resembled El's in the Twinwood Forest. Only this time, without the layer of frost. In the middle of the outcropping, an assortment of tents and foot-made paths snaked throughout the camp. Makeshift traps comprising spears and ropes caused any would-be intruder to slow. Dozens of boxes of supplies acted as barriers to entering the camp, not that it was too difficult simply to walk around them. *More of Jovy's bombs?*

They walked around the personal firepits that extended from each shelter to the front of the largest tent at the center of camp. El lifted the flap and waved everyone through. The entrance to the tent made everyone, especially Krag, duck to enter, but a large beam lifted the center, allowing the space to accommodate a large crowd. A large table wrapped around the beam, and various papers were knifed into its surface.

Krag smacked Daegon on the back and glared at Gallant. *There had to be a better way for him to get his attention.* "He smells like Congregation." Krag grabbed his axe and filled his chest, glaring down on the former Fluidguard.

"He may have been." El placed her hand on Gallant's shoulder as he attempted a comeback at the enormous man. "But we're all on the same side now." Krag's hand pulled from his weapon at the command.

Jordell pushed the pace of the conversation. "We mustn't stay here too long. El, who can we talk to about our plan?"

Aramide and El paced to the center of the room and waved for Fabian. "While I'm away, Fabian is in charge of the group." Fabian scooted and shimmied through the mass of people before El pulled him closer. "Since he's joined us, he's helped us convert more and more Conjuror's to our cause."

Gallant shot out from the crowd. "Doesn't that go against everything you were taught?"

Fabian passed glances between El and Gallant before returning an answer. "You're currently working with the Forlorn to attack what? The capital or the Congregation? I would ask the same of you?"

Gallant was caught. Between two worlds. The one he'd lived his entire life. The one he'd espoused and protected. But also, what he'd learned was a lie. He was in no position to criticize Fabian. Realizing his conflict, Gallant said, "What did they say to you? How did you come to learn about the Congregation?"

Fabian's expression softened, and he explained, not realizing that it came off more like a sermon. "If you remember, I was already doubting the purpose of the Journey. Then I met her." He diverted his gaze to El. "She told me about the group and how they were tracking the *Scourge's* movements, noticing that it wasn't chasing any stones but appeared to be acting on orders."

El put her arm around his shoulder and continued his story. "I didn't realize it fully yet either. We were always told to avoid having too many Conjurors together for fear that it would cause the *Scourge* to target you. But as we amassed more and more to our cause, the attack never came." Her hand squeezed into a fist. "The only sensible reason would be that someone, or something, had to know about the group." It wasn't the stones.

Aramide said, "We were already pretty skeptical about the Congregation and their Journey. It always seemed barbaric. Archaic. There had to be a different way. After what happened to Raynor, well. The root of our mission was always to protect Conjuror's from becoming the very thing that they set out to destroy."

Gallant shook his head. "How could you not just tell everyone? Why was it a secret? Still a secret?"

Aramide opened his mouth, but Fabian held his arm out to answer. "Would you not have killed the person for heresy? Or at least imprisoned them? Silenced them? You sure seemed to want to arrest me that time around the fire. The Congregation programmed you to keep the order. Keep their cycle going."

The overfilled room warmed from the mass of bodies engaged in the heated discussion, and a bead of sweat dropped from Gallant's forehead, but he shook it off, acknowledging the semblance of truth in Fabian's assertion.

Fabian continued, "The Forlorn is much larger than the Congregation knows. Their roots...our roots run deep. Waiting for the opportunity to make a tangible difference."

Jordell parted the crowd and approached the center. "We have the difference. We need your help."

Fabian turned his attention toward Jordell. "El just gave me a rundown of what all needs to happen. We're happy to help. We just have to figure out the best method of doing so." He turned his head and scanned the crowd. "Anyone have any ideas?"

"Bombs!"

Jovy's shrill voice bounced off the back wall of the tent. It actually wasn't a bad idea. But how would they execute that?

Vrest stood tall above the crowd. "Bombs? What do we do? Take them to the front gate and storm the city?"

Jordell interrupted, "No, Vrest, bombs might actually be the answer. We're entering through the tunnels. If we could set off explosives outside of the front gate, we might divert enough attention to sneak in unseen."

Jovy's eyes grew enormous at the opportunity to use explosives again. Against the leaders of the opposition, nonetheless. Fabian quieted the growing fervor of the crowd just as a thin man wearing Forlorn gear sped into the front flap of the tent. He wheezed, and his sudden appearance made Gallant pull his spear.

"That's ours." Fabian waved for Gallant to lower his spear. "I was given notice of our meeting and had him scout ahead to Corporeal. What is it?"

The man's face was pale, and his chest churned. As if he sprinted from Corporeal to the camp without stopping. His mouth opened wide, shaking at the words. "It's...it's the *Scourge*." Quiet gasps rippled through the air. Aramide asked the boy to continue. "The...the *Scourge*...it's just hovering outside of Corporeal."

Vrest couldn't help but scoff. "That essentially confirms our theory that the Congregation is controlling the monster."

Aramide pressed the spy further. "Have you heard anything about the Conjuror?"

"Only that she is being held in the Congregation's central chambers. She's alive as of this morning."

Daegon's eyes slammed shut, and he took a relieved breath at the news. *As of this morning.* The news wasn't instant. Any and everything could have happened between now and then. He wanted to go, but he knew they needed to complete the plan. If they could just do it a little quicker.

"They are planning a ceremony for tomorrow, though. I got word of that. Their obelisks are shooting bolts of lightning into the air. I assume it has to do with her."

Aramide met the man and put his hands on his shoulders. "You risked your life for this mission. The Forlorn thanks you greatly." He gave the man a strong pat on the shoulders and ushered him out of the tent. "I think our mission is clear. Fabian, you'll take your men to the front of Corporeal. I don't need it to be a dangerous mission. I only need you to make as much noise as possible. We'll sneak in through the tunnels and try to be out before they even notice. Before the *Scourge* descends."

Fabian nodded and directed Jovy and Krag to set up the supplies. El clapped her hands. "First thing in the morning, we're going to save your Conjuror."

The completion of the plan brought the scattered clatter of armor exiting the tent. The bleeding sun dropped over the forest, casting an orange glaze over the campsite. Thin wisps of smoke drifted through the makeshift alleys of the camp, signaling that dinner was in the works. On the outside of the tent, Daegon took a seat on a stack of barrels. Despite the noticeable absence of rain, the ground squished beneath his boots. He wiped a bead of sweat and waited. Jordell poked through the opening, and Daegon pulled him aside.

Jordell grunted. "Daegon? You can't spook a man like that."

Daegon sighed and found a barrel. He lowered his head and sloshed his boots through the damp soil.

"What is it, Daegon?"

Daegon stared at the ground. "Keep the Memory."

Jordell's eyebrows shifted. "Keep the Memory? What about it?"

Daegon crossed his arms. "I've figured it out. Everything."

"Oh?"

Callah implied that the *Aether Stone* was the missing piece of the Conjuror's Journey. But Aramide's assumption that the *Aether Stone* was a concoction of all elements, split among the five nations, sat at the forefront of his thoughts. Fermenting. The Great War. A bastion of memory. Controlling Reality. It was supposedly destroyed to appease the *Scourge*, but he'd seen it. Jordell had seen it. Felt its power. Its warmth. "We're the Memory."

"What?"

"You said that the *Scourge* protected the lands surrounding Malachi. In all the maps I reviewed at Aramide's tavern, there was never mention of a city."

"Well, yes, a hidden city wouldn't appear on a map." Jordell approached a pole and rested his arm, his face twisting with thought.

"But no maps? A whole kingdom hidden from the world?" Daegon stood from the barrel. "It had to have been created. Imagined. The *Aether Stone* has the ability to control reality, right?"

Jordell brought his hand to his chin. "So the tombs say."

Daegon drew shapes in the mud at their feet. "The stones found in each city. They all correspond to a unique element. Shishbash. Water. Territoria. Earth. Embre."

"Fire."

"Yes, and then there's Luminary. Light. And Corporeal. Darkness. But *we* also had a stone, didn't we? In the center of Malachi? It was just something that existed. Thought nothing about. But I could feel it." Jordell's eyes widened, the glint of a terrifying truth sparkling within them. "The books Callah gave me. The stories Aramide told me. This world is missing the *Aether Stone*."

Jordell had considered that outcome, but Daegon's conviction darkened his eyes. "And our stone is the *Aether Stone*? Creating our bastardized version of Malachi?"

Daegon nodded, sitting at the information. "That makes us...memories. Side effects of the Stone maintaining the Kingdom. That's why my father is in the history books, and I'm not. He *did* exist. I'm just...a part of that memory's history."

Jordell stumbled, grabbing the pole to stay upright. His face flushed pale as the truth settled behind his eyes. "We're what... ghosts? Why?"

"Memories...but I haven't figured that part out. There's something in Malachi the Congregation must want to keep. Something that was destroyed in the Great War. A cherished memory?" Daegon reached his hand for Jordell and brought him over to a large crate to sit. "Since I've been here, I've been trickled bits of information. The small pieces never made any sense, but now. Now it's all I can think about."

Jordell's eyes grew wide, and he snapped his fingers. "That's it."

Daegon cocked his head.

"That's why they took Layla. Why the Reapers didn't simply end her at the camp."

Daegon's mouth dropped as the pieces clicked into place. "Because we can end the cycle. They're trying to replace Raynor with Layla."

"Because of Raynor, the *Scourge* is bound to the Stone, just like us. If we are creations of the *Aether Stone*, then we are made of the same power as the monster. We can hurt it. We can end the cycle, but..." Jordell closed his eyes. "If what you say is true..."

"I know." Daegon squeezed his eyes shut. "But if what I'm saying is true, destroying the *Aether Stone* would end the Journey."

Daegon nodded and stood from the barrel. He recalled Jordell's description of Raynor succumbing to the *Scourge*, imparting the soulless eyes onto Layla. He winced, and a tear rolled down his cheek. "I've lost my father to that monster. I can't let the same fate happen to Layla."

"We won't let it happen." Jordell stood from the barrel.

"Thank you." Daegon stepped forward and embraced him. It wasn't a King hugging his mentor; it was a son hugging his father. "Keep the Memory."

Chapter
Thirty-Nine

The slick black walls of Corporeal drank in the scorching sun. Daegon stood ankle-deep in the lake, scanning its depths for the supposed tunnel leading into the city. The water refracted the dark walls, scattering the image into its murky depths. There should've been more resistance. More opposition to their getting this close. And yet, they walked right to the edge of the city. No guards. No Reapers. No *Scourge*. It was a city too brazen to know about its subtle weaknesses. Daegon stepped out of the water, passed through a thicket of tangled briar, and found Aramide. "Are we sure there are tunnels down there?"

Aramide stood with his hands pressed against his hips, leaning back comfortably against a large tree. The surrounding forest shrouded their attempt into the city. He was indiscreetly contemplating something. Maybe the plan? Whatever it was, he maintained a blank stare as he responded. "The maps aren't often wrong, kid."

Daegon's eyebrows lifted, and he turned his gaze to Jordell, who offered one of his trademark grins. Were they messing with him? He returned his attention to Aramide. "But they have been before?"

Aramide pushed off the tree and pressed a device into Daegon's chest. "Oh, you mustn't worry too much." He handed the small devices to the rest of the crew.

Don't worry? They'd already taken one too many detours. And Layla was still in the Congregation's possession. With the looming *Scourge*, they had only so much time before they performed whatever sadistic ritual on her. *A replacement ritual.* Daegon winced while rotating the grooved gray device in his fingers. A singular mouthpiece poked from the thick, ribbed crevices.

A splash rippled from the lake. El waded into the water with the device pressed into her mouth. She dove under the surface for an uncomfortably long time. That was until the purpose of the devices became clear. Minutes later, El resurfaced. "Not far down! There's the tunnel from the map."

Aramide flashed a smiling thumbs up before she dove back into the water. Content with his maps, he smacked Daegon's shoulders. "Time to put your breather in! Let's go save your Conjuror."

Daegon waded into the water. Slowly at first. Was he really to trust these breathing devices? There wasn't much time to contemplate whether he'd be able to survive under the dark surface. It was already cresting his shoulders. The cool, dark water enveloped him, pulling him deeper into its unknown depths. The only way to save Layla was down. And that was all the motivation that he needed. Milky weeds flogged his vision, but he followed Gallant's boots until a flicker of red and yellow light stabbed through the darkness.

He burst from the water, the splashing pool echoing against the tiny chamber. They surfaced in a small, brightly lit corridor, paved with dusty black stones that contrasted the slickness of the black brick he'd passed before. El had already lit the nearby torches and pressed deeper into the chamber, scouting ahead as the rest of the crew surfaced.

The passage was a tomb. A relic of old Corporeal, sealed off from the city itself. Small vestiges of the city before the Great War were carved into the narrow tunnel, just wide enough for two people to walk side-by-side. Their footsteps echoed and sloshed as they followed through the chamber, and the dusty floor acted like snow, both subtly dampening the noise and providing a well-worn path for them to follow in the event of a quick escape.

El led the group, waving her torch at both the ceiling and the floor as she stepped through the unknown passage. *It wouldn't be booby-trapped, would it?* "Don't worry, Daegon, we won't leave you behind this time."

Daegon shook his head and bit his lip as Jordell gave him a cocked expression. It was too much to explain, and Daegon waved the conversation away before crashing into Gallant's back. The same dusty brick that had lined the tunnel now created a wall that prevented them from moving any further. Aramide traced his gloved hand along the crumbling mortar. "This must be why we haven't come up against any obstacles."

Vrest sarcastically quipped, "A wall? How ever are we going to make it into the city now?"

El waved him off, not easily amused by his terse attempt at humor. She kneeled, pulled a knife from her belt, and carved a brick from the bottom of the wall. She scratched and shook the brick free from the mortar, revealing the signature shiny black surface of the Corporeal architecture. A flickering fire-light blazed from the hole, showing life. And potential enemies.

Aramide put his hand on El and addressed the group. "Remember, Fabian's crew is going to set up a distraction in the front. That should allow us to get in relatively undetected. Once we're through, we wait for the signal that they've started their front."

Everyone nodded in agreement. El removed more bricks from the wall, creating an opening just big enough for everyone to slip through. Aramide poked his head out into a long, narrow corridor with torches evenly spaced. It was sterile but maintained. Two doors dotted the exits of the path. Opposite directions.

"Alright!" Aramide clapped his hands, now dusty and covered in chiseled mortar. "Jordell, Vrest, and I are going to head right. Daegon and Gallant head left. El, I'm going to need you to keep watch over our escape route."

"I feel like I would be much more helpful in the city," El said.

"I know you would, but if our only safe means of escaping is compromised, we're setting ourselves up for a suicide run."

El huffed before ultimately following orders and leaning against the dusty wall. Aramide pointed his eyes at Daegon. "Once you've rescued Layla, immediately return to escape through the tunnels. There's no need to wait for the others. It's in and out. Got it?"

Daegon nodded, beginning the mission. They slid through the opening. Fewer torches than expected lit the hallway; the shining black bricks strategically bounced the light through the hallway. The mortar crackled behind as El ground the bricks back into their original position. If someone were to stop by and stare at the wall, they could notice a difference, but a wanton guard simply walking through should be oblivious to the hidden escape.

Daegon and Jordell gave one another a long glance before they split their separate ways. Like old times. Vrest walked backwards. "First one to find the Conjuror, then." His chuckle emanated from within the clean walls.

Daegon and Gallant approached their door, and a bright light shone from underneath. Daegon creaked open the door, revealing a burning fireplace. The hallway's black bricks faded to a more natural gray, and multiple cots sprawled on the far side of the room. Large openings spanned the front, allowing light to flow into the homey interior. Two soldiers conversed, their gazes fixed on the city beyond. Their conversation was inaudible, but their inky black armor absorbed the light ricocheting within the room. The soldiers' shoulders displayed the familiar eye—the crest of the Congregation. Of Corporeal. Of Malachi.

Daegon and Gallant gave each other a long look. The look of conversation and planning, all without a syllable being uttered. The two soldiers waved their hands in conversation before they simultaneously dropped to their sides and collapsed to the floor. Two knives lay burrowed into their necks, subduing them into an eternal slumber.

Their ornate armor easily slid from their bodies. Daegon slipped the dark piece of metal over his clothes. He cinched the breastplate tight, smelling of sweat and oil, and held out his arms to Gallant. "How do I look?"

"Like you're ready to do everything you can to protect the Cardinals." Gallant pulled the last of the dark boots over his feet.

"That's what I was going for!" Daegon smeared a piece of blood from the shoulders. "You look like someone who was born to wear the armor."

At any other time, on any other day, Gallant would have taken that as a compliment. Since the revelation that his entire life was a lie, it was difficult for him to take those sorts of comments in jest. What normally would have been an opportunity for him to quip back with some jaded remark turned into a frown. He rubbed the raised eye on his shoulders.

They sat for an extra moment and waited for the signal to descend deeper into the city. Daegon rose and stood at the edge, peering into the sea of darkness. The smoothness of the buildings flowed like waves, slowly sucking the sun into their dark facades. The Congregation's obsidian temple bloomed in the distance, surrounded by four obelisks emitting purple crackling light. *That's where Layla's being held.* Past the walls of the city, plumes of purple and green smoke crested over the horizon.

Daegon shuddered, his fingers tracing the hilt of his sword. "The *Scourge*." Those words meant a lot more knowing the truth.

Gallant jumped through the opening and followed Daegon's gaze. "I just don't get it. If the Cardinals are in control of everything, why would they call that monster to Corporeal? We saw what happened to Terratoria. It will destroy the entire place."

Daegon peered at his hands, remembering his conversation with Jordell. It didn't matter how, but they needed to rescue her. If it were true, her survival became immensely more important. He breathed a sigh at the mounting odds, feeling a firm hand on his shoulder.

"Remember. We don't know how much of Raynor is still there." Gallant squeezed his hand, competing with the ill-fitting dark gloves. "Are you okay?"

Daegon stared into the distance, nodding. And just like that, an explosion rattled on the far side of the wall. A plume of black smoke puffed over the top, drawing the attention of the guards. An alarm blared along the streets, prompting Daegon to pull his sword. That was the signal.

Chapter Forty

Aramide, Jordell, and Vrest crept through their door leading to a market of people flocking through the streets. They slipped into the bustle, listening for clues to Layla's whereabouts, but the roar of the marketplace drowned out any specific conversation. The black bricks from the tunnel comprised every building. Other than the occasional tree strategically sprouted to give the city some contrasting color, every point, turn, and alley was aimed at efficiency. A group of people pushed them along, eventually spitting them into a section swarming with Corporeal soldiers, all adorned with their traditional black armor.

Jordell pulled Aramide and Vrest to a wall, and they peeked at the mass of guards surrounding a door adorned with the eye of Corporeal. "Aramide, is this familiar? Back together, protecting a Conjuror?"

Aramide chuckled, flattening himself against the bricks to stay hidden. "Like old times."

"I'm thrilled that I'm in the hands of two of the very best Protectors." Vrest rolled his eyes at their obvious pleas for validation.

Aramide reached and patted him on the back. "Oh, believe me. You are. When we're all said and done, maybe you too will turn into a monster."

Vrest wasn't well enough acquainted with Aramide to tell if he was joking or not, but took it in stride, returning the back-pat with a soft and cautious pat of his own. "So. My Protectors. What's the play? That room obviously has some importance if there's that many guards protecting the front."

"Yes. I would agree." Jordell leaned around the corner, eyeing the various options. "Where is Fabian? They should've made their attack by this point."

Suddenly, the soldiers began to shift and run. The entire city shook. Supplies dropped from the various shops that dotted the streets. In the distance, over the walls, a dark cloud of smoke plumed. The soldiers scattered, pulling their swords and sprinting toward the blast. An alarm blared. Initially in the distance, but the wave of noise soon flooded the streets. The plan was working. Fabian had done his job. After the commotion and chaos, one soldier remained to protect the entryway.

"I know just what to do." Vrest slipped to the front and flicked his wrist. Shadows leaped from the corners of the space, binding themselves across the guard's eyes like a blindfold. The man reached with his hands and attempted to grab onto anything in his immediate area. "Hurry and take him out."

Jordell hustled to the flailing soldier and slammed him into the wall. His body collapsed to the stone floor, leaving the door unattended. Jordell checked the man's breathing, confirming his unconscious state, and gave a thumbs up to Vrest and Aramide. "I think we're good to enter."

Vrest stepped over the soldiers with a theatrical flourish and cracked the door. Slivers of darkness swallowed any light emanating from the crevices. Vrest peered behind the door, gazing into the suffocating black. A long staircase, periodically laced with pockets of flickering torches, hugged the wall into the pit. Vrest took a step back and gestured toward Aramide. "After you."

Aramide shook his head and descended the staircase. Jordell trailed, closing the door behind them. On the right, the staircase continued with no definitive end. Stray torches lined the wall, guiding them deeper. On the left, an open chasm without a discernible bottom called to them.

Vrest poked his head over the edge. "They could at least include a handrail."

Jordell nudged him forward, carefully navigating each shaking step caused by the explosions above. Small pieces of dust and stone cracked away from the ceiling, clattering and echoing on the floor below. Still, they trudged forward. That mass of soldiers had to be guarding something.

Aramide called back, "You know, Jordell, you didn't have to leave."

Jordell traced his hand along the wall. "We needed to find the answers to what happened to Raynor. And I found them."

"You don't think that I wanted answers too? Did you think I was just running home to start up a tavern? Call it a day?" Aramide scraped his fingers along the wall, crumbling bits of mortar onto the staircase.

Jordell slowed his pace. Every decision he'd made angered somebody. "It all just happened so fast. I had to dig. I had to search, and I couldn't stop."

Aramide spun toward him. "And look where it got you. Followed. Attacked by the Congregation. Because you got too close. Without a plan." Vrest pinned himself against the wall, avoiding the clashing stares. "You're lucky I never gave up either. I built the Forlorn to defeat the Congregation. Avenge Raynor."

"I know. I appreciate everything you've done. But I had to get back to Daegon. That boy needed someone."

For once, Jordell wasn't hiding behind lies. Leaving something unspoken. His entire persona was about Daegon. And Aramide could live with that. Aramide nodded and descended the steps once again.

Frozen to the wall, Vrest was unsure whether to follow or run away. "Very well. Let's not fight. We still have a mission to resolve. Once we return, we can work on your marital problems."

Jordell shook his head, pressing Vrest to continue. They eventually reached the bottom of the long shaft. Their footsteps echoed across the seemingly hollow chamber, and the entrance behind loomed like a speck of light in the distance. The three regrouped at the base of the staircase, unsure of the next move. Without torches, they were surrounded by a wall of endless black.

Jordell's nose flared. "Do you smell that?"

Aramide sniffed the air and agreed. The air had been sterile. Cold and empty. But now it was thick. Musty. Smoky. They'd smelled it before.

"The *Scourge.*"

All three pulled their weapons and backed into one another to prepare for any unforeseen assailant. But nothing came. They were alone. Their echoing footsteps filled the void. And yet, the smell consumed them, pulling them deeper into the dark. Jordell lowered his weapon and snapped his fingers, unleashing a bolt of fire that floated above his outstretched fingers.

Vrest gasped. An army of Reapers lined the empty corridor. But instead of attacking, they stood frozen. Rows of hollow helms, waiting for a command that hadn't yet come. Searching quickly revealed that the only opportunity for escape was above. Trapped.

Chapter Forty-One

Daegon and Gallant descended the steep staircase into the city below. A city so familiar, and yet so foreign. As if it were molded after Malachi. The same curved, clean architecture and expansive use of brick imbued every structure. Statues of the stoic founders of Malachi rattled along their descent as explosions rippled in the distance, sending a wave of soldiers flowing across the street below.

The two cautiously trekked into the city, following a wide main street peppered with stores and peddlers. The plan had gone smoothly thus far. They'd alerted no guards or tripped any traps. They just wandered, their hands firmly on the hilts of their weapons, prepared to strike. Guards trickled from one of the hidden alleyways, sprinting toward the noise created by Fabian. As the soldiers unknowingly passed them, they continued unabated.

Despite the chaos, citizens continued their everyday lives with anxious glances at the sky. Daegon paused, pressing himself into the shadows. In the street, children played with paper streamers, laughing, completely ignorant of the threat looming just beyond the wall. The threat controlled by the very people they called their leaders. His father. He wanted to scream at them to run, but silence was his only armor.

Daegon looked up. Faint wisps of purple and green seeped over the distant city wall. It wasn't consuming yet, but moving. Stalking. Waiting. Lightning crackled from their destination, matching the purple hue of the incoming monster. The citizens around Daegon stopped. The four corners of the building focused the electricity deep into the sky, and the lightning split the clouds, bathing the city in a blood-red glare. This was it. This was the ceremony.

As the lightning struck, a citizen slammed into Daegon. The Cardinal's ceremony mustn't have been a common occurrence, judging by the chaos that suddenly developed not just on the wall, but in the streets. People screamed. Slamming doors mixed with breaking glass and echoing footsteps. The *Scourge* flowed into the city, casting its rancid stench into the mix. It's happening again. Daegon couldn't move. All he could do was stare. Stare at the chaos of yet another city sent into disarray.

Gallant grabbed his arm and yanked him out of his despondency. "We need to go now!"

Daegon shook his head, caught his feet under him, and followed closely behind. Despite the importance of their rescue, Gallant upheld his silent oath to protect and aided civilians as they sprinted through the street. He assisted an elderly man who had fallen among the wave of disorderly escape. Daegon lifted a child onto his shoulder and ushered her into an open door. A closed door would do nothing if the *Scourge* attacked, but the illusion of safety was all he could provide.

For every person they assisted, another two requested help. And they obliged, carrying them to safety, despite the wave of fleeing citizens. In the middle of it all, Corporeal guards, donning their black armor, also assisted. While the guards initially ignored their presence, instead focusing on providing safety to the various unfortunate individuals, eventually their gaze shifted to Daegon and Gallant, and they turned in their direction. Despite the façade of a good Corporeal soldier, the enemy had pierced their identity. Maybe. There wasn't really an opportunity to know if their cover was blown because Gallant thrust his spear in their direction.

Gallant's spear impaled the first soldier, who gurgled, eyes widening in shock, before falling limp to the ground. The sneak attack was successful, but they were obviously not part of their army. Three more soldiers pulled their swords, just as black and ornate as their armor, and waded through the chaos toward Gallant. Gallant deflected multiple strikes and parried their attacks to the reflective stone floor.

Daegon jumped into the fray of combat, dodging the passing civilians and pushing the soldiers back. The soldiers were no match for the two. Through their adventures, they'd learned each other's movements. Their tells. Daegon had learned the rhythm of Gallant's strikes. His timing. And they used it to dispatch their attackers quickly, flipping over one another's backs and coordinating their attacks with deft precision.

After another soldier succumbed to Gallant's spear, the remaining two soldiers fled into the throng of people still swarming to the exit. Daegon flashed Gallant a large grin, to which Gallant lifted his fist and angled it in his direction. Daegon met the fist with his and the two focused their gaze back on the tower, now with thick, persistent crackling spikes rippling from its obelisks. Explosions shook the city, but at this point it was unclear if it was Fabian's diversion or the *Scourge* savoring its meal.

At the far wall, the *Scourge* had fully entered, flowing into the city streets, but coalescing around the tower. The Cardinals had to be calling it, if not controlling it directly. Any idea to the contrary seemed impossible. And if their theory were true, then there wasn't much time left before their opportunity to save not only Layla, but the world, slipped through their fingers. Daegon and Gallant exchanged glances one more time before disappearing into the crowd toward the tower.

***

Jordell's hollow footsteps rattled through the empty chamber as he walked among the rows of Reapers. Their menacing forms shuddered at the presence of his manifested ball of fire, flowing between his fingers. And yet, their helms stared aimlessly, absent in their scarlet glare. As if in stasis, on-call for orders to attack. The darkness in the cave extended through each of the Reapers, spreading up the walls. The only reprieve was the distant, faint outline of the door at the top of the staircase.

A cool breeze slipped along Aramide's spine, causing his hair to rise. A breeze requires an opening at some point. He brushed his torch toward the vacuum of darkness. Nothing. Explosions rippled dust and debris onto the cave floor, raining on the pristine black armor of the frozen monsters. Fabian had done his job. They hadn't come up against any unwieldy guard presence, and he should've been preparing to leave at this point. There wasn't much time left.

Vrest slinked through the tightly spaced Reapers, brushing his fingers on their skull-encrusted armor. Dust failed to cling to his fingertips. He grimaced and flinched under the relentless explosions before shaking his head and cautiously continuing his examination. He wrenched a smile. "So it's true about these people... these...monsters." His hands slid off the smooth metallic armor, and he made his way to the front of the chamber. "I guess I wasn't as crazy as everyone made me out to be."

Aramide sat on the cool brick floor, letting out a sigh of pain. "Even after creating the Forlorn, I didn't think their infection would amount to this."

Jordell pushed his flame to fill the dark void. "We were all pawns in their game. All willing participants at one point."

Aramide gritted his teeth and shook his head. "It just feels disgusting to look at all of this. How many innocent people had to die for their charade to continue?"

"Too many!" Vrest ran up to a Reaper and smashed its face with his fist, causing the motionless body to topple over. A tear sifted out of his eye, bouncing onto the stone floor.

Aramide jolted from the floor and rubbed his hands together. "Something's not right." He glanced down. A waft of purple smoke flowed along the floor where he had sat. "Jordell."

"It's here. In the city." Jordell unlatched his sword and steadied his feet, balancing against the shaking chamber. The air grew thick, and the overbearing smell of fire and sulfur pushed out the oxygen. "We should get out of here."

Suddenly, the eyes on the Reapers lit up a menacing red that dotted the darkness. Their arms and legs shifted, emitting a machinelike crackle. They were awake. They were alive. Within seconds, their bodies pivoted toward the deep side of the cave. Toward nothing. Until a white light opened, temporarily blinding the group and unleashing a blast of cool air. The city. The Reapers marched toward the light in eerie synchronicity.

Without a second thought, Jordell heaved a large fireball into the center of the progressing troop, sending them scattering. They quickly pivoted their gaze before drawing their oversized swords and stepping in their direction.

Jordell yelled, "We can't let them into the city!"

Left with no choice, Aramide and Vrest attacked, and because of Jordell's desperate fireball, they had to think quickly. Vrest jumped and dove between two slicing blades, pulling three bricks from the back wall and smashing them into the Reapers' heads. Despite destroying one Reaper, another two took its place, causing him to bound out of the way.

Jordell and Aramide were back-to-back, deflecting the oncoming heaving slashes. What the Reapers lacked in speed, they more than made up for in power. Even one nick of their sword would cleave off a limb, ending the battle before it even started. Jordell rubbed his blade with his fiery hand, casting it aflame, and swung it at the beast. It clanged and slid from the metallic armor, leaving little more than an indentation in the monster. Sweating and surrounded, Jordell braced himself as a large arm shoved him onto the floor.

Aramide deftly spun between the creatures, blocking and counterattacking when he could. But he wasn't like Vrest. He wasn't like Jordell. Unable to conjure, he had to rely on his physical skills. And as he wasn't a spring chicken anymore, he could only maintain his dexterity for so long. He dodged the falling blade of a Reaper and pressed forward for an attack, digging the blade between its eyes. Despite the kill, a surrounding Reaper crushed his ribs, causing him to crash next to Jordell.

Blades passed through empty air as more enemies poured in. They were a never-ending flood of inescapable death. Designed killing machines meant to protect the *Scourge*. They couldn't let them into the city. Jordell wiped the blood from his chin and stood, readying his weapon at the two Reapers angling in his direction. He deflected their swords and released a flood of fire at their feet, separating the enemies and causing him to flash backward, smacking against the hard wall. He heaved in exhaustion, but the enemies continued to press.

A fatal swing came down on Jordell, but Aramide rushed and deflected it to the ground. "I can't let you go out like that." Aramide's back pulsed.

At this point, the end was determined. Reapers continued to fill the voids that Aramide and Jordell created, pushing them to the brink of what was possible. Vrest appeared and pierced an attacking Reaper with his rapier. A large scratch opened across the side of his face, and his hair glistened with sweat. "This isn't going how I thought this was going to go."

Aramide let out a grim chuckle. "How did you think this was going to go?"

Vrest pushed out with earth, creating a short-lived wall around the group, and scanned the room. "The city is above us, right?"

Aramide returned with a nod. "What are you thinking?"

Vrest grinned. "I have an idea."

He reached toward the ceiling. Slow cracks of light appeared, causing larger pieces of dust to collapse to the cave floor. The entire cave teetered, ready to drop. The Reapers continued to home in on Vrest, but Aramide and Jordell jumped in to protect their only viable plan. Their clanging steel paled compared to the deep, resonating cracks of the city floor above. Larger chunks flaked off, collapsing into the cave and crushing the monsters.

The Reapers suddenly pulled away from their attacks and scattered for an escape. But it was too late. Vrest screamed into the void, and the entire ceiling gave way, falling to the ground and smashing the monsters. The red eyes of the Reapers faded to black.

Chapter Forty-Two

C hunks of black stone collapsed to the floor as explosions rattled the city. The ornate walls of the Corporeal Temple gleamed unabated onto the crumbling streets. Daegon and Gallant huffed, unrelenting in their pursuit, slowing only to check the surrounding guard towers. They remained unoccupied. The purple and green smoke slowly circulated among the city's streets, increasing in both density and intensity. The familiar smell of fire and death tore at Daegon's nostrils, burrowing into the faded memories of his precious city.

They attached themselves to the decorated walls and slowly slid their way through the purple wisps toward the wooden entryway door. From the moment Fabian's distraction started, Gallant and Daegon balanced against the violent tremors, muscles twitching with every ripple.

Boom.

A sudden shockwave swept them off their feet. The temple's foundation cracked, splitting the black marble and forcing Daegon and Gallant to duck for cover. In the distance, buildings sank into the city's floor, and a cloud of black smoke mixed with the *Scourge's* signature haze.

Daegon held his hand on the wall, bracing for a potential aftershock. "What was that?" He covered his face, preventing the thin cloud of smoke from shooting into his mouth.

"Nothing good, that's for sure." Gallant pointed at the guard towers. "Whatever it was, we need to get inside. Between Fabian and the *Scourge*, there's no one guarding the front gate."

Daegon turned his back on the crumbling city and pushed the door open. The door fought against their shoves, but with Gallant's help, it shot open, allowing them to enter the dimly lit chamber. The *Scourge's* fingers attempted to stretch into the room, but Gallant thrust his back into the door, slamming it shut and sealing the monster out.

Filtered dust spanned the inside of the temple, which was decorated with strategically placed pillars holding the history of Corporeal. The paintings mirrored the history and wars of Malachi. But the victories conflicted with the stories he'd grown up with. The stories that he'd been taught. Daegon grabbed a torch from the wall and inspected the artwork, his feet barely echoing across the thick red carpet.

Gallant stayed at the door. "What is it?"

Daegon narrowed his eyes on the image of a Malachinian King, wielding a fiery sword. It looked like his father. In fact, it wasn't a resemblance. It was him. Fighting in the great battle between the City of White and the City of Black. What he'd learned from Aramide to be the great battle over the *Aether Stone*. Memories of the shining stone at the center of Malachi flooded his mind—the feeling it emanated to all his citizens. The power. The reason for all of this. *What is going on, Dad?*

Lightning crackled above, causing the hair on Daegon's arms to rise. The obelisks. The crackling increased in volume, accompanied by the faint drone of an ominous chant. In synchrony, the low hum of an ancient ritual had begun. Gallant followed Daegon and snuck through the room, eventually happening upon a large splitting staircase that led to the second floor. The red carpet stretched along the staircase, providing a cushioned walkway for them to sneak.

They readied their weapons and trod up the staircase. One step at a time, accompanied by the slow rumble of the collapsing city. It split into two paths that both curved onto the second floor. They stuck to the path to the right, using their weapons as guides that led them to the wooden floor above.

The red carpet ended at the top of the staircase, replaced by polished wooden planks. The air was sharp. Despite consuming everything around them, the *Scourge's* acrid aroma was noticeably absent. The purple lightning from the obelisks extended past the tips, flowing freely across the ceiling. The only way out was the staircase and a long, dimly lit hallway on the opposite side. In the center of the ceiling, an oculus leaked purple and green smog through its opening. It was here.

Five individuals dressed in blood-red robes gathered around a pedestal containing a young woman with black hair. *Layla!* She lay there, unmoving. Daegon's muscles coiled, urging him to jump in and rescue her, but he'd been lectured enough about attacking without a plan. It was five on two, combined with the potential for that monster to join the fray.

The leaking smoke flowed with slick vigor, reaching for the sacrifice. The chanting intensified, perfectly encircling her in dissonant harmony. Their voices bounced off the walls, filling the room and competing with the crackling above. Gallant squeezed his spear, his focus locking onto the leaders of the Congregation. The leaders of his lie.

Gallant and Daegon scanned the room. They needed a plan, and they needed it fast. But there really was nothing. Daegon quietly pressed Gallant, "We need to do something now, before it's too late."

The smoke filled the outside of the room, and the noticeably absent scent started to intrude. Burning flesh flared Daegon's nostrils, obscuring the ritual in the center of the room. Suddenly, a roar shook the chamber. The Cardinals raised their gaze at one another and said in unison, "It is here."

The oculus above cracked, widening enough for the smoke to flow freely. The dreaded mouth of the *Scourge* waited patiently in the crackling sky for its offering. There wasn't any time left. It had to be now. *Who needs a plan?* Daegon held his hand up to Gallant, jumped from his crouched position, and bolted at the Cardinals with his sword raised high above his head. Cardinal Bilari was the nearest enemy, and before he could react, Daegon's blade swung cleanly through his torso, cutting him in half. Blood splattered across the wooden floor, leaving Daegon's eyes wide at the clean kill. The nearby Cardinals jumped back from their partner's severed remains.

Except one. Cardinal Sooman. He stood at the head of the table, his hands clasped together in front, his voice unnervingly calm despite the surrounding chaos. "Daegon, there's no reason to resort to violence."

Sooman's eyes morphed to black beads, devoid of life, and the chamber succumbed to the darkness. The crackling lighting. The whirling clouds of his monstrous father. Layla. All gone. Daegon swung his sword at the void, only to meet air.

Just him and the splashing echoes of his footsteps. The floor sprouted figures, swirling into shapeless forms. They reached with their claws, dragging their formless bodies against the slick floor. Daegon tried to dodge them, but like the *Scourge*, they were oppressively everywhere. All he could do was survive. He slashed his sword at the nameless beings. "Layla!"

But there was no response.

Gallant crouched in the shadows. Daegon stood motionless, in a trancelike state, feet stuck in the pooled blood of the slaughtered Cardinal. The purple smoke obscured the room, blurring the chaos unfolding within, but Cardinal Sooman aggressively waved his hands in Daegon's direction. The remaining Cardinals pulled long, serrated daggers from their robes and circled him. At that cue, Gallant burst from the smoke, his lungs heavy from the thickness, and tackled Sooman to the ground, breaking the Cardinal's concentration.

The void shattered like glass, and reality ripped back to Daegon. He swung his blade just in time to deflect the incoming daggers. Gallant flailed on the floor, trying to maintain his spear toward Sooman. The Cardinals, who had attempted their attack, drifted off into the barrier of the consuming storm. They accepted it. Like it was their own, and they disappeared into the cacophony of destruction. He pivoted. Layla's hands and feet were bound on the table. His blade sliced cleanly through each of the straps, and he heaved her over his shoulder. It was difficult to bark any commands, but he threw his voice into the crackling roar of the storm. "Gallant, we have to go. Now!"

Gallant pushed from the older Cardinal and stood. They were trapped. Surrounded by a vortex of purple and green death. Daegon had lived this exact scenario before, but this time felt different. This one felt more exact. More final.

Cardinal Sooman pushed off his knees, shakily standing to his feet. "It's too late. We have to complete the ritual. The *Scourge* needs a new host."

Daegon spat in his direction. "You mean my father wasn't good enough."

Sooman's smile had grown vicious. Replacing the careful leader was a maw that resembled the *Scourge* itself. Blood dripped out of the corner of his mouth. "Your father is part of the cycle that keeps our world alive. Our city, alive."

Daegon threw his arm at the old man. "What do you mean?"

Sooman raised both of his hands and cackled. "You thought we were doing this for what? For power? We already had all the power we could have ever wanted."

"Then why…" Before Daegon could complete the question, multiple beams of colored light blasted from the cloud.

He skirted the shots and oriented himself in their direction. The hidden Cardinals had reemerged from the smoke, changed, deformed. Snaking vines of black sludge draped their bodies. Their hollow eyes stared, and their hands pulsed with energy.

Sooman took the distraction as an opportunity to move closer. Gallant raised his spear at the old man, the point digging into his flesh. Sooman said, "What did you think was going to happen coming in here? What was your plan?"

He was right. Between the swirling vortex of death and the three Cardinals poised to attack, they were stuck. Daegon spun, looking, desperate for an answer. The cloud acted as a wall, preventing life from pushing through. He looked up to the open oculus, straight into the eyes of the *Scourge*. His father's eyes, hoping that he would be there for him, just this once.

The room shuddered, and the roar of the storm became more literal. Like a beast, hungry for flesh, willing to accept the next closest approximation to food. Cardinal Mesa gasped as a barb ripped through her chest, splattering blood across the platform. Blood spewed from the corner of her open mouth. Her eyes drifted to her chest, and she tried to grab the barb. But it quickly withdrew into the smoke, leaving her body crumbling. Cardinal Luminara and Cardinal Drone jumped from the smoke, ignoring Daegon and Gallant. The vortex sucked at Cardinal Mesa's body, haphazardly scraping it across the wooden floor. The wet crunch of her corpse temporarily satiated the hidden roars.

Daegon continued to spin, holding back the invisible enemy with an outstretched sword. Gallant backed closer to Daegon, but the swirling chaos was going to explode. The Cardinals no longer had control. How anybody ever thought they could control that monster seemed like a far-off idea. The wall of death crept closer, exerting its suffocating presence. Even the Cardinals trembled at the swirling cloud, exhibiting the first sign of genuine fear. The oculus above overflowed with smoke, hiding the *Scourge's* face deeper within the cloud.

"There's no stopping the exchange." Cardinal Sooman stepped closer to them, despite the outstretched blades. His typically stoic voice grew desperate. "The *Scourge* needs Layla!"

Gallant jabbed his spear in front of Sooman. "Why should we believe you? The Congregation is a lie! Everything is a lie!"

Sooman winced, tipping the point of Gallant's spear away from his chest. "Sir Gallant. While I admire your bravery..."

Gallant interrupted the man. "You were supposed to protect us from the *Scourge*. Not wield it for some insane machinations."

"You do not understand the world like we do! The pain it can cause. The treachery. The betrayal." His voice petered out, exhausted by the memory of some hidden pain.

Gallant's tears streamed down his face. "I know! I was taught by you! I upheld your rules. Limited the amount of conjuring. The number of Conjurors. For what?" He stepped closer to Sooman. "Now I know the Congregation was hoarding power for themselves?"

Sooman's hands dropped to his side. His voice had grown hoarse from the yelling, and he shook his head in disbelief. "You know nothing, Sir Gallant. This land had its chance at peace without death. Corporeal betrayed everyone, and yet, who suffered? What these cities did to Mala..."

Gallant drove his spear into Sooman's chest. The Cardinal reached and grasped the shaft, but Gallant pushed deeper. Stabbing at the essence of his pain. Of his existence. Gallant let out an explosion of breath before collapsing to his knees, tears streaming down his face. "I'm sorry."

Sooman's voice shook, and his eyes grew wide. He stared at Daegon. "Keep the Memory."

He stumbled backward toward the smoke. A barbed tentacle stretched from the darkness, attaching to his shoulder, dragging him closer before ghost-white teeth erupted from the cloud and burrowed into his neck. Blood gushed from the wound, rendering his once screaming voice little more than a quiver. *No one, not even Cardinal Sooman, deserved a death like this.* In an instant, the cloud consumed him, pulling Gallant's spear into the chaos.

The roar of the cloud grew animalistic and swallowed the chamber. It still hungered. The clouds restlessly spiraled with the spark of the obelisk's persistent lightning. The heavy, sucking smoke quickened and spread across their feet. Screaming out in a moment of panic, the two remaining Cardinals spun blindly and dropped their hands.

Daegon lifted his feet from the carpet of smoke. The suction wasn't as powerful as expected. He murmured to himself, staring up at the smog piping into the room, "What are you doing, Dad?"

The swirling cloud grew more violent. Like the strong current of a river, Cardinal Luminara was swept off her feet, screaming as the smoke dragged her into its depths. The remnants of her screams died off quickly, replaced by the insatiable roar of the *Scourge*.

Daegon looked at Gallant. "There was a hallway right through there?" He pointed into the cloud, which had no discernible exit.

Gallant's mouth dropped. "You want us to run through that? Have you not seen what's happening to everyone?"

Daegon squeezed Layla. "I know it sounds crazy, but you have to trust me."

Gallant shook his head, forcing himself to believe. There was nowhere to go except through. Death was inevitable regardless of the option. He put his hand on Daegon's shoulder and followed him into the miasma.

Chapter
Forty-Three

The heat from the smoke filled their lungs, fighting for every scrap of oxygen. The cloud was suffocating, thick as tar, continuously pulling them to a halt. A terminal halt. Their sprint morphed to a lumber, and visibility reduced to mere inches. The purple lightning of the obelisks had fully mixed with the smoke, creating a blinding and powerful storm of chaos. Daegon shuddered as a scream rattled nearby, followed by the wet crunching of flesh. There wasn't time to survey what had just happened. Gallant's hand pulled at his cloak, and Layla was securely on his shoulder. Safe. He continued pushing forward toward the hopeful end.

They collapsed onto the floor of an ornate hallway, once decorated with commissioned paintings of Corporeal's past and ancient artifacts resembling times forgotten. Now, those same pieces of art were being used as shrapnel. Crushed, shattered, and destroyed. The *Scourge's* foul cloud ripped through the building with ease.

Gallant started laughing. "I can't believe that worked."

What brief reprieve from death existed quickly vanished when a long, barbed tentacle shot from the cloud and grabbed Gallant's ankle. He let out a scream, but the tiny needles of the creature's arm had dug in, pulling him ever closer to the cloud of doom. Daegon sliced through the tentacle, sending Gallant rebounding into the dimly lit hallway. Gallant shuddered as Daegon firmly placed his hand on his shoulder. "We're not through this yet."

Gallant nodded, took Daegon's hand, and they scurried down the hall. Searching for an escape. There had to be an escape. But every door they passed spewed that purple smoke. Every window shattered, the shards snapping under their boots. Layla's weight became cumbersome, but they trudged through the corridors, kicking through doors, and ignoring the roars that slowly closed in. The howling sky opened itself, ripping bricks from the ceiling and tearing down the surrounding walls. The *Scourge's* hunger was insatiable.

At the end of the hallway, they made their way to an outdoor balcony overlooking the city. The *Scourge's* smoky fingers firmly laced throughout the buildings. Daegon's heart raced. It was all too familiar, playing out like a bit of déjà vu. *What would Jordell say if he were here?* One by one, buildings slowly descended into the murky depths of the *Scourge's* hunger. His hands clutched the stone pattern of the railing. He needed an answer.

Tentacles wound their way up building after building, squeezing the life from every structure. Daegon covered his face as the statues above them were freed from their supports, barreling into their balcony. Suddenly, the balcony shifted, leaning into the city itself. Burdened with Layla, Daegon now had to balance to maintain his footing. The stone floor splintered between them, and the railing shriveled away into the cloud below. If only Layla were awake to hold the balcony together. He leaned against the angled floor as it started careening down; the cloud opened its mouth to their inescapable death.

A voice echoed amidst the noise, and the building froze midair. "Hey Daegon, Gallant, need some help?"

Vrest thrust his hands from a rooftop next to their collapsing building. Jordell, Aramide, and he had seen better days. Dust caked the dried blood smeared across their scarred faces. With shaking hands, Vrest lifted a bridge of debris between them. Aramide waved them over. "Hurry! He's not going to be able to hold it when the entire building collapses."

Daegon and Gallant jumped onto the makeshift path and scurried across. They collapsed onto the other side, keeping Layla safely on his shoulder. Jordell patted him on the back and pulled him up. "We're not through just yet. Come on!"

Daegon turned toward the temple one last time. Like a fungus consuming its host, the purple and green cloud swallowed the building, interlacing its tendrils through the windows and out every crack and fissure. The building collapsed in on itself, pushing the cloud of destruction deeper into the city. Daegon, now shaking with exhaustion, looked at Jordell. "Can you take Layla?"

Jordell nodded, throwing the Conjuror over his shoulder. They spun out of the rooftop and descended an outside staircase onto the now empty city street. Other than the subtle hints of purple and green smoke, they were free of monsters. But the *Scourge's* unmistakable smell permeated the air. At the end of the street, the exit stood atop the enormous staircase used to enter the city. They only had to make it.

Roars ripped through the alleyways. A small trickle at first. Then an all-out flood. It was coming for them. Wanted them. Needed them. Layla's head carefully bobbed on Jordell's shoulder. They couldn't have her. Small black vines wove their way through the mist, snapping at them with sharp tendrils, but they swung out at the attempts. Three menacing monsters pounced into their path, forcing them to stop. Their taut skin ripped open, gassing a purple and green cloud. Thundering steps announced additional beasts were already on their way. The cloud nipped at their heels.

Vrest jumped in front and heaved mounds of earth at the creatures. "Keep going! I can hold them off."

Gallant reached for the Loneseeker. "You can't defeat them!"

Vrest's laugh became stuck in his throat, and he pushed out a wall of stone, knocking Gallant back. "I don't have to defeat them. You helped me reveal the lies of the Congregation. I wasn't wrong." He created a Territorian wall between the monsters and pushed. "I only have to get you an opening. So, take it!"

Gallant closed his eyes and nodded. They pushed past the monsters, who desperately clawed for a piece of flesh as they swung their barbed tails and razor-sharp claws. Vrest's constant use of stone shields blocked every attempt.

The creatures tried to follow the group, but Vrest screamed, hurling block after block of stone. "Hey! Look at me!"

The monsters obliged, turning back toward him and letting out a wretched screech. Vrest pulled his rapier and readied the weapon's point at the creatures. He had run away from the *Scourge* and the Congregation for so long. Now was his opportunity to stand up and fight back. He closed his eyes and steadied his feet. The cloud slowly converged. The monster's fangs opened, and its claws splayed for an attack. Purple smoke smothered the battlefield, leaving behind the muted sounds of clanging metal. Daegon didn't look back. The triumphant roars of the monsters drowned out the hope. Their howls distracted them from their ultimate defeat.

They arrived at the staircase leading to the cave tunnel. El was at the top, inside the guard's quarters, rushing everybody inside. "What took you all so long?"

Aramide shook his head. "If you couldn't tell, we were a little busy." He gave her a gentle hug before descending into the tunnel.

Jordell, Aramide, Layla, Gallant. One by one, the group entered the tunnels, ready for their escape. As El entered the door into the hall, a thick wave of smoke surged through the room, slamming Daegon onto the floor. The *Scourge* wasn't done with him. The purple smoke filled every inch. Daegon rose from the floor, brandishing his father's sword. He yelled at El, "Close the door!"

This wasn't the first time she'd left him for dead. Hopefully, it wouldn't be the last. She closed her eyes and pulled the door closed, leaving him face to face with his father. The *Scourge* roared, and the purple smoke crackled with ferocious green lightning. Daegon stepped into the center of the room. "You want me, Dad! I'm right here!"

He walked to the doorway leading into the room and came face-to-face with the toothy maw of the *Scourge*. Of his father. The beady black eyes pierced the back of his skull, castigating him for yet another error in judgement. Always messing up. Daegon pulled his sword to his chest and screamed, "What are you waiting for? Come and get me!"

The *Scourge* took the challenge and charged, its heinous, fiery smoke filling the room, cutting off all light. The harsh crunch of the surrounding stones filled his ears before the entire building collapsed, adding to the carnage of the beautiful, black Corporeal floor.

Chapter Forty-Four

Daegon searched through the now smooth surface. His hands struggled to balance, and his eardrums screamed, blotting out any competing noise. The last memory was the collapsing crunch of the building, and then nothing. His eyes struggled to open, but a blinding light rendered objects into fuzzy, indiscernible forms. Almost indiscernible. Through his haze, the outline of a man's boots stepped closer.

"Wake up, kid."

Daegon's eyes cracked open, battling the pristine white light. He rubbed the fog away. The truth hit him. It couldn't be. The crest of his sword. The beast that destroyed his city. The man who led his city to salvation. Crouched in front of him, dressed in flowing black robes, was none other than the King of Malachi, Raynor. Daegon opened his mouth, but his father cut him off.

"It's good to see you, kid."

Raynor helped Daegon off the ground. He rose quickly; his injuries were more mental than physical. A large fountain cascaded through the middle of the courtyard. Just above, a balcony overlooked, staffed with soldiers wearing white armor. They were expressionless and stood ready. Above everything, the stark eye of Malachi watched over them. As he steadied himself, what had been an empty courtyard shifted into a busy market. Hundreds of people materialized from nowhere and went about their lives. His people. He recognized everything. The blinding white architecture, clean white attire—he was home. Daegon braced himself against the view of the city. "What's going on? Am I...am I dead?"

"Dead?" Raynor's deep, scratchy voice offered subtle comfort. He shook his head and pointed through the mass of people to the edge of the courtyard. "You still have to complete your Journey."

"My Journey?"

Raynor put his hand on Daegon's shoulder. "Like me, kid. You have to stop the *Scourge*."

Daegon looked past his father's finger to a younger blonde man dressed in pale white robes, carrying a bouquet of honeysuckles and peonies into a small stone shack. The man was familiar, yet the name remained just out of reach. An attractive young woman gave him a kiss on the cheek, and a child sprang to his shoulders. Their laughter cut a smile on Daegon's face. "Who are they?"

"Who?" Raynor folded his arms and stoically faced the family. "You don't recognize Grand Cardinal Sooman?"

Daegon's smile fell, and he stepped back. "What? He died!"

Raynor's voice answered in a quieter tone. "Relax, your knight friend ended him." He jerked his head back toward the family.

Daegon turned. The scene had changed. The surrounding figures scattered like mist, replaced by the white stone carvings of a new section of the city. As the new area materialized, he placed his hand on the adjacent wall. "Dad, where are we?"

Raynor didn't turn around, instead eying the sky. "You really can't tell? We're home, son."

Obviously. "How? Why are we here? How are we here?"

"Have you not learned?"

Daegon looked up. Shimmering above them was the light from their stone. *The Aether Stone*. In all its radiance, emanating its celestial power throughout the city. He'd always felt the power. The warmth, pulsing through him, but it wasn't until now that he truly understood its beauty. *It's everything.*

Raynor finally turned and smirked. "Everything is possible through the *Aether Stone*, Daegon."

Daegon looked back at his father. The scene changed again. His city had been set ablaze. Infernos tore through buildings, and citizens screamed in the streets, brutally being struck down by soldiers clad in black armor. Sooman's house returned. And then it was gone. Not in a haze of dreams, but in a ball of fire. The explosion collapsed the building, sending ripples throughout the city. The once joyous family that greeted the Grand Cardinal struggled to escape, and the flame consumed them, sucking them into the void of despair.

Daegon stepped back and looked for an exit, but Raynor raised his voice. "Relax! You can't be hurt here."

He was right. Daegon ran his fingers through the scattered embers consuming the nearby wall. Cool to the touch, not even acknowledging his flesh. Attacking soldiers ran right through them, slaughtering the innocent civilians fleeing for their lives. It was all too much. *Not again.* "What are we doing here?"

Raynor turned his back to Daegon and walked. "I'm showing you the history of our people. Or more accurately, our final minutes."

Daegon sighed and looked back at Cardinal Sooman's home. The Cardinal kneeled in front of his downed family, weeping over their bodies. The insatiable inferno spread but inexplicably shied away from the grieving man. Daegon closed his eyes and turned back to Raynor, and the scene had shifted once again. They were now in the center of Malachi, with the *Aether Stone* squarely in front of them. Its pulsating presence pushed against the destruction. The screaming pleas for help had died off, replaced by the ripe smell of charred flesh and soot.

Raynor paused and held out his arm as a barrier, gesturing for Daegon to watch. Five individuals, all dressed in blood-stained white robes, surrounded the *Aether Stone*. They chanted the same hymn he'd heard as they offered Layla to the *Scourge*. A beam of lightning shot between each of their hands, causing the *Aether Stone* to emit a white light that spread through the city, stretching into every void. Their eyes grew an eerie red, and they synchronously turned in Raynor's direction.

Raynor's hand dropped. His mouth stretched, revealing the familiar deep purple and green cloud that had followed Daegon from the destruction of Malachi. It gassed out of him and spread along the charred floor of his city. His father had been set loose like a disease. Daegon looked back at the Cardinals, their chanting growing in ferocity. *Or a cure?* The screams that rattled his core were no longer just of his people. Whether it was the attacking soldiers or his civilians, his father didn't discriminate. He slaughtered everyone. He destroyed everything. Until nothing remained.

The smoke filled the space like a smoldering campfire. It couldn't touch him, yet the scent remained as oppressive as before. Daegon swatted through the cloud, brushing away some of the blinding chaos, and through the darkness, the *Aether Stone* began to shatter. The five figures circled it, raising their arms in unison. Then everything went black. Or white? A powerful gust of wind smashed into him and forced him to the ground.

But it wasn't hard. It was soft. Daegon landed on a tufted carpet of green grass. A cascading mountain range circled a field and the burning in his nose vanished. The foul smell of the *Scourge* was replaced with a fresh spritz of honeysuckle. His hands splayed through the blades of grass. Behind him lay a wide lake. And his tree. Where it all began.

"Let's try this again." Raynor materialized and pulled Daegon to his feet.

Daegon faced the tree he'd used for fencing practice, practically taunting him for a rematch. But he knew there'd never be another fight. "Malachi was destroyed?"

Raynor nodded. "To prevent Corporeal from taking control of the *Aether Stone*, the leaders of Malachi banded together and destroyed everything. To them, the power to conjure was too powerful to be wantonly wielded."

"By creating the *Scourge*?"

"They did what needed to happen." Raynor turned toward the open field.

Daegon stared at his fingers. "Then...then what are we?"

Raynor stayed silent. He gazed at the field. Cardinal Sooman appeared, shaky and caked in dirt. The blood of his city stained his once-white robes. He held a glowing white shard, pulsing with a familiar, warm energy, and walked to the center of the field, where he collapsed. As he lay there, weak and battered, he buried the shard under the grass.

A beam of light erupted from the ground and pierced the sky. The ground around Sooman shifted, cracking and opening crevices of darkness. A white hue sprouted from the depths. Like a geyser, pristine marble bricks combined, building into the familiar architecture he'd always known. It spread over the field, eventually blotting out the soft grass. Daegon spun around. He stood in the middle of Malachi Manor with its towering walls and spraying fountains.

"What is this?" Daegon ran to the fountain and slid his hand through the water.

Guards filed in above them, their armor clanging as they patrolled the grounds. The town had come to life. Out of nothing. And it looked like home. Expansive buildings revealed a life untouched by the *Scourge*. Life absent of any knowledge of the atrocities of the Congregation.

Raynor walked to Daegon. "This is home, son." He walked through the courtyard, gesturing for Daegon to follow.

Daegon darted after him, childhood memories rushing back. From the bubbling curiosity of the apothecary to the melodic banging of the armorer, everything was familiar. Like he'd never left. Like they'd never been attacked. This was the Malachi he remembered. This was home. The memory that the Congregation desired to keep.

A still disheveled Cardinal Sooman rushed across the street and ran toward the house that'd been destroyed in the war. As he fervently knocked on the door, a woman and child greeted him, and he broke down into their arms. She rubbed his back, and the child squeezed his leg. Daegon looked at his father, who had a tear cascading down his cheek. They made their way into the home, disappearing into the faded memory. Raynor stepped backward, rubbed his face with his sleeve, and strolled down the revitalized street.

When Daegon turned around, they were face to face with the *Aether Stone*, transplanted and reformed in all its immense power. Daegon flexed his fingers, the opacity flickering. The beating energy of the stone had always been there. The intoxicating power that surged from it. But that very power was the answer to the *Scourge*.

Daegon said softly, "So what does this mean?"

Raynor didn't look at Daegon. He stared at the stone, basking in its transcendent warmth. "I think you know exactly what it means. You and Jordell have already figured it out."

Daegon nodded and put his hand on the hilt of his sword, his thumb tracing the encrusted symbols. "You know..."

Raynor interrupted Daegon, turning his head to look down upon him. "I'm proud of you."

Tears welled in Daegon's eyes. *What?* "I've hated you for so long."

Raynor chuckled. "Oh, believe me. I know."

Daegon reached and embraced his father, who firmly squeezed him back. His father nestled his head into his hair before pushing him away. Raynor shed a smile. "I'll see you soon."

Daegon fell backward, collapsing onto the white marble floor. His head bounced off the bricks, and everything dissolved into a fuzzy void. Aches radiated through every limb. He coughed and sat up, eyes wide open. *Where was he?*

"It's about time you woke up," a familiar voice said next to him. The concerning rhythmic beeping bounced next to his ears. Daegon looked down. Bandages covered his wrists and wires attached him to machines. "You're probably not feeling too good, huh? Take it slow." Daegon turned toward the voice. Jordell sat pensively, reading a book. A smile cracked Daegon's face.

Red hues bathed the room. A hospital? Multiple empty cots spanned the walls, complete with machines Daegon had never seen before. "We were right. Are right, Jordell."

Jordell cocked his head to the side. "I'm not sure what you're talking about."

"About the *Scourge*. The *Aether Stone*. All of it." The beeping of the machines grew quicker in pace and volume.

Jordell waved for him to calm down, his hand landing on Daegon's bandaged shoulder. "Alright, alright. We can talk about it later. I'm just happy that you're alive."

The beeping initially slowed down, but sped up when Daegon yelled, "Where's Layla!"

A nurse burst through the door, dressed in a tight blue uniform. "You're awake!" Despite the beeping of the machines, she calmly adjusted the settings on his monitor and pulled out a stethoscope to check his chest. Daegon shuddered under the cool steel but winced as his body creaked. "I'll alert Aramide that you're awake." She walked out of the room.

Daegon took a breath, continuing his question to Jordell. "Is Layla okay?"

Jordell stood from the chair and smiled. "Layla is alive thanks to you." He walked to the end of Daegon's bed, and the smile faded from his face. "It's the *Scourge*."

Daegon pushed onto his forearms. "What's happened, Jordell?"

"I'm not sure. Since the attack on Corporeal, the *Scourge* has been spreading indiscriminately to the core cities. The Forlorn cell in Embre recently went dark. It's getting bad."

Daegon stared at the pillows stacked under his legs. "It's because of us."

"Oh, kid, don't think like that."

Daegon's gaze rose. "It is. Without the Cardinals telling it what to do, it's going to continue to spread. It's going to protect Malachi."

Jordell ran his hands over the beeping monitors. "Well...we're going to have to figure out how to stop it then."

Daegon bit his lip. His father. "We already know how."

They stared at each other before Jordell shut his eyes and nodded. "I'll let Aramide know that there's a plan."

Chapter Forty-Five

Daegon was alone. His mind preoccupied with the constant beeping of the flashing machine, proof that he was alive. Or was he? Through the rotating flashes of the buttons, the room echoed with footsteps from behind the wooden door. Instead of the nurse who'd periodically checked on his vitals, a guard in leather armor entered. Their armor resembled more of an unfinished tanned hide than something that could stand up to the thin side of a blade.

The guard ground to a halt and locked his arms to his sides. "If you're up to it, Aramide would like to see you."

A wince accompanied Daegon's nod. As he lay in bed, he'd gotten used to his injuries. The extent of the damage had become a familiar throb. But now moving. Moving was unlike anything that he'd expected. The guard threw Daegon's arm around his shoulder and carried him away from the hypnotic trance of the beeping machines.

On the other side of the door, a dark hallway burrowed into the earth itself. Half-empty lanterns hung along the wall, providing just enough light to guide their steps. The right side of the hallway opened into a wide chasm. Voices echoed and metal bounced throughout the hollow space. Daegon approached the ledge; signs of life sprinkled among the darkness. People moved across makeshift bridges and down carved stairs. The never-ending network of caves spiraled to the bottom, which was filled with tunnels spanning in every direction.

All it took was a little movement for Daegon's body to function again. He dismissed the assisting guard, who motioned him along the pathway to a cracked door where a familiar voice barked commands. Aramide was at the front of the room lecturing to a group of Forlorn soldiers. He spun a knife between his fingers and gestured toward diagrams and maps pinned to the cave wall. Dozens of soldiers listened, in various states of excitement, prepared for a mission.

"You're alive." Aramide broke from his mission plans and directed everyone's attention toward him.

A murmur of approval rippled through the room, growing into a roar, and boots stomped against the stone floor. Daegon brushed his hair and scanned the hundreds of eyes that were solely on him. He didn't recognize anybody, yet their support was palpable. The chaos of the celebration made the dark room even more claustrophobic. He tried to step back, but the gloved hands of a Forlorn soldier joyfully pushed him back into the fray. The crowd pulled him through, ignoring his cries of pain, and brought him to the front.

Aramide grabbed his shoulder and jerked him close. "Without this man, our mission would have failed!" The crowd erupted again in a fervor of excitement. His name quietly built into a chant. "The man who took down the leaders of the Congregation! The masterminds of oppression!" The crowd's energy electrified once again.

Daegon leaned into Aramide and yelled a whisper, "Where are we?"

Aramide smacked his back. "You sir, are in Alexander. The home of the Forlorn!" He had a knack for riling up the crowd into excitement.

Arms waved in front of him, casting flickering shadows on the documents pinned to the wall. They were tracking the *Scourge's* movements. Black marks scratched Corporeal and Terratoria from the picture, and a blue peg stabbed the outline of Embre. His eyes tracked across the room. Layla stood in the back, biting her thumb as the praise flooded over him. She raised her eyebrows and offered a small wave. He wanted to run to her. Right there and then.

Daegon turned back toward Aramide. "I know how to beat it."

"Beat it?" Aramide quieted the crowd.

"The *Scourge*. I know its weakness. I know how to end the cycle."

Aramide stroked his mustache, scanning his sea of people. "Do you? And how did you find this information?"

Daegon turned toward the crowd. "My father. He showed me everything." The crowd erupted in quiet gasps and grunts. His secret must not have been a secret.

Aramide leaned back against the wall. "And how do you know the *Scourge* isn't just leading us into a trap? Why would it tell you how to defeat it?"

"My father is still in there." Daegon looked at Layla. "I trust him."

Aramide sighed. "I suppose we don't have many other options at this point." He pushed himself off the wall and stared at the *Scourge's* tracked trail. "What's the plan?"

"It's the *Aether Stone*." Aramide's head shot around at him. "The Cardinals destroyed Ancient Malachi to ensure that Corporeal couldn't possess it."

"Right. The story goes that the *Aether Stone* was separated into the five nations we know today. I learned history too, kid."

"That's the thing. The *Aether Stone* was never destroyed. It still exists." Daegon walked over to the map. "It's where it's always been." He paused. The memory of when he entered this world returned. Where his father first entered the world. He pointed at the Twinwood Forest. "It's home."

Aramide crossed his arms. "And what makes you think it's there?"

"In the dream...or vision...or whatever it was, I knew the landmarks. The Cardinals planted the seed of the *Aether Stone* to create a New Malachi, its citizens. The *Scourge* exists to protect it."

"And you're saying that if we destroy the stone..."

"It should destroy the *Scourge.*"

"And everyone in it." While finishing the sentence, Aramide walked over and put his arm on Daegon's shoulder. That was it. That was the plan. Aramide stood broadly in front of the room. "There you have it! We're going to the lost city of Malachi!"

The hushed crowd burst into cheers. Daegon searched the sea of people, but Layla no longer stood against the wall. When did she leave? How much did she hear? After he made it past the wall of people, he ducked into the nearest hallway and darted down a corridor. Everything was a tunnel. Dark. Enclosed. Endless. He peeked his head into every open room, but she was gone. Out of breath, he checked the dark chasm. In the distance, a figure climbed a set of stairs. Layla. *How to get there?* He bolted in her direction, ignoring the fire in his ribs, and found a narrow bridge leading to her location. The eerie sound of hollow footsteps rattled the room as he crossed the worn path. The air was stagnant, and the bridge rippled with unsettled dirt. He made his way across and climbed the staircase.

It emptied into an open chamber with a small hole of daylight peeking through the ceiling. The first sign of life in this entire underground city grew on the walls. Thick layers of wet moss provided much-needed color to the otherwise drab tunnels. A cool breeze pricked his skin as he climbed the last step. Layla stood at the rail, looking up at the sky.

Her voice echoed through the empty chamber. "Thank you."

Daegon stepped closer, the breeze catching his cloak. "Layla."

"For saving me. For not letting them turn me into that..."

Daegon wrapped his arms around her. "I know."

There it was again. That comfort. That safety. Nothing else mattered. He released and stood at the rail beside her. "We could run off, you know?"

She laughed before responding, "Run off? And leave millions of people for dead?" Daegon stared over the edge. His comforting smile had faded, but her soft voice was a precious melody to his ears. She said, "Maybe there's another way? There's always another way."

Daegon cracked a weak smile, and a tear welled in his eyes. "When I said that before, I think this was the other way."

Layla closed her eyes and took a deep breath. She shook, but pulled herself together, turned to the void and screamed. Daegon jumped back at the sudden noise. She let out another scream, refusing to hold back the pain. Daegon put his hand on her back and chuckled. She fell back into his arms, returning the laugh.

Daegon asked, "Do you feel better?" She smiled and gave him a hug. Daegon reached his hands through her hair and brushed her black locks. "I'm just a memory to be forgotten."

Layla pulled back and laced her fingers between his. "I will never forget you, Daegon."

She leaned in, and he met her halfway. It was a kiss of desperation, of promise, of goodbye.

Chapter Forty-Six

Distant footsteps echoed in the hall, waking Daegon from his sleep. Panting, he rolled over and smiled. Layla lay bundled in a thin cotton sheet. Her silky dark hair was perfectly bunched on the pillow. He lay back down, but his thoughts betrayed him. The flicker of the lone candle tried to outpace the darkness that sprawled across the flaky ceiling. Jagged edges reached for him, and the faint ripple of laughter broke his resolve.

He left the bed and creaked open the heavy wooden door, careful not to flood the room with light. The hallway was comparatively bright; a rough tunnel generously lit with candles. The right side of the tunnel had that singular opening overlooking the chasm below. Daegon stared into the depths of Alexander; pockets of houses were sprinkled amongst the assortment of chiseled paths and carved stairs. The chamber spiraled to the bottom where all the winding paths funneled to an endless number of tunnels, shooting in every direction.

"Daegon!" A voice echoed from down the hallway.

His head whipped around. Jordell, Aramide, and a handful of Forlorn soldiers sat around a dying fireplace. They had been there for a while, clear from the multiple bottles of booze strewn across the table, and the biting smell of something too sweet.

But they were still going strong. He entered the room. A rhythmic ticking drew him closer. Among the assortment of empty bottles scattered throughout the room, multiple clocks hung on the wall. The ticking of the clocks and the subtle cracking of the fireplace blended into the hollow, claustrophobic cave.

Jordell sipped his drink, grimacing as the fire raced down his throat. After completing the task, he raised his glass in Daegon's direction and said, "Your father would be proud."

Daegon froze at the door. His face contorted at the sudden comment, but he brushed it off and took a seat in one of the open chairs opposite Jordell.

Aramide sat up in his chair and scooted closer to Daegon. "You know. He talked about you a lot?"

What was with the pestering about his father? Aramide pushed the bottle of brown liquid in Daegon's direction, which he accepted. He grabbed an empty glass from the table and poured some of the mixture. He allowed the drink to enter his lips, and as he did, the hair on his neck rose. His throat scorched with a pleasant pain, pushing out the thoughts of the future.

Aramide laughed and leaned back in his chair, staring at the shadows on the ceiling. "'Everything was,' 'I can't wait for Daegon to see this,' or 'Daegon would love this.'"

His memories clashed with Aramide's words. He was always so callous toward him. So indifferent. Anything he did was never good enough. But what if he had changed? What if that vision was not simply an encounter with the *Scourge*? What if that truly was his *father*?

Daegon watched the ice cubes float in his glass. "Do we have a plan to get into Malachi? The last I remember, the *Scourge* destroyed it."

Jordell swirled his drink around. "Oh, it's still around. The *Scourge* can't hurt the thing it's protecting. When it brought us here, it shouldn't have been long before the *Aether Stone* recreated the city." He took a swig and raised his glass. "It'll be like nothing even happened."

Like nothing even happened. Daegon eyed the empty bottles scattered across the table. "Then I should be able to just walk right in, then? Right? I am the King, after all?"

Aramide rubbed his red mustache and kicked his feet onto the table. "You know. It might actually be that easy."

Jordell leaned forward in his chair. "It might be. I assume the *Scourge* knows what we're going to do, based on it essentially telling you how to kill it." Jordell reached across the table and poured the rest of the bottle into his glass. "I would expect heavy resistance of some type."

Daegon took another sip of his drink, no longer affected by the fire. "How so?"

Aramide glanced at his soldiers and hissed through his teeth. "I have intel that the Reapers are migrating to the forest north of Shishbash."

Daegon asked, "North of Shishbash?"

Jordell sat there, unmoving, his voice taking a more somber tone. "Right where you ended up. The Twinwood Forest."

Aramide said, "Like we said in the debrief. Your killing of the Cardinals has caused the *Scourge* to enter an unpredictable pattern of behavior. It used to follow the rules laid out by the Congregation. But now it's attacking everything... Corporeal... Terratoria... Embre...it won't be long before it comes for Shishbash."

Daegon set his drink on the table. "What do you think it's targeting?"

Jordell stoically said, "That's the thing. There's no clear sign. It's razing everything. Slaughtering innocent civilians and destroying the very villages that have helped us so much."

Aramide spread his hand on the table, closer to Jordell. "We're not sure."

Daegon interlaced his fingers. "I can take a guess." Aramide's eyes turned toward Daegon. "The *Scourge* was created to protect the *Aether Stone*, right?" Aramide nodded his head at the known information before Daegon continued. "If everything but Malachi was destroyed, who would pose a threat?"

Aramide rubbed the rim of his drink. "I see." He sat swirling his glass, the ice crackling in the amber liquid. Aramide threw the drink down his throat and slammed the glass on the table. "Then we'd better finish this quickly!"

Jordell laughed and followed Aramide's chug. "Who would've thought that we'd have two chances to save the world?"

The joining soldiers threw their drinks back as well. Aramide stood and brushed off his pants. "Let's meet at the bottom of Alexander tomorrow morning. We can use the blast tunnels." He walked out of the room and laughed. "I'd better get paid handsomely for returning a King to his kingdom."

The fire sizzled as the soldiers doused it with water, the smoke filling the already enclosed space. Daegon watched the white wisps rise and balled his fist before turning to walk out of the room. But Jordell called for him.

Jordell, who had enjoyed more than his fair share of drinks, carefully navigated the room. He held himself up on the wall with one hand. "You know, regardless of what happens, this will be our last adventure." Jordell pushed himself off the wall and stood confidently in front of Daegon.

Daegon knew the end. He'd already lived the outcome in his mind multiple times. With his father. With Layla. Now with Jordell. He nodded, the stale ticking of the clocks filling the silence. Jordell reached out and threw his arms around Daegon's shoulders. Was it the booze, or genuine affection?

Jordell whispered in his ear, "Your father was always right about you."

Why did everyone know his father better than him? Pushing through Jordell's toxic breath, he said, "My father never gave me the time of day."

Jordell's face softened as he pulled back. "He was harsh, yes, but he cared." Jordell dropped one of his arms from Daegon's shoulders. "Aramide was right. He talked about you all the time. With every new thing he encountered, he couldn't wait to bring it back to his son."

Daegon eyed Jordell's burned hand. "You'd returned all those years ago. Why couldn't you just tell me what happened?"

Jordell let out a hearty chuckle. "Between the Congregation knowingly letting me return to Malachi, and the slow realization of what we were, did you want me to just drop that your father had been transformed into a terrifying smoke monster?"

"It would have been something." Daegon's biting retort caused Jordell to drop his other arm.

"To be honest…I didn't know how to tell you." Jordell's eyes drooped to the floor.

Daegon inhaled and closed his eyes. He remembered everything Jordell had done for him. The sparring matches. The political games of a leader. The leader he needed to be. Daegon was alone until Jordell returned, removing some of the sorrow that plagued his childhood. He had every right to be upset with the man for concealing the world from him. But he couldn't. Daegon let out a soft, "Thank you."

Jordell's eyes glossed over. "I trained you to the best of my ability. And look at you now." His hand returned to Daegon's shoulder. "Raynor would be proud of you." Daegon's eyes mirrored Jordell's before Jordell continued. "I am proud of you."

Tears blurred his vision, and he pulled Jordell into a powerful hug. Jordell patted his back. Daegon didn't know what to say, defaulting to the only phrase that seemed to work. A phrase that had been uttered so many times that night. "Thank you."

Chapter
Forty-Seven

Daegon awoke to the synchronized march of soldiers traversing the halls. Alexander came alive. Stinging steel clashed amongst the burrows; the rapid clatter of climbing feet charged through Alexander's dense maze. Daegon took the nearest flight of stairs and descended into the depths of the city, where the flicker of faint candles illuminated a growing group of soldiers. Upon reaching the bottom, a troop of Forlorn escorted Daegon to the network of tunnels where Aramide waited with Gallant, Layla, and Jordell.

At least thirty tunnels extended in all directions. The faint repetition of life echoed from the depths, though the exact tunnel was impossible to pinpoint. Wooden carts with wide wheels extended from the nearby wall to the floor above. The tunnels pulled him closer, beckoning him to join before Aramide nudged him.

Aramide said, "The blast paths are pretty incredible. They're how we get around so quickly."

"Blast paths?" Daegon glanced at Layla, then back to the tunnels.

"Yeah. With the help of a little conjuring," Aramide gestured toward two women wearing brown cloaks. "We're able to send our carts here in all directions, arriving at just the right location.”

“And one goes to Malachi?” Daegon eyed the shadows.

“Well, no…the Twinwood Forest. Right outside Shishbash. But if what you and Jordell said is correct, it should be right there.”

Daegon climbed into the thick steel cart with Gallant, Layla, and Jordell. Scratches scuffed the sides, and burn marks dented the rear. A faint track hid in the stone surface below, flowing into the path.

Jordell gripped the cart. “Will you be joining us?”

Aramide walked beside the cart and rested his hand on the cool steel. “We’ll be there shortly after to assist. I’ve delivered word to nearly all my Forlorn sects to meet in the Twinwood Forest on orders to delay any threats as long as possible.” His eyes tracked to Daegon. “I don’t know how long we can hold the Reapers off.”

“I’ll get it done,” Daegon said, Layla’s soft fingers intertwining with his.

She silently mouthed, “We’ll find a way.”

Gallant slapped his hand on the metal cart, sending an echo into the darkness. “I think we’re good to go, then. Let’s return this King back to his castle.”

Daegon bit his lip and shook his head. “The last time I saw Malachi, the *Scourge* was leveling it. I can’t shake the smell of the city out of my memory.”

Gallant put his hand on Daegon’s shoulder. “Hey. We’re going to do this.”

Layla put her hand on his other shoulder. “Together.”

From the front of the cart, Jordell delivered an affirmative nod.

Aramide smacked the cart and yelled to the Forlorn Conjurors. It was time to go. The cart wheeled to the front of the tunnel. It shook and clicked, locking into a section of the track. Two Conjurors stood close. Aramide delivered a nod, and the two threw a mountain of fire at the rear of the cart. Daegon's back slammed into the metal and the darkness blurred against the whipping walls. An explosion roared through the tunnel, fading the passing sections of the track. The track went dark, but a flicker of light gleamed at the end of the tunnel. While faint at first, the speed of the cart made it expand quickly. Instead of the expected crash, the cart came to a soft stall under a metal grate. Grass reached through the rusted holes, pulling a sweet trickle of whispering insects.

Daegon pushed the grate; the familiar scent of honeysuckle greeted him. His hands met a soft carpet of dense grass. A cool breeze whistled over the tunnel, and the push and pull of a nearby wave crashed against his ears. He helped the others through, freezing at the white marble of Malachi's walls peeking over the canvas of emerald trees. *Home.*

Jordell placed his hand on a nearby tree, surveying the forest. "Be prepared for anything. We're in the *Scourge's* territory now. I'm sure it already knows we're here."

Layla nodded, igniting a small fireball in her hand. Gallant pulled his spear from his back and angled its point. Daegon drifted toward the city, his sword slicing across the blades of grass, but hesitated at the quivering branches above scraping across the rustic bark. A clamor reverberated from deep within the trees. The group backed into one another, their weapons prepared for an incoming foe. The noise morphed into a rush of hooves beating against a treaded path. Daegon's heart met the pace of the hooves, but dropped at their presence. He knew the riders. He lowered his weapon and stepped forward, the cavalcade of soldiers circling with swords drawn.

"King Daegon! Sir Jordell! You're back!" the lead knight in full plate said, ripping off his helmet.

Daegon stepped away as the horses kicked up dust but returned a smile at the instantly recognized face. "Sir Geoffrey!"

The horses shifted from side to side, clanging the riders' armor against their saddles. "We thought you were lost."

Daegon put his hand on Geoffrey's horse. Its deep beauty coursed underneath his fingers. "What happened here, Geoffrey? What do you remember?"

Geoffrey's dark brown eyes rose. "What do you mean?"

Daegon turned to Jordell. "The day we vanished. What do you remember? What happened?"

Geoffrey searched the stretching trees, shifting under the persistent breeze. The quiet chirps of birds vanished. He turned back to Daegon. "You and Jordell were on a hunting party after your coronation." Geoffrey returned his attention toward Jordell. "And never returned."

Daegon stepped away from the horse and put his hand on Jordell's shoulder. "I see...well, we're back now. And these are our friends Layla and Gallant from the nearby city of Shishbash."

"Shishbash?"

Daegon chuckled. "We're not as alone here as we thought, are we?"

Geoffrey, who at first looked confused, cracked a smile. It dropped quickly as the forest moved beneath their feet. Daegon knew that feeling. The thunderous footsteps radiated from deep within the forest but quickly approached. The silent birds ripped from the canopies and scattered. Daegon spun through the group. "We have to get to the city. Now."

A shadow stretched through the woods, emanating the deep, vibrant colors of the forest itself. Daegon looked up, praying for a rain shower, but his stomach squirmed at the purple and green tinge that stalked them. The vibrations shook tree trunks, dropping stray branches onto the forest floor. The horses whinnied and jumped onto their hind legs, pleading for Daegon to move. He grabbed Layla's hand and started for the castle. Jordell and Gallant readied their weapons, following closely behind. Geoffrey pulled at his helmet, commanding his troop to join.

The horse's hooves clanged against the path, filling the forest with a frenzy of scattering wildlife. The field in front remained bare, littered with a stray tree that shielded a passerby from the glaring sun. Malachi never had enemies. Traps and barriers were a foreign concept to a city too proud for its defense. Unbeknownst to the city, the *Scourge* acted as a perpetual watchdog. His sparring tree, shifting at the pulsing ripples of Lake Kimset, greeted him with familiarity. His sword firmly entrenched within its bark. If times weren't so dire, he would've taken time to savor the moment. He turned to the group. Black metal glinted in the trees—hulking, skeletal monsters.

Geoffrey sped through the forest, his troops close behind. His reign as head Kingsguard would end quickly. A giant sword erupted from a bush and swiped with haste, cutting through his midsection. His eyes grew wide. The pain was sudden, but the wave of anguish ceased as his top half sloughed off the horse, collapsing to the forest floor. The horse, coated in red, quickened its pace and whinnied, fueling the footsteps into an aggressive fervor.

Daegon lowered his face. While Geoffrey and he weren't always cordial, their relationship was one of respect. Geoffrey had always done his job, protecting his father with a passion that was becoming of a Kingsguard. Even in Raynor's absence, he'd made sure that the city was safe. That he was safe. And for that, he'd be forever grateful.

Daegon sprinted alongside the others, waving his hands at the guards manning the front gates. "Open the gates!" The deep vibrations and clicking hooves drowned his voice. "Open the gates!" Barring a feat of conjuration, he did everything to get their attention.

The white marble he'd snuck in and out of for so many years finally creaked, the turning gears entering into a chorus of noise. The gate hefted open. Soldiers stared, mouths agape at the return of their King. *With the Scourge and Reapers following behind, was the bewilderment because of the monsters or of him?* The gate opened just enough for them to slip into the city. After everyone entered, Daegon yelled for the guards to seal the gate, to which they obliged with a hearty salute.

As the gate closed, the stalking footsteps of the monsters ceased. The Reapers stood lined at the edge of the forest, perfectly spaced with their weapons sheathed on their backs. Their glowing red eyes fixed on the city, unmoving and ready; the *Scourge* loomed ever closer.

The gate slammed shut, and the locking mechanism clicked into place. Daegon faced the wall of Malachinian citizens. Their surprise mirrored his own. Whispers of his name scattered amongst the group, but Daegon pulled his sword and pointed it at the sky. "Malachinians! Prepare for battle!"

These were his people. This was his kingdom. For a moment, he feared they might overthrow him or reject him as their King. He'd disappeared. Left the city to fend for themselves. It would make sense. Instead, the lag in the crowd's response erupted into a wave of cheers that radiated into the pit of the city. Armored soldiers clanged their shields, and sword blades stung the air.

Daegon brought the group to the top of the wall, their presence taunting the purple and green cloud that stretched over the city. The vibrations that haunted his memories returned. Daegon looked out at the distant battlefield. The Reapers began to stomp their feet.

Daegon grabbed Layla. "We have to get to the *Aether Stone*. It's the only thing that can end this."

Daegon signaled Jordell to lead the army on the wall before darting into the city with Layla. The thundering boots of the Reapers pushed forward, creeping their way closer. Gallant followed Daegon, but Jordell jerked him by the cloak.

Jordell said, "Where do you think you're going?"

Gallant shook his shoulder. "Daegon and Layla may need my help."

Jordell dug into his pocket, pulling out a rattling chain. The gold had faded to a warped black. "I pulled it from the fire that night. Figured you might need it again."

Gallant twisted the discarded necklace between his fingers. The Eye of the Congregation. He looked up at the flag flying at the central keep, bearing the same all-seeing eye, and squeezed the necklace into his fist. He turned to Jordell, eyes glassy. "Thank you."

"All of that training. Under its watchful eye. Let's not let it go to waste. This city needs a captain. Be the leader you were born to be." Jordell pulled his sword and faced the wall, giving Gallant an approving nod.

With a thunderous voice, Gallant said, "Malachinians, you heard your King! Rain fire!"

Chapter
Forty-Eight

Daegon and Layla descended the stairs, joining the throngs of screaming people scattering into the nearby buildings. Above them, streaking fireballs spat out from the wall and crashed into the outside offenders. The *Scourge's* green and purple cloud roared overhead, emitting crackling scratches of light that blasted the city with unrelenting devastation. The smell of death flared Daegon's nostrils. *Just like Corporeal and Terratoria.* Below, his citizens floundered against the unknown enemy.

The city violently shook, raining white bricks from the tops of the buildings. The *Scourge's* lightning scarred the city as the cloud flooded the streets. Swirling plumes of destruction reached through the courtyards, collapsing buildings and plucking citizens from the safety of their windows. Crunching stone railed against the Malachinian soldiers, their shields failing at deflecting the jagged debris. It was happening again. But this time, there was a plan.

Daegon checked a side street; a plume of purple, crackling smoke flooded toward them. He grabbed Layla's hand, pulled her into the nearest room, and slammed the door just in time. The door bowed, rattling at the hinges. The cloud outside searched for life. Any life. Wet gasps for breath replaced the screams that had joined him in the courtyard. They backed away from the door and searched the room, made difficult by the roar that hungered just outside. It was a storehouse. Half-empty crates of unworked leather and polished steel stacked against the back wall. Several small candles lay on the boxes, creating pockets of light for them to search. The narrow windows leaked putrid purple smoke. At the rear of the room, a stone staircase led to the second floor.

Daegon pulled Layla up the staircase, their footsteps drowned by the outside noise, and pushed through the door. The building opened onto a rooftop that stood squarely in the vision of his father. They stopped, the destruction of Malachi burning into the mind like a memory played on loop. Daegon squeezed her hand and shook his head. Despite knowing the truth, he still felt their pain. Their fear. The *Scourge* ripped through the streets like a broken dam, swallowing the city whole. And there was nothing he could do.

"Daegon!" Layla pointed at the large crystal emanating from the center of the city.

There it was. The cause of all of this. Daegon nodded and sprinted to the edge. The roofs of the nearby buildings lined up perfectly. He yelled through the destruction, "I think we can make the jump!"

There were few options. The crunching stone beneath them opened into the swirling cloud below. Daegon and Layla sprinted for the edge, held hands, and jumped. The deadly smoke flowed beneath, reaching for their feet, barely missing its target before they collapsed onto the adjacent roof. Daegon pushed to his feet, but Layla lay there laughing, staring at the churning sky. *At this moment?* He envied her ability to find levity in this chaos. He took a moment to smile before reaching out a hand and continuing onto the next roof.

They bounced from roof to roof, approaching the heart of the city. Daegon winced at the sickening snap of nearby bones, and the smell of fresh iron flooding the air. It would all be over soon.

The *Aether Stone* was fully within view. It pulled at him, and a piece deep down wanted nothing more than to succumb to it. Daegon closed his eyes and embraced the warmth. He looked down at his hands, the faint flicker of opacity rippling from its power.

Layla stepped behind him and grabbed his hand. "We're going to find a way."

He wanted to believe her. He needed to believe her. But he was on a collision course with what his father had brought him here to complete. The Journey. His fate was erroneously tied to the cloud that so callously stoked fear into everyone he loved. He knew the way. The only way. If only he could relive the previous night, lying there with Layla, their bodies intertwined. He closed his eyes and pulled his sword, a glint of blue shining against his boots.

The roof rattled and bowed toward the center, pulling them from the edge of the building. A loud screech shot from the alley, hungering for the opportunity for flesh. Long, jagged nails reached over the railing, ripping into the stone. It pulled onto the roof. A grotesque, malformed monster bled from its maw. Slender, bladelike arms extended into the stone floor. Stretched skin ripped at the seams, exuding a purple and green mist, and a set of razor teeth screamed with pain.

Daegon jumped in front of Layla and pointed his sword at the creature. She placed her hand on his shoulder. "We do this together."

A fireball shot from beside his ear and blasted a hole in the creature. It screamed. Festering black liquid spilled onto the ground, but the mist stretched from its crevices, mending the wound. Daegon rushed with his sword, backed by the constant barrage of fireballs. It met the creature's bladed arm and sparked to the ground. The creature countered with the opposite arm, and Daegon jumped over the attempt. He swung, severing the arm, and the creature staggered.

It sprang toward Daegon. He deflected the relentless attacks, but the severed arm slowly repaired itself. He had to do something. It snapped at him, but a fireball met its mouth at the last second. Daegon swung his blade through its jaw, separating the two halves from one another. It fell to an exposed knee, but Daegon pushed the fight, slicing at the monster vertically. Daegon's sword embedded itself in the roof, and the creature lashed out with its arm. A wall of earth erupted from the ground, catching the attack before it hit. Daegon pulled his sword from the stone and cut through the clamped arm.

Its now disfigured face screamed. Layla threw three more fireballs at the monster, while Daegon slashed at its belly, separating the creature into two sections. The mist from its stretched skin reached for the halves, attempting to repair itself, but it couldn't move. Layla stomped her foot. A fire ignited within her, exploding out. She screamed, and a pillar of stone erupted beneath the beast at a sharp angle, launching it off the roof.

Sweating and ash-stained, Daegon cracked a smile. Layla's hair gently fell back over her face, and she lowered her hands, shaking but standing tall. The sky rumbled above them, split, and struck the roof with a green bolt of lightning. White light engulfed the rooftop, and the force of the concussion pushed Daegon and Layla into the misty streets.

Breath rushed from Daegon as he crashed onto the hard marble street, now painted with a slick layer of blood and ash. The street twisted with a persistent ping, and a beacon of light stretched through the cloud, forcing Daegon to his elbows. The sticky burn of the fog stabbed at his lungs. As he staggered to his feet, he swung his sword at the surrounding darkness, meeting nothing but the hollow wisps of fog.

Layla. Where is she? Against his better judgement, he screamed into the void, "Layla!"

Silence. Only the distant screams of his civilians fading to their inevitable end. In front of him, the *Aether Stone*. He covered his face and pushed through the darkness. She couldn't have fallen much further. Static and heat rippled across the hair on his arms; an orange hue added to the colored smoke. Fireballs exploded, crumbling the remaining walls of a nearby building. He picked up his pace. *Please be alive.*

Layla deftly avoided the attacks of multiple smaller creatures, their sharp skin leaching the purple mist. She was winning. Fireballs rained from the air, ripping through the creatures with ease.

Daegon yelled out for her.

Dirt glazed her purple robes, and she bore the scorch marks of a fireball placed too close. Despite being in the throes of battle, she flashed Daegon that smile. That real smile. Daegon rushed to her, but she yelled, "Get to the *Aether Stone*! Finish it!"

Daegon hesitated. She had everything under control, but he couldn't abandon her. Not again. He took another step, but she held out her hand. She raised a block of stone and dropped it on an attacking monster, flooding its acrid blood across the street. "I'm fine! Get to the stone!"

Daegon took a step back, then spun, running for the light. The cloud enveloped him, coating him in a cloak of toxic smoke. The purple, flowing walls of the *Scourge* closed in. But only temporarily. The *Aether Stone's* light pierced the veil, opening the courtyard and drawing Daegon closer. He was now within feet of his existence.

The crested jewels on his father's sword vibrated against his palm, knowing what would happen the second he plunged the blade through the stone's shell. He had arrived at the end of his Journey. Despite what Layla wanted. What he wanted. There really was no other way. His entire journey. His life had led to this specific instance. It's what was supposed to happen. It's what Raynor wanted to happen. To finish what he had started. To follow in his footsteps.

Daegon raised his sword and plunged it into the *Aether Stone*. The roaring clouds above descended and pushed into a thick wall around him. Then stopped. Time stopped. Everything became silent. The screams and crashing stones faded to a quiet whisper. The pulsing glow of the stone taunted him.

"I can't believe you thought that would work."

Daegon stared at the blade, supposedly plunged into the *Aether Stone*. Another sword with identical runes parried the attack. His father. The long dark hair he'd always known flowed from a man standing next to him, but there was something off. Something dark. Compared to his encounter after the battle of Corporeal, this Raynor was slumped at the shoulders, and his hair fell in front of his eyes. He was hollow. Like a husk filled with hate. A marionette of death and destruction.

Daegon withdrew his sword. "Dad?"

Raynor's face failed to move. He picked up his sword and swung it at Daegon. The movements, while robotic and lifeless, were deadly. He alternated between slicing and stabbing, but Daegon parried the attacks, continuously blocking Raynor's sword into the white marble courtyard. He countered an attack, swinging his blade across Raynor's chest. A deep gape ripped into his flesh and green mist flowed from the wound. Raynor remained unfazed, refusing to react as his chest filled with the cloud. Relentless swings hacked at Daegon, trying to protect the stone.

It was just them. Their clanging swords provided the only proof of life within the frozen swirl of purple. Daegon blocked an attack and threw Raynor to the ground. "Dad! Are you in there?"

The lifeless body rebounded from the floor and sprang at Daegon, its sword chopping and swinging at anything it could touch. Daegon's training with Jordell replayed in his head. Retreat, step, push step, and swing. The dance of sword fighting had become second nature to him. Every battle he'd ever fought culminated here. In this moment. The supposed nameless, faceless opponents he'd fought always had a face. And it stared at him now.

Their swings aimed high in the air, and sparks spat onto their heads. The beady, soulless eyes stared into Daegon's, ready to pounce. Raynor opened his mouth, but the green mist had infiltrated every crevice. As if his entire body were a vessel for the *Scourge*. "You were never good enough."

The phrase that defined his childhood. It was his father's voice. But the *Scourge* vibrated the disappointment. Failures flashed through his mind. His failure to live up to his father, failure to be the King Malachi needed, failure to protect Layla from the Reapers. Through those failures, he persevered, embraced his father's criticism, and followed in his footsteps. He shook his head at his success: crowned King of Malachi, saved Layla from the Cardinals. And he was going to end the *Scourge*.

Daegon pushed the swords into the air, recoiled and stabbed his sword right through the heart of Raynor. It cleanly pierced the flesh, but hit resistance. He pushed harder. The roaring clouds that had been placated by the stone flooded back into the courtyard. Raynor's beady eyes exuded a bright white light, and his body faded away, transforming into the *Aether Stone*. The entry point splintered, exploding with a bright white light.

The surrounding clouds dispersed, bringing the white marble courtyard into view. The slick brick buildings he'd grown up with overtook the dark destruction of the purple cloud. He wasn't alone in the courtyard anymore. As the cloud dissipated, armored guards with drawn swords trickled into view. Daegon's sword remained firmly in the stone as he turned, using the hilt as a crutch. The beauty of his city revitalized. One last time. A bright light silently extended from the stone and ran through the city.

Chapter Forty-Nine

Layla smashed a fireball into the creature's chest, but it pressed the attack. A bladed arm reached out with a deft slice, and she ducked and bounded backward. Another monster crept up the building behind her, purple mist seeping out of its razor teeth. Her arms grew heavy, and the once powerful fireballs faded to a spark. She only had to hold on until Daegon could destroy the *Aether Stone*. Whenever that was. The faint outline of the Stone glowed through the purple mist, but there was no sign of Daegon, left alone to battle whatever demons lay in the darkness. She stood firm and hissed as two creatures crept toward her, their bladed arms dragging across the ground.

Layla plunged her foot forward, screamed, and pushed with everything that was left. Fire erupted from her hands, consuming the monsters. Their screams sizzled underneath the blazing streak of color. A white light flashed through the streets, and her blaze sputtered. Under no control of her own. She flexed her fingers; the last wisps of flame faded away. When the ball of fire had subsided, the creatures were gone.

Layla spun as the smoke dissipated around her. The ominous purple and green cloud faded to the brilliant sunshine that reflected across the white marble bricks of Malachi. However, one bright light was gone. *The Aether Stone.* Layla waved through the vanishing smoke. Daegon stood in the center of a nearby courtyard, his sword plunged into the now cracked and colorless stone.

Dozens of soldiers and citizens made their way out of hiding and into the streets, basking in the warmth of life. They survived their bout with the *Scourge*. Layla avoided the soldiers, jumping over the carnage and sprinting to Daegon. He held himself up with his sword, huffing. She threw her arms around him. "You did it!"

Daegon cracked a smile. "We did."

Gallant and Jordell pushed through the crowd. They plodded through the rubble and ripped bricks. Battered and broken. Jordell's armor splintered off his body, and whatever remained wasn't very functional. Gallant's precious spear was gone, lost to the chaos, replaced by a scavenged, dented longsword. They flashed a smile from across the courtyard and quickened their pace.

Gallant said, "Aren't you all a sight for sore eyes."

Daegon pressed off the sword and staggered to his feet. "How was leading the Malachinian army?"

Gallant huffed and placed his hand on Daegon's shoulder, but the hand slipped through. Gallant gasped at the lack of resistance. Daegon looked down at his shoulder and closed his eyes, meeting Jordell's somber gaze.

With a shaky voice, Gallant said, "No, no, there's got to be something we can do?"

Jordell stood unmoving. "Gallant." They all turned to Jordell, whose form was already flickering like a dying candle. "We all knew the cost when we came here."

Tears welled in Layla's eyes. Daegon stared at his hands. The marble bricks behind him were visible through his chest. He looked up at her and forced a weak smile, fighting the truth.

Layla screamed, "No!" She dashed to hug him, desperate to meet something, but collapsed through his body onto the cold ground. Tears stained the courtyard. Her voice struggled to solidify her words. "We said we'd find a way."

Daegon whispered, "Layla." There wasn't much he could say. He knew the cost of coming. She knew the cost. There would never be another way to defeat the *Scourge*. "I'm sorry."

Her back heaved. She wiped her eyes, standing from the ground. She couldn't bear to see him become nothing. With her back toward him, she buried her face in her hands. "I love you."

Then, warmth. His arms wrapped around her body. It wasn't physical, but the phantom warmth wrapped around her, a memory truer than the ground beneath her feet. He rested his chin on her shoulder and held her waist. They closed their eyes and savored the moment. In that moment, the destruction was absent. The surrounding carnage was irrelevant. This was their last moment. A moment to remember forever. A memory to keep.

He let go, the pain of escape hurting more than the bladed arms of the *Scourge's* minions. Tears sparkled in his eyes as he made his way to Jordell. He wiped his eyes and gave Layla one last smile. He muttered under his breath, "Keep the Memory."

Jordell gave one of his hearty laughs and grabbed Daegon's shoulder, pulling him close.

At the opposite end of the courtyard, a man with long dark hair and flowing blue robes stood patiently. The man smiled—not a smirk, not a grimace, but a smile of peace. Daegon exhaled. He nodded and put his hand on Jordell's back, ushering him in the direction. Slowly, their form faded until they were no more.

Layla stood frozen. The person she'd shared the most intimate moments with vanished. And not just the person. The ground beneath her crumbled away. As if the forest were sucking the marble back into the earth. The buildings slumped, eventually becoming nothing more than stones in the ground. Before long, the hidden city of Malachi was no more. The *Aether Stone* stayed planted in what was the center of the city, but it no longer exuded its light. Instead, it stayed nestled in the dirt, hollow and lifeless.

Gallant's hand on her shoulder made her jump. She reached and covered his hand; her gaze lost in the tree line. Aramide and his troop of Forlorn dotted the distance. Despite everything they'd accomplished, everything was so empty. It was selfish, but a thought scratched at the back of her mind. *Was it worth it?* She shook her head at the idea as Gallant waved both his hands at the soldiers.

Was it worth it?

Chapter Fifty

Layla sorted through the wreckage of dusted sandstone and chipped mortar. The edges were sharp, concealing all that she once knew of this once beautiful city. A great city. Not in the time she'd visited, but in the stories told by Gallant. By Sir Maybin. Now, Terratoria's rubble remained, and the once impenetrable walls let intruders pass without a glance. The Cardinals had the citizens believe it was a product of disobedience, but it was worse. The malfeasance they held most sacred lingered on every overturned stone. Every splintered log and collapsed building echoed with the fears and lies of the Congregation.

"Help!"

Layla hurried over to a Forlorn soldier lifting a large wooden beam from the rubble. She attempted to push out with her feelings, but nothing came. She instead resorted to a simple shoulder. It wasn't heavy, but the angle of the rubble wedging the piece of wood fought back. With two people, though, it was quick work. A bundle of green fabric splayed out underneath, prompting Layla to break off from the man. Layla reached down and wound her fingers in the soft fabric, biting her lip as she recalled the marketplace. Where he took her. Where they'd shared their first time alone.

A tear rolled down her cheek, succumbing to the sand at her feet. Despite the fall of Terratoria being months ago, she could still taste the fire in her mouth. It was under control, but the slow embers of the city periodically ignited under the hard-to-reach destruction. Layla stood from the fabric and stared at the mass of soldiers and weary citizens, with their green tunics laced over their bodies, restoring this once incredible city back to a semblance of normalcy. The *Scourge* had overtaken many of the cities, leaving deep scars that would be felt for many generations.

But they would move on. That's what Aramide said. That's why he told her it was important for her to be here on this day. Leaders from the five cities were all gathering in Terratoria to start over. Create a new government led by the people. By the very individuals who suffered in fear at the hands of the Congregation. And who better to be here than the one who ended it? The one who completed the Conjuror's Journey and defeated the *Scourge*. Once and for all. At least, that's how Aramide pitched it. And Gallant urged her to go. Everything she'd been through. Everything she'd grown up believing ended in this very moment. A united people, safe to wake every day without the fear of death.

Despite the jovial attitudes of those around her, excited to return to their homes, she couldn't help but feel the biting edge of completion. What would she do now? She had devoted her entire life to the Congregation's teachings. And not just her life. But her father's life. She looked at her hands, and a tear collapsed into her palm. *We did it, Dad.* She had to fight to hold back anymore tears. Now was not the right time.

She wiped her hands on her white cloak and moved stones once again, chuckling to herself, remembering Daegon attempting to barter with the Terratorian salesman. She didn't say it at the time, but he was terrible at it. A true King. A large stone failed to move under her force, prompting her to step back and push out with her hands. But the stone stood immovable, mocking her lack of power. She hadn't gotten comfortable with her inability to manipulate the elements. After so long on the Conjuror's Journey, it had become a part of who she was. Another piece of her the Congregation had wiped away. All that remained of her power was the small piece of the faintly glowing *Aether Stone* that she kept in her pocket. A small memory of Daegon. Of what was.

She dropped to the ground and put her hands behind her, pulling her hood over her head. Despite the heat from the desert climate, the unrelenting sun was a more oppressive enemy. The slow crunch of shifting rubble quieted, and she turned around to see Gallant watching her with crossed arms. He wore thin leather armor with a refinished spear attached to his back. His golden hair shifted in the subtle breeze that teased the heat.

"How long have you been standing there?" She whispered, turning her head toward the sand.

He walked over and kneeled next to her. "Long enough." He put his hand on her shoulder. Despite the Journey being over, Gallant still watched out for her. He was still her protector. It was hard to turn that off. "Are you okay?"

She turned to look at him. "I will be."

"Good." A smile spread across his face. "They're almost ready for you."

She reached for his arm, and he pulled her to her feet. "I don't know if this was a good idea."

"Nonsense." He brushed the dust from her shoulders. "With what you've done for everyone." He paused and tracked his gaze across all the soldiers who were now finishing their shift. "They're honored to have you speak. It is the first general assembly after all."

Layla blushed and nodded. He was right. The cities needed someone to look to in a time of reconstruction. While she didn't like the idea of being a spiritual figure, she recognized the importance for symbolism. For what she represented. An end to pain and suffering. "Thank you, Gallant. I wish he were here to enjoy today."

Gallant quietly huffed. "I know. The kid grew on me."

"Did you really just acknowledge that you cared?" Layla poked at him.

Gallant slyly grinned. "I hope you remember that. You probably won't hear something like that again."

"Oh hush. I knew you were a softy."

He reached with one arm and pulled her in, giving her a hug. Their heads jolted at the loud roar of fire. *Was the city going up in flames again?* A large flame blossomed atop the wall, followed closely by another. Within seconds, the great wall of Terratoria was ablaze with its legendary flame, on guard for the city once again.

"I think that's our cue," Gallant muttered.

Gallant ushered Layla through the rubble to the center of the city. Before she could leave, she turned back one final time, appreciating every speck of dust that'd followed them along the way. Despite her rather limited and unfortunate time in Terratoria, tokens of poignant memories continued to reach out to her. A painted eye with a slash through the center poked from the crumbled stone. Crushed and incomplete stone masks dotted the pathway out of the city, each displaying unique marks. There was beauty in the memories that lived on.

The city cleared the tunnel into the outdoor auditorium more than other parts of the reconstruction. It was relatively hollow, recently cleaned, and decorated with pieces of art pulled from destruction. As she passed through, the art had no discernible pattern but contained works from the various sects of the city. Images of stone giants hoisting the impenetrable walls detailed the history of Terratoria. Their massive arms planted the front gates, and wiped their fingers across the top of the wall, igniting the flame of protection. Was there a better place to have the first convention of the new Congregation than in the city that could never be defeated?

A low murmur of a crowd echoed near the end of the tunnel, reminding her of her stone ceremonies. All here. For her. That's what she'd say to herself prior to the events. This time was different, though. This was reversed. She was here for them. A symbol necessary for the continuation of life. Her eyes winced at the end of the tunnel as the sun's rays cracked through, and her audience streamed into view. Thousands of people lined the stands. People stood on the rubble of the destroyed half of the auditorium. As soon as she stepped into view, the fervor of the crowd increased.

Layla froze at the entrance, but Gallant gestured for her to come forward. *Always there.* Aramide, with his red, knotted hair, stepped to the edge of the stage and assisted her to the center.

"Pretty impressive, isn't it?" Aramide chuckled. "We let them know two days ago about the construction of a new government, and people from every city answered."

He wasn't joking. Layla stared at the assortment of people. Clothing from every major city represented the crowd. The traditional green cloaks of Terratoria. The shimmering crystalline blue chain mail from Shishbash. Even the Embrens attended, with their breathing masks removed and wrapped around their necks. Layla's eyes continued to wander among the crowd, and she gasped at the appearance of what looked to be Daegon in the front row, casually smiling at her. *How?* She took a step forward and blinked, causing him to disappear. Shocked, her head spun around, trying to determine what had just happened.

She shuddered at the presence of a hand on her shoulder. Aramide leaned into her ear. "Relax, my lady. We would be honored for you to give the first speech."

She continued scanning the crowd, trying to find Daegon. Just to see him one more time. But he was gone. She looked back at Aramide and nodded. Gallant reached out with his hand, which she accepted, and led her to the podium.

Though it was constructed hastily, it allowed her a good vantage point to judge the people's reactions. The applause of the crowd died down as she stepped up. She took a deep breath and looked at Gallant, who nodded with approval.

Layla closed her eyes. "We will write the story of our people. And that story will be filled with many chapters. Adventure. Destruction." She paused and scanned the crowd. "Love. It was...It will be difficult to read some of those chapters. To remember what was lost. What could have been." She looked at Aramide, who stood at the side with his arms crossed. "But every chapter is finite. Every chapter has an end. And with every end, comes a bit of hope." Her voice sharpened. "When I look out into you, I see that hope. I see the wall of Terratoria burning bright. I see a collection of...".

She froze at the sight of five red cloaks standing with their arms entrenched in their sleeves at the top of the stands. Darkness concealed their faces under their hoods, but their menacing gazes burned into her skin. *They couldn't be here.* She rubbed her eyes, and they vanished, replaced with five citizens intently listening. Aramide coughed, and Layla's head spun. Gallant stepped up behind her.

He whispered, "Is everything okay?"

Layla nodded, gripped the podium, and continued. "I see a collection of people determined to create a better ending." She cleared her throat. "And this isn't the end of our story. It takes all of us striving for that unreachable completion. But I believe in us. I believe in a better tomorrow." She stood tall and placed her hands on the top of the podium. "Thank you. For everything."

The crowd rose to its feet and erupted in a loud cheer. Layla absorbed it but continued scanning the crowd. First Daegon, then the Cardinals. Maybe she was tired? Maybe the Terratorian sun affected her. She stepped back from the podium, and Gallant assisted her. Aramide nodded and continued the event as Gallant led her offstage. With the subtle speech being delivered behind her, Gallant asked, "What happened up there?"

"I'm not sure. I think I'm just tired." She responded while her eyes fluttered, still replaying the scene in her head.

Gallant frowned. "I know you, Layla. I can tell when something's bothering you."

Layla closed her eyes. "I saw Daegon. I saw the Cardinals."

"Where?"

"In the crowd. They were watching. They were present." Her voice had grown strained from her speech.

"That's not possible." He looked down at his hands. "I killed Cardinal Sooman."

"I think I'm just seeing things. We've been through a lot. And coming back here has made me remember our Journey. It's not the easiest thing to do." Tears welled in her eyes.

"Hey." He reached out and squeezed. "Whatever happens. We'll be there together."

"Do you think there's a way to bring him back?" She wiped her eyes, but the dust had already invaded, causing them to swell.

"I'm not sure. Without the *Aether Stone*, conjuring seems to have vanished. But if that's where our next Journey takes us, I'll be your protector."

Layla smiled. "You don't have to do that. The Journey is over."

"As your protector, the Journey never ends."

"Thank you, Gallant." She reached for another hug. As he wrapped his arms around her, she reached for her pocket, fingering the glowing shard. Despite the *Aether Stone* being destroyed, the shard pulsed against her fingertips. Warm. Alive. *There has to be a way.*

www.ingramcontent.com/pod-product-compliance
Lightning Source LLC
Chambersburg PA
CBHW051256130726
47987CB00004B/1551